'In this acidly smart thriller, Nicholas Coleridge takes the lid off the glossy-magazine business ... Coleridge writes superbly with both pace and depth – never an easy combination. He leaves you feeling you know everything there is to know about periodical publishing and more than a little about the stink of corruption that is power's closest companion' *Sunday Times*

'I was glued to the thriller ... the plot grips to the end' *Literary Review*

'Pacy, polished and exciting, it gives a riveting insider's view of a fascinating and frenetic world. Nicholas Coleridge, whose beady eye misses nothing, is expert at putting across unpatronisingly a great deal of inside information. Much of it is extremely funny' Selina Hastings, *Evening Standard*

'A riveting and well-informed read' *Spectator*

'Mercilessly accurate, great descriptions. All the drama and glamour is here. It's as funny, in its way, as *England, Their England*' *Mail on Sunday*

'Pacy and full of jet-set action ... The magazine scenes are bitingly realistic and are likely to cause much glossy-magazine corridor debate' *Tatler*

'It's a real page-turner' Ken Follett, *Vogue*

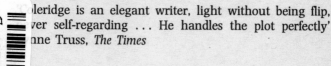

...oleridge is an elegant writer, light without being flip, ...ver self-regarding ... He handles the plot perfectly' ...nne Truss, *The Times*

Nicholas Coleridge is Managing Director of the British Condé Nast magazines. He lives in Oxfordshire and London with his wife, Georgia, and children Alexander, Frederick, Sophie and Tommy.

Nicholas Coleridge

# WITH FRIENDS
# LIKE THESE

**ORION**

An Orion paperback
First published in Great Britain by Orion in 1997
This paperback edition published in 1997 by
Orion Books Ltd,
Orion House, 5 Upper St Martin's Lane,
London WC2H 9EA

Third impression
Reissued 2002

A CIP catalogue record for this book
is available from the British Library.

ISBN: 0 75280 947 4

Typeset by Deltatype Ltd, Birkenhead, Merseyside
Printed and bound in Great Britain by
Clays Ltd, St Ives plc

*For Georgia, Alexander, Freddie*
*and Sophie Coleridge*

This is all fiction, not a *roman-à-clef*. The names, characters, companies and institutions, other than where indicated, are drawn from the author's imagination. Any resemblance to actual persons, living or dead, is entirely coincidental.

# PART I

---

20 June – 6 July

# 1

It wasn't even twelve o'clock and already it had all the hallmarks of a deeply stressful day. I'd spent forty minutes with the circulation director and no matter how you spun the figures, they were badly down. Then the publisher of *Smart Living* had rung through to warn me they'd be seventeen advertising pages off forecast for the August issue. I'd been snappier than I'd meant to be. Seventeen pages is a heap of money: £110,500 after agency commission and the usual discounts from ratecard. I'd asked her what the hell she needed eight sales people for if they could only move twenty-seven pages between them in a month, and she'd got defensive. I'd have to drop by later on and spread a bit of morale about. Now apparently I couldn't get a table for lunch anywhere within walking distance of our offices in Park Place, which meant I'd have to go somewhere by cab which I hate doing.

Then Micky Rice from *In Society* loomed into my office and announced a possible problem with the Anastasia Fulger profile.

'She's insisting on copy approval,' said Micky. 'She's rung twice herself and her lawyer's biked round a letter. They're threatening to injunct.'

'But we never give copy approval,' I said. 'You know that. And anyway the issue's at the printers. Tell the lawyer it isn't even a starter.'

Micky Rice looked uneasy and began fiddling with the gold buckle on his leather trousers. I groaned. Now I knew we were in trouble.

'Micky. You *couldn't* have.'

'I didn't promise her copy approval, honestly. I just said she could have her quotes read back to her.'

'Are you crazy? She'll want to retract half of them now.'

'She does.'

'You can't let her. It'll ruin it. This isn't a puff piece.'

'Her lawyer says some of the stuff about Bruno is *sub judice*.'

'Jesus, Micky. Did you put anything in writing?'

'No.'

'Thank God for that at least.' If nothing was in writing we could bluff it out. The issue would be on the streets by lunchtime on Friday and once it's out it's almost impossible to injunct anyway.

Micky still looked shifty. 'Actually there might have been *something* in writing. Only on a postcard. At the end of a thank you note for lunch I might have mentioned something about reading back the quotes. Sorry.'

'What were you doing lunching with Anastasia Fulger anyway, for God's sake?'

Sometimes I worried about Micky. He was a pretty good editor most of the time, but had a serious flaw. He was too keen on socialising. It wasn't enough for him to run articles about celebrities, he wanted to play with them too, wanted them as friends. It was compromising for the magazine. Once you've had dinner with the cover story, it's going to end up bland. Micky tampered with his contributors' copy, took out the bite.

Trust him to have lunch with Anastasia Fulger. Mrs Bruno Fulger, soon-to-be-divorced wife of the German steel billionaire, was exactly the sort of nightmare he'd make a bee-line for.

'Where'd she take you for lunch anyway, just so I can picture it?'

'Harry's Bar. Honestly, Kit, it was just a girls' lunch. I needed to be there for the magazine.'

'Does Anna know about all this?'

Anna Grant was one of our contract journalists. Probably our best. She had a real talent for writing on the

4

line, so her subjects could never tell whether she was playing it straight or sending them up. As soon as the Fulger exclusive came up, she was the obvious person to write it.

'That's really why I came up to see you,' said Micky. He wouldn't meet my eye. 'Anna says if we touch one word of her copy she's resigning. She's being hysterical. In fact, she put the telephone down on me when I was trying to calm her down. She deserves to be fired.'

Just then Suzy my secretary put her head round the door.

'Sorry to interrupt, but I've got Anna Grant on the line. I said you were in a meeting, but she's insisting. And there's a taxi waiting downstairs to take you to Daphne's.'

'Daphne's? That's halfway across London.' I sighed. 'Who am I having lunch with anyway?'

'The French people from Mouchette. All the numbers are in the folder.' She handed me a sheaf of figures and file notes in clear plastic. Mouchette are our fifth biggest beauty advertiser. The top sheet showed that they spent £426,015 with us last year across four magazines. The lion's share goes to *Couture*, but we sell them pages too for their aftershaves in our men's book, *Man Alive*, plus scent strips in both *In Society* and *Smart Living*.

'Thanks, Suzy.' I really couldn't live without Suzy. People always say that about their secretaries, but with Suzy it was true. Since my wife left me, or I left her or whatever, Suzy's done more and more for me. Food shopping, collecting dry cleaning, buying my daughter's fifth birthday card and present. The only person who understands me. Maybe she should simply move into the flat too. Some days, when I felt really down and Suzy showed up to work in her short leather skirt, I came close to suggesting it.

'Oh – Suzy.' I called through into the outer office. 'Tell Anna I'm not avoiding her but I just can't talk to her right now. And would she like to have supper tomorrow evening.' I threw in this last bit specifically to annoy

Micky. It evidently worked, because his face clouded with annoyance.

'I'm leaving now to schmooze the French. Haven't they got some big new launches coming up in the autumn?'

'All in the folder,' said Suzy. 'A skin rejuvenator and a new fragrance called Chromosome. Smells like Givenchy, bottle like Obsession, packaging like Trésor. The budget for print is three million.'

'Three million francs, I expect, when it comes down to it.

'Oh and Suzy.' I was halfway out of the door now. 'Cancel all meetings tomorrow morning, and keep the loonies at bay. I need total, absolute calm. I need to think.'

# 2

I had always got into the office early. Now I was on my own I arrived even earlier. I missed those mornings at home, when Cazzie came down into our bedroom and Sally read her stories while I had my bath next door. Oddly enough I didn't particularly enjoy it at the time, I hated the way Cazzie forced open my eyelids with her fingers, but now it didn't happen, I missed it.

So I had a taxi collect me at six-thirty and was at my desk by ten to seven. Suzy left coffee set up in the percolator and all I had to do was switch it on. The newspapers were piled up outside the door, so I spent an hour or so scanning them. Sometimes I spotted freelance pieces by our contract writers. Even when they write under pseudonyms I can generally recognise them anyway by their style. Sometimes I raise a stink; sometimes I don't bother. Depends on my mood. There's a piece in *The Times* today about the return of the bespoke Savile Row suit that I would take a large bet was written by a staffer on *Man Alive*.

I love my office. It is very minimalist. Big black leather sofa, black conference table, six heavy chrome and leather chairs. White walls of course. Some black and white photographs from the *Couture* archives. My desk is a glass Corbusier one with no drawers, which means no clutter. There's no place to stuff anything away and just forget about it. This requires discipline but it makes me feel good. Since Sally and I split I've streamlined my life a lot. I didn't take anything with me from home, just my clothes, and I still don't want anything either. She's welcome to it.

My big concern at the moment was the circulations.

Yesterday's meeting with Norman Turner, our circulation director, had been disturbing. We couldn't get final audits on any issue for a month after it came off sale, but there was a four o'clock monitor each Friday afternoon and the indications were usually pretty accurate. A team of merchandisers goes into two hundred newsagents during Friday morning, all over the country, and physically counts the copies on the shelves. From this they can work out how many have sold in the week. Two hundred newsagents isn't even seven per cent of the outlets, but it's amazing how closely they reflect the trend. What's selling in London is selling in Newcastle, most of the time.

For fourteen weeks our news stand sales had been stalling.

'I've been ringing around the trade,' said Norman, 'and it's soft everywhere. It's not just us.'

Circulation directors always said that. They believe in trends. The whole market is up, the whole market is down. They like to see the magazine industry moving as one entity. In fact they like the whole notion of a magazine 'industry', full stop. It makes them feel secure.

I've never seen it that way. Magazines succeed or fail on their content. Readers either want them or they don't. They can love a particular magazine for years and years and then go off it, lose attention, move on.

That's why it bothered me when the magazines began to lose impetus at the news stands. It was a big problem. *In Society* looked particularly sick. Week after week we'd lost sales, anything up to thirty per cent against the equivalent issue last year. Unless we could reverse the trend quickly, we'd be massively down in the next round of audited figures.

At twenty past seven Norman Turner turned up in my office. I wasn't pleased to see him, and glared, but as usual he didn't notice and sat himself down in one of the leather visitors' chairs opposite my desk. When I first began coming into the office extra early no one knew and I could get on undisturbed. Now people come in early too when they want to catch me, knowing that the protection, Suzy, won't yet be on guard.

Norman seemed pleased with himself, claiming to have some 'industry intelligence', as he likes to describe the third-hand gossip he picks up from the distributors.

'You're going to enjoy this, Kit,' he assured me, buttoning his suit jacket over his increasingly prominent roll of stomach fat. 'Can't name my source but suffice to say it comes from very high up in a certain prominent retail chain.'

That meant W. H. Smith or John Menzies, or at a stretch Martins or Forbuoys. One of Norman Turner's abstruser fantasies about himself was that he had a special relationship with the top brass in the newsagency world and could obtain inside information about our competitors. Frequently this turned out to be inaccurate.

'What if I told you,' said Norman, 'that *Town Talk* has Brad Pitt on the cover this week.'

Now that *was* interesting. If true, it was a colossal misjudgement on their part. We'd twice put Brad Pitt on our own covers and he didn't sell. Successful cover personalities are difficult to predict. A Hollywood star can put out an Oscar-winning performance but flop on a cover. A different star might be going through a professional famine but still shift magazines. Certain actors like Kevin Costner, Hugh Grant, Michael Caine and Johnny Depp always sell. They're bankers. Barbra Streisand's a banker. Roseanne Barr's a banker. Uma Thurman too. Elizabeth Hurley does it for certain titles but not for others. Kate Moss works where Elizabeth Hurley doesn't. Princess Diana was once worth a fifteen per cent boost but then it stopped working. Oprah Winfrey doesn't even pass go. You learn these things as you go along. And one thing we knew for certain was that Brad Pitt on the front cover was an out and out bummer.

'So it's Brad Pitt up against Anastasia Fulger.'

Norman nodded. 'Shame we haven't got Uma Thurman. We'd wipe 'em out.'

Norman hadn't been in my office for two minutes and already he was irritating me. He had an immense capacity for this, of which he was entirely unaware.

'Norman, we had Uma Thurman on the cover two weeks ago. So we can't possibly have Uma Thurman again, can we, even assuming we had another cover picture of her in the drawer, and a new article to go with it?'

If circulation directors were editors you'd only get six cover personalities on a loop, round and round again. Except at Christmas when there'd be a heavily decorated Christmas tree with sprigs of holly around the logo. And all the cover lines would be about sex and relationships and there wouldn't be any green logos or blue backgrounds because they don't sell. And all the fashion models would be blonde and smiling and wearing red jackets and be called Claudia Schiffer.

'This Anastasia Fulger woman, though,' said Norman. 'I mean, will the readers know who she is?'

'They damn well ought to. She's been plastered across the newspapers for a month.'

'But she's only of interest, surely, to people in high society.'

'That's the point. That's why we've put her on the cover of the magazine of that name. *In Society*. Truly, Norman, trust me. People all over Britain, all over Europe, New York too, are discussing this divorce. It's a hot story.'

'Well, you're the guvner,' said Norman doubtfully. 'I'll have an early indicator for you tomorrow as usual at four o'clock.'

Painful as it was to admit it, there was something in what Norman was saying. That was his main usefulness as circulation director, to provide the common man's view. You could depend on Norman to be the last person to catch on to any new thing. He was like a normal reader. He wouldn't recognise a new Hollywood actress until he'd seen her twice at his local cinema in St Albans. And he was right: Anastasia Fulger wasn't a banker. We'd probably sell better with an old black and white shot of Jacqueline Onassis waving a gloved hand. But it was the right story at the right time, bang on target for the magazine's profile and long on kudos. And we needed some of that.

*In Society* had been off the boil for six months. It was difficult to define exactly why, but I could feel it instinctively. It wasn't just the news stand sales. People were talking about it less. I wasn't seeing it about so much in friends' houses. And it was beginning to show in the advertising bookings too. They were down. Advertisers buy into hot books. If this carried on, we could be in a serious hole by the autumn, and Barney Weiss, our number-crunching proprietor, would be on my back.

Outwardly, of course, *In Society* looked exactly the same as usual. If I were honest, I hadn't a clue what was going wrong, just knew that it was. The formula hadn't changed, nor had the contributors. Perhaps that was the problem. There were interviews with film stars and rich people saying the same sort of stuff, plus photographs of parties, restaurant reviews and the arts pages which research shows nobody much reads but we put in anyway. Arts journalism is fig-leaf journalism, providing a veneer of respectability. Some people are embarrassed to be seen reading *In Society* and like to pretend they get it for the opera reviews. So we give them opera reviews.

Magazine formulae are delicate things. The first editor I ever worked for, straight out of university, liked to compare it to mixing a cocktail. You need exactly the right combination of spirits, mixers, salt, etc., he'd tell me. Add too much lemon juice or sugar syrup and the whole thing's fucked up and then it's hard, if not impossible, to salvage. He was a great editor and right about magazines being cocktails. But he forgot one important thing and it was his downfall. People's taste changes. They don't know it themselves half the time, but it happens. One day they wake up and they don't like their cocktail mixed that way any longer. They want sherry in there too and horseradish and less Tabasco. One morning, after I'd been at the magazine eight months, we were all called together round a desk by a man we'd never clapped eyes on before from the management floor and introduced to the new editor. The old one, my mentor, had resigned to pursue his own interests. Later, the security men from lobby reception came into the office and tipped all his belongings out of his desk drawers into cardboard boxes. It made an impression. Maybe it's why I have no drawers in my glass desk.

I turfed Norman Turner out of the office, closed the door and told switchboard to take calls. If *Town Talk* really had a bum cover this week then this was an opportunity to pull ahead.

*Town Talk* was *In Society*'s most direct competitor and as such needed to be kept in a perpetual state of inferiority and disarray. It was owned by Incorporated Periodicals, our number one rivals, and recently it had had a run of alarmingly strong-selling issues and was gaining market share fast.

But first we needed to establish whether or not they really had Brad Pitt on the cover.

Suzy turned up right on cue looking fantastic in a red suit with brass buttons. A little overweight, perhaps, but that gave her a wholesome look that was in short supply elsewhere in this building. She was in her mid-twenties, small, with blonde hair cut into a bob. And I needed her badly for her telephone skills.

'Sorry, Suzy. But it's the old Mike Yarwood routine again.'

Suzy does brilliant impersonations and has a whole range of accents. I sometimes get her to ring up our competitors and discover things, pretending to be somebody else. One of her best is the dimwitted retail promotions girl from a supermarket chain, and she didn't let me down.

'Hello,' said Suzy in her finest Dagenham whine. 'Is that Incorporated Periodicals? I wonder if you can help me. I need to speak with the person in charge of your in-store promotions. We've got a query about your displays.'

She was put through to Incorporated's circulation department, and repeated the same routine.

'What I need to confirm,' she went on, 'is whether it really is Brad Pitt on the cover of *Town Talk* next issue. Because if it is, we thought he's such a pin-up, you know, and so much in the public eye, we might be able to offer you point-of-sale merchandising services at check-out, at a substantial discount.'

I could hear the girl at the other end consulting her boss, who plainly thought she was being sold a last-minute cancellation and was irritable. The message came back: 'Yes, we do have Brad Pitt, but I'm afraid we haven't any budget left for point-of-sale.'

Suzy slammed down the receiver and we laughed like children.

'Never fails,' she said in her own voice.

'Like lambs to the slaughter.'

I called a meeting for ten o'clock. The publisher and editor of *In Society*, circulation director, production director and the magazine's PR. I had an idea and if we wanted to do it we needed to move quickly.

It was risky but then we were in a risky predicament already. *In Society* was soft and we were already more than halfway through a circulation period. Every six months we had to have our figures independently audited and fourteen weeks had gone by already. As a weekly, the magazine had twenty-six issues in each half year, so that meant there were only twelve left to go. Last time round our circulation had been 146,000, of which 16,000 had been pre-paid subscriptions and 130,000 bought at news stand. This time, on present performance, we'd be lucky to scrape 110,000 at news stand, making 126,000 in total. The trade magazines would roast us alive and it would probably make the media pages of the nationals too. If *Town Talk* actually overtook us, which seemed all too possible, then Incorporated would crow like roosters. I could imagine their press releases already, and the smug bearded face of Howard Trench, my opposite number, looking out of *Campaign* and boasting about his brand values. Worst of all, we'd be beaten to pulp by advertisers. I couldn't see an agency in London agreeing to pay the current rates if we dropped circulation by 20,000. It would be a bloodbath.

To make up the lost ground would be tough; according to Norman, impossible. Over the first fourteen issues we'd lost a total of 280,000 copies. To make them back in twelve weeks meant selling an extra 23,300 copies a week, in other words 153,000 at news stand for every single issue.

But there's an old bit of folklore in magazines that I'd never actually put to the test, and if it turned out to be true then maybe we could just do it. According to this theory, if you can make a huge impression with one issue, get the whole world talking about it and send the circulation into orbit, then a lot of these new readers stick. People who've never thought of buying you in their lives before, try it and like it and buy it again. Lapsed readers return to the fold. News vendors display you on the very front of their kiosks. The prodigal magazine returns in glory.

On the other hand, it's chancy. It means printing tens of thousands of extra copies and flooding the market, which in turn means persuading the newsagents that you've got a big scoop, a dead cert. Otherwise, they don't want mountains of extra copies clogging up their shelves. And if, in the end, the issue doesn't sell through, they feel duped, and cut back future orders to the bone. It can backfire badly.

Then, in order to sell the copies, you've got to get coverage in the national press, acres of it, with all the papers picking up on your story and running with it for several days without reprinting the whole thing. It's a fine line. If you give them too much, people feel they've read the story already and don't bother buying the magazine.

14

The ten o'clock meeting was circling my outer office and Suzy let them in, offering tea or coffee. I must say, I really hate the tea and coffee ceremony at meetings. With five or six people it takes for ever – 'White with? Black without?' – but it's expected and causes offence if you don't lay it on. So we frittered away several minutes passing the milk jug around, and eventually got down to business.

'What I need your advice and help on,' I said, 'is a major push on tomorrow's *In Society*. I mean *mega*. I've decided we should blitz the market.'

There was a flurry of interest around the table. Norman Turner, predictably enough, looked sceptical.

'When you say "blitz the market", guvner, you don't mean put out extra copies?'

'I certainly do. I was thinking of a print run of 250,000.' Normally we distributed 160,000 to sell 110,000 so this was a huge jump, probably unprecedented.

'The news trade will never wear it, sorry, guv. You might be able to swing out another twenty thousand but never a quarter of a million.'

At this point our production director, Megan Whiley, interrupted. She was an impressive woman in her mid-forties who'd started life as a printer on Teesside. These days she wore Louis Feraud suits with power shoulder pads but had lost none of her northern bluntness.

'What are you proposing to print all these copies on, anyway?' she asked. 'We haven't got enough paper.'

'How about next week's stock? That must have arrived by now.' Weekly magazines normally get their paper delivered to the printers a fortnight in advance.

'Well, what about the following week's issue, then? There'll be a shortfall.'

'I'm sure you can handle it, Megan. Borrow some.'

Norman was still shaking his head from side to side in the way of all professionals faced with the misguided enthusiasm of amateurs.

'You know what I'm thinking, guv,' he said. 'It's not that I'm against the idea of a blitz *per se*, quite the reverse in fact. You know me, always game for a little excitement to brighten up our lives. It's just that you could be backing the wrong horse here. Now if you'd suggested this two weeks ago with Uma Thurman on the cover, I'd have been right with you. But this German lady. I asked the wife when I got home last night if she knew about her and she'd never even heard of her.'

At this Micky Rice rolled his eyes and muttered 'Oh puhleeze' under his breath.

I said, 'Micky, perhaps you'd like to defend your scoop.'

'I've brought up the page proofs,' said Micky, 'and the colour chromalins so you can see the pictures.'

He spread them out on the conference table and we looked at a large opening photograph of Mrs Bruno Fulger sitting perched on an expensively upholstered sofa surrounded by cushions. She was a highly strung blonde in her early thirties, pin thin, dressed in a pink beaded Lacroix suit and a serious pair of Kutchinsky diamond earrings. At her side on the sofa sat a miniature black Pekinese which Micky said had been produced from nowhere by the Filipino housekeeper seconds before the photograph was taken.

Despite the best efforts of a make-up artist and subsequent precision airbrushing by our retouchers, Anastasia Fulger still looked neurotic and distraught. And who could blame her, I thought, married to one of the biggest shits in Christendom. Bruno Fulger was one of those men you felt you knew because you'd been reading about them all your life in gossip columns. At seventeen he had inherited from his father something like $500 million, a yacht, three Titians, a castle near Munich and a passion for screwing anything that moved. After twenty years of being linked with everyone from a Monégasque princess to a well-thumbed Venezuelan hooker, Fulger had met and married Anastasia, a nineteen-year-old model twenty years younger than himself. Their wedding and subsequent costume ball had been one of the splashiest events of the decade. More than a thousand guests had flown in from all over the world, many by private jet, and for days helicopters chartered by *Hola!* and *Paris Match* overflew the castle snapping celebrities with long lenses. Mick Jagger and Jerry Hall had been there, the Thyssens, the brothers Flick, Andy Warhol, a whole raft of Hapsburgs and most of the inhabitants of the Studio 54 nightclub in New York. It had been the Eurotrash beanfest of all time. After the ceremony in the Fulgers' private chapel, guests had convened in the Great Hall of Schloss Fulgerstein dressed as aristocrats or executioners from the French Revolution. There were tumbrils filled with crushed ice and oysters and a life-sized guillotine wreathed with wild roses. Bruno, for some strange reason, came dressed as Count Dracula, with bloody fangs and a black cape, but Anastasia was ravishing as a whippet-thin Madame du Barry in a cream hooped dress so wide that the double doors of the ballroom had had to be specially enlarged to allow her through. Jimmy Goldsmith came as Cardinal Richelieu. Henry Kissinger as the Scarlet Pimpernel. Even Barney Weiss, not by then our proprietor, had somehow wangled an invitation and once produced for me a framed photograph of himself as the Marquis de Something or Other with his second wife Bonnie as the Marquise. But since he'd replaced Bonnie with Lola as wife number three, the picture didn't get desk space any longer.

Now, twelve years on, Bruno and Anastasia's marriage was on the rocks. To most people the only surprise was that it had lasted so long. For several years now the Fulgers had increasingly operated independently, with Anastasia flying off to Paris for weeks on end for the fashion collections and Bruno chasing wild boar and pussy as the mood took him.

It was a perfect story for *In Society* and the kind of exclusive I liked best.

I began copy tasting the page proofs and could see at

once that Anna Grant had done a great job. Some journalists know how to set up a colour story and others just don't. You could lock them in a room for a week with the Princess of Wales and a notebook and they'd still ask all the dud questions. Anna was a natural. She would kick off her shoes, tuck her long legs underneath her on the sofa and lock on like radar. I called that expression of hers 'rapt sympathy'. Whatever was said, she agreed, whether she did or not, and coaxed out a little bit more. In forty minutes her subject was her best friend and was pouring out her soul.

Ellen Durlacher, our PR, slid me a second set of proofs with certain passages scored in yellow highlighter.

'I've marked the juice for you,' she said. 'Three of these quotes are dynamite.'

Each quoted Anastasia Fulger verbatim.

The first read: 'At first it was OK having sex with Bruno, despite him being uncouth, you know, in bed. He had no manners. Maybe he hadn't made love to a real lady for a long time, I don't know, just those damn hookers. Anyway I became pregnant with Natascha who I love very much, and after that, nothing. Bruno and I haven't slept together for five years. Not even any pretence. Believe me, ask anyone. Ask my maid.'

The second read: 'This divorce has been terrible for me, just terrible. Each day lawyers, lawyers. It's OK for Bruno, he has all the money, he couldn't spend what he has. It's a game for Bruno. But for me, how can I pay these lawyers? I'm not asking for half his money. What would I do with half? I like to live simply, it is better, I think, for the soul. I ask only ten per cent of his fortune as it stands today. One hundred million dollars, not so much, no?'

The third was the most damaging: 'There is so much treachery surrounding this whole divorce thing. I ask some of our oldest friends to swear affidavits on the things they've seen, things Bruno did and said to me in front of many people. It happened, but they won't sign. They say, "Oh Anastasia, I don't remember that happened. I must have been outside the room." You know why? Bruno has got to them. Sometimes with money. Sometimes they are afraid of him. Bruno is very powerful and he knows how to use money.'

When I'd finished reading I said, 'This is even hotter than I imagined. No wonder Anastasia Fulger's having second thoughts. Have we heard any more from her lawyers by the way, Micky?'

'Nothing yet. I sent a stalling letter.'

'Ellen, what's the PR programme?'

'The *Daily Mail* I think. They know we've got it and they're gagging for it.'

'OK, but where else?'

'I've promised the *Mail* an exclusive.'

'Not enough. We need this story everywhere if we're aiming to shift a couple of hundred thousand copies.'

'The *Evening Standard*?' suggested Ellen. 'The *Mail* could break it and the *Standard* follow up tomorrow afternoon.'

'No, I mean everywhere. *The Times, Telegraph, Guardian, Express* for God's sake. The *Sun, Mirror, Independent*. Then all the Sundays.'

Ellen looked scared. 'I can't do that. Honestly, Kit, I just can't. They'll only touch the story if they think it's exclusive, and if I give it to them all at once I'll blow my contacts for ever.'

'Blame it on me. No, this is better, pretend there was a leak. An early copy stolen from the printers. You'll think of something.'

I liked Ellen. She tried hard. If you threw a stick and said 'Go fetch', she went. All she wanted out of life was a pat on the head and a company car with a soft top.

'If you're really telling me I've got to do this,' she said, 'I'm going to have to crack on. That's a lot of calls of make.' Then she said, 'While I'm still here, have we a front cover? Presumably you want me to make it a condition they show it as part of any coverage.'

Micky was even now propping up the cover proof on my leather sofa. The sofa was where we always looked at front covers. It was exactly the right distance from the conference table. The mistake you can make is to choose covers from too close up, which isn't how readers see them. They see them from fifteen feet across a newsagent amidst a jumble of competing titles, hundreds of different images and logos jostling for attention. If it doesn't stand out instantly, it's failed, and by then it's too late.

By this criteria, Mrs Bruno Fulger was a flop.

The image was a close-up of the photograph inside, with Anastasia facing forward and smiling thinly. She looked ghastly. The pink beaded jacket fused with the pinks and blues of the sofa cushions making it hard to tell where one ended and the other began. Worse were the cover lines. Against this jumble of textures, they were all but illegible. In a valiant but misconceived attempt at good taste, the art director had chosen to set the words in a grey serif typeface. For sheer impact, it scored one out of ten.

Norman Turner looked physically pained, and I didn't blame him. Even Micky Rice, sensing our reaction, had taken on a hangdog air.

'Is this really all there is?' I asked.

''Fraid so,' said Micky. 'She only gave us forty minutes.'

'And there's nothing better from a photo agency?'

'Nothing that hasn't been seen before.'

I was seriously considering aborting the whole push on the issue when Micky said, 'It's such a pity we can't use the sexy one.'

'Which sexy one?'

He sucked in his breath. I think he regretted saying it the moment it slipped out.

'Well, Anna Grant found this old picture. Anastasia in a swimsuit with one breast popped out. Taken just before she was married.'

I asked him to have it sent up and with reluctance he rang down to the art department. A minute or two later the photograph was brought upstairs.

It was simply brilliant.

She was standing on a jetty, it looked like the South of France, her hair tumbling over her shoulders and her eyes gazing straight at the camera. She was smiling and looking happy. The swimsuit was yellow and covered with daisies and was still wet from the sea. One of the straps had fallen down exposing her left nipple.

It was the cover.

'How did Anna get this?' I asked. 'Not from Anastasia Fulger surely.'

'From a French photographer,' said Micky, 'so she told me. Someone she met. Used to be a boyfriend of Anastasia's, apparently. Maybe Anna's too.'

If he said that to hurt me, it worked.

'It's fabulous,' I said.

'We can't use it,' said Micky.

'Why?'

'Lots of reasons. We don't have copyright clearance for a start. And anyway, I promised Anastasia we'd use the portrait.'

'Since when was Anastasia Fulger the editor?'

Micky fell silent. I knew I'd pay for that later. He hated criticism, particularly in a room full of people.

'Norman. What do you think? Will it sell?'

'Like hot crumpets, guv.' He looked like a man reborn.

'Kay? Which gets your vote?'

Kay Lipschwitz Anderson, the publisher, smiled. 'Oh, the swimsuit shot for sure. Some of the advertisers won't like it, too sexy, but I can square it with them.'

'Ellen?'

'I just love it. It's retro and modern at the same time.'

'Sorry, Micky,' I said, 'you're outvoted.' I could see he was already sweating about Anastasia's reaction. No more Harry's Bar for a bit, that was for sure. Actually I felt sorry for him, and a bit guilty. So I said, 'Blame it on me, won't you?'

'Oh, don't worry,' he replied tartly. 'I will, I will.'

'If we're changing the cover at this late stage,' said

Megan, 'I hope you appreciate there'll be five thousand pounds in overtime. And we need to send it off right now.'

'Fine. We'll just rejig the cover lines.'

It took five minutes. When you've got a great story why mess about? Keep it simple. So we just put HOW TO LOVE AND LEAVE A BILLIONAIRE. *Exclusive interview: Mrs Bruno Fulger on Sex, Divorce and Bribery.*

The telephone rang and it was Suzy. 'Sorry to disturb you,' she said, 'but Mrs Fulger's solicitor is on the line. He's rung before. It sounds urgent.'

'Let's face the music, then. Put him through.'

I switched the button on the squawk box and the voice of Rudolph Gombricht echoed around the room.

I'd had dealings with Gombricht before and hadn't enjoyed the experience. He was Swiss by birth, from Zurich, but was married to an Englishwoman and had practised in London most of his adult life. He had an office in the City in Broadgate and I occasionally ran across the Gombrichts at the chillier kind of cocktail party. His specialities were international tax and power divorces.

'Am I connected now to Mr Kit Preston?' he asked in his still-strong Swiss-German accent. I agreed that he was.

'Then I am first of all obliged by law to tell you that this conversation is being tape recorded. Do you understand this?'

'Yes I do.'

'All right then. It is eleven-sixteen a.m. on Thursday June 21st. I am speaking with Mr Kit Preston, Managing Director of Weiss Magazines Ltd. Is that correct?'

He blathered on in this officious tone for a few more minutes before reaching the meat.

'I am instructed by my client, Mrs Bruno Fulger, to inform you officially that unless certain passages already indicated are deleted from the next issue of *In Society* of tomorrow's date, then an injunction will be served at the High Court, binding on all parties. Mrs Fulger was given an explicit undertaking by a senior member of your staff that she retained full control over her quotes for publication. Mrs Fulger contends that her opinions have been misrepresented and quotes selectively taken out of context by the journalist, Miss Anna Grant, and that the article as it stands does not accurately reflect her views and opinions on the subjects concerned. The injunction will be served at both your registered office at 32 Park Place and upon your printers. Is that clearly understood?'

'Perfectly,' I replied. 'Which isn't to say I accept anything you've just said. Obviously I need time to decide what to do. I'll need to talk to our own lawyers of course.'

Rudolph Gombricht chuckled drolly. 'I think, Mr Preston, when your lawyers give you their advice, it will not be to lock horns with Mr Bruno Fulger or Mrs Fulger. That would be most imprudent. I don't need to remind you, Mr Preston, the Fulgers are not without influence.'

'I'll certainly bear that in mind, Mr Gombricht.'

Then I added, 'We begin printing at ten o'clock tomorrow morning, so maybe we should talk again just before then. Either we'll have edited out the bits Mrs Fulger objects to or you'll have your chance to injunct.'

'Till ten o'clock tomorrow, then,' said Gombricht. 'I am confident you will make the right decision.'

After he'd gone we all sat in silence for a bit in a mild state of shock. I must confess I hadn't got a clue what I was going to do next. The cover with Anastasia Fulger falling out of her bathing suit was still on the sofa. God, I loved those new cover lines. Hot or what. But I hadn't bargained for Rudolph Gombricht taping our conversation. What had I said anyway? Not a lot, so far as I could recall.

'Well?' said Megan. 'What's it to be? One way or the other we've got an issue to put to bed.'

Think! I stared out of the window and up the street in the direction of St James's. Down below I could see some *Couture* fashion assistants returning from an early sandwich run.

'You know what,' I said to Megan. 'If you really pleaded

with the printers, I mean went down on your knees and begged, do you think they could advance our print slot?'

'*Advance* it? Surely you mean delay it.'

'No, advance it. Say they started printing at nine tonight. It could be finished by four or five o'clock in the morning, couldn't it, clear of the plant by six? If we hired special trucks – I know it's expensive, Megan, don't tell me, but if we did – we could have the issue on the streets by breakfast, anyway in London. By the time Gombricht got his injunction together, half the copies would be out and no judge is going to force us to recall them.'

'You're quite mad, you do know that,' said Megan. 'Seriously barking.'

'Think you can square it with the printers?'

'If I can't,' she said mysteriously, 'then the favours I'll be calling in weren't as memorable as I thought they were at the time.'

'I hope you've factored into your plans that we're all going to end up in the slammer,' said Kay Lipschwitz Anderson sardonically.

'Not us, *him*,' said Micky Rice. 'Kit's already volunteered to take the rap.'

'Thanks, Micky,' I said. 'You sure know how to make a guy feel great.'

But actually I did feel great. In fact I felt terrific.

# 3

I didn't bother going home after work. These days I keep a cupboard full of clothes at the office, so I had a glass of wine at my desk at about six o'clock, changed into jeans and took a cab along the Bayswater Road to Lancaster Gate. There's a side gate into the park there that gets you right into the heart of the good bit, past the Italianate pumping house and downhill to the Serpentine.

Most English think Kensington Gardens is hell on a summer evening, which is why you don't see any English there, just Arabs shuffling along in family groups and American investment bankers pounding the perimeter in trainers and sweat bands. Personally, I don't mind, I can rise above it. And to be truthful I get a bit of a buzz out of dressing up in a baseball cap and rollerblades and melding into the diaspora.

Not that I'm any great hero on rollerblades. I'm OK, but that's it. Anna says I lean back too much; it's a common failing. At least I fall over less than I used to.

Anna was already there. Normally, she's notorious for being late, but not tonight. I could see her from half a mile away as I freewheeled down the path towards the bridge, practising her side flips. Anna's a more adventurous rollerblader than I am. Once I even discovered a magazine about it lying about in her flat, full of photographs of black kids doing the wall of death on some council estate.

One reason I think she rollerblades is that it gives her an excuse to show off her figure. She wears one of those skintight Lycra affairs, cut like a wetsuit, and her legs go on for miles. Usually she slips an old leather flying jacket on top, cut short so it doesn't cover her ass.

She spotted me slaloming unsteadily towards her and her face took on a cross expression. She's actually a very laidback person but once in a while, if she thinks something bad is happening to her professionally, she puts on this tough act. I'm sure it comes from living on her own and paying all her own bills.

'Don't say anything, Kit, just one word, "yes" or "no", OK?' she said as I skeetered to a halt beside her. 'Have you allowed them to censor my piece about Anastasia Fulger or haven't you? Level with me, yes or no?'

'Well, when I tell you that the Fulgers' lawyer is Rudolph Gombricht and he's threatening an injunction on the printers ...'

'Yes or no, Kit.'

I laughed. It felt so great being the good guy for once. 'Actually, Anna, the answer's no. We haven't cut one word.'

I've never seen anyone look so delighted. She threw her arms into the air, whooped, kissed my cheek and then scooted off on her blades, zigzagging and circling back along the path.

'You know,' she said, 'I was convinced you were going to cave in. Micky Rice was a bitch on the phone, you'd think he was Anastasia Fulger's personal publicist.'

'There's been a lot of pressure on him. On all of us, actually.' Then I told her about increasing the print run and Rudolph Gombricht's warning and how we'd substituted the old cover at the last minute for the swimsuit and nipple one.

'You won't regret it,' said Anna. 'You'll see. This story's going to be huge. It's exactly what people want to read.'

Anna had a spot-on instinct for what magazine readers really want. I'm supposed to have that myself, but Anna's far better at it. It's an advanced form of intuition and she just had it. One day she'd start talking about this great new actress or this Chinese playboy who'd just hit town, and she'd do a story about them, and three months later you'd be reading about them everywhere.

She had no time for make-space journalism, as she called it, the kind of pieces editors sometimes feel they *ought* to be publishing, for the moral good of the readers and themselves. She hated profiles of high-minded philosophers, tedious Eurocrats and unknown fringe theatre directors. What Anna liked to write about were movie stars, young royals and flamboyant tycoons. These she found genuinely fascinating, and she wrote about them in a way that was starstruck and teasing at the same time. Her profiles of Cindy Crawford, Taki and Kerry Packer are models of their kind, brimming with energy and juice and wry detail. In their way, they're quite anarchic.

We were halfway round the north shore of the Serpentine, blading past the boathouses. Anna was twenty yards ahead, weaving between joggers and pedestrians, I could hear the grating sound of her wheels as they shot sparks on the asphalt. She was so fast. Sometimes she looped back around me to show off some funky new manoeuvre. She had one of those lovely faces without any visible artifice, like a model made up to look like she's wearing no make-up in a skincare advertisement. Always suntanned (she made no secret of using the 'Electric Beach') with soft freckles and big, clear, brown eyes. She wore her hair long, except at the typewriter when she would gather it up into a soft roll and stick a pencil through it.

We arrived at the cafeteria at the head of the water, a Festival of Britain relic, all glass buttresses and concrete walkways and bored-looking ducks. God knows why we went there but it has become a kind of tradition, rollerblading with Anna followed by a bottle of wine and a tuna salad. At lunchtime I took her to Italian restaurants, but that was work. In the evening somehow I wasn't ready yet to take her out to a proper place.

'Seen Cazzie?' she asked.

That was Anna's way of raising the whole question of my divorce: Sally, how I felt about it lately, everything. We were almost a year into our official separation. Thirteen more months and I'd be single.

'Fine,' I said. 'I'm taking her to the park on Saturday morning.'

'Is she taking it well?'

'Hard to tell. We don't discuss it. I turn up, ring the bell, say goodbye to Mummy, off we go. Park, hamburger, home.'

'And Sally?'

'Easier. Slightly. Unless we have to talk about anything, then she's a pain.'

Out on the lake there were two rowing boats full of Indians who were fooling about with the oars, trying to push each other off into the water.

'What do you think will happen next?' asked Anna.

'With Sally? We'll get divorced. She'll get a ton of money and the house. Then it's anyone's guess.'

'Actually, sorry, I meant about the Anastasia Fulger article. Sorry, that was thoughtless of me.'

'Don't worry. In fact I find I prefer talking about work at the moment. Must be a phase in the cycle. I'm sure it's very well documented. As for the Fulgers, who knows? They'll be furious, but I don't see they can do much about it. Anastasia gave the interview voluntarily, all you did was write down what she said.'

'Those kind of people can be quite dangerous, though,' said Anna.

'You're starting to sound like Rudolph Gombricht.'

'I'm serious, Kit. You've got to remember that about rich people. They're used to getting their own way. I see it time and again with my articles. They start off very friendly and relaxed, send their plane for you, give dinners for you, and then it hits them they haven't got final control over what you're going to write. They can tell you everything they want you to say, project themselves in a good light, but in the end it infuriates them that this girl is going back to her office and can write whatever she likes about them.'

'Well, that's journalism, isn't it?'

'But they don't think of it that way. They have this

28

absolute image of themselves, very dignified, respected, cultured, and to their faces nobody ever departs from that. Not the people who work for them, not even their friends. So when they think some little upstart – that's how they think of you – some little upstart is about to burst the bubble and say what they're really like, they get mad.'

'That's why you're so clever at writing these pieces. You read them and see in them what you like. Your profile of Ivana Trump, for instance. I bet she read it and loved it and stuck it in her cuttings book, but ninety readers out of a hundred must have thought "What a nightmare woman".'

'I've got a real balancing act coming up with my next one,' said Anna.

'Who's that?'

'Erskine Greer for *Man Alive*. I wanted to ask you about him.'

'I don't know him that well. I had to go and see him once in Nassau when he was thinking of buying the magazines. Before Barney Weiss. Billy Heathcote sent me out as part of the sales effort, to tell him how successful the company was. He didn't fall for it. Much too smart. It was a very odd trip actually. He took me scuba diving off his boat with some weasel-eyed accountant who was going through our books. Nasty piece of work. I was glad to get back to the surface, I thought he might cut through my respirator with a knife.'

'What did you make of Greer?'

'Clever. Well informed. Mercurial. Less pompous than I'd expected. Completely ruthless, I'd have thought.'

'Honest?'

'Not particularly. Depends what you mean by honest. I imagine the airline's pretty kosher, and my friends who work for him in Hong Kong are absolutely straight. If you mean, "Do I think he's cut corners on the way up?" then I'm sure he has. Why do you ask?'

'I've heard some funny stories about him, that's all. Several different ones. An arms dealer I met at a party last week went all mysterious when I mentioned his name. I'm going to follow him up for some leads.'

'When's the Erskine Greer interview?'

'Saturday morning, while you're having quality time in the park. Eleven-fifteen in Hyde Park Gate. He's given me an hour.'

'Short.'

'This is only the warm-up, not that he knows that yet. My plan is to get him to take me to Palm Beach next weekend on his plane to watch his polo team in action.'

'Be careful of him, won't you?'

'Now it's you who sounds like Rudolph Gombricht. Why should I be careful?'

'Because he's rather your type. Older, rich, houses all over the place.'

'Then I'd better not be *too* careful, had I? I'll be thirty-two in September.'

We left the Serpentine and rollerbladed across the park to the Prince's Gate and out into Queensgate. Anna lived in a flat in Harrington Gardens, on the top floor of a redbrick building with a lot of ugly, elaborate masonry around the window casements. Flowers and thistles and rambling briars. I think the style is known as Pont Street Dutch.

We'd almost arrived when I suddenly remembered I'd forgotten to ring Barney Weiss. It was one of the rituals of my job that every Thursday evening at eight o'clock I had to ring the proprietor. It didn't matter where he was in the world, night or day, he wanted to hear from me at eight o'clock London time. Generally I didn't know where he was anyway. His office and main home, or 'residence' as he called it, was in Chicago, but he travelled a lot. He'd given me his digital world-phone telephone number which worked everywhere. The number would ring in shrill electric bleeps and there was Barney.

'Only time you'll find the machine switched off,' he told me, 'is when I'm on the Concorde. They make you turn it off there. Interferes with the electronics or something.'

At first I was a bit reluctant about these calls, in case I disturbed him in the middle of lunch or a meeting, but as I got to know him better I understood that this was exactly what he liked best. The telephone would ring and I'd hear him at the other end saying, 'Excuse me a moment, folks. It's my conference call with my magazines,' and then we'd go through this whole pantomime of me telling him how it was going and Barney repeating any significant names out loud to impress his friends. I'd find myself mentioning articles that I'd normally never bother mentioning at all, just to afford him the pleasure of participating. So I'd say, 'The pictures of Brooke Astor's house in Maine are going to look great, Barney,' and he'd say, 'Brooke Astor's mansion, eh. Well, be sure to say nice things about Brooke, won't you, she's a fine lady.'

Sometimes, to my great embarrassment, he'd pass the telephone along to someone else, some new friend he and Lola were cultivating, and encourage them to give me free editorial advice at long distance. Once the phone was passed round a whole table at some country club in Martha's Vineyard, and ten or a dozen people, all rather drunk, made suggestions about vacation spots which I pretended to write down.

Periodically, when he was in a foul mood and felt like kicking ass, he'd bawl me out about some bad numbers that had caught his eye in the monthly accounts. This, too, was mostly for the benefit of his audience. Barney Weiss the tough cookie.

Once when I rang he snapped, 'Mind ringing back in an hour, Kit? Lola and I aren't through screwing yet.'

Anna's flat was on the top floor and since there was no lift you had to climb ten flights of stone stairs. These deteriorated in quality as you got higher. The hallway was almost smart, with an Edwardian mosaic of entwined serpents set into the tiles, but the common parts soon relapsed into a succession of fire doors and timer-lights that allowed you insufficient time to reach the next floor. Her flat itself was tiny, it had been advertised as a studio,

31

and I was struck by how ironic a magazine journalist's life can be. Anna made her living writing about rich people but she wasn't rich herself. For her piece on Erskine Greer she'd make a thousand pounds maximum, and it would take her at least a fortnight. And at the end of it she'd turn in an article so confident, so insider in tone that you'd believe she was born an heiress.

But within its limitations, she had decorated the place beautifully. Almost everything was white, the curtains, sofas, chair covers, but there was nothing clinical about it. It reminded me of a beach house with its stripped wooden floor and decking that extended outside on to a small area of flat roof. Propped up on the mantelpiece were three or four bright orange starfish. The only painting in the whole flat was a beautiful Craigie Aitchison of a canary, bright yellow in gouache, which he'd given her years before as a present for something she'd written about him. She liked to point out that it was the only gift she'd ever received from 'my victims'.

I picked up the telephone and dialled Barney Weiss's world-phone number. It bleeped three times and then I heard a deafening clatter like a mini rockfall.

'Barney?'

I could hear someone cursing and, distantly, a cringing foreign apology.

Eventually Barney came on to the line, booming. 'You're not going to believe this, Kit, but some clumsy Spick's tipped an ice bucket over the mobile.'

'Where are you, incidentally?'

'Where are we? Three guesses.'

Barney Weiss loved this game. We played it most Thursdays.

'Palm Beach?' They had a holiday home on Ocean Boulevard and it was always worth a shot.

'Gawd, no. And here's the clue: much closer to you.'

'Cap Ferrat?' The Weisses had a big thing at the moment for the Hôtel Bel Air. Someone had told Barney it was the priciest place on the Côte d'Azur and he'd loved it ever since.

'No. Even closer. Last guess.'

Closer than the South of France. Jesus, this was getting worrying.

'Paris? The George V?'

'You lose, sucker. We're at the Dorchester. Right round the block.'

'You are? What a great surprise.' I hoped I sounded more enthusiastic Barney's end. 'How long are you staying?'

'Just the weekend. We're taking the seven o'clock Concorde to JFK Sunday night.'

'Anything we can do for you while you're in town?'

'Nothing I can think of right now. We've got seats for the men's singles at Wimbledon tomorrow. That's Centre Court. If Lola needs anything special to wear round her neck, I guess one of the girls from *Couture* could drop by with a selection.'

'Sure,' I said lamely.

'We hope too you'll both be able to join us for dinner Saturday evening in the restaurant here. They have a fine reputation by all accounts.'

'That would be great. But you haven't forgotten Sally and I are sadly not together any longer.'

'You're not? I remember now, you told me that before. Well, boy, probably no bad thing, time to trade her in for a younger model. Anyone else you'd like to bring along instead?'

I looked at Anna and raised my eyebrows entreatingly. She crossed her eyes and mimed slitting her throat, but then relented and nodded yes.

'I'll try and get Anna Grant, who writes for the magazines,' I said. 'I know she'd be honoured to meet you.'

'Fine,' said Barney, 'so long as she's cute. Get over here at seven-thirty and have them call up to our suite.'

# 4

The press coverage on Friday morning was even better than I'd dared hope. Ellen Durlacher had done a great job. Every newspaper had cleared the decks for Anastasia Fulger. The *Daily Mail* ran a cover flash above their masthead with our front cover inset, and had turned over the whole of page three and the centre spread to the story, plugging *In Society* in every paragraph. *The Times* had devoted their basement – the quirky slot along the bottom of the front page – to it, recycling all the key quotes and attributing them to us. *The Daily Telegraph* put it on page three with a front cover, and the *Daily Express* on page five. The *Sun*, who hadn't actually been sent an advance issue by Ellen, simply pirated the front cover and splashed it across their whole front page under the headline 'Hands off my Assets'. In the cab into work I heard the presenters of the *Today* programme discussing it, with Anna Ford questioning whether it was ethical of us to publish an old picture of Mrs Fulger half-naked.

I arrived at the office to find Ellen already waiting.

'Have you seen the papers yet?' she asked.

I kissed her on the cheek. 'It's just brilliant. You've done brilliantly.'

'They're going to massacre me,' she said. 'Half the stories have Exclusive on them. I'm dreading the calls.'

'Don't take them. Hide behind your secretary.'

'She's scared too.'

'Then hire a temp for the day.'

Kay Lipschwitz Anderson came into the office with a full set of newspaper cuttings, already reduced on the photocopier to A4 size.

'Isn't this something?' she purred in her Brooklyn drawl. 'I'm having the girls run off two hundred sets of everything and bike them round to the top spenders.' She flashed an inventory of advertisers under my nose. 'I've drafted a Publisher's Letter about success for us translating into success for them.'

'Are the copies actually on the news stands yet? I didn't notice any on my way in.'

It was seven-forty-five. If the system had worked they should be arriving right now. It was crucial they were available by eight o'clock, at the railway stations especially, otherwise some of the impact of the newspaper coverage would be lost. The commuters had to pour off the trains and see the issues on the station bookstalls.

'Where's Megan anyway?' I tried her office but no one answered.

The telephone rang. 'It's Megan. Look, I'm still in Peterborough at the printers. The fucking binder broke twice during the night, but don't worry, it's OK. Half the copies left here at six o'clock. They're going to make it. My God, Kit, I've never seen so many trucks waiting.'

'You all right, Megan? You sound like you ought to go to bed.'

'Don't tell me, love, I'm going. Alone unfortunately. Just me and an Irish coffee.'

Ellen, Kay and I decided to walk up to Piccadilly and see whether any copies had arrived yet. Directly opposite Prince's Arcade there's a large newsagent which stocks all the magazines as well as expensive greetings cards and tacky souvenirs of London. On the way we ran into Micky and he joined us. He looked elated by all the attention but also jumpy. I didn't blame him. I think we all felt a bit like that.

The first thing we saw as we went through the door was *In Society*. Four full facings, which means four piles side by side on the shelf with no overlapping. They hit you right between the eyes. I defy anyone to have gone into that shop that morning and not noticed them. The cover was very strong. It had that magnetic quality that's difficult to achieve except by luck, and what in the mag biz we call 'icon' quality.

We stood there, the four of us, admiring the impact when a woman in her twenties came in, browsed along the shelves, picked up *In Society* and bought it. It was a good omen.

'Nice reader to have,' said Kay Lipschwitz Anderson. 'You noticed her bag came from Dolce & Gabbana.'

My morning in the office was punctuated by updates from Ellen about the progress of her PR blitzkrieg. She had got Anna Grant on to a lunchtime talk show and promised to video it for me. At midday she appeared with an early edition of the *Evening Standard*. On page three was a photograph of Bruno Fulger coming out of the Connaught hotel, looking ballistic and refusing to comment on his wife's remarks. I hadn't realised he was in London. The knowledge was oddly disquieting.

For now I had other things to think about. My lunch yesterday with the French cosmetics people from Mouchette had not been one hundred per cent reassuring either. Being French, and knowing that I was picking up the bill, they had made it plain they expected three full courses with wine, liqueurs, the lot. They had then proceeded to criticise the food dish by dish, while pursuing a similar tactic on our stable of magazines. This is standard practice in the advertising world. First denigrate the medium. So they told me that for them, at this time, radio was much more potent than magazines and had an immediate impact on sales over the counter. They told me that 'our partners in retail' were urging them to drop magazine advertising altogether and divert the entire spend on to TV. Then they told me they were very disappointed with the level of editorial coverage they'd been receiving in our titles for their new gentle exfoliating scrub and eye-contour gel. It was the classic beat-up routine.

Jean-Marc LeNoy, Président du Conseil de Mouchette SA, was a smooth, rather dissolute man in his late fifties.

The sum total of what I knew about him was that he had an apartment in the place de la Madeleine, of which he was very proud, and a mistress somewhere in the Marais who accompanied him on his frequent overseas trips.

You have to be very careful in the way you handle clients like LeNoy, because their business decisions aren't based on any kind of logic. Everything is an extension of their vanity and ego and personal prejudices. If you turned down an invitation to one of LeNoy's launch parties or dinners, he'd wipe *Couture* off the advertising schedule without a moment's hesitation or regret. I don't suppose he even bothered to glance at the reader profiles and magazine demographics we sent him. His principal concern was whether and how often his own photograph was published in the party pages. If he was missed out (as sometimes happens when you're choosing six pictures from six hundred) he'd ring me up from Paris and whinge for a full half hour.

'It isn't for me personally that it matters, you understand,' he'd say. 'You know me – *pah* – I don't give a damn if I'm in this magazine or that magazine. It is *Mouchette* you have insulted. When people see these pictures and they know I was present but there's no picture of me, they ask themselves, "For what reason has *Couture* excluded Mouchette?"'

That explains why you see so many more photographs of Jean-Marc LeNoy than he genuinely merits.

He had arrived with two of his marketing people in tow, the chief of whom, Pierre Roux, was a Euro-class slimeball. I'd only ever seen him in one uniform: blue blazer with gold buttons, grey flannel trousers and a silk Hermès tie with a pattern of yellow and green giraffes. Probably he slept in it too. His complexion – and this was unlucky considering the extravagant claims of his company – was terrible, with angry red blotches and open pores. He had recently graduated from INSEAD and travelled everywhere with an Apple powerbook. On the slightest pretext he would magic up a set of pie charts on screen, demonstrating Mouchette's ever-growing market share in fragrance and skincare.

I must say I treated these statistics with extreme caution. From what I heard from their competitors, Mouchette was in trouble, possibly even terminal decline. It was a pity because they were almost the last French beauty company not to have been swallowed up by one of the big boys like L'Oréal or Louis Vuitton-Moët Hennessy, LVMH. As magazine publishers, we preferred them to stay that way. The conglomerates have a nasty habit of collectivising their ad-spend and ganging up for special deals. Mouchette would have to look out if they wished to stay independent. And with LeNoy and Roux in charge, I didn't hold out much hope.

Pierre Roux waited until the digestifs to fire his salvo. A lot of second-raters in marketing do this, I've noticed. They pussyfoot about for the whole of lunch, talking about their children and whingeing gently about the economy and magazines, then launch into the important stuff when you're ready to leave.

'I am now going to say something very serious for you,' he announced. 'If you will just take a look at the screen here.' He slid a switch and a thicket of bar charts appeared on the powerbook. I squinted. Against the terracotta walls of Daphne's it was hard to distinguish anything very clearly.

'This,' he said, indicating the first column, 'is our current advertising investment in Weiss Magazines. While over here,' he pointed to the adjacent column, 'is the same information for Incorporated Publications.'

I nodded. Nothing he was showing me surprised me. We track our competitors' revenues account by account.

'Now I am going to tell you something which will maybe shock you a little,' he said. The self-importance of the man was beginning to get to me. I felt certain his ancestors had been slavish denouncers of the bourgeoisie in the Reign of Terror.

'For this year,' he said, 'Mouchette will no longer be

splitting its budgets in the same ratio. Instead we will do it like this.'

He pressed a button and a single enormous column flashed on to the screen.

'One company will have everything,' he said. 'Nine hundred thousand pounds of advertising for the winner. Nothing at all for the loser.'

As a strategy for selling face cream it sounded just about the dumbest I'd heard, but Pierre Roux seemed delighted with it. Doubtless it was a technique he'd learnt at INSEAD.

'And the rationale behind this?' I asked.

'Commitment,' he replied. 'We're looking for one publishing house to forge extra-close ties with. To be our partners in progress. We would make a very substantial commitment to you in advertising pages. In return we'd expect you to make a very substantial commitment to us.'

'Meaning what, exactly?'

'That's up to you. It could be a question of additional volume discounts, it could be other things too. Editorial commitments, special endorsements of our new products by your beauty editors.'

'As you know very well, Pierre, we don't tell our editors what to write.'

He snorted sardonically. 'Well, as I said, that's entirely up to you. It's not for me to tell you how to run your business. But I'm sure your editors won't find it beyond them when you explain to them what's at stake.'

'As a matter of fact, Pierre, I won't be telling the editors about this at all. This is a commercial matter, not editorial.'

I hated the turn the conversation had taken. And I was cross with myself too for letting it rile me. Heaven knows, the Chinese wall between the editorial department and commerce is thin enough on magazines, virtually transparent sometimes, but there is still some vestige of integrity and I was proud of that. I found it insulting that

Pierre thought he could buy our editors by holding us to ransom.

I asked Pierre, 'What's the time frame on this Dutch auction, then?'

'Dutch auction?' He looked blank. Evidently they don't teach them that module at business school.

'It's an old English expression,' I said. 'It's the reverse of a normal auction. The price keeps on going down.'

'Kit,' he said, 'I'm disappointed in you. You shouldn't adopt this attitude. It's bad business. I'm sure Mr Weiss wouldn't find anything unusual in what we're proposing. Howard Trench certainly didn't when I made the same presentation at Incorporated. He seemed keen to get the extra volume.'

I bet he was.

'As for the time frame,' said Pierre, 'how about next Wednesday afternoon in Paris at four o'clock. At the avenue Montaigne.'

Three working days. Bastards.

The bill when it arrived came to £234 of Barney Weiss's money.

All this was going through my head as I sat in my office in Park Place that Friday afternoon, waiting for the four o'clock circulation figures.

As it turned out, we got them slightly early. Norman had spent most of the day on the distributors' backs and they'd responded by processing our data first. In addition he'd had his entire circulation department conduct their own monitor, ringing key newsagents and railway stations direct. At lunchtime he'd rung to tell me the issue was 'going like a train'. Now, at a quarter to four, he was ecstatic.

He burst into my office followed by most of his department, grinning from ear to ear. Phil Burton, our news stand manager, was punching the air in triumph.

Norman was brandishing the figures that had just come through on the fax.

'This is bloody fantastic, guvner, that's all there is to it,' he announced. 'Eighty-nine per cent sell-through in the first six hours. Technical sell-out. Two hundred bloody thousand copies. My contacts at Menzies say they've never seen anything like it. Listen to this. It's a list of all the places that have sold out completely. W. H. Smith in Sloane Square. Smiths, High Holborn. Smiths, King's Cross. Smiths, Epsom High Street ...'

'That's OK, Norman. I think we've got the picture.'

Suzy, who knows the appropriate gesture for every situation, appeared through the door with champagne and a tray of glasses. 'I've invited Micky Rice, Kay Anderson and Ellen Durlacher to join you too,' she said. 'They're on their way up. And some of the *In Society* staff. Megan still hasn't got back from Peterborough. We think she's out cold in some motel on the ring road.'

A second bottle was opened, then a third. Even Micky Rice began to unwind a bit.

'I've got to hand it to you, Micky,' Norman in his euphoria was telling him. 'When I heard you were putting that German bird on the cover, I never believed it'd work. But it's bloody marvellous. She's selling like stink. Don't ask me why, I'm only the circulation man. You fellows are the creative geniuses. And it's bloody marvellous, that's all. Not that I see anything very special in this Anastasia myself. Give me Uma Thurman any day.'

A toast seemed to be called for, so I asked everyone to top up their glasses and said, 'To Micky, for taking *In Society* through the two hundred thousand barrier.'

There was a roar of agreement and cries of 'Well done, Micky!'

Then I added on the spur of the moment, 'And to Anna Grant, who sadly isn't here too. For writing such a great piece about Anastasia Fulger and for bringing us the scandalous picture on the front cover.'

A second cheer. Unconsciously I found myself looking at Micky. It might have been my imagination, but I was pretty certain that his nose had suddenly been put badly out of joint.

The party was still going strong when a telephone began ringing in the outer office and Suzy diverted it through to my desk.

'Mr Kit Preston?' It was a heavy accent, Swiss-German. 'Rudolph Gombricht.'

I motioned the others to shut up, and the laughter subsided into a gentle murmur. I think those colleagues standing closest to me realised this was an awkward call, and watched me nervously.

'You appear to have made a fool of us,' said Gombricht. 'I hope you're feeling pleased with yourself.'

'I'm sorry, I don't know what you mean.'

'Grow up, Mr Preston,' he snapped back. 'You know perfectly well. And if you're wise you'll listen to what I'll say next very carefully. Mr Bruno Fulger isn't happy about what happened today, and nor is Mrs Fulger. Please don't imagine we don't know all about how you placed those stories in today's newspapers. You've made Mrs Fulger a laughing stock and Mr Bruno Fulger's wife is never a laughing stock, not even after they're divorced.'

I began to say something about the article being an accurate reflection of what Anastasia Fulger had said, but Rudolph Gombricht cut me short.

'Don't interrupt, Mr Preston. You're in enough trouble already, printing a stolen photograph of Mrs Fulger for which you have no copyright clearance whatever. And which you published against the explicit advice of the editor. Don't sound surprised, we know everything, Mr Preston.'

I glared at Micky across the room but he didn't notice me. He was still basking in compliments on his issue.

'Where's all this leading, Mr Gombricht?'

'For the moment Mr Fulger is considering his position. But, make no mistake, my client isn't often crossed. And when it happens, he is quite unforgiving.'

'That isn't a threat, is it?'

'Not a threat. A polite warning.'

After that the party broke up. I wouldn't say it had been

exactly soured by Rudolph Gombricht's telephone call, but I certainly felt that a shadow had fallen across it, and it was hard to recapture my high spirits.

For a couple of years now I've suffered from mood swings, probably my separation's got a lot to do with it. I can feel great one minute, down the next. It's nothing to worry about, just mild occupational depression.

I headed home to my flat. Suddenly I was very tired. The flat felt cold and unlived in and I wished someone had been there for me. I rang Anna but the answering machine was on, so I left a message about how well the issue was selling, and good luck tomorrow morning with Erskine Greer and we'll liaise nearer the time about getting to the Dorchester. I stood for a minute or two by the french windows watching the river down below. The tide was very high for June and the current strong. Then, without bothering to draw the curtains, I went to bed.

# 5

I'd got my weekly visits to Cazzie down to a fine art, requiring the minimum interaction with Sally. I'd arrive at our old house off Clapham Common at ten o'clock, double park the car with the hazard lights flashing and walk up the path to the front door. It still felt strange ringing the doorbell of my own house. Sally was usually watching out for me anyway and I'd hear her call, 'Cazzie. Quickly now, Daddy's here,' and there'd be a series of thumps on the staircase as my daughter ran down to find me.

I'll give Sally this, she's never tried to poison Cazzie against me or anything. On the surface it's all very civilised, all very considerate, we tiptoe around on eggs for Cazzie's sake.

'Got your shoes, darling? Come on, hurry up, Daddy's waiting for you.' Sally fusses around her, helping her get her things together. As soon as she's handed her over, she'll drive over to the big Sainsbury's at Nine Elms and do the weekly shop.

I stand about in the hallway. We bought the hall table together when we first married, but it doesn't mean anything to me now. I'd never choose it again.

Next door in the sitting-room everything looks exactly the same as it always did, the chair covers, the lamps. The only difference I notice is that our wedding photographs have been taken off show. In their place are pictures of Cazzie everywhere. There's a new school one of her in an oval frame wearing a gingham smock.

'Everything OK?' I asked Sally.

'Fine,' she replied. 'Oh, I don't know what you've

planned for today, but if you're taking her to the children's zoo at Battersea Park can you please leave out the snake house? She had nightmares afterwards last time.'

'Sure,' I said. 'We'll miss out her favourite place. Great.'

'I'm serious, Kit. It's not you who has to sit up half the night with her. She was very frightened.'

'Point taken.'

We went out into the street where I transferred Cazzie's child seat from Sally's Renault into my BMW. As usual the seat belt wouldn't disengage from its clips and I became testy.

Sally and Cazzie stood on the pavement watching me struggle with it. Sally in blue jeans, a blue cotton jersey and a silk scarf tied round her neck. Her hair was short and blonde, she'd had it cut since last Saturday.

'You will strap that seat back properly into my car afterwards, won't you?' said Sally. 'Last time you didn't.'

'Sure,' I called back.

'Well, you say that, but last time you didn't.'

I fixed the child seat and Cazzie climbed in.

'I can do my own straps now,' she said proudly. 'And my own seat belt.' Her little hands fumbled with the metal ends and slotted them in.

'Well *done*, Cazzie.'

Sally put her head through the back door, kissed Cazzie goodbye and dropped a plastic bag on to the seat beside her. 'One pink Power Ranger,' she said. 'Two spare pairs of knickers. Baby wipes. Bring them all back please, Kit.'

We drove to Battersea Park and put the car under a tree near the Buddhist temple. Battersea is my favourite London park. As a child I lived just across the river and walked there over the Albert Bridge every afternoon. In those days there was a great attraction called the Tree Walk, which was a wooden walkway that ran for about a hundred yards between the branches of the sycamores. You went up a flight of steps, walked along and came down at the other end. One of my earliest memories is of running ahead along the Tree Walk, and my mother shouting after me to take care. It disappeared long ago but I still had a special attachment to this park.

Cazzie said, 'Can we go to the zoo today?'

'But we went to the zoo last weekend.'

'Again, Daddy. Oh come on, Daddy. 'Cos it's got some really good things. Let's go and see the scary snakes.'

'Well, I don't know.'

'Please, Daddy. Please, please, please. Say yes, Daddy.'

She was hopping from foot to foot and pulling my hand. Some days she looked extraordinarily like her mother with her straw-blonde hair and big imploring eyes. She was wearing a blue denim dress, stripy tights and little blue button shoes, shiny with polish. I don't know whether the polish was in my honour. She always looked neat and tidy, I'd give Sally that too. Cazzie had recently started minding about what she wore, Sally told me. Today her hair was pulled up off her face in a pink elastic band, like the crown of leaves on a pineapple.

'OK,' I said at last. 'The zoo it is. But not the snake house, Mummy says it gives you nightmares.'

I picked her up and swung her around and hugged her. For some reason I never do this at the house, I wait until we get to the park. Maybe I feel inhibited by Sally being there or something. Anyway Cazzie must have picked up on it because she's not demonstrative with me either until we're on our own.

She wound her arms around me for a bit and we kissed and then I put her down and we walked together to the turnstiles of the children's zoo.

Our visits always followed the same routine. First we went straight through to the fenced-off farmyard area where you can touch the animals. There's a goat and a large pink pig and baby lambs that stagger about. Then we go and make faces at the capuchin monkeys. Then we visit the rabbits in their hutches, followed by ice creams.

'Can we see the snakes now, Daddy? I won't be frightened, I promise.'

'Not today, darling. Mummy would be cross with me.'

'But we don't have to tell her. Let's just go.'

Our first secret.

So we pushed through a plastic curtain into the temperature-controlled clamminess of the snake house. Along the walls of a long, narrow room were brass-bound aquaria of iguanas and dark cases ostensibly containing snakes. Saturday after Saturday we peered into these cases, Cazzie and I, our eyes scouring the backlit habitat of logs and pebbles, but the snakes were either deep in their holes or coiled up asleep. No hissing or dancing on their tails. Nevertheless something about the place must have rattled her because as soon as we were inside she put her hand in mine and dragged me round as quickly as she could.

As we were walking back to the car I noticed two men watching us from the trees. When I looked at them they turned away and pretended to walk off, but when I was lifting Cazzie into her car seat I saw them again through the rear windscreen, still looking in our direction.

We drove over the bridge to Tootsies for a hamburger and on the way I stopped to buy the Saturday newspapers. The *Daily Mail* had followed up yesterday's article about Anastasia with one about Bruno Fulger: The Billionaire and his Women. Someone in the photo library had collected together every picture ever taken of him with a girlfriend over thirty years and a facetious paragraph about each one had been appended underneath. None of it was liable to improve Bruno's mood.

We ordered a chocolate milkshake with two straws and played a game to see how quickly we could finish it, both of us sucking like Hoovers. Then we ordered a strawberry one and did it over again.

'Are you going to sleep at our house tonight, Daddy?' Cazzie suddenly asked.

'I don't think so, darling. Daddy has his own flat.'

'But you *used* to sleep there.'

'I know that, darling. But I have my own flat now. One

day you can come and stay with me if you want to. Would you like that?'

Cazzie shook her head. 'But there won't be any *toys* at your house.'

'Oh yes there will be. We'll buy some specially at the toy shop and take them home with us to play with.'

'Can I come and stay with you *tonight*?'

'Not tonight. But one day.'

When I dropped her home Cazzie went rushing into the kitchen where Sally was ironing.

'Mummy, Mummy,' she called out. 'Daddy bought me an ice cream, a hamburger, two milkshakes which we shared and we saw the snakes in the snake place. And Daddy says one day I can sleep in his house and he'll buy lots of special toys for us to play with.'

'Well,' replied Sally grimly. '*What* an exciting day.'

## 6

I'd expected to find a message from Anna at the flat, but the answering machine was clear and there was no e-mail either. So I rang her at Harrington Gardens and spoke again to her machine. 'Anna, this is Kit. It's ten to four, Saturday. I'm back home now. Please ring me about tonight when you get in.'

I took a shower then mooched about the flat in a towel doing domestic chores. For some reason after my Saturdays with Cazzie I always feel rather resentful loading washing into the machine. Sally used to take care of everything like that, and to be honest, until the day I walked out, I hadn't set the dryer or ironed a shirt in seven years. I put on a CD and the warped, fragmented lyrics of Sheryl Crow boomed around the flat. One of the bonuses of living in these rather soulless service apartments is that every single room has a speaker.

I was unloading glasses from the dishwasher when I saw them again. Out of the kitchen window overlooking the car lot at the back of the flats, the same two men from the park staring up at the outside of the block. I stepped back so they wouldn't see me, then edged forward again for a better view. Anyway my flat's on the sixth floor, so it was easier for me looking out at them than for them looking in.

This time I could see them quite clearly. There was an older man, early forties, in jeans and a brown suede jacket zipped up at the front. And there was a younger one, mid-twenties it looked like, in a black track suit. The younger one had a moustache and looked Greek or Egyptian or

Lebanese, something swarthy. The older one could have been a driving instructor, he was that nondescript.

They stood there for five or ten minutes, then got into a car and parked up at the end of the street. It was a fawn Sierra, unfortunately too far away to read the number plate. It crossed my mind to go down and tap on the window but something stopped me. The younger guy in particular looked tough and in any case I was in a towel.

The entryphone buzzed and I lifted the receiver.

'Hello?' I said cautiously.

'Kit. Is that you? Your voice sounds different.'

It was Anna. I let her in and waited for her by the lifts.

'Hope you don't mind me coming straight here,' she said, 'but I've only just got away from Erskine Greer. The interview went fantastically, right until the end when I think I might have blown it.' She dumped her duffel bag and a tape recorder on to the sofa and threw off her jacket.

'Did he invite you to Palm Beach?'

'Need you ask? I was all over him. Even before lunch he'd invited me. Hope he doesn't revoke it now.'

'Why would he?'

'Because I got totally carried away and asked him about arms dealing. I must be crazy.'

'It sounds like you did pretty well anyway to get four hours. Were you on your own or was there a minder?'

'No, just us. And a Filipino housekeeper who I swear was only four foot six. When she served lunch she could hardly reach the table.'

'Listen,' I said, 'come into the kitchen with me. Slowly now. We've got to approach the window without being seen.'

Anna laughed. 'What is this? A stake-out?'

'That's exactly what it might be. Two men have been watching the flat for almost an hour. And they were in the park earlier on, watching me and Cazzie there too. If you look carefully you'll see they're parked down by the garages in a Sierra.'

But when we looked out, the car had gone.

'I know what you're going to say next,' I told Anna, '"You imagined it."'

'Well, I could. But I won't. Considering you're the least fanciful person I know. Who do you think they were? The Fulgers' footmen?'

'It already crossed my mind they could be working for Bruno. But I can't see what's in it for him.'

'Unless it's just to scare you. Put the wind up you a bit.'

'Could be.'

'For daring to publish articles by a girl like me.'

We were sitting next to each other on the sofa, me in a towelling dressing gown, Anna in a pink linen dress, very short and sleeveless. Her small vaccination scar was the only blemish on her long brown arms. She'd kicked off her shoes and her brown legs were only a few inches away from mine.

'What do you mean, "a girl like you"?' I said. 'Clever, witty, intuitive.'

She raised her eyebrows. 'That all?' she said. 'What about sexy as hell?'

'I wouldn't know about sexy. Great looking, certainly.'

I swallowed. Suddenly it became rather hard to say anything else. I guess I'd wanted Anna for months now without admitting it to myself. I leant across and kissed her, laying my hand on the hem of her pink dress.

'More compliments first, please,' she said, smiling.

'Beautiful skin,' I said, kissing her neck. 'Beautiful legs. Beautiful breasts.'

'You haven't seen them yet,' she said, pulling me down on top of her.

Our lovemaking was OK but I don't think either of us would pretend it was the fuck of the century. Probably it was my fault. I hadn't done it for eighteen months, not since Sally, and had lost the rhythm. It was as though I was attaching too much importance to each movement.

We persevered.

At some point in the proceedings Anna's bag tipped on to the floor with a crash.

'Fuck it,' said Anna. 'No, don't stop, not now, it's OK.'

'I've been longing to do this for ages, you know,' I said.

'You should have told me,' she replied. 'I love it too. Very, very much.'

After fifteen minutes of stop-start exertion, we pulled apart and rolled on to our backs, short of breath, sweating on to the sofa covers.

For a while neither of us said anything, just watched the patterns of the water reflecting on to the ceiling from the river down below. My solicitor had made a big thing of warning me not to get involved with anyone during the separation, it can be used against you in the settlement, he'd said. And I'd missed it.

Jesus, I thought suddenly, could the men in the car have been private detectives sent by Sally, to see who came and went? The idea was much too farfetched, surely. Well, if they were, they'd have seen Anna Grant arrive at the flat at five to five. Nothing incriminating in that presumably, not in itself.

Anna leant over and kissed me on the cheek. 'Thank you for that,' she said. 'It's a funny thing, I always feel like sex after doing an interview. It leaves me kind of hyper from the adrenalin.'

'Not sex with just anyone, I hope.'

'Only someone I like.'

She stood up and gathered up her clothes from the floor. 'This poor dress is all crumpled,' she said. 'I hate linen. Have you got a steam iron? I'll need to get the crinkles out before tonight.'

Then she disappeared into the bathroom and I heard the shower come on, and a bit later she came out again, naked apart from a towel wrapped into a turban around her head. I must say that her figure, now that I could see it properly, was quite magnificent.

'You know the best thing about Erskine Greer,' she said. 'He has very good manners. Didn't you find that too?'

'Always offering drinks and asking if you have every-thing you need in your room. Yes. He's quite solicitous in that way. I suppose it's easy to be thoughtful if you have a lot of help to make it happen. In Nassau there were about six maids hovering about and a black butler in a green waistcoat.'

'He's good at asking questions too. Most people couldn't care less about the person who's interviewing them, you don't exist except as a conduit to good publicity. But Erskine Greer knew a lot about me already and asked some interesting questions. He'd obviously been briefed, but it was quite flattering all the same.'

'I thought that was the first rule they teach you in journalism school. Never talk about yourself. It wastes time.'

'Don't worry, I pumped him non-stop for the first two hours. Didn't waste a second. I kept thinking any moment he'll say "time's up" and chuck me out. The telephone kept going and each time I thought this'll be it, he'll get the maid to show me out.'

'Maybe he fancied you.'

'Maybe it was my questions he found fascinating.' Anna rummaged in her duffel bag for cigarettes and lit up.

'You know what he told me,' said Anna. 'This is the first interview he's given for fifteen years, apart from ones to financial journalists who only ask about the figures. The first magazine interview with proper questions. Nor-mally he turns everything down.'

'I wonder why he agreed now.'

'Why does anyone agree? Maybe he just felt like pouring out his life story. Or swanking. "The charmed life of Erskine Greer: his yachts, his houses, his Lear jet, his opinions on the future of the world."'

'Was he forthcoming?'

'Enough. At least he told me what he wanted to. He's pretty controlled. I don't suppose a single word he said was genuinely spontaneous.'

'Vivid, though?'

'Quite. He was very good on his childhood in Scotland in Dumfries-shire. His father worked for Jardine's in Hong Kong so his parents lived out there, and it was too far for Erskine to go out except in the summer holidays. He was at prep school in England and the other two holidays he spent virtually on his own in Scotland. A housekeeper looked after him. Tragic, though he makes light of it of course. Says he didn't mind.'

'How does he say he made his money?'

'Trading with the Chinese. In the 'sixties. The house is full of the most amazing paintings of the Far East. There's one in the dining-room, an old oil painting of ships in Hong Kong Harbour that's just incredible. It fills an entire wall.'

'What kind of house is it?'

'Big. Unlived-in feel. It reminded me of a suite in an hotel, rather impersonal. Very smart of course. Patterned carpet everywhere, all very David Hicks. But the pictures are amazing, especially in the drawing-room. It's like a modern art gallery. Cy Twombly, Georgia O'Keeffe flowers, one of those big scribbly paintings by Willem De Kooning. And in the hall there's an Andy Warhol of Chairman Mao.'

'How did you pull off the invitation to Palm Beach?'

'Heavy hints, you know me. Actually it was surprisingly easy. I just carried on asking about his team and their prospects until he popped the question. Then he asked me to stay for lunch too.'

'Maybe he did fancy you.'

Anna blushed. 'Perhaps he did a bit. He's quite attractive too in a very restrained way. I can't imagine him making a pass unless he was absolutely certain of success, but probably most women would say yes to him anyway.'

'But you only said yes to lunch.'

She laughed. 'I certainly said yes to lunch. He only suggested it at ten to one and by one o'clock there was this huge Chinese feast laid out in the dining-room. About fifteen different dishes all in blue and white china. I suppose if he hadn't asked me to stay he'd have sat there all on his own eating it. Anyway, there we both were in the dining-room which is painted like the inside of a red lacquered box, and I'd drunk a couple of glasses of Chablis and it was all going so well, when I don't know what came over me but I started asking him these questions about arms dealing.'

'What questions?'

'Rubbish questions. Gossip I'd picked up about him at that party. Like was it really true he'd sold armaments to the Vietcong during the Vietnam War.'

'Christ, that *is* bold. What on earth did he say?'

'Well, that was the strange thing about it. He wasn't at all annoyed, not at first. Took it completely calmly. He gave me this long, cool stare and said, "Is that so very disgraceful? A few rocket launchers to Hanoi could hardly make much difference. The American government supplied seven hundred billion dollars' worth of arms to Saigon over the course of the war." That's almost word for word. He was virtually admitting it.'

'What happened next?'

'I blew it. I should have let it go, switched the subject back to polo or something, but instead I carried on. Asked him how he justified himself morally, that kind of stuff. And whether the airline and trading company are just a front for arms dealing. Anyway he heard me out, very patiently considering, and then he said, "Finished now? With all due respect, Miss Grant, I'm afraid you don't know what you're talking about. Total balls, frankly, from start to finish. I only wonder at your impertinence, coming to lunch at my house and proceeding to lecture me like some feminist from Greenpeace. Perhaps now you've finished your food you'd like to leave." He didn't raise his voice once, didn't even look particularly annoyed, it was one of the coolest displays of controlled anger I've ever seen. He simply rang a little bell and told the Filipino I was leaving. And that was that.'

I whistled softly. 'Well, it certainly doesn't sound worth packing your suitcase for Palm Beach. Have you got enough material to write the piece without? It sounds like you have. That arms dealing stuff will be dynamite in *Man Alive* and with a quote on tape from Greer, even an oblique one, we're covered legally.'

'I know,' said Anna. 'With a little more digging this could be a serious scoop. Bigger than Anastasia Fulger. It's got substance as well as glamour.'

'Which issue's it for? September?'

'That's the idea. Spike's got it on the board for September. The copydate's next week some time, but I could probably get an extension if Palm Beach happens. I haven't given up hope.'

'I'd have thought Erskine Greer would run a mile.'

'That depends, doesn't it, Kit, on whether he can forgive me in time.'

We made love again then, more slowly. And this time it was great. Anna's body was very strong, the product of hundreds of hours in the gym. It makes a difference. She was a direct and energetic lover and after twenty minutes of extraordinary pleasure we staggered, all fucked out, through to the bathroom, and then rushed about the flat in a panic about being late for dinner. The thought of Mr and Mrs Barney Weiss and the Dorchester left me cold. I'd like to have holed up in bed with Anna and done it all over again. The whole thing felt so right and inevitable, I could feel my whole future opening up. I loved Anna so much. I wanted to tell her but instead I threw on a suit while Anna ironed the pink dress and shook out the contents of her duffel bag on the carpet to find her lipstick.

'No time to repack all that,' I shouted. 'It's ten past seven already. Grab your keys if you need them and let's get out of here.'

As we drove out of the car park I was relieved to see no sign of the two spooks in the fawn Sierra.

# 7

The Weisses' suite at the Dorchester was pretty much as
expected, big and Araby with plenty of closet space.
Barney was watching the tennis on a large-screen television built into a French cabinet, with an open bottle of
champagne in front of him in an ice bucket. Of Mrs Weiss
there was no sign.

I introduced Anna and Barney looked her up and down
appreciatively. 'You people like Cristal champagne?' he
asked. 'I'm just watching Becker here. He's pretty fast on
his feet for a Kraut.'

The same could not be said of Barney Weiss. His own
physique at the age of fifty-nine was anything but agile,
he lumbered around the suite, weighed down by an
enormous girth which spilled over his suit trousers which
were held up by a belt. The only aspect of his appearance
with any zip were his eyes, which darted about like a pair
of piranhas in a tank, missing nothing.

We sat in front of the tennis for a few minutes, drinking
champagne and watching the ball being slammed to and
fro across the net. Then Barney said, 'You ready for dinner
yet? I sure am. I had room service send up some servings
of canapés earlier on, but the portions were the size of a
Chinaman's dick.'

'Is your wife joining us?' I asked.

'Lola? She's sick today. Must have eaten something on
the Concorde.'

'How disappointing. Please give her my best wishes,
won't you?'

'You can see her if you want. She's through there in the
bedroom.' Before I could dissuade him, Barney Weiss

rolled over to the connecting door and shouted, 'Lola, you decent? I've got some folks out here want to say hi.'

There was a reluctant cry of assent, the door was flung open and there was the third Mrs Weiss, propped up in bed against a battery of pillows, reading American *Vogue*. To my eyes, she looked perfectly fit though rather peevish. I guessed her sickness was simply an invention to get out of dinner with us. Or, more likely, to get out of dinner with Barney. From the expression on her face I didn't give that marriage another year. They'd stuck it out for four already and it only seemed a matter of time now until Lola waltzed away with sixty or seventy big ones from LoCo Inc.'s President and CEO.

We trooped down to the Terrace dining-room where the head waiter greeted Barney with a virtuoso display of delight and deference. Barney returned the compliment by palming over a twenty-pound note as he led us to the best table.

'Did I ever tell you my secret of successful travel?' asked Barney. 'Cultivate a *maître d'* and a concierge in each city. Look after them so they remember you, get a dialogue going, and they'll put themselves out. You should have them do an article on that some time.'

Menus were distributed and the wine waiter appeared with a heavy tasselled folder which Barney proceeded to discuss with him for several minutes.

'You like something a little special tonight, Mr Weiss? This is a celebration?'

'I don't know about celebration,' said Barney. 'This guy who claims to work for me,' he nodded in my direction, 'I took a look at his numbers on the Concorde and they're shit.' Barney laughed heartily at his wisecrack and the sommelier, not understanding and consequently not knowing whether or not to join in, smiled politely.

'Made up your mind what you're eating yet, Anna?' asked Barney. 'Let me guess. Fish. The ladies always choose fish.'

'Actually I think I *will* have fish,' said Anna. 'The monkfish with *provençale* sauce sounds delicious.'

'I just knew it,' proclaimed Barney. 'Didn't I tell you she'd go for the fish, Kit? The ladies just love their fish. There you are, there's another article for you. Who needs expensive editors anyway?'

'The fish for you too, Mr Weiss?' asked the waiter, taking orders.

'No way,' said Barney. 'There's never enough taste on a fish for me. I'll take chopped steak, french fries, garden salad and blue cheese dressing. The chopped steak well done.'

Across the table I caught Anna's eye and winked. She smiled, then turned towards Barney and did the best job of buttering him up I've ever seen. Fifteen minutes of unalloyed flattery, grade A quality, the whole performance carried off without the merest intrusion of irony. She questioned him about LoCo and expressed admiration at the rapid growth of his budget supermarket chain across the Midwest.

'At this rate,' she said, batting her eyelashes, 'you're going to be bigger than Wal-Mart.'

'Well, that's the general idea,' replied Barney. 'You probably know we made it already on to the *Fortune* list of America's top two hundred companies.'

'Of course I know,' said Anna. 'Everyone's watching LoCo. Erskine Greer was talking about you only today at lunch.'

'The Pacific Rim guy? I was reading about him someplace only the other day. It's a big operation he's got going over there.' Barney looked chuffed. 'Is that right, Erskine Greer talking about me? Maybe we can get together some time and do some business.'

He gulped back most of a glass of Château-Lafite – I forget which fancy year it was – and savoured the moment.

'What exactly was it he was saying about me anyway?'

'Oh, just how well your corporation is doing. And how

shrewd you were buying the magazines out from under everyone's nose.'

Well done, Anna. In fact, the Heathcotes had been thoroughly relieved when Barney Weiss took the bait. There were no other bidders and the media brokers had run out of leads. After twenty years of keeping the torch of journalism alive, at a subsidy of half a million pounds a year, the Heathcotes were desperate to pass it on.

I remembered the first time Barney Weiss had entered our lives. Billy Heathcote, our Chairman, Managing Director and proprietor since the 'fifties, had heard from God knows where about this grocery millionaire up in Chicago who might conceivably be interested in a stable of British magazines, and I was sent out, as his appointed deputy, to investigate. Billy knew next to nothing about Weiss except that he'd made his money manufacturing plastic straws and beakers. The company was much smaller five years ago than it is now and there wasn't much in the newspaper cuttings. It was called Suck-U-Like Corporation and had posted profits the previous year of $190 million.

Barney, it turned out, wouldn't be back in Chicago for another week, he was out on the road making sales calls, but Billy Heathcote was panicking badly about the losses by now and had me go and see Barney in Cleveland. I'd met him at lunchtime in the cocktail bar of the old Stouffers hotel, a room so dark and panelled that we could barely see each other across the table, and afterwards he took me with him to case a supermarket he was thinking of buying on the edge of the city. We'd been driven there in a chocolate-brown Cadillac reeking of cigarette smoke through the roughest inner city I'd ever seen, while Barney explained to me the margins on waffle syrup and frozen pizza.

In return, I'd sold him the idea of becoming the sole proprietor of the Heathcote Magazine Company Ltd and of changing its name to Weiss Magazines. I'd spun him an alluring picture of the power and social cachet that went

60

hand in hand with being the owner of *Couture, In Society, Man Alive* and *Smart Living*. I hinted with exactly the right degree of subtlety at the invitations that would surely be forthcoming for the man who owned such institutions of discrimination. And I suggested that this influence would have currency not only in London, but in Manhattan and Paris as well, in fact wherever the smart set congregated. I said everything in fact, except that he'd be buying a lemon and that he was the last hope on the planet for saving the magazines.

The more he heard, the more the idea grew on him. At dinner that night he asked me to travel on to Chicago with him the next day to meet Bonnie, the second Mrs Weiss. When he said that, I felt we were halfway there.

Bonnie, who so closely resembled Lola her successor that I can never clearly remember when the handover was effected, saw the point of owning the magazines at once.

'But it's perfect, don't you see, Barney?' she'd said. 'We know some of the people they write about already. We met with them at the Fulgers' ball.'

'Bonnie's referring to Bruno and whatshername's wedding ball at their castle in Germany,' said Barney. 'We were invited guests and it was quite an occasion. Bruno was a very happy stockholder in Suck-U-Like at one point, before I took the company private again. One day I'll show you the photograph of Bonnie and me dressed as French aristocrats in period costume.'

When Barney stepped out to the john, I took the opportunity of reminding Bonnie that, as the wife of the owner of *Couture*, she'd be entitled to front row seats at all the fashion shows in Paris.

'No kidding,' she said. 'Right up front with Mrs Gutfreund and Mrs Taubman and everyone?'

'*In front* of them, Mrs Weiss. Their husbands don't own *Couture*.'

It was all over bar the shouting. Pretty soon afterwards

Barney said, 'What kind of money are your people looking for anyway?'

I had no idea. I was pretty certain Billy Heathcote would be only too pleased to give the company away.

'Ninety million dollars,' I said. 'We may not be making much at the moment but the potential is huge. These are blue chip titles.'

'Sounds on the steep side to me,' said Barney. 'I'll bid you sixty.'

'I'll have to check that with Mr Heathcote of course,' I said, trying to disguise my astonishment. 'If you can just lend me a phone somewhere private.'

Three minutes later we had a new proprietor.

Within a month Billy Heathcote had cleared his office and vamoosed to his manor house near Ipswich with the cheque. I've never seen anyone bank something more quickly; I don't think he really believed in the money until he read it on his bank statement.

For several weeks my own role seemed in jeopardy too. I thought Weiss would send some financial hitman over from Chicago, but he didn't, and in due course I was confirmed as Managing Director and moved into Heathcote's old office. It's the office I still work in today. Once the oak panelling had gone and Billy's beagling trophies, it looked pretty good.

And one thing I'll say for Barney Weiss, he knows how companies work. He taught me about cashflow and cost control and told me what he expected, and then pretty much left me to get on with it. I'm under no illusions, if I screw up I'm out. But the place is more focused with Billy Heathcote off the scene, and I took the opportunity to retire a lot of other dead wood too. Within a year we were in profit after overheads and by year three even Barney found the return on capital acceptable.

Whether he found the return in status as great as he'd hoped, I never dared ask. You certainly read more about him these days, but that probably has as much to do with his hostile takeover of LoCo as his ownership of the magazines. He read the individual titles only sporadically so far as I could tell, and never had much to say about them beyond suggesting friends' houses for inclusion in *Smart Living*. This presented a constant problem for the editor, Meredith Carew-Jones, since they were invariably hideous, full of reproduction French furniture, with all the loose covers, drapes and bedspreads made up in the same blinding chintz. It took all Meredith's ingenuity to extricate herself politely from Barney's rash promises.

Tonight I said, 'Barney, did you have a chance yet to read Anna's brilliant article about Anastasia Fulger? It's doubled the circulation of *In Society*.'

'Not yet,' said Barney. 'I've been stuck into this tennis. I trust it's complimentary anyway, the Fulgers are wonderful people, close personal friends of mine.'

'It's Anastasia's side of the story. She gave Anna an interview. You know they're splitting up.'

'That's too bad. I went to their wedding at that castle of theirs someplace in Germany. Since Lola's not here I can mention this, I was still with Bonnie at the time. We went dressed in costume as French aristocrats.'

'Well, it's all over now,' said Anna. 'Anastasia is quite bitter about it.'

'That's too bad,' said Barney. 'I must give Bruno a call.'

We talked business a bit which gave Barney a chance to share a little perspective from the discount supermarket scene. He never had the slightest doubt that what worked in a warehouse in Indianapolis would have relevance to magazines in London.

'You people still experiencing a strong downward pressure on margins?' he asked.

'We certainly are,' I said. 'Tougher all the time. Next week I've got to go to Paris to pitch against Incorporated for the Mouchette business.'

'Mouchette, eh?' said Barney. 'I know a little about that outfit. It's a listed company on the Bourse and underperforming. Half the stock is still owned by the founder.'

'You're very well informed.'

Barney shrugged. 'I read the *Wall Street Journal* pretty much front to back. It's enough. That and *Playboy*.' He laughed suggestively in Anna's direction.

'You know there's a great story to be written about Mouchette,' said Anna, 'though I doubt any of the magazines would touch it, because of advertising. I'll probably have to write it for a newspaper.'

'Beauty journalism isn't usually your thing,' I said.

'It's not beauty journalism. They're real sleazoids at Mouchette. I've got this bearded brother who's a conservationist out in Brazil and he says they're doing terrible things in the rainforest.'

'This isn't the Greenpeace feminist talking again, is it?' I said teasingly.

'Aw,' said Barney, 'all those big cosmetic guys are out there someplace looking for some new iguana tail to grind down and put in a pot. Lola's a real sucker for all that stuff. They try and charge me overweight on the Concorde just for her vanity case.'

Dinner over, Barney and I kicked our heels in the lobby while Anna went to the cloakroom.

'That girl's work as good as her butt?' asked Barney.

'Even better. She's a great writer. Once she gets her teeth into a story she never lets go. That's why we use her.'

'That's quite a build-up,' said Barney. 'She's cute.'

Anna returned and we began our goodbyes, but Barney interrupted. 'I've got a car and driver sitting outside on round-the-clock call. Say, Anna, let me run you home, I could use some fresh air before turning in.'

We went outside into Park Lane where an elderly chauffeur was dozing at the wheel of a black Mercedes. Belgravia Limousines. We use the company sometimes in the evening for work. I was following Anna into the capacious back seat when Barney turned to me and said, 'Maybe it's best if you take a cab home tonight, Kit. It's a little tight inside for three.'

I caught Anna's eye and she winked and rolled her eyes. It was a look that said 'It's OK, I can handle him.'

So I said goodbye to Barney on the pavement, waited while the chauffeur shut the door with an expensive clunk, and then watched as the long black car pulled away from the kerb and merged into the Saturday night traffic.

I got home, scanned the car park for evidence of spooks, and considered ringing Anna to make sure she'd got back OK. The flat was strewn with evidence of our hurried departure, the contents of the duffel bag and her notes and tape recorder where they'd fallen behind the sofa. It occurred to me that Barney might have inveigled himself upstairs into her flat for a drink, in which case it would look rather uncool if it appeared like I was checking up on him. But just then the telephone rang anyway and it was Anna.

'As for Barney,' she said, 'talk about unsubtle. I nearly died when he manoeuvred you out of the car.'

'Did he try anything?'

'Did he *try*? He was all over me. Hands everywhere. I nearly had to tell the driver to pull over and make a dash for it. I wish you'd been a fly on the ceiling, you'd have loved it. For the first ten minutes he put on his hilarious pseudo-sensitive face and talked about journalism, if you can believe it. He was actually quite high minded. Then, just as we were turning into the Cromwell Road, he lunged. I'd have elbowed him in the balls if he wasn't the great paymaster.'

'So you didn't ask him up.'

'No way. Which didn't stop him asking himself.'

'But you got out of it.'

'Just. I had to promise to have dinner next time he's over. Just the two of us.'

'Talking of coming over,' I said, 'why not come over yourself right now? All your stuff's here and I'm missing you. And we could do brunch somewhere tomorrow.'

'You know something,' said Anna, 'I think I'll pass. I'm

65

here now and it's been a long day. A *great* day actually. But I'm tired. I'll ring you for sure tomorrow. I need the tape recorder anyway, I want to make a start transcribing Erskine Greer.'

We said goodnight and confirmed we'd talk in the morning.

'Oh, Kit,' said Anna suddenly. 'I meant to say this, I loved this afternoon. Really loved it. I might have forgotten to say so at the time.'

'You did, actually. But keep saying it. Because I loved it too.'

# 8

I woke late and padded to the front door and fetched the Sunday papers. They were waiting outside on the mat like a big slab of tofu, vaguely threatening in their enormity. I fixed a pot of coffee and put on a CD. Nirvana. Every Sunday morning it has to be Kurt Cobain, he catches the mood.

Back in bed I made a start on the papers, first removing those sections like Appointments and Personal Finance that I had no intention of reading. I had hardly opened *The Sunday Times* when I saw this big photograph of Anna looking out at me, surrounded by several smaller pictures of her standing side by side with various celebrities. The headline said 'Meet Anna Grant (but only if you're rich and famous)'. There followed one of the nastiest hatchet jobs I've ever read, so manipulative and shot through with half-truths it made me feel slightly sick. Obviously the peg for the piece was Anastasia Fulger, whom *The Sunday Times* presented as this pathetic, duped woman, cynically befriended by Anna and later betrayed. It said that Anastasia had no idea that Anna was a journalist when she'd met her, that she'd confided in her as a friend, woman to woman, and that Anna had either fabricated the quotes or interpreted them in such a way that they were utterly misleading. The specially taken portrait photograph of Anastasia on the sofa, which rather undermined the theory that she hadn't known she was being interviewed, was explained away rather ingeniously, with Anastasia claiming she'd agreed to be photographed for a quite separate article about charity queens, which was to have highlighted her fundraising efforts for children with cystic fibrosis. When she'd seen the magazine, she said, she'd felt terrible, 'practically like I'd been raped', she couldn't understand how people could write these things when she was already so depressed about her separation from Bruno.

The article went on to say that Anna Grant had a reputation for ingratiating herself with the jet set, posing as a friend and then knifing them in the back. Several sharp quotes were reproduced from her profiles of Kerry Packer and Ivana Trump as evidence of the sort of betrayals she was capable of, though I knew for a fact that both those interviews had been set up through their PR people.

This was followed by some sleazy personal innuendo. There was a suggestion that Anna had obtained her first commissions by sleeping with the editor of a national newspaper, and there was a list of other men she had apparently been 'close to', which could mean anything from a dinner date to an old lover. Some of this was quite well informed and I wondered who'd been helping with the piece. There was a poisonous quote from 'a friend' that could only have come from someone quite high up at Weiss Magazines. Some friend. He went on to say that unless you were rich and a celebrity Anna wasn't interested (a modicum of truth in this, as subjects for her writing) and that she was haughty in the office (total rubbish).

Finally, and this was the most offensive bit of all, there was a lot of stuff about Anna's background, 'revealing' that she wasn't born into the smart set at all and that her mother was a teacher at a private day school in North London. It stated that Anna was ashamed of her home and never talked about it. The 'friend' had something to say about this too, claiming that Anna liked to pretend her mother lived in Chelsea rather than Belsize Park. It was all such a travesty I wanted to hit someone. Anna never made any secret of her North London origins. In fact she was proud of them. About six months ago we'd had supper together at a place up in Chalk Farm and afterwards, on the spur of the moment, she'd taken me round to meet her mother. Mrs Grant had been a delightful person, a widow, correcting exercise books to Mozart in her ground floor flat. She was evidently very proud of her daughter and Anna had been affectionate to her, telling her about the articles she was working on, and asking her for news of the school. I hated to think of Mrs Grant reading this kind of crap in the newspaper.

The article was bylined 'Carol White' which didn't mean anything to me. Doubtless she was one of those braindead I-was-only-following-orders hackettes who do the dirty work as directed. I was certain the article wouldn't have been Carol White's own idea. The subject and tone would have been suggested by someone much more senior on the paper. I wondered who. The editor, Colin Burns, was quite capable of it, a class warrior with a deeply schizoid take on high society. It could have been Burns on his own. Or he could have been put up to it by someone else, like Bruno Fulger or Bruno Fulger through Rudolph Gombricht. I'd have to find out.

But first I needed to ring Anna. She might not have seen the article yet, I doubted anyone would deliver newspapers to a top floor flat, and I wanted to warn her. Or, better still, scoop her up in the car and get a couple of drinks inside her before letting her read it. I was certain she'd take the article badly. Journalists who dish it out are meant to be able to take bad publicity, but Anna would be deeply wounded, I was sure, by something so unjust and unprofessional. Her own articles, however uncomfortable for their subjects, were always meticulously researched, and I had never known her to manufacture a quote or suppress an inconvenient fact that didn't fit in with her theory. She'd hate the way the piece questioned her professional integrity.

I could hear the phone ringing three times at the other end, then click, it was the answering machine. Probably she was out buying the papers. I left a message for her to ring me.

Thirty minutes later, having heard nothing, I tried again. Still the answering machine.

I wandered around the drawing-room straightening the place up, and stuffed Anna's junk back into her bag: lipsticks, eyeliner, spare tapes, her pocket address book – one of those calf leather Smythsons ones divided in sections for London, Paris, New York – and a wedge of yellow Post-it stickers and dry-cleaning tickets. Then I gathered up her notes and began putting the pages in order. As I did so, I read. They were her background research on Erskine Greer consisting of thirty or so pages of people's opinions on him. Anna had evidently been ringing around getting a preliminary fix on his character. Quite a number of the quotes were from prominent socialites who more or less moved on the same circuit as Greer. Several had the words 'NB – not to be quoted by name' next to them where Anna had evidently guaranteed anonymity as the price of an off-the-record appraisal. Ironically these opinions were mostly anodyne or laudatory. Sentiments like 'charismatic', 'so charming', 'quite brilliant' and 'generous host, holiday on a yacht from Bodrum to Fethiye' were scattered liberally about.

It didn't surprise me all the same that so many of her informants had chosen to keep their identities secret. This happens a lot when you profile tycoons, particularly when there are negative things that might come out elsewhere in the article. Even if you are quoted saying only the most praising things, if the overall tone of the piece is nasty, you are in jeopardy of being found guilty by association. It is an old trick to say something laudatory for attribution, while dishing the dirt off the record. It happens. Which is why most socialites talk strictly for deep background.

Further on, Anna had headed a sheet 'Erskine Greer as womaniser?' There was some gossip, unattributed and not specific, about an old love affair in Hong Kong. Below that she had written 'Amandari Hotel, Bali?'

And later there was a sheet headed 'Erskine Greer as Businessman. Strategist or lucky?' There was a list of people Anna was proposing to ring later in the week, including Henry Keswick, the former taipan of Jardine Matheson, the Chinese entrepreneur David Tang and the banker Rupert Hambro.

I ran a bath and carried the remaining few pages of notes into the bathroom with me to read. Before getting in, however, I made a third attempt at ringing Anna. Still no luck. Where the hell was she? It was half past eleven and more than an hour since I'd first tried. A wild idea came into my head that she'd already read the article and gone to ground to lick her wounds. Or else she was tracking down Carol White with the intention of inflicting some grievous bodily harm.

Of course there were plenty of perfectly innocent explanations. She could be at the gym. She could be rollerblading in the park, though if she were I was a little put out she hadn't asked me to join her. She could be at some twenty-four-hour deli in the Gloucester Road stocking up her fridge.

I made a snap decision not to wait around any longer. It was a beautiful, warm June day and I wanted to get some air. These flats are so badly designed, the balconies overlooking the river aren't deep enough to sit out on. So, abandoning my bath, I threw on a pair of shorts and a shirt and made for the park. It crossed my mind to ring Sally and see whether she'd mind if I took Cazzie along with me, but I didn't think it would go down well, she's very strict about adhering to the small print over access.

I went out into the car lot. There was no trace of the Sierra or its occupants. Then along the Albert Bridge Road and into the park, no sign of them there either. Several times during my walk I made a point of suddenly turning round, until I satisfied myself I wasn't being followed.

I had almost – almost but not quite – started to believe I'd imagined the whole thing.

I walked for about ninety minutes right round the

perimeter, then cut back across the sports fields and lay down on the grass and let the sun beat down on my face. I love the sun. I like to stare directly up at it for a couple of seconds, then close my eyes and still see the white fireball imprinted like a photographic negative on to my eyelids.

At half past one I returned to the flat where a shock awaited me. As soon as I got out of the lift I saw my front door was hanging open on its hinges. I shouted, 'Hello. Anybody there? Hello.' Then I rang my own doorbell. If there was a burglar inside I'd rather let him rush past me here on the landing than come face to face inside the flat. I'd already decided not to tackle him, unless it was a nine-year-old kid or something when it would be embarrassing not to. More likely it was youths from the estate round the back, they were always breaking into these flats. I doubted they'd be armed but they could have a jemmy with them, and I wasn't volunteering for a crack on the head.

'Hello. Is anybody there? If so, please come out now. I'm unarmed and won't give your description to the police.'

Heaven knows why I said that last bit. If I had been armed I'd have gone right in and shot the bastards. Defending hearth and home against intruders. Not a jury in the land would have convicted me for that in the present climate. As for not giving a description to the police, I was already bracing my visual memory for the photofit.

There was still no reply, so very gingerly I inched my way inside. It's funny how in these circumstances you notice things you've never seen before. Like a useless three-point electrical socket and telephone point in the skirting bang next to the front door.

I made it into the sitting-room and it was deserted. The place is pretty bare anyway so there's nowhere much to hide. Thank God I left the furniture with Sally.

I edged towards the kitchen. There was a blind spot behind the fridge freezer and I stood motionless at the door, listening. Absolute silence. No one was hiding there.

That left the bathroom and bedroom. I recrossed the

sitting-room and slammed back the bathroom door against the side of the tub. Nobody behind it. The plug was still in the bath and the water at the same level I'd left it.

Finally the bedroom. As I approached the door, which was ajar, I saw that the drawers of my chest of drawers had been pulled out. Blast. It meant they'd got the gold cufflinks and Dad's old watch. Then I noticed my wallet and chequebook were missing from the top of the dressing table, and the silver frame with the picture of Cazzie.

I was quite angry now. 'If you're fucking well in there, come out now. And you can leave the wallet and picture frame too. You won't get more than a fiver for the silver, it's only plate, and I'll stop the credit cards in any case.'

Did that mean I was giving them the cufflinks and watch? I wasn't sure.

I smashed back the door. Beside a lot of clothes thrown about the place, there was nothing at all. Whoever it had been was long gone.

I walked back to the front door, still feeling jumpy, dragged it shut and put on the security chain. Too late, the horse had already bolted, but it made me feel better. Then I checked the whole flat a second time, opening every cupboard, and rang the police. Not that I held out much hope of seeing my stuff again, let alone an arrest, but the jewellery was insured and I needed one of those police incident chits to make a claim.

There wasn't a lot of enthusiasm for the case down at the Battersea cop shop, but they said they'd send some-body over in the next half hour and I thanked them for that.

While I was waiting for them to arrive, I rang the various charge card companies and cancelled the stolen plastic and, this done, began making a full list of everything that was missing.

Nothing had gone from the bathroom or kitchen so far as I could see. From the sitting-room they'd taken about eight CDs and the CD player. I looked about for Anna's tape recorder and found it still lying on the floor next to the sofa, half-hidden by the skirt of the loose cover. A lucky escape. I'd have hated to have told her she'd lost that on top of everything else.

Then I noticed Anna's duffel bag and the Erskine Greer notes had disappeared too.

I'd left them on the sofa, face up, and they weren't there.

I searched around the flat in case I was mistaken. In the bathroom I found the last few pages that I'd taken through to finish, but there was no doubt about it, the rest had been stolen.

Why on earth would anyone want to take a stack of notes? It didn't make sense.

The police turned up in the guise of a young constable, serious and thorough, who took down the details and then led me round the flat, room by room, advising on additional security devices I might like to install. He had no doubt the burglary was the work of kids from the estate, 'probably not older than fourteen or fifteen'. American videos had a lot to do with it, he believed, and he was disappointed that the government wasn't tougher on people who rented them out to underage youngsters. He reckoned that a fine of a thousand pounds or six months inside would make them stop and think.

I gave him my list of everything that was missing, including the notes (which he wrote down as 'personal papers'), and told him about the two men in the fawn Sierra, watching the flats.

'Quite likely to have been casing the joint,' agreed the constable. 'They're very professional, some of these criminals, probably knew exactly what they were after before starting the job. Electricals, stereos. Could have been stealing to order. Someone wants a CD player, they get him one, no questions asked.'

Abandoning his earlier conviction that it was kids from the estate, the constable became increasingly taken with his new theory, adding that several gangs were operating in exactly this way all over the patch, up as far as Brixton and Streatham.

'You didn't happen to note down the registration number of the Sierra by any chance, sir?'

Had I done so, I would hardly have kept it to myself. But I just said, 'Sadly not. It was too far away to read.'

'Probably a stolen vehicle anyway,' he said. 'Stolen to order.'

After he'd gone I tried Anna again but there was still no reply. I was even more anxious to talk to her now, to tell her about the bag and notes. So I sat at my PC and typed her a message through e-mail to her mail box at grantanna@easynet.uk.co. 'Where are you? I've been trying all day. Probably filled your whole answer machine with messages. Make contact.'

I must confess that at this point a small and unworthy suspicion crept into my mind. I wish it hadn't, especially under the circumstances, but it did. Was it possible Anna was with Barney Weiss? Ridiculous, I know, but when you've spent most of a day talking to an answerphone, paranoia can take hold. I rang the Dorchester to be told that Mr and Mrs Weiss had checked out of the hotel half an hour ago at three o'clock but that if it was urgent I could probably catch them later in the Concorde lounge at Heathrow airport.

One final idea occurred to me. Could Anna have been so upset by the article that she couldn't face talking to anyone in the business, and had gone to spend Sunday with her mother? There are pages and pages of Grants in the telephone directory but only four in the Belsize Park area, and as luck would have it I struck gold first time.

'Mrs Grant? This is Kit Preston, we met once when Anna brought me to your flat after dinner.'

'I remember very well. You work with Anna, don't you?'

'That's right. And I was just wondering if by any chance she's there with you, I've been trying to get hold of her all day.'

'She's not, no. And I wish she'd ring me herself, I was hoping it was her now. Did you see that idiotic article in the newspaper?'

'That's why I wanted to talk to her. To make sure she's OK.'

'I don't take *The Sunday Times* myself, but my neighbour does and he passed it on to me. He can't have read it very carefully or he wouldn't have bothered.'

'It was very unpleasant. Entirely untrue, of course, from beginning to end.'

'Oh, don't worry, I know that. It wasn't Anna they were describing there, it was like reading about a total stranger. But tell me, as a fellow journalist, why would they write something like that? It was so cruel.'

'God knows. Jealousy I expect, because she's such a good writer.'

'Well, it was nice of you to ring anyway,' said Mrs Grant sadly. 'If Anna gets in touch, I'll tell her you were looking for her. Goodbye.'

# 9

I always wake up slightly apprehensive on Monday mornings with a fear born of horrible imaginings about the week ahead, but the minute I walk through the lobby of Weiss House and along the corridor to my office I feel a great surge of energy and cruise back into top gear. Arriving at my desk I spent an hour thinking through a strategy for the Mouchette pitch which I'd test drive on the publishers tomorrow morning. Time was getting tight on this. We'd have to agree our proposal by Tuesday afternoon so Suzy could type it up before the Paris presentation on Wednesday.

Later in the morning I saw I had a big *Couture* fashion meeting coming up, and departmental budget reviews back-to-back in the afternoon.

Suzy turned up at nine looking exhilarated from her weekend. She'd been pony trekking in the Brecon Beacons with a bunch of friends and staggered cheerfully about the office complaining of saddle sores.

'I bought *The Sunday Times* in Builth Wells,' she said, 'and read that ghastly article about Anna Grant. Did you see it?'

She carried a tray of coffee cups to wash up in the kitchen and returned ten minutes later with her hot gossip face on.

'Guess what I've just heard from Micky Rice's secretary Delphine, that ditzy girl with red hair. Apparently Carol White, who wrote the thing about Anna, rang Micky Rice on Friday for the lowdown on her. Delphine had been going through the post with him and he chucked her out of his office. Then they talked for twenty minutes with the door shut. What do you think of that? It means most of that rubbish came from Micky.'

'That would certainly explain some of the detail. But why the hell would Micky do that? Anna's his star writer.'

'That's exactly what I asked Delphine and she thinks it's because he's jealous of her. It really annoys him that Anna's a friend of yours and that you have lunch. He probably thinks you're going to give her his job.'

'That's crazy. Anna wouldn't even want to be an editor.'

'Micky doesn't know that. He's totally screwed up anyway, Delphine says. She read his diary one lunchtime and the things he gets up to after work are really sordid.'

'But I still don't see why he'd invent all that stuff about Anna. It'll just make it more difficult for *In Society* to get interviews. People won't talk if they think they'll get stitched up.'

'I suppose he thought it was worth it to get at her. He's quite spiteful. Apparently, he's sitting in his office looking incredibly smug and telling everyone how sorry he feels for her.'

At eleven o'clock I went down to the *Couture* floor to look at the shoots for the September issue. This monthly fashion summit is the forum at which the editorial and commercial requirements of the magazine are reviewed in tandem. In other words, the editor and fashion editors give us a preview of the upcoming fashion stories, and the publisher and I ensure that no vital advertisers have been missed out. This is very important, since both sides of the magazine have their own, sometimes conflicting, agendas. The young fashion editors are interested only in the cutting edge. If Anna Sui or Jean-Paul Gaultier produce a brilliant directional collection, they will happily jettison every other designer and devote all the pages to them. Worse, if some new shooting star blazes across the fashion firmament from a warehouse garret in Brick Lane, their passion for his Perspex and sheet metal garments can eclipse any other look in the magazine.

The advertising department, however, needs the editors to act like jugglers, keeping dozens of different fashion houses happy at the same time. It is no good saying that Krizia or Fendi have had an off-season and aren't going to be covered, if you want to retain advertising month after month in the magazine.

At the same time these meetings are useful for reviewing the programme from the readers' standpoint. Although the median age of a *Couture* reader is twenty-nine, our richest readers are considerably older. It is important to show clothes that this constituency wants to buy too. So as well as juggling the advertisers, we juggle the different kinds of readers. This sitting is for fashion-forward art school types, this one for Cartier-wearing ladies who lunch, another for professional women who need suits for the office. Success depends on achieving the perfect balance. Too conservative and we alienate the opinion formers who look to *Couture* for fashion leadership; too crazy and we are accused of being an 'art house book' with insufficient power to shift clothes at retail, which in turn leads to a fall-off in advertising.

By the time I arrived, everyone was already squashed into Leonora Lowell's office, and a projector and carousel had been set up on the aluminium conference table. Ten fashion editors on aluminium stools lounged back against the walls clutching black notebooks while a ponytailed art director in a sleeveless T-shirt adjusted the focus. Leonora herself sat imperiously behind her desk flanked by her deputy, Tasmin Feeley, and the executive editor, Loella Renouff-Jones, whose job it was to keep track of the fashion credits. In front of her lay a sheaf of computer print-outs which showed precisely how many times outfits by Donna Karan, Karl Lagerfeld, Ralph Lauren, Escada, Jil Sander, etc. had been shown in the last three years.

Outside commentators writing about the *Couture* fashion room often erroneously talk about 'the *Couture* look' as though there was only one. In fact there are two, and as I gazed around the office that morning, both were in evidence. Leonora, with her short black hair brushed straight back across her head, and her two principal deputies were dressed for the meeting in sharply fitting suits, respectively red Chanel, navy blue Valentino and beige Armani. Tasmin had on in addition a pair of wraparound sunglasses, their lenses so impenetrably black that it was doubtful she could see anything through them.

The fashion editors and assistants, however, wore either long, droopy skirts or no skirts at all, just skintight black leggings, and black shirts with strangely large neck-holes that hung limply off their thin, bony shoulders. One wore a shrunken orange cardigan with its buttons fastened into the wrong holes, a garment so ugly and grungey that nobody could have got away with it other than this strangely beautiful gamine creature. These juniors reminded me of tadpoles, black-haired and incredibly pale and skinny. To be in the fashion room at *Couture* was the only thing that mattered in their lives, and they would rather pack suitcases and tape the soles of shoes in that particular room in Park Place than work on any other magazine.

'Shall we make a start?' said Leonora briskly. 'Three of the sittings for September are already here and we've made a real effort to get everyone in this year.'

'Including Müller, I trust,' said Kevin Sky, the publisher. This was a reference to a German fashion house that had somehow been excluded in the spring, costing us £127,000 in cancelled advertising.

'Yes, don't fret, Kevin, Müller's in there,' said Leonora in a pitying voice. 'It was almost impossible to find something to shoot. The whole collection's pass the sickbag.'

'It may interest you to know,' retorted Kevin, 'that in the latest *Couture* reader research eighteen per cent of your core purchasers said they bought one or more outfits from Müller a year.'

Leonora rolled her eyes disbelievingly while the fashion assistants looked frankly stunned. It was clear they had never seen, let alone met, a Müller wearer in their lives and doubted they ever would.

'Let's just leave it, shall we?' I said. 'It's in and that's great. Can we see the pictures now?'

'The lead story,' explained Leonora as the blinds were lowered, 'is the ready-to-wear shot on location in Jamaica. The photographer's Yando. The only annoying thing I should warn you is that I asked him to shoot colour but it's ninety per cent black and white.'

'There are plenty of shots around the hotel, aren't there?' said Kevin. 'Don't forget we promised the Jamaica Creek Resort Hotel there'd be lots of branding in return for the accommodation.'

As the slide show began, however, it was only too clear that nothing of the kind had been achieved. In fact, it would have been impossible to have conceived a fashion shoot less likely to attract hordes of holidaymakers to Jamaica. For a start, the photographer had chosen for his backdrop the most rundown backstreets of Kingston.

The models, on whom the clothes were scarcely visible as they lurked in rum shops and behind trash cans, had been teamed up for the shoot with a variety of Rastafarian dopeheads and crack dealers. These rather dominated the pictures at the expense of the models who were relegated to supporting roles.

'Jesus,' said Kevin. 'Where the hell did those drop-outs come from?'

'They're the chefs from the hotel,' said the fashion editor responsible. 'They were really cool.'

In the next picture a particularly big black man with dreadlocks was shown performing a voodoo ceremony with a dead chicken.

'Who's he, then?' said Kevin. 'The pastry cook?'

'No, that's Yando's boyfriend. Yando threatened to pull out if we didn't bring him along. It was rather annoying because we hadn't budgeted for him and he needed a first-class air fare.'

Leonora had been correct in alerting us to the preponderance of black and white pictures, but nothing had prepared us for their enveloping gloom. Some were so dark and fuzzy they might have been taken in a dust storm, rather than on a Caribbean island. One of the great mysteries of fashion photography, incomprehensible to outsiders though entirely logical to those in the business, is why pictures are always exactly the opposite of what you expect. You can fly a fashion team halfway across the world to a sun-drenched island and they'll return with black and white shots, complaining the light was too bright. Send them on location to Bucharest, however, or some equally grey and soulless former Soviet satellite, and they'll overdose on colour film.

The sole colour picture in the Jamaica shoot was of two hookers standing on a street corner in red rubber dresses, looking bored and poor, while a crack dealer plied his trade in a doorway behind them.

Then slides of the next shoot began clicking through the carousel.

This time we were in Paris, in an eau-de-Nil suite at the Hôtel Ritz. The subject was evening wear and in order to accentuate the new longer line, the photographer had piled more than a dozen little gold chairs one on top of the other. Perching precariously at the apex of this wonky-looking pyre was a devastatingly beautiful supermodel, Marja, her hair piled into an elaborate beehive.

'Just a moment,' said Loella, the executive editor, as the sitting flashed past. 'I had this down for eight pages but there are only seven pictures.' She began leafing backwards and forwards through a sheaf of merchandising before announcing, 'Valentino! Where's the Valentino? The dress arrived at the shoot but there's no picture.'

One of the fashion editors looked uneasy. 'Actually, Loella, there was a problem with that. We were about to do the last picture when Marja fell off the chairs. We had to rush her to some hospital on the Périphérique and she's broken her tibia.'

'We've got to get Valentino in somehow or other,' said Kevin. 'You can't publish a Collections issue without Valentino. Surely you can re-create the picture.'

'Not without spending £28,000,' said the managing editor. 'That's what the Ritz shoot cost in the end.'

'Twenty-eight thousand pounds?' exclaimed Kevin. 'For seven photographs? That's more than the down payment on my present mortgage.'

'And in any case,' went on the managing editor, 'we can't get Marja. She's in plaster up to her thigh. And Rico the hairdresser is working for Guess jeans in New Orleans.'

'Surely it must be possible to get hold of a Valentino evening dress, in fact it needn't even be an evening dress, a Valentino *anything*, and take a photograph of it,' said Kevin, increasingly exasperated.

'Not without spending a *minimum* of £4,000 and that's not even for a good girl. And we've already blown the entire editorial budget for the issue, overblown it, in fact.'

All eyes looked at me.

'Kit,' said Kevin, 'seriously, we've got to. Otherwise they'll go mad in Rome. It could take a year to get them back in.'

'OK,' I said. 'But for God's sake try and bring October in under budget.'

'The third main story,' said Loella, 'is my favourite. Very hot colours. Great-looking girl. You're probably not going to like it because it's futuristic.'

In fact, she was wrong about this, I loved it. The pictures were incredibly strong, with the shortest purple slips photographed against flaming reds, and lime-green corsets against acid yellow. The model stared out of them as though she was floating in an aquarium, the pupils of her eyes intensified with the photographic technique called ringflash. They were the kind of remarkable images that remain with you for years afterwards and eventually end up in books about the decade. I felt sure these pictures would be chosen as representative of the nineties when the moment came: the kind of pictures *Couture* can produce better than anyone else.

'Aside from that,' said Leonora, 'we've got the medieval varlet story that was coming through very strongly at the shows and the New Puritan look inspired by Newt Gingrich. Very Shaker.' Then, seeing Kevin Sky's despondent face, she added, 'You'll love it, Kevin. Lots of Ralph Lauren in there.'

'May I raise one point?' said Kevin. 'I know I'm not creative and I've never pretended to be, but perhaps you could just tell me what's in this issue for the normal AB woman to wear to work. You're not telling me she's meant to turn up dressed like one of those streetwalkers in a red rubber dress.'

At this, Tasmin Feeley, who had hitherto kept her own counsel behind the wraparound shades, exploded. 'I'm not sure how much more of this I can listen to. I'm sorry, Kevin, but why don't you just go and sell a few pages and leave the editorial to the editors. *Couture* isn't a bloody *catalogue*. It's not *Marie Claire's* 101 ideas.'

'It seems to me,' I said, rising to my feet, 'that we've just about wrapped it up now. To quickly recap, the Müller credit is in and won't be dropped under any circumstances, Valentino is being reshot using extra budget which will be clawed back later in the second half, and if you think there'll be a problem with the Jamaica Creek Resort, Kevin, it's probably best to work something out with them now rather than after the issue appears.

'And for October, Leonora, may I suggest you commission at least ten pages of wearable suits for women who work in offices. And, please, not shot by Yando.'

About every six weeks, when I haven't got a lunch, I take Suzy to a Korean barbecue place round the back of the office. I like it because it's the only restaurant within walking distance where you're guaranteed to find no one from Weiss Magazines. It is too scruffy and insufficiently pricey to be used by people with expense accounts, but slightly too extravagant as an alternative to the sandwich bar. Another reason I like it is for the kimchee, the pungent Korean cabbage fermented in garlic and vinegar. I have a real passion for kimchee. It stinks to high hell but some days it hits the spot like nothing else.

As usual, the place was practically deserted. Somebody once told me that in the evenings it livens up and is packed with officials from the Korean embassy who are offered special sexual services in upstairs rooms, but at lunch it's a tomb. Three, sometimes four, pretty waitresses greet you at the door and explain how to use the barbecue: 'Dhon tush, it howt.' However often you eat there, they never seem to recognise you. Maybe we really do all look alike.

Today we were shown to the table underneath a framed poster of the island of Cheju. The caption, which never fails to amuse, says 'You are welcome to the honeymoon island of Cheju.' Several years ago, on the way home from a trip to Japan, Sally and I spent three nights in Cheju, but as I recall it was no second honeymoon.

I told Suzy about the break-in at the flat and the two men who'd been watching me. She agreed it was very odd and shared my scepticism that it had been a local gang.

'Why would they have to watch a flat if they were going to nick a CD player and cufflinks?' she asked. 'It's not logical to say they were stealing to order. You can't see what's inside through a brick wall.'

'Then who were they? Anna suggested they might have been working for Bruno Fulger, to put the wind up me. But I don't see why they'd want to break in, unless it was retribution.' I put on my Bruno Fulger German accent. 'You have made a laughing stock of my wife, Mr Preston. For that you will lose your father's watch. The one he gave you for your twenty-first birthday.'

'Is he capable of arranging that sort of thing?' asked Suzy. 'I don't know much about the Fulgers except what I see in *Hello!*'

'They've been in *Hello!*?'

'Pages and pages in their castle. I promise you, it went on for twenty pages, with pictures of them posing in every room. It just went on and on. In the ballroom, in their bedroom, on the drawbridge, sitting in an open-topped carriage. The wife had changed into a different outfit for each picture but Mr Fulger – Bruno – just wore the same tweed jacket.'

'I'd love to see it.'

'I'll get it for you. It was some time last summer, the issue with Fergie on the cover in an aqualung.'

'You know what would be helpful too,' I said. 'Find out for me whether Bruno's still in London. There was a picture of him in Friday's *Standard* coming out of the Connaught. I'd like to know whether he's still there, and if not, exactly when he left.'

As soon as we got back to the office I tried Anna again. She still didn't know about the break-in. It surprised me she hadn't rung me back, but I'd been so occupied with meetings in the morning it had temporarily slipped my mind.

This time the telephone was answered on the third ring.

A man's voice. 'Hello.'

'Is Anna there, please?'

'Who is this speaking?'

'Kit Preston.'

'Miss Grant cannot come to the telephone.'

'What on earth do you mean? Who are you?'

'This is PC Murray from the Metropolitan Police.'

'How extraordinary. Not arresting Anna for anything, I hope.' I said lightly. 'She hasn't been rollerblading on the pavement again?'

'Actually, sir, this is no laughing matter. There's been a serious accident.'

I felt my heart miss a beat and a sudden coldness in my legs.

'What kind of accident? Is Anna there?'

'I'm afraid I can't tell you, sir.'

'Look, I'm a friend of Anna's and I also work with her,' I said. 'In fact, I'm her boss. Where is she?'

'As I said, I'm afraid I'm not allowed to give out any details, sir. We were called out about fifteen minutes ago by a Portuguese lady who I understand cleans the flat.'

'For God's sake,' I said, 'this is terrible. Can I do anything to help?'

'Everything's in hand, sir. The emergency services have been notified.' He coughed. 'I'm sorry to have to say this, sir, but it might already be too late. Miss Grant appears to have been dead for some time.'

In the pit of my stomach there was a terrible lurch. My hand holding the receiver started to shake and sweat. My throat was dry, so dry I could scarcely speak.

'But I saw her yesterday, Saturday rather. Saturday night. We had dinner. She was perfectly all right then. She can't be dead.'

The policeman told me to hold a moment but stay on the line, and I heard him saying something into a police radio in another part of the flat.

Then he returned. 'Mr Preston, I've just been talking to the officer in charge of the case over at the station, and he's asked me whether you can get down here yourself as soon as possible. An ambulance is due any moment but if, as we suspect, Miss Grant is dead we'll need somebody to formally identify the body. The Portuguese lady is rather distressed, you see.'

The whole conversation was so surreal I couldn't begin to take it in. Two minutes earlier I'd been taking off my suit jacket and hanging it over the back of the chair. Now Anna was dead. A policeman was asking me to go over and identify her body.

I said, 'Of course, if you want me to. By taxi I can reach Harrington Gardens in fifteen or twenty minutes. I'll be there as quickly as I can.'

I grabbed my jacket, money and bolted. In the outer office Suzy was making coffee for the first budget meeting of the afternoon, and some of the participants were already gathering in the sheep pen. I touched Suzy's elbow and wheeled her back into my office.

'This is a nightmare, Suzy, something terrible's happened to Anna Grant. I've just been talking to the police, but there aren't any details. I've got to go straight over, so cancel the meetings and invent some excuse. Don't tell anyone what's happened, not anyone – I know you wouldn't anyway – I may be back later, depending.'

I found a taxi outside the *Economist* building and sat in the back hyperventilating as it drove down Piccadilly and through the Hyde Park Corner underpass. Along Knightsbridge, left into the Gloucester Road then right into Harrington Gardens. It took fourteen minutes. Outside the flat an ambulance was double parked with its rear doors open and a policewoman standing guard on the steps.

She radioed the flat, then told me to go straight on up. 'Right to the top floor, sir. An officer will be looking out for you.'

Was it really only Thursday evening that I'd last been there? Not even four days. I could see Anna walking up the stairs ahead of me, carrying her rollerblades and rummaging in her pocket for the door key.

The senior officer, Superintendent Barratt, was waiting outside the door. We shook hands and he thanked me for coming over. 'Once we go inside, sir, I must ask you to touch absolutely nothing. I also need you to slip one of these oversuits on top of your clothes.'

He produced a white jacket and trousers made of thickened paper. The trousers had an elasticated belt. Then he handed me a pair of thin plastic overshoes like airline slippers, which expanded to fit over my brogues, and flesh-coloured surgical gloves.

'Now, as we proceed inside the flat,' said Superintendent Barratt, 'I want you to stick as closely behind me as possible. Wherever I step, you step – got it? As we cross the living-room we're going to follow a prescribed pathway so as to keep the disturbance of any forensic evidence to the minimum.'

In the sitting-room Maria, Anna's cleaning lady, was collapsed on the white sofa wailing, while a forensic officer worked stoically behind her, dusting the french window on to the flat roof for fingerprints. Another was working his way across the carpet, lifting threads and fibres with a pair of tweezers and placing them in a sterile container. Next door in the bedroom I could see the green-tunicked back of a paramedic leaning forwards over the bed, and watched him stand up, shake his head sadly and start to repack his gizmos. A police photographer was taking pictures.

Anna was stretched out on the bed, her face grey. Even I, who know nothing of medicine, could see she was long dead. Next to her on the bedside table were a novel by Gabriel García Márquez and a fat red book with a Kensington Library bar-code on its spine called *Who's Who in Hong Kong Business*.

The paramedic was talking to Superintendent Barratt and I heard him say, 'The pathologist will get a better fix on this, of course, but my first estimate of time of death would be some time early yesterday morning. Any time between midnight Saturday and noon Sunday, no later. Judging by her body temperature, she's been dead twenty-four hours – minimum.'

'And cause of death?'

'That's for the pathologist too,' said the paramedic, 'but on the face of it, no question it's strangulation. The bruising round the neck's clear enough. And entirely consistent with the estimate of time of death. See, the bruises here are on the turn.'

It sickened me to look too closely, but around Anna's neck was a greeny-brown weal of bruising, which was starting to go black.

'Murder, then?' asked the Superintendent.

'Jesus,' I said.

'Certainly looks like it,' said the paramedic. Then he added, 'There's also evidence of damage to the back of the skull. It'll need to be X-rayed, but I'd say there's a hairline crack here.'

'Caused by a fight prior to the murder?'

'Most likely. If you've no objection, I'd like to have the body bagged up and taken over to Horseferry Road mortuary. I'll inform the coroner's office, but the sooner they make a start on the post-mortem the better.'

'Agreed,' said Barratt.

After he'd gone, I formally identified Anna's body.

It was a curiously artificial experience, almost cursory. Yes, this is Anna Elizabeth Grant of 195E Harrington Gardens, London SW7. Yes, the deceased has been known to me for six years and I can positively confirm that this is her. I added that her next of kin was her mother, whose Christian name I thought was Bridget, of Belsize Park, and that there was a brother too who I understood worked abroad.

When I'd finished, I felt dizzy and asked if I might fetch a glass of water from the kitchen. Next to the sink were a couple of dry tumblers upside-down on a plastic draining board, probably the glasses I had drunk from on Thursday night. While I was running the tap cold I noticed, lying on the bread board, a spare set of keys to the flat; not Anna's main bunch but the single Chubb and Banhams she lent to friends on the rare occasions anyone stayed. On the spur of the moment, for reasons which even now I can't explain, I picked them up and slipped them into my suit pocket.

I edged back through the sitting-room and did my best to comfort Maria, of whom I already knew a great deal. Anna had turned the turbulent private life of her cleaning lady into a long-running soap and I had followed at second hand Maria's marriage and separation from a waiter from her village, with its many attendant rows and reconciliations along the way. Now Maria had another tragedy to cope with.

'She was such a beautiful lady,' Maria kept repeating.

'Beautiful. So happy. For why would someone kill her? For what reason? You tell me why.'

Superintendent Barratt joined us and took a preliminary statement, warning me I'd probably have to make a fuller one later on. I told him about our dinner on Saturday evening and how Barney Weiss and his chauffeur had dropped her back at the flat at about eleven o'clock. I said that we'd spoken on the telephone shortly afterwards, and at that time Anna was in good spirits and, so far as I knew, alone.

I thought of telling him about Anna's article about the Fulgers, but decided it would be premature. If there was a second interview I might mention it, if it didn't seem too melodramatic.

Nor did I tell him about our lovemaking on Saturday afternoon.

Superintendent Barratt thanked me for my help and said he would be in touch in the not too distant future.

I left the flat feeling shaken, exhausted but something else too. I felt that something I'd seen wasn't right, something was missing.

It was only when I was halfway back to the office that I realised what it was: Anna's AppleMac. It had gone from the sitting-room. Normally, it was set up on a small, painted trolley next to her desk, with the modem and printer on the lower shelf. The printer was still there, but where the computer had been was now an empty space.

I found a cab in the Gloucester Road and was back at Park Place before four o'clock. The lobby, with its backlit display of magazine covers, looked exactly as it had done when I left an hour earlier. Charlie, the commissionaire, was still smoking a cigarette behind reception and watching cricket on his mini television with the volume turned low. A group of fashion assistants from *Couture* was dragging trunks of clothes from the lifts, ready to be collected for a shoot, while two delivery men edged through the revolving doors carrying an upholstered armchair for *Smart Living*. Everything was different, but nothing had changed.

Suzy was stationed outside my office looking worried.

'How was it?' she asked softly.

'The worst. She's dead.'

Suddenly I felt not sadness but anger. I wanted to strangle Micky Rice. It wasn't logical, because I didn't seriously make any connection between Anna's murder and that *Sunday Times* hatchet job, but I didn't mind Micky thinking I did. How could he have fed those things about her? I wanted to face him with the fact that I knew it was him, and watch him squirm.

'Suzy, will you get Micky Rice up here now.'

'Are you sure that's wise? Wouldn't it be better to talk to him tomorrow?'

'Because you think I'm emotional? That's precisely why I want him here now. While I'm still mad.'

'Whatever you do, don't drop Delphine in it.'

'That should be the least of your worries. You should warn me not to hit him.'

I heard Suzy ring Micky's office and tell Delphine it was urgent. Four minutes later Micky himself appeared at my door looking cocky in blackwatch trews and a black Yohji Yamamoto jacket. His hair, unless it was my imagination, was a shade or two blonder than it had been at Friday's party.

'Sit down,' I told him.

Something in my tone must have alerted him to a mood change, because he switched in a second to petulant.

'I'm going to ask you a straight question, Micky, and I want a straight answer. Just yes or no.'

Micky nodded in a what-is-this kind of way.

'Did you or did you not talk to Carol White of *The Sunday Times* about Anna Grant?'

'Oh, for God's sake,' said Micky. 'So this is what it's about.'

'I said yes or no. Did you talk to her or didn't you? Answer me.'

'No, I didn't.'

'I'm told you did. You spoke to her from your office on Friday.'

'Who told you that? My secretary, I bet. I'm going to fire her, she's totally incompetent anyway, ask anyone.'

'Actually,' I lied, 'I heard from *The Sunday Times* end. So they *were* your quotes.'

'Only the complimentary ones. You should have heard what other people were saying. Carol White read some of them back to me, which is why I agreed to be interviewed, to redress the balance. Anna Grant isn't popular, you know, or perhaps I shouldn't say that since she's a friend of yours.'

'A lot of that stuff – the total crap – could only have come from someone inside the office. You know that.'

'If you mean me, that's a slur you'd better withdraw. A lot of people in the office hate Anna Grant, as a matter of fact, and I can tell you, if it wasn't for *In Society* and the subjects we give her to profile through our contacts, she'd be nothing. *Nothing.*'

'Micky, that's rubbish. You know as well as I do Anna sets up all her own interviews.'

'Well, they need an awful lot of rewriting when they come in. Ask anyone. I know you think the sun shines out of her arse, but you should see her raw copy. Takes a week's editing.'

'Look, I'm not getting into a debate about Anna's talent as a journalist, beyond reminding you she's contracted to two of our magazines and I've never heard anything from anyone else about rewrites. Quite the opposite. What amazes me is why you co-operated with Carol White in the first place. You've already told me you knew it was going to be a knife job. All you've done is damage *In Society*. That article's achieved nothing except put people off being interviewed by us.'

Micky Rice, cornered, flailed. There was something a little manic about his eyes.

'If we're talking about damaging *In Society*,' he said,

'then the ones who've done the damage are Anna Grant and you. People are up in arms about that cover of Anastasia Fulger. I hope you realise that. We've had two cancellations of interviews already. Arianna Stassinopoulos Huffington and the Duchess of Albi. Both have pulled out and it's taken months to get them to agree. Anastasia Fulger is ringing round everyone she knows telling them not to talk to us.'

'You know perfectly well why we ran that cover. And it didn't give you the right, as Anna's editor, to invent gossip stories about her and feed them to Sunday newspapers. The word around the building is that you did it because you're jealous of her. If that's true, it's pathetic. She's your star writer. When she produces a scoop, the kudos reflects on to you.'

'Obviously, we can't use her any longer,' said Micky viciously. 'Everyone agrees that, not after the Fulger piece. None of our cast of characters would ever give her an interview again. She's blacklisted. When her contract comes up in September I don't want to renew.'

'Renewing her contract,' I said steadily, 'won't be an option anyway. Anna's dead.'

Micky reeled back. It was a shit's trick I'd played, but for that look it was worth it.

'How do you mean, dead?'

'She's been found in her flat, dead since some time over the weekend.'

'I just can't believe this,' Micky was saying. 'It just isn't possible.'

'Perhaps you'd like to go back downstairs,' I said, 'and break it to the staff. I'm sure even the ones you assure me "hate her" will be devastated to know their best contributor is dead.'

Micky stood up and tried to avoid my eye as he left the room. But as he pulled the door shut I got a clear look at his face. There were so many emotions there: shock, fury, excitement and one other too. Triumph. There was definitely something triumphant in the mix. It was troubling.

# 10

I was still furious with Micky the next morning. And furious with myself too for getting involved in a slanging match. And sad and tired and flat and demoralised.

Suzy fetched me three Solpadeine painkillers dissolved into a tumbler of fresh orange juice with two tablespoons of demerara sugar. Not something I'd like to do every day, but for an instant high it's hard to beat.

At some point around three o'clock in the morning I'd woken up, and found myself lying in a pool of sweat. I was shivering. I must have been dreaming about Anna because her face remained vivid in the afterglow of sleep; her hair loose over her bare, brown shoulders and pink linen shift. The image was so strong that, with my eyes still closed, I reached out to touch her. I wanted to kiss her. But as my fingers brushed her cheek, there was nothing there, and I remembered with dreadful clarity that Anna was dead.

After that, I had been unable to drop off to sleep again. Micky's face, that glimpse of triumph, had kept drifting in and out of focus and my brain seethed with wild conspiracies. Was it possible Micky had had something to do with the murder? If he was jealous of Anna, and if he really did believe there was a chance she'd replace him as editor of *In Society*, then it was perfectly conceivable he'd try and manoeuvre her out of the way. But would he kill her? The magazine was Micky's life and he wasn't the kind of editor you could easily imagine working somewhere else. If he lost his job with us, I couldn't see one of the competitors picking him up nor one of the Sunday colour supplements. He was too brittle and had made too many enemies.

Thinking about him made me realise how little I really knew about Micky Rice. He'd been editor of *In Society* since before I'd arrived, for six or seven years at least, and deputy before that to the legendary Buffy Lejeune. It was always said (especially by Micky) that in the last few years of Buffy's reign he'd done all the work anyway, while Buffy ate her lunch in the Causerie at Claridge's wearing a hat. Buffy, who everyone had thought would go on for ever, choked on a mini sushi one evening at a launch party for an exhibition of tableware and was rushed into intensive care at the King Edward VII Hospital. For three months she held on to life while suffering almost total amnesia brought on by lack of oxygen to the brain. Micky held the fort as acting editor. When Buffy eventually expired, I suppose that Billy Heathcote hadn't the heart or courage to bring in anyone else over him. In any case Billy probably didn't know the names of any other editors by then. So Micky Rice, for so long the bridesmaid, was officially appointed editor of *In Society*.

Outside work, I knew almost nothing about him. He lived in a flat in a block off the Marylebone High Street, which belonged to a charitable trust so the rent was low. Nobody from the company had ever been there, so far as I was aware. When he entertained he did so in restaurants, paying with a company credit card. His dinner dates, I'd learnt from signing his weekly expenses, tended towards camp elderly actresses, strapped-for-cash aristocrats and rich foreign Eurotrash like Anastasia Fulger.

Something else had occurred to me in the middle of the night too.

If Micky was responsible for Anna's murder, and if Anna had really died some time on Sunday morning, then he'd either have had to have rung her after eleven on Saturday night, or else very early the next day. That's assuming he made an appointment to go round. He could, of course, have just turned up.

I knew from experience that if you rang Anna early in the morning, particularly a Sunday morning, it took several rings before she answered. In fact, she was so slow that, as often as not, the answerphone had activated before she picked up the receiver. You heard her prerecorded voice on the tape tell you nobody was there right now, and then the real Anna would cut in sleepily, asking 'Who is it?' The answerphone would continue running while you talked, so the whole conversation was taped.

Let's assume Micky had rung her at seven or eight o'clock on Sunday. Anna would definitely have still been asleep. Chances are, everything would have been caught by the machine. Which meant the evidence could be sitting in her flat in Harrington Gardens. *The flat to which I had a spare set of keys.*

I took a decision: I would go over there tonight, after work. It was a bit of a long shot, but it was just possible it could land Micky in it.

The only other explanation, of course, was that it wasn't Micky. Which led us back to the Fulgers.

'Suzy,' I called through into the outer office. 'I meant to ask you, what did you find out from the Connaught about Bruno Fulger's movements?'

'Oh yes, I spoke to the reception manager yesterday evening. He said he checked out quite late on Sunday. Apparently he's in St Moritz now.'

'So he was in London all Sunday morning.'

'Definitely. You know how discreet they are at the Connaught, they never tell you anything about who's staying, so I'm afraid I told a bit of a white lie. I said I was ringing from his tailor and we'd got a suit to deliver. They said, "Then you're a day too late, I'm afraid. Mr Fulger left us at seven o'clock yesterday evening."'

'You know there's another thing I'd love you to do,' I said, 'and this is going to take a bit of ingenuity. In fact, it may not even be possible to find out. But when I was over at Anna's flat yesterday afternoon I noticed her computer was missing. It's probably nothing and just being serviced or something, but I'd like to be sure. Could you look up all the service centres in South Kensington and check whether it's there? Or maybe you could ask the IT Systems boys downstairs. It was an AppleMac. For all I know there's a central AppleMac maintenance place. All I'm sure is that it was there on Thursday evening and it's not there now. So she'd have to have had it collected some time on Friday, or Saturday morning.'

Suzy rolled her eyes and laughed. 'Any time frame on this?'

'How about Thursday first thing? After I'm back from Mouchette in Paris.'

'Talking of which, you haven't forgotten you've got the strategy meeting with the publishers this afternoon? I've set it up for two-thirty. Early I know, but I assume you'll want me to type up whatever you decide and make about twenty million copies in plastic folders to take to Paris.'

'Well anticipated.'

'Then tomorrow, while you're swanning about on the Rive Gauche, I'll spend an exciting day ringing round computer shops.'

'Before we even begin this meeting,' said Kevin Sky, 'I'd like to put two things on the record. Firstly, since *Couture* quite rightly gets the lion's share of the Mouchette spend, I'd like to state quite emphatically that I'm not reducing their rates by one penny. In fact I'm looking for a six per cent increase. And secondly, if they cut back on volume to anything below thirty-eight pages, I'm going to tell the beauty editors never to mention their products again. None of them.'

'That's all very well for *Couture*,' said Kay Lipschwitz Anderson, 'but I'm afraid at *In Society* we're not in a position to be quite so arrogant. We're not even a core title. And if you're going to go strutting about the place making threats, we'll all be off the schedule.'

Three of the four publishers were in my office, each armed with thick buff files labelled 'Mouchette 1987–96'.

Inside was the client's ten-year business history: numbers of advertising pages booked, prices paid for each individual brand, volume discounts and the impossibly complex agreements on special positions. In certain months, for instance, advertisements for Mouchette face cream were guaranteed to be the first double page advertisement for a cosmetics company – known as the first cosmetics spread. In other months, however, they could be preceded by advertisements for Clinique or Lancôme. Three times a year Mouchette had first option on the back cover, or inside front cover, or the page opposite the horoscopes. They paid extra for these specified positions which were hotly competed for by newer, less established advertisers. Once in a while a big new cosmetics company, usually American or Japanese, would try to 'buy out' the best positions, offering up big premiums to bounce the incumbents. Normally we said no. Special positions in glossy magazines work on the principle of squatters' rights. Providing you carry on occupying them and don't whinge too much about the neighbours, you have first refusal in perpetuity. We talk about it as loyalty, but special positions are useful bargaining chips too.

'I think we should make a start,' I said, 'if we're all here now. Where's Kathy from *Smart Living*?'

Suzy was coming in with a tray for the tea ceremony. 'Delayed at the Interior Design Fair, but she's just dictated her targets to me for next year, which she wants you to incorporate in the pitch tomorrow. Last year apparently they got three pages of Mouchette advertising and three scent strips. Next year she's hoping for fifteen pages.'

'Fifteen!' Kevin sounded personally affronted. 'Why on earth would a cosmetics company want to put all that into a wallpaper magazine?'

As Suzy passed round the milk she said, 'Actually I asked Kathy the same thing. She says that in the latest TGi attitudes research, more *Smart Living* readers identified with the statement "I love to indulge myself with expensive fragrances" than the readers of any other upmarket monthly.'

'Jesus,' said Kevin. 'If we start diluting the Mouchette business across every magazine, all it'll mean is fewer pages for *Couture* where the margins are better.'

'What we've been asked to do,' I said, calling the meeting to order, 'is very specific. It's totally crazy, of course, but if they want us to pitch for everything against Incorporated, then there's not a lot we can do about it. We take part, and either win or lose, or else we don't take part, in which case Howard Trench is going to suck it all up anyway like a vacuum cleaner.'

'You know what I find so damn weird about this whole business?' said Kay. 'How the hell could Mouchette seriously consider putting all their spend into Incorporated? Those titles they've got, they're just so *second rate* for God's sake. *Ladies' Home Cookery, Girls on Top, Town Talk*. It's just orgasms and chicken recipes.'

'Nevertheless,' I said, 'I have it from the lips of Pierre Roux that they easily might. Their combined circulations are a lot bigger than ours, and their rates are lower too.'

'Low,' said Robin Reese, the publisher of *Man Alive*, 'is an understatement. I meant to tell you this. I heard it yesterday at an agency. Guess what they sold the inside back cover of *Town Talk* to Audi for last week? Twelve hundred pounds. Pathetic, isn't it? Twelve hundred for an inside back.'

'If we're going to win this,' I said, 'it can't simply be a question of price. Otherwise, we've lost already. We know Trench will underbid us. What we need to concentrate on is added value. Extra things we can do for Mouchette to help promote their brands.'

'Like what?' said Robin. 'Like sending Kevin up and down Oxford Street with a sandwich board?'

'How about direct mail?' suggested Kay. 'We could offer a special mailing to our database, endorsing their autumn launches.'

'Paid for by us or by them?' asked Robin. 'The postage to 626,000 people would cost a packet.'

'Paid for by us,' I said, 'but piggybacked on our subscription and subscription renewal mailings. Then the cost would be pretty well negligible.'

'Another thing we could try,' suggested Kevin, 'is a tie-in with a department store. Some kind of offer where you get a free sample of their rejuvenating cream when you take a copy of *Couture* to the counter.'

'Or *In Society* of course,' said Kay sardonically.

'Darling,' said Kevin. 'We're talking about response here. Big numbers. Which means *Couture*. Three point two million readers.'

'Actually,' I said, 'I think it would work best as a companywide promotion. If we're pitching corporately then the gizmos should be corporate too. If the department store promotion lasted a month and was national, we'd need all four magazines to pull the numbers.'

'What do you think Incorporated will come up with?' asked Robin Reese. 'Just discount?'

'Not what I hear,' said Kay. 'Apparently Howard Trench is going over himself to pitch and has put together some secret new presentation.'

'Good news for us, then,' said Kevin. 'It's bound to be embarrassing.'

'We shouldn't underestimate him,' I said. 'If they come up with a couple of original ideas and combine them with rockbottom rates, they could win.'

'I'll tell you one thing,' said Robin. 'If Mouchette pull out of *Man Alive* I'll never give them those special positions back. They'll have lost them for ever. Calvin Klein and Hugo Boss are both desperate for them. In fact it would give me quite a bit of satisfaction to tell Jean-Marc LeNoy and that marketing prat they'd lost the sites for ever. We've done so much for Mouchette at *Man Alive*, and this is how they thank us.'

'And another thing,' said Kay. 'It'd be the last time Jean-Marc LeNoy gets his face in *In Society*.'

'Maybe we should consider going over their heads,' I said. 'Fabrice Mouchette is still their Chairman and owns half the company. I could catch an earlier flight to Paris tomorrow and drop in on him on the way. Don't forget we gave his granddaughter work experience last summer.'

'Dangerous though,' said Kay. 'It can backfire, going to the owner. It can piss everyone off.'

'OK, then we'll keep that in reserve for now. But we still need something extra. The database idea is good, and so's the store tie-in, but we need to undermine Incorporated's position somehow.'

'Is there anything at all helpful in the research?' asked Robin Reese. 'I'm talking demographics, household incomes, comparing our readers with theirs.'

'Nothing obvious. Statistically they're pretty much indistinguishable, unfortunately.

'On the other hand,' I added, 'there is one thing we might try. It's pretty low. But you know how snobbish those Frenchmen are, and if we do this properly it could just work. But we're going to have to move like lightning. We need the last eight issues of every Incorporated magazine and our own. And we're going to need some new slides made up overnight.'

At dusk I drove across London and left the car in a mews behind the Tara Hilton hotel. From there it was three minutes' walk to Harrington Gardens.

Returning to Anna's street made me feel wretched. Throughout the day, I had somehow contrived to postpone the pain by refusing to focus on it. Instead, her death had hovered at the edge of my consciousness, like a dark blanket waiting to envelop me. How I'd got through the meeting with the publishers, I will never know.

In my pocket was Anna's bunch of keys. I thought I'd worked out which was which: the fat gold Chubb for the downstairs entrance, then two silver Banhams for her flat. It wouldn't look good to fumble about too much on the doorstep.

I wondered whether the police would have sealed the flat. I'd seen that done on television: they cover the door jamb with electrical tape so no one can get in or out. Just in case, I'd slipped into my jacket pocket a small kitchen knife – a Kitchen Devil – and a pair of suede gloves.

When I reached the building there was a girl outside in a Metro backing into a parking space, so I continued circling until she'd gone. More than anything, I didn't want to get caught breaking in. As one of the last people to see Anna alive, it would look suspicious. In fact I didn't even want to be seen near the building. I'd been here often enough: some of the neighbours must know my face.

Next time the pavement was all clear, I tried the Chubb. The key turned and I was inside. The hall with its Edwardian mosaic tiles was dark and cold and deserted. For a moment I just stood there, without turning on the lights, listening. From inside one of the ground floor flats I could hear a television, some kind of quiz show. In time my eyes became accustomed to the dark and I began walking upstairs.

On each landing I stopped and listened. Surely the police wouldn't still have a man guarding the flat? They're always claiming to be under-resourced, but you never can tell with the police. From the first and second floor flats there wasn't a squeak; they must be out.

I had reached the third landing when the dog began yapping and scratching at the door. It felt only a few feet away; a dachshund or a terrier. I froze, then retreated down to the half-landing. The dog continued yapping. At any moment I expected the door to open and the lights to come on. But then I heard a voice – an old lady's voice – telling the dog to shut up: 'Back in your basket, you tiresome animal,' and I crept past up to Anna's floor.

There was no tape on the door. And no constable on guard. In fact nothing to suggest a suicide or murder had recently taken place.

I unlocked the deadlock and slipped the last key into the

top lock. The door opened silently, I stepped inside and pulled it closed behind me.

It was hot in the flat and muggy. Evidently the windows hadn't been opened for a week and the sun must have streamed into the sitting-room every day. Anna once told me that on hot afternoons she wrote in just her underwear, with the french doors open on to the roof.

I crept around the flat, checking each room. The bath and basin were already gathering dust. With no one to pay her, Maria had presumably packed in the job. I opened the fridge door and saw it had been cleared. Maria? Or Bridget Grant? Somebody had at least thought of that.

On the shelf above Anna's desk I found the key to the french doors and, on an impulse, unlocked them and walked out on to the decking. There was a warm breeze and I could hear blackbirds. Across an expanse of rooftop the lights from the Gloucester Road glowed orange.

I felt desolate and strange, alone in Anna's flat. This would probably be my last visit. Soon, no doubt, it would be sold, and Bridget Grant would take Anna's things away and the majority of the proceeds revert to the mortgage company. Would they tell the next purchaser a beautiful girl had just been murdered here? Was there a full-disclosure clause for this eventuality?

If I had my life over again, I'd have married Anna four years ago, before our work friendship got in the way. I knew, even then, I wasn't really happy with Sally. At least I think I knew, even before Cazzie was born, as long ago as that.

On a worktop in the kitchen was the answerphone and the red light was signalling a message waiting. Good. I clicked rewind and went right back to the start. It took longer than I'd expected. There must have been fifteen minutes of listening time, half the cassette. I perched on a kitchen stool and began listening.

Click. 'Hi, this is Kim from the picture desk at *Man Alive*. It's Friday evening at five-forty. Please ring me really early on Monday morning because we've got to begin picture research on Erskine Greer. Have a good weekend.'

Click, click. 'Hello Anna, this is Kit, it's Friday evening about – uh – eight o'clock.' I sounded tired and rather slurred. 'Look, just to say that the new issue is selling brilliantly, a sell-out, everyone's gripped by Anastasia, and best of luck tomorrow morning with Erskine Greer. Ring you tomorrow some time about dinner with Barney Weiss. Sleep well.'

Click, click. 'Anna, this is Kit. It's ten to four, Saturday. I'm back home now. Please ring me about tonight when you get in.'

Click. 'This sounds like the voice of the dreaded peacenik, Anna Grant.' The laugh of an older man. 'This is the arms dealer. I've spoken to my secretary and she is going to contact you on Monday about the arrangements for Palm Beach. Another thing I should have told you is bring jewellery. They wear it to swim in, probably to sleep in too. If you forget, I can buy you some out there. Goodbye.'

Click, click. 'If you are hearing this, Anna Grant, then why don't you come to the telephone?' A woman's voice, foreign and hysterical. 'Don't try and hide behind this bloody machine. What you wrote in the magazine was lies, I trusted you and you betrayed me. Bruno is wild with fury. He wants to kill me, and you too. Why did you write those things, they weren't meant to be printed? Please ring me, my number is 581 15 — No, don't ring the house, I'll ring you. You have ruined my entire life.'

Click. 'Is this the correct number for Miss Anna Grant? This is Rudolph Gombricht speaking, the solicitor of Mr Bruno Fulger. You have been a very foolish young lady and will have cause to regret it. Mr Fulger asked me to convey that to you. Goodbye.'

Click. 'Anna, it's Kit, Sunday morning ten-thirty. You're probably out buying the papers unless you're in the bath. Shall we have lunch or brunch or something? Please ring me. Lots of love.'

Click. 'Anna, me again, it's eleven-thirty.' God, I was persistent. 'Where on earth are you? I'm going for a walk in the park, be back later.'

Click. 'Hi, sweetheart, it's Peter.' He sounded a long way off, the line was terrible. 'When you get in, please ring me urgently. I'm at the river lodge for twenty-four hours. The story's really hotting up and I wonder how you're getting on your end. Lots to tell you. This is important worthwhile stuff. Bye, sweetheart.'

Who the hell was Peter and since when was Anna 'sweetheart'?

Click. 'Darling? This is your mother. I'm telephoning to say how stupid I think that article is in today's newspaper. It doesn't sound like you at all. The man upstairs, the concert pianist, gave it to me. If you'd like to, come over and have tea this afternoon. I'll be out at lunchtime but back here by three o'clock.'

Click, click. 'Hi, sweetheart, this is Peter again. It's now four o'clock in the afternoon which I guess makes it seven your time. I'm still at the lodge but only until tomorrow morning. So ring me tonight, it doesn't matter how late, I've got to speak to you. Even if you don't listen to this until Monday morning, ring me here. It's important. Bye, sweetheart.'

The tape ended and clicked itself off, so I ejected the cassette and slipped it into my pocket. There had been no message from Micky Rice. If he'd rung Anna on Sunday morning she must have picked it up before the answerphone cut in.

I was relocking the french doors on to the roof when I heard a rattling sound coming from the hall. It stopped, then began again.

*Someone was unlocking the front door.*

I could hear metal turning in the lock. At any moment the door would open. But then there was more rattling. Whoever was trying to get in didn't have the keys: *they were picking the locks one by one.*

I thought of shouting something out loud, or ringing the police. To say what exactly? That I'd broken in first?

I heard the second turn and they moved on to the second lock. The easy one. Fifteen seconds later the door began to open and I saw a black gloved hand appear around the jamb. As silently as I could, I stepped out on to the roof and pulled the french doors shut behind me.

There were two of them. One stocky, the other taller and slimmer. They wore track suits and zipped leather masks covering their faces: pervert masks I'd describe them as, built for dungeons and role-play.

I pressed myself against the wall, behind a tree in a terracotta pot, praying not to be seen. The french doors hadn't fully closed, they were half an inch ajar. I tried to edge them shut from outside, but they wouldn't stay. The men moved about the flat with the lights off. I stood motionless. From across the Gloucester Road I could hear the dull thump of disco music.

They were leaning over Anna's desk, going through the drawers. They had a torch. One of them carried a bag – it looked like a dustbin liner – and they were piling her stuff into it.

I could see their shapes moving about the flat. One of them passed the french doors. He was six feet away from me now. Any moment he'd notice the doors were open and come outside. I was numb with fear. In my mouth was a putrid taste, as though adrenalin had driven half the contents of my gut back up my throat.

The second man, the stocky one, came into the sitting-room carrying the answerphone with the wires trailing behind it across the carpet. He dropped it into the bag and returned to the kitchen.

Around the edge of the roof was a wooden balustrade and beyond that sloping rooftops. On one side was a gap of several feet above a sixty-foot drop, but on the other the roof joined on to the building next door. To get from one to the other would mean climbing over the balustrade, down the tiles into the dip and then up the steep pitch on the far side. I was sure I could manage the first part, but the climb up again looked tricky. It was ten feet and I couldn't see any handholds. From the next roof it might be possible to get into the adjacent flat, or else continue along the block until I found some other way down.

I inched my way across the deck, conscious of the first man still in the sitting-room.

Then the french doors blew open.

I saw him turn, stiffen on seeing me, then advance through the doors and out on to the decking. He moved slowly but deliberately, testing each footfall. The leather mask must have been impairing his vision, but he was heading straight towards me.

I backed off, but he kept on coming. He was only five feet away now. I had retreated as far as I could. My calves were pressing against the crossbars of the balustrade. I saw him pause and consider what to do next. His gloved fists were clenched, his legs slightly bent as though ready to spring.

I wasn't sure, if I clambered over the balustrade, whether I could make it before he reached me. It would mean turning my back on him. I'd be vulnerable.

My eyes flickered over his shoulder towards the flat. Through the sitting-room I could see the open door to the staircase. Five strides would take me to the hallway. I took two of them, but he'd seen my eyes move and blocked my way.

I was trapped.

I reached into my jacket pocket and grasped the handle of the knife. I waved it about in front of me and he leapt back in surprise. The blade flashed white in the evening sun. Now I was armed and he wasn't. If I could clear a path to the door, I had a chance of escape.

He continued backing off, but he'd regained his composure and the balance of power was less obviously mine. The knife was small and he was protected by leather. He began advancing on me again.

We were standing in parallel, equidistant from the french doors.

'Let me out,' I said, 'and I'll just go. I won't ring the police.'

He moved closer, without responding. I stayed absolutely still. He wasn't even a yard from me now. I could hear him panting behind the mouth slit of the mask.

His gloved hand lunged at my wrist. He was trying to snatch the knife. As he moved, I saw a flash of pink skin between the top of the gauntlet and the sleeve of the jacket, and plunged at it with the blade. There was a spurt of blood and the man clutched at the wound with his other hand.

I sprinted to the door and into the sitting-room.

As I did so, the second man, hearing the yells from the roof, emerged from the kitchen. He was smaller than the other, but compact and moved dangerously.

*And he was holding a knife.*

It was a serrated bread knife, twice as long as mine and with the grey-silver sheen of sharpened steel.

For the second time I found myself backing away, but now the space was more confined. My back was pressed against the mantelpiece, the shelf digging into my shoulders. Anna's white sofa blocked the route to the door.

I snatched a starfish from the mantelpiece and lobbed it at his head. Then, in the split second he turned his face away, I bounced across the sofa cushions and up over the back.

I nearly made it. Two more strides and I'd have been out of the door. What I hadn't noticed was the first man, still nursing his hand, who had edged into the room and now darted forwards and grabbed hold of my jacket.

He spun me round, cracking my head hard against the wall. Involuntarily, I groaned, loosened my grip on the knife, and saw it fall on to the carpet. I had barely steadied myself when the second man caught up with me, raising the bread knife towards my neck. I could see every crenellation of the blade. He was going to kill me. There was no way I could get to the door now. There was nothing I could do but stand here while they cut my throat.

Instead, I threw myself back over the sofa, feeling a rush of pain as the knife carved into the side of my neck below the ear. I clenched my teeth and clambered up from the floor and out again on to the roof. Behind me, the two men cursed and hurried around the sofa. The pain was extraordinary, my head swam and I felt sick. I was approaching the balustrade now. I had to reach it before they did. I was staggering as I climbed on to the crossbar, then leapt down into the dip between the roofs and began to struggle up the other side.

I could hear the men close behind, scrabbling down the tiles. At any moment one of them would catch hold of my ankles and drag me back down.

Some of the tiles on the incline were badly chipped and I used them as handholds. The sharp edges cut into my fingertips. Then, within reach, was a length of guttering and I hauled myself up.

The men were following up the tiles, but their leather gauntlets wouldn't grip. The stocky one, unable to gain a proper hold, tugged them off with his teeth and let them drop. Now he was catching up. He grabbed the guttering with both hands and began pulling himself up. In front of me on the flat rooftop, next to a cat's cradle of television aerials, lay a broken concrete slab. It was heavy, but I was able to lift it.

I cracked it down with all my strength across the knuckles of his left hand and heard them crack beneath the skin. He screamed, then tumbled back down the tiles into the dip of the roof.

The slimmer man, already slowed by the gash in his wrist, had stopped and was bent over his partner.

Then slowly, painfully, the whole side of my face throbbing from the slash of the knife, I clambered across the rooftops until eventually I found a metal fire escape that led down the side of a house to the street.

I didn't stop running until I reached the car.

*

111

Charles de Gaulle airport in June is my idea of hell. I'd prefer to have gone over by train but for some reason the Eurostar schedules are organised to make it impossible to arrive in Paris in sensible time for a four o'clock meeting without wasting the whole day. So I fought my way through the crowds of holidaymakers at Terminal Two, queued for forty minutes the other end for a taxi, then sat baking in the back as we crawled into the centre of the city. My neck was throbbing badly. The wound was covered by a homemade collage of bandage and waterproof tape under a cashmere polo-neck. When I'd got home last night I'd caked it in Savlon and trusted to luck. I'd thought of going to the hospital with a story about being mugged in the street. They'd have believed me, no question, but who needs it?

Between bouts of nausea, I read and reread the presentation until I almost had it by memory, and crammed the competitive demographics. The trouble with these sorts of shoot-outs for advertising is that you have no idea what the inquisitors might spring on you. Some clever-dick marketing shark can suddenly start asking why *Ladies' Home Cookery* has more mascara-wearers in North Humberside than we have.

The headquarters of Mouchette SA is a large brick and glass building on the avenue Montaigne, near the intersection with the place de l'Alma. It is entered by a marble and brick lobby featuring a small waterfall and a large chrome sculpture of a lipstick blasting off like a rocket into outer space. Behind the front desk a hard-as-nails receptionist took care not to catch my eye too quickly. Eventually she relented, muttered into a telephone, then told me peremptorily to 'Wait downstairs. They are not ready for you yet.'

Twenty minutes passed slowly. I hate hanging about before important meetings at the best of times. I find the adrenalin goes and I lose momentum. Today, I was worried I might keel over.

In the lobby, a succession of French cosmetics executives came and went like boulevardiers off to visit their mistresses, which they probably were. I wished Anna had been there with me. She would have known exactly how to describe them. She'd been out with enough of those kinds of men.

I heard English voices as one of the doors in the big bank of elevators slid open. Out stepped three people: Howard Trench and two apparatchiks, whom I recognised as his corporate sales director and marketing manager. Trench was striding angrily on ahead, while the others hastened behind carrying a carousel of slides and a projector.

'I'm just so sorry, Mr Trench,' the marketing manager was saying. 'I did check, or rather my PA did, and they definitely said we didn't need an international adaptor to work the projector.'

'It was a fiasco,' Howard Trench snapped without looking round. 'I'm afraid I am left with no alternative but to comprehensively review the parameters of corporate responsibility within our company.'

'How was I to know the voltage is different here anyway?' muttered the marketing manager. 'I'm not an electrician.'

Then they saw me.

Howard Trench's face clouded for a moment before he recovered himself and bounded up with hand outstretched. We have an odd relationship, ostensibly friendly but also guarded. We compete for everything: circulation, advertising, staff, kudos, and sometimes it gets personal. When we win something off them, it's Howard Trench's bearded face that comes first into my mind. I like to imagine him smarting a bit. And when we lose, I have this unpleasant sensation of Trench gloating in his big office full of fake antiques.

'How nice to see you, Howard,' I said with every appearance of genuine warmth. 'I hope you haven't grabbed the whole budget already and have left a bit for us.'

'Actually,' replied Trench, 'we at Incorporated no longer think in simple terms of advertising pages. We like to offer a total integrated package of communications.'

'Bells and whistles, you mean.'

Howard Trench laughed superciliously. 'Not exactly, Kit, not exactly. I'm referring to our new programme for speaking interactively to our nine million woman readers through the print medium. As we point out at Incorporated, every three seconds an Incorporated woman reader buys an Incorporated brand.'

'Very impressive,' I replied. 'I hope that leaves them enough time to buy Mouchette face cream too.'

The sales director with the slide carousel giggled, and Trench glared at her.

'While you're here, Kit,' he said, 'I understand from my circulation people that you flooded the market last week with copies of *In Society*.'

'Yes, we did have rather a hot issue.'

'Well, I wish you wouldn't,' he said. 'At a time when the whole magazine industry is committed to saving paper, all you're doing is inciting the paper merchants to raise their prices even further, which they will do if they see increased wastage.'

'Fortunately,' I replied, 'it wasn't wastage. The issue was a sell-out.'

Trench said nothing while he took this in. You could see his brain whirring. He was weighing up whether to believe me or not. If true, then they'd lost more market share than he'd realised, and he would have to take it out on his editor. If I was making it up, then I might have some other motive, such as encouraging Incorporated to raise their print-runs to match ours and lose money.

In the end he said, 'Nevertheless, Kit, I'd rather you didn't increase wastage like that. I was talking to a Finnish pulp manufacturer earlier this week, and they are planning to raise the tonnage price by a further twelve per cent in the autumn.'

This was classic Trench. You tell him something – 'The issue was a sell-out' – and instead of incorporating the new information into his thinking, he ploughs on as though you hadn't said anything.

The receptionist called out to me to go up, and Howard Trench watched me collect together my notes, mini projector and slides.

'I notice, Kit,' he said, 'you are on your own today. Not, I take it, a sign of economy at Weiss Magazines.'

'Not at all,' I replied. 'I was going to bring one of the publishers with me, but they're all at the great Tiffany event, of course.'

Howard Trench looked puzzled. He didn't know anything about an event at Tiffany the jewellers, which wasn't surprising since I'd just made it up. But it would give him something to fret about on the flight back. He hated us to be at something without his lot.

'Also,' I went on, 'these modern projectors are so compact and light, you really don't need an assistant. Even the international adaptor is built in.'

Up on the fourth floor, Pierre Roux's secretary was waiting by the lifts to show me to the conference room. Inside, across a vast expanse of Stilton-coloured tabletop, sat Jean-Marc LeNoy, Roux, several assistants with electronic powerbooks and a secretary taking notes.

LeNoy, dressed for the library of a French château in tweed jacket and a canary and grey bow tie, stood up and offered me a cup of tea or a glass of Perrier. Pierre Roux, rather ominously, remained sitting. Clearly he had been designated as Mr Nasty for this presentation.

I arranged my slides and looked expectantly across the table.

Roux, having glanced first at LeNoy for a go-ahead, launched into an unnecessary preamble.

'As you remember well, I think, from the restaurant,' he recapped, 'we are this year dividing our marketing budget in a new way. For four months now, we have been new thinking here at Mouchette. In order to move forwards, such new thinking is absolutely necessary.'

I stole a look at Jean-Marc LeNoy, the living embodiment of old thinking, for any sign of reaction, but he was engrossed in the lighting of a large Montecristo cigar.

'So,' said Roux, 'today we are looking for new ways to forge relationships with publishing companies. Instead of supporting several houses with our advertising budgets, we will select just one company. That successful company will henceforth become our partner in progress, working together with us towards one common aim: the development of our respective brands in the marketplace. You follow me so far?'

I nodded. I longed to get going.

'Already,' went on Roux, 'we have seen three publishers. And I must tell you that one company in particular – a big rival of yours I think – impressed us very much. Why have they impressed us? That is easy to say: *new thinking*. At Mouchette, let me tell you, we no longer think in simple terms of advertising pages. Our strategy is a total integrated package of communications.'

I blanched. This was going badly wrong. Pierre Roux was quoting Howard Trench's gobbledygook verbatim, and if he was fool enough to swallow that, then I was going to have to be very nimble on my feet.

In fact I was doubtful that, whatever I said, I could swing the deal with Roux. Better to address my remarks to LeNoy, if I could draw his attention away from his cigar, and go for broke.

'Let me make a start,' I said, clicking the first slide on to the screen, 'by talking not about us at Weiss Magazines but about *you* at Mouchette. Too often,' I went on, 'magazine publishers take up your time by talking only about themselves – how many readers they have, household incomes, statistics of all sorts, trying to blind you with research.'

Pierre Roux looked profoundly nonplussed, but LeNoy

nodded softly to himself. Clearly Howard Trench had stupefied him with precisely these kinds of facts.

'Instead,' I said, 'I am going to focus on you. On *your* position in the marketplace – and what a fine position it is – and how we can help you to maintain your brand image as the number one quality cosmetics and fragrance house in Europe.'

I flicked on to a slide of the ten leading Mouchette products, which one of our art departments had photographed rather tastefully on the hall table of an imposing Belgravia house.

'Here,' I said, 'are your products. Each one a leader in its field. Your eye-contour gel in our latest *Couture* research came out as the number one favourite with our readers. Your fragrances, Mesdames de la Nuit and Aurora, consistently poll number one in all Weiss Magazines research. Now, it seems to me that what all your products have in common are three things.' I paused impressively. 'Three things: quality, discrimination and a high unit price.

'It's a question of targeting,' I said, 'which brings me on to the central theme of my presentation: niche marketing and the primacy of media environment. Your products, as we've established, are premium priced. How much will a fifty-ml bottle of your new men's fragrance Man Friday retail at? Thirty-nine pounds. A medium-sized jar of the skin renovator? Forty-two pounds. Both priced significantly above the competition. Clearly you are not aiming them at people on government benefits, are you? You aren't targeting the poor and dispossessed.'

'Indeed not,' protested LeNoy. 'For fifty years Mouchette has been synonymous with wealth and privilege. Princess Grace swore by our products.'

'Then you should beware,' I said, 'of devaluing all that you've built up by a misdirected advertising strategy. Think of the damage that could be done to the brands in just one year if you changed the perception of your loyal customers about their value. At the moment,' I went on,

'Mouchette is spoken of in the same breath as Chanel, Givenchy and Lancôme. But if you get the advertising wrong, in one year – *one year* – you could become associated with the cheapest supermarket brands.

'Never forget the old adage,' I said, 'that a man is judged by the company he keeps. You, Monsieur LeNoy, are known to mix freely with only the cream of French society. Indeed, you have been awarded the Légion d'honneur for your contribution to Parisian cultural life. And I know that you bring the same discrimination to your business life.'

LeNoy bowed his head in acknowledgement of the egregious flattery poured upon him.

'I am now going to show you ten slides,' I said. 'Each one is of a cover line – a headline from the front cover telling readers what's inside. And each is taken from a different magazine. Five of the cover lines are taken from Weiss Magazines, five from magazines belonging to our main competitor Incorporated. But I'm not going to tell you which is which. I just want you to sit back, read them and see what you feel about them.'

The first slide came on: 'Penile Dementia. You tell us about oral sex with older men.'

The second: 'Whipping it up. Why teenage prostitutes say spanks for the memory.'

Slide three: 'Sex in jail. Meet the intimate inmates.'

Slide four: '"I married a forty-stone truck driver" says schoolgirl hitch-hiker.'

'This is grotesque,' I heard Jean-Marc LeNoy whisper to Pierre Roux. 'Imagine writing about truck drivers in a luxury magazine. I hope we weren't supporting that issue with our advertising.'

Slide five: 'Size does matter! Read the results of our most candid-ever sex survey.'

Then pausing only to allow the secretary to catch up, I moved on to the next five slides.

Slide six: 'Brilliant ideas for summer beauty. How to look instantly desirable.'

Slide seven: 'The world's most intelligent women: New York, Paris, London, Rome.'

Slide eight: 'The Princess of Wales. Could she remarry less than $100 million?'

Slide nine: 'The 100 best holiday houses to rent in Tuscany, Provence, Corfu and the Hamptons, and who goes there.'

Slide ten: 'Scent of money: the world's most eligible men behind the world's finest aftershaves.'

'Aha,' broke in Jean-Marc LeNoy. 'I can already guess which one that is from. *Man Alive*. They mentioned me in that article.'

'Do I need to tell you,' I asked, 'which were which? Perhaps it is kinder simply to say that one company speaks to the rich, the confident and the intelligent, while the other addresses the sad, the depraved and the very likely out of work who read for cheap thrills.

'Think about it in terms of your own life, your own customers who you know better than anybody,' I said. 'Are Mouchette customers the sort of women who rent holiday villas and take trouble over their appearance? Or are they hitch-hikers who chase after overweight truck drivers and finish up having weird sex in jail? I don't need an answer to that question, but I'd like you to reflect on it while I tell you what Weiss Magazines would like to do to help you build your business.

'First,' I said, 'I am going to show you some original research. Nobody has seen this before. And in fact we don't intend to show it to any other cosmetics or fragrance companies for obvious reasons. Because Mouchette comes out so strongly that if any of the others got hold of it, they would despair. I am now going to show you twenty slides. Each one is of a real reader of Weiss Magazines who responded to our research. Many are well-known people, and I must ask you to keep this information absolutely confidential. Can I ask for your assurance on this?'

LeNoy nodded emphatically. I could see that I'd got his

attention. But Roux tilted his head sceptically, unconvinced by where all this was taking us.

The first slide showed the wife of a prominent auction house owner, smiling out of a party scene. There followed in quick succession similar pictures – all captioned – of a well-known businesswoman, television presenter, two young socialites, an art historian, a political hostess, a titled banker's wife and so on for three minutes.

'Every single one of these beautiful women,' I said dramatically, 'has revealed to us that she prefers Mouchette products.'

I allowed this to sink in. 'Prefers Mouchette. Over Chanel, over Clarins, over Lauder.'

Jean-Marc LeNoy was licking his lips, his social antennae throbbing. We had spent much of the previous afternoon in the office selecting women he would certainly have heard of, but probably hadn't met.

'What we're proposing as part of our added value programme,' I went on, 'is that Weiss Magazines will co-host a party with you in November and invite every single woman on that list. And not only them. Each of the twenty will in turn suggest twenty other women, so in all we will have four hundred of Britain's most significant opinion formers in one room. I was thinking of the ballroom at Claridge's. The invitation could say "Jean-Marc LeNoy, Président du la Conseil de Mouchette, and the Publishers of Weiss Magazines" in that order. The publicity and PR will be phenomenal. With a guest list like that there'll be photographs in the evening paper, everything.'

LeNoy, eyes gleaming, began leafing through his pocket diary for November dates, but Roux cut him short.

'This idea is all very nice,' he said, 'but what can I tell my regional sales teams is the value of such a reception? I hardly think a party at Claridge's will sell much of our new ultra-mascara in – how do you pronounce this place – Doncaster.'

'An excellent point,' I said. 'And in order to answer it, I

need to tell you a little of our latest thinking on the relationship between publisher, client and global marketing. As retail markets change, increasingly we feel that traditional relationships are changing, *have* to change in fact. At Weiss Magazines we no longer think in simple terms of advertising pages. That kind of transaction, in the new world of the interactive information superhighway, is outdated. What we like to offer is a total integrated package of communications. Call it database marketing. Call it niche marketing. Both have equal validity. But more than anything we see our role as *bringing together* the reader and the marketeer. The modern magazine is quite simply the pimp that engineers the transaction between the punter and the product.'

Roux was tapping away furiously into his powerbook, scrolling down competitive data.

'Nevertheless,' he said, 'the market penetration of your stable of magazines compared to Incorporated's is not so good, no? I am comparing your coverage of BC1 women aged twenty-eight to forty-four. Weiss Magazines have thirty-two per cent coverage against Incorporated's fifty-two per cent.'

'You're absolutely correct,' I said, 'but there's a lot of duplication in their numbers. If you run the reader profile of *Ladies' Home Cookery* against their decorating magazine *Genteel Living* you'll see a seventy-eight per cent crossover. And of course they perform much less well than we do on TGi lifestyle analysis, and we have a much stronger story among ABs in London and the South: people who can actually afford to buy products.'

Roux looked unconvinced and I could see him moving on to the National Readership Survey (NRS) where Incorporated also beat us on coverage. But at that moment Jean-Marc LeNoy, evidently bored by four long meetings in succession, rose to his feet, advanced towards me around the table and laid his arm across my shoulder.

'Enough,' he declared. 'Enough, enough. We could spend the whole afternoon debating this figure or that and still be none the wiser. Sometimes, you know, I think these statistics actually confuse the situation, not make it clearer. For next year, I have decided, Weiss Magazines will be our – what was the expression you used, Pierre?'

'Our partners in progress,' said Roux through clenched teeth. He was clearly furious at his boss's intervention.

'Exactly,' said LeNoy. 'Now the most important thing is to fix the date for this reception very soon, since of course my schedule gets very booked up at that time of the year. And, Kit, I thought it would be amusing to take thirty or forty people on to dinner somewhere afterwards, perhaps to Mark's Club. Which I think, my friend, you can pay for, since we are giving you £980,000 in advertising revenue.'

Normally I get a real kick from closing a deal, but today the usual elation wasn't there. For a start, I felt nauseous. The pressure of the presentation had temporarily banished the pain, but now it came rushing back, along with the deeper pain of losing Anna. And then there was Pierre Roux. It always makes me uneasy when the president and marketing director of a company have different strategies, and when our success is dependent upon the senior man pulling rank. As a company we have always had close relationships with chairmen, CEOs, big bananas everywhere. It's our secret weapon. But unless you can win the hearts and minds of the decision makers lower down too, it's a short-term advantage. So our business strategy at Weiss Magazines is to bond with advertisers on at least four levels simultaneously: my job is to schmooze the presidents and managing directors, the publishers schmooze the managing directors and marketing directors, our advertising directors schmooze the marketing directors and media planners while the advertising managers and sales executives schmooze brand managers and media buyers. The advertisers' PRs, meanwhile, schmooze our editors with baskets of cosmetics and cachepots planted with orchids.

What worried me was Pierre Roux's hostility and loss of face. As Billy Heathcote used to say, you haven't made a sale until the signed order's in your hand, and we were still a long way from that. In the next twenty-four hours I needed to get a firm date for the party into LeNoy's diary, and a confirmatory fax from Mouchette's media-buying agency in London.

My taxi crawled back around the Périphérique to Charles de Gaulle, along one of the ugliest airport highways anywhere. Worse than Moscow. Worse than Bangkok. Anyone who says every inch of Paris is a national treasure hasn't been there.

After I'd checked in, I rang Suzy from one of the callboxes on Satellite Five next to gate fifty-four.

'Any news?'

'Several people rang from the magazines,' she said, 'but nothing urgent. The most important thing is Anna Grant's funeral which is going to be tomorrow morning at twelve o'clock at a church near her mother's flat. I've shifted your paper-buying meeting to the afternoon. A lot of people from here are going to the church so I've ordered some cars, I hope that's OK.'

'Great. If the funeral's allowed to go ahead, it must mean they've released the body.'

'They have,' said Suzy. 'It's in the evening paper. And Superintendent Barratt called you half an hour ago. He wants you to ring him back. I've got the number here if you've got something to write with.'

I didn't feel like talking to the police from an open bank of phones, so I searched about in my wallet for my executive club card and headed for the British Airways lounge. Normally it never quite seems worth the palaver of checking into a special waiting room unless the plane is delayed, but at least there are telephones where you can't be overheard.

I rang Chelsea police station and was put through to Barratt.

'Kit Preston,' I said. 'I understand from my office you want to talk to me.'

The Superintendent thanked me for ringing back and asked if I might be able to come over to the station, there were some questions he needed to ask.

'Not right away, I'm afraid,' I said, 'I'm at Paris airport. I won't be back in Central London for a couple of hours.'

'Well, if you've got a few minutes now, we could talk on the phone.'

'Fine. I gather they've done the post-mortem.'

'That's just it,' said Barratt, 'if I can just locate my notes on the screen. They're here somewhere, here we are. Yes, the pathologist completed his examination and there's no doubt that strangulation was the primary – and sole – cause of death.'

'Anything to go on yet?'

'Still early days, Mr Preston. The coroner's office has officially opened the inquest, but that's a formality. We're still concentrating on house-to-house inquiries, abandoned vehicles and so forth. Routine police work.'

'So nobody's helping you with your inquiries yet, as you put it?'

'As we *don't* put it actually, sir. That's strictly TV-cop stuff. The real force doesn't touch it.' Superintendent Barratt sounded mildly peeved. 'What I need to ask you, Mr Preston, is about Miss Grant's state of mind. Would you say she was prone to depression?'

'Not at all. I'd say she was very much an optimist.'

'Not worried about anything or anyone so far as you know?'

'Well,' I said, 'there was one thing. There was a very rude article written about her in the Sunday papers. *The Sunday Times*. Extremely cruel and unfair. I suppose it's possible that could have affected her.'

'And the content of the article?'

'It said she was a social climber and only wrote about rich people. It was largely provoked by a profile Anna had written the previous week about a woman called Anastasia Fulger, the wife of the German steel tycoon Bruno Fulger.'

'I see,' said Barratt. 'And is it possible this could have a bearing on her murder?

'Conceivable,' I said, 'but to be honest I haven't any hard evidence.'

I told him about the men in the car park watching my flat 'who were possibly looking out for Anna'. But I didn't mention last night's fight on the roof. I felt it would be difficult to explain without raising unnecessary suspicions about my motives.

'Another point I'd like to confirm with you, sir, is the exact time of your telephone conversation with Miss Grant on Saturday evening. When we spoke on Monday at the flat in Harrington Gardens you told me you thought it had taken place at about eleven o'clock.'

'Certainly around then. We left the Dorchester where we'd had dinner around ten-thirty. We can't have spoken much more than half an hour later.'

'Which would seem to fix eleven o'clock as the last time we know for certain Miss Grant was alive.'

'You might also like to double-check with the man who dropped her back home. We had dinner on Saturday evening with my American boss.'

'I'm aware of that, sir. I already spoke to Mr Weiss's office in Chicago. He confirms Miss Grant was very much alive at ten minutes to eleven.'

In the Club Class lounge they called my flight and all around me passengers began clicking shut their briefcases and folding away laptop computers.

'I'm afraid I've got to run,' I told Inspector Barratt, 'or I'll miss my flight.'

'One quick final question, sir, before you go,' he said. 'I hope you won't find it intrusive but it has to be asked.'

'Sure.'

'What exactly was the nature of your relationship with Miss Grant?'

What indeed? I had thought about that myself often enough over the last few days.

'She was a very close friend,' I heard myself saying. 'We worked for the same company so I met her originally through journalism, and then we saw each other a bit away from the office too.'

'Was she your girlfriend?'

'No, no, you couldn't describe her as my girlfriend.' Somehow, standing there in the departure lounge, girlfriend seemed too possessive, too intimate a term for Anna. It was presumptuous. I didn't want to explain the fragile, powerful threads of our relationship to this policeman. I couldn't even bear to think about them myself. I could feel tears prickling under my eyelids and I blinked fiercely. Just then I missed Anna so much.

So I said, 'No. I wasn't going out with her, if that's what you mean.'

'Thank you, sir,' said Superintendent Barratt. 'You've been very helpful. For the time being I don't think there's anything further I need to ask you, but you'll have no objection if anything comes up?'

'None,' I mumbled.

I just made it on to the plane and fell into my seat with my head in my hands. The stewardess offered hot towels and newspapers and I took an *Evening Standard*. On page nine I found it: 'Police open inquest on tragic Anna.' Just three paragraphs, very factual, and a big picture of Anna laughing. I wondered what Carol White of *The Sunday Times* would be thinking as she read this.

As usual the flight was delayed into London. Three times we banked over Hammersmith and Kew as a dozen other aircraft landed ahead of us. Then we taxied along the perimeter fence for a further twenty minutes while they found a free gate to attach us to. At some point during this frustrating waste of time I began to feel anxious about going back to my flat. Probably it was just a delayed reaction to last night, but I was definitely jumpy. Physical violence wasn't something I was familiar with. You just don't find it in the magazine world. Psychological violence, yes, an everyday occurrence, but not physical. On the whole I wasn't unhappy about my performance on the roof, but I was unsure how I'd handle a second encounter. It was hard to predict. When I walked out on Sally, one of her more thought-provoking analyses of the event was that I never let people stand in my way. At least I deduce that's what she meant; she dressed it up more psychologically. At the time it rather annoyed me, but maybe it was mental toughness she was getting at. That's something I do admire. Anna certainly had it in bucketfuls. If she hadn't become a profile writer, she'd have hacked it equally well as a war correspondent. Whether I had the same mental toughness myself, though, I was far from sure.

One thing I did know, these men were dangerous. They would have killed me on Anna's roof, I was quite certain.

And if they'd tried it once, I'd have to watch out.

# 11

Anna's funeral was in a High Victorian church in a road off Belsize Park. About sixty people turned up, thirty of us from the office, her mother, neighbours and twenty or so friends, many of whom she'd first met through interviewing them. I recognised a young dress designer and a fashionable chef, and a girl who made expensive shoes and handbags. Micky Rice had arranged for the *In Society* party photographer to cover the service and I hoped he wouldn't have the bad taste to publish the pictures in the magazine. When I asked him, he looked prickly. 'Oh no,' he said. 'These are strictly a private record. I've asked the art department to make up a little book of remembrance for Mrs Grant.'

The church, being Tractarian, was now far too big for the congregation so the service took place in a partly modernised side chapel; we sat on fold-up chairs facing a brick altar overlooked by posters for famine relief and UNICEF. The bleakness of the scene was at least partly relieved by the beauty of the flowers. The magazines had sent enormous bunches: all white lilies and roses and tulips from *Couture*, mixed colours – very bright – from *In Society*. *Man Alive*, being less practised at sending flowers to contributors and designers, ordered something smaller and less dramatic. I suppose that Weiss Magazines had paid for all of them, one way or another. Barney himself, whom I'd telephoned in Chicago on Tuesday to break the news about Anna, had sent a bouquet – a dozen large red roses wrapped in Cellophane. When I'd told him about her death he'd sounded shocked. 'That's too bad,' he kept saying. 'That's too bad.' Probably he'd been looking forward to the dinner *à deux* on his next trip over.

The vicar tried hard to raise our sights above the sadness of the moment. He said that Anna would have wanted her mourners to have a party here today, and that it was Belshazzar in the Book of Daniel who had attached such importance to the celebration of life that he had commanded the golden and silver vessels to be taken out of the temple so that the king, and his princes, his wives and his concubines might drink therein. It didn't make a lot of sense and it was clear he didn't know much about Anna, but he did his best and what can you say anyway. Anna, who was so beautiful and talented, was dead and that was the end of it.

I sat several rows back between Suzy and Leonora Lowell from *Couture*. It was all unutterably sad. The funeral of a very young person has a special tragedy about it, and I think those of us who work in magazines come particularly unprepared. We are better accustomed to the artifice of novelty and success than to the dull finality of death.

Several times during the service I felt the psychotic stare of Micky Rice boring into the back of my head. I would have looked round if I hadn't thought it would afford him some perverse satisfaction. Evidently he was still fuming from the conversation in my office.

After the service I waited to offer my condolences to Mrs Grant. She stood on the front steps of the church, shaking hands with every mourner and thanking them for coming. I thought how empty her life would be from now on. Although her job at the school was far removed from the world that Anna had moved in, she had in some ways lived vicariously through her daughter's triumphs.

When I reached the front of the queue she took my hand and said, 'I know who you are, of course, Kit Preston.'

'How clever of you to remember.'

'I'm still quite sharp, you know. Especially at remembering faces. You have to be at school, with so many children coming and going each term.' She smiled weakly.

'One thing I want to say,' I heard myself telling her. 'Anna was one of the most brilliant writers I've ever met. Truly. I'm sure you knew that already, but I just want to say it here.'

'She did seem to have a talent for it,' said Bridget Grant. 'I could see that, even when I didn't know the first thing about the people she wrote about. Don't know where she got it from. Not from me. My tutor at Girton once told me I could regurgitate all the facts in the world and still send her to sleep with my essays.'

'You know she had become a good friend of mine. We'd become very close recently.'

'I knew that,' said Bridget Grant. 'Anna told me that.' She held my gaze for a moment. 'The saddest thing for me,' she said, 'is that now we'll never know what might have happened in Anna's life. So many good things lay ahead of her. Different phases. We'd only really seen one side of Anna, the Anna who loved parties and razzmatazz. But there was another side to her too, you know, the home girl, and that would have come through.'

'I can see that,' I said, though actually I hadn't really thought that about Anna.

'I think you might have done,' said Mrs Grant. 'You might have been quite surprised.'

Outside the church a fleet of taxis and minicabs was waiting to ferry the magazine staff back to Park Place. I didn't feel like going straight back to work, so I sat on the church wall for a bit, watching the last mourners disperse. While I was sitting there I was approached by a tall, gangly man with long streaked blond hair whom I'd noticed earlier on at the back of the church.

'Kit Preston, isn't it?' he asked.

'Yes.'

'I'm Simon Beriot.'

The name meant nothing to me. In the church he had

looked twenty-five, but in the strong June light I could see he was twenty years older. He had one of those lined, lived-in faces that suggested at some point he'd taken a lot of drugs and booze, and which often goes hand in hand with a Peter Pan character. He struck me as someone girls would initially find attractive, but who would flounder from lack of substance.

'You don't know who I am, do you?' His voice had a slight accent, French or Italian.

'Forgive me, I'm clearly being slow here.'

'We haven't met, but I take pictures for *Man Alive*. Still lifes. They never give me as much work as I'd like, but that's another story.'

'Well, good to meet you.'

'Actually,' he said, 'I'm fucking pissed off with you.'

'You are?'

'You really don't recognise my name at all, do you?'

'Listen, I'm awfully sorry, but I've no idea what this is about. If I can help, tell me. But don't play games, I'm not feeling up to it just now.'

'You used my picture on the cover of *In Society* last week. The one of Anastasia Fulger. I took that. You used it without permission and it's gone and got me into a lot of trouble. And I'm telling you, it could get *you* into a lot of trouble too.'

Now I knew who he was. The old boyfriend of Anastasia Fulger. The French photographer Micky had implied might have been an ex of Anna's too.

'I'm sorry if it's made things difficult for you. Was Mrs Fulger angry with you?'

'I haven't spoken to her. A German bloke called Rudolph Gombricht rang me at the studio and threatened me. Friday lunchtime he rang and again Friday evening. Now he rings every day. Very heavy conversations.'

'Does he want anything in particular from you?'

'It's not what he wants *from* me that ought to worry you,' said Simon Beriot, 'it's what he wants to *give* me.'

'Like what?'

'Like I'm not fucking telling you, mate. Why should I? You didn't tell me you were using my photograph, you got Anna to steal it from the studio. It isn't even a good picture. We were just mucking about.'

'Look, maybe we can talk about this another time, if you think there's anything I can do to help.' There was something flaky, and frightened too, about Simon Beriot. It was clear he wasn't going to tell me anything today, if there was anything to tell. But the line about Gombricht giving him something worried me. It rang alarm bells. I couldn't imagine what it might be.

'I've told you,' he said. 'It's not you who can do anything to help *me*. It's me who might be able to help *you*. There again I might not. I might not feel like it.'

He turned away. 'See ya,' he said. 'And next time you might just recognise one of your contributors when you meet them at a funeral.'


I left the office punctually and walked all the way home, across St James's Park in the direction of Victoria, then right along the Embankment to Battersea Bridge. It was raining but I didn't care. Walking suited my mood and ensured privacy. The worst thing about my job is that I'm never alone. From eight o'clock in the morning until closedown I'm ambushed by questions: the interactive superhighwaymen. Once, as an exercise, I kept a count of all the separate conversations I had in a week and it came to over two hundred.

Was it really only last Thursday I'd been rollerblading with Anna? A week later and she was dead and buried. The strange thing was, events had moved so rapidly I hadn't even had time to feel proper grief. Since identifying her body on Monday afternoon, I'd been in three long meetings, bollocked Micky, had a knife-fight on a roof with two masked psychopaths and attended her funeral.

There was a lot to think about, not least Bridget Grant's remarks to me on the church steps. I wondered what exactly Anna had told her mother about me. The idea of girls discussing their love lives with their mothers has always struck me as rather mawkish. I certainly never told my own mother a damn thing while she was alive, neither of us would have felt comfortable with that level of intimacy. Could Anna really have believed we had a future together? Our relationship until Saturday afternoon had been so circumspect and dependent on work I hadn't dared risk a move in case it spoiled everything. Perhaps, all the time, she'd been waiting for me to do just that. What was it she'd said when I admitted I'd been wanting to make love with her for ages? 'You should have told me.' Now I wished I had, but now it was too late.

Back at the flat, I stripped off my wet clothes, ran a hot bath and lined up a couple of beers on the bathrack. I peeled off the plasters, millimetre by millimetre, and was pleased to see that my neck was beginning to heal. It still hurt like hell when I touched it, but the skin would join up again quite quickly. After that I felt much better. Hot baths always do it for me, the hotter the better. Sally never understood this. When we were together, she always wanted to share my evening bath and add more cold water.

I'd never really considered Anna as a wife. I thought of her as a free spirit. But in fact her mother was right, it was surprisingly easy to make the transition. Anna had always been practical and I could imagine her coping rather well with the exigencies of children and domesticity. On the one occasion I'd introduced her to Cazzie she'd been brilliant with her. I suppose I shouldn't have been surprised, instant rapport was her stock in trade. As I lay there, stewing, I reflected on what married life with Anna might have been like and the thought of it, now that it could never be, made me unbearably sorry.

Through the open bathroom door I could see right down the passage into the sitting-room, where my eye alighted on a small black box on the coffee table. Anna's tape recorder. It had sat there since I'd retrieved it from underneath the sofa on the afternoon of the burglary.

I was suddenly overtaken by a strong desire to hear her voice. It frightened me a bit, because I guessed it might be painful, but I hauled myself out of the bath and dripped along the corridor to fetch it.

Back in the bathroom I rewound the tape, propped up the machine behind the taps and adjusted the volume.

There was a series of bumps and crackles and then Anna's voice, incredibly close by, echoed around the bathroom.

'Testing, testing. One, two, three, testing. Oh fuck, is this machine working? I do hope so. It's ten past eleven and I'm standing at the end of Hyde Park Gate. In five minutes I will ring Erskine Greer's doorbell which I can just see on the next corner. Testing, testing.'

The tape switched off, then back on again. Now we were evidently inside the house. I could imagine the machine positioned on a stool in Erskine Greer's drawing-room, with the microphone angled towards him. Anna must have been sitting opposite him, behind the recorder, because her questions were quieter than his replies.

She had broken him in gently, saying how much she liked this area of London and singling out certain paintings on the wall for praise. Erskine Greer had replied rather noncommittally as he sized her up, asking her not to mention any of the artists by name 'in case it encourages the criminal fraternity while the house is left empty'.

Anna replied she didn't think many cat burglars subscribed to *Man Alive*, to which Erskine Greer had said, 'I wouldn't be over-confident about that myself, Miss Grant.'

At this point there was a series of metallic crashes as the Filipino housekeeper put down a tray of coffee near the microphone. I could hear the sound of pouring and Greer spooning sugar crystals into his cup.

'Remind me,' he said, 'who owns this rag *Man Alive*?'

'An American named Barney Weiss,' said Anna. 'He's

from Chicago. He bought several glossy magazines over here about four years ago.'

'I remember now,' said Greer. 'I was offered them myself. Some chap who'd lost a heap of money was trying to get shot of them. I seem to remember he sent a gofer out to Nassau to give me the hard sell.'

'Well, they were bought by Barney Weiss.'

'Idiot,' said Greer. 'Never buy media. The good stuff never comes on the market and the rest's rubbish. Quickest way to lose your shirt. Only reason to buy media is prestige and there are plenty of other ways of getting that.'

'Like becoming the patron of a polo team?'

Greer laughed. 'That certainly is one way, as I'm rapidly discovering to my not inconsiderable cost.'

I put the tape on pause, turned on the hot tap with my big toe until the temperature came close to boiling, then resumed listening. There was something rather eerie about hearing Anna at work, but after a bit I became absorbed by her interview technique. Sometimes she would come over as formal and respectful, questioning Greer about the early days of Greer & Company when it was a modest trading house with offices in Hong Kong, Macau and Shanghai. Then, in an instant, she'd switch tack and tone, pumping him about his holidays and exactly how many friends he could fit on to his boat.

I admired the way she angled for an invitation to Palm Beach. She made the idea of him flying her out in his plane sound so normal, so inevitable a part of the process of writing the profile, that it was practically a foregone conclusion.

And, let's face it, she wasn't above a little flirtatiousness either. Even on the tape you could pick up on it. 'I'm told by people in Hong Kong you're regarded as the most attractive spare man on the island. How do you feel about that?'

'How do I feel? Well, you're asking for a reaction to something I've never given a moment's consideration to in my life. In fact, on that one I'd question your whole premise.'

But you could tell he was flattered, and from there on his answers were more confiding. You could hear him trying not to disappoint her.

The tape ended and I flipped it out and turned it over. The interview continued uninterrupted. Anna was asking him about professional polo players and mentioned she'd always had a secret passion for Carlos Gracida.

'Never get involved with polo players,' said Greer too quickly. 'Those hired assassins, they're all the same.'

Had she really said it just to make him jealous? If so, it had worked.

They went through into lunch with the tape still running. You could hear them helping themselves to food while the housekeeper hovered about passing dishes. Erskine Greer, none too subtly I thought, asked whether Anna was married or involved with anybody. Anna avoided answering. She said she'd been to a fortune teller who'd told her she wouldn't settle down until her mid-thirties.

'You should try a Chinese fortune teller,' said Greer. 'There's a man I use, he comes to see me in my office, who's quite uncanny. You must come and try him.'

Then Anna started on arms dealing. Her account of the conversation had actually been quite accurate. Even when I knew what was coming I was still rather surprised by her gall.

'I keep being told,' she said, 'that you supplied weapons to the Vietcong during the Vietnam War. Wasn't it rather immoral as well as illegal to do that, when you knew they were being used to kill young American conscripts?'

Greer took a long time before replying and you could hear the tension on the tape.

'You may be right. I can see that to somebody of your generation, particularly if they were impressionable emotionally, it might look that way. But don't forget,' he continued steadily, 'that nobody other than Beijing was

136

sending anything to Hanoi, and the Chinese weapons were either basic or redundant issue, didn't work half the time. Whereas Saigon was being shipped several hundred million dollars' worth *a month* by the Americans, probably seven hundred billion over the course of the war. Heinous waste of money, of course. It'd have been far cheaper, as I never tire of pointing out, to have presented each and every member of the Vietcong with a villa in St Tropez and a staff to run it.'

Anna had persevered, pressing him for details on his arms deals, but then Greer had very calmly and deliberately brought the conversation to a close, and I heard him ask Anna to leave the house. 'I only wonder at your impertinence,' he said, 'coming to lunch at my house and proceeding to lecture me like some feminist from Greenpeace.'

There was a scraping back of chairs and a click as the tape was switched off.

I imagined it was the end of the interview and sat up in the bath to turn off the machine. But as I leant forward, there was a further soft click and the tape was playing again.

This time it lasted only half a minute and was very muffled. It sounded like the recorder was inside Anna's bag and had reactivated itself by accident. I could hear Erskine Greer saying something partly drowned out by the sound of traffic, as though they were standing on the doorstep.

'After that little performance, Anna, maybe my lifelong evasiveness where female journalists are concerned has been unwarranted.'

Anna giggled. 'Well,' she replied, 'then I'll see you next Friday, if not before, at the airport.'

'Bring nothing except yourself, blue jeans and something pretty for the evening. They tend to rather expect one to dress up in Palm Beach.'

'And my notebook, of course.'

Erskine Greer laughed wearily. 'Oh yes, and the dreaded

notebook. I was beginning to forget that was the point of this whole thing. Are you all right to get home? Do you have a car or something?'

'Fine. I'll get a cab at the end of the street, there are plenty.'

'Goodbye then, Anna.' I heard them embrace. And then the click click of Anna's heels as she skipped down the front steps.

This surprise epilogue to the interview left me with plenty more to dwell on, and none of it uplifting. There had been such a mood change between the episode in the dining-room, with Greer expelling Anna from his house, and the scene on the doorstep when they seemed to be reconciled, it was hard to square the two. For one thing, what period of time had elapsed between the conversations? If Anna had gone straight from the table to the front door, it couldn't have taken more than half a minute and yet here was Erskine Greer reconfirming her invitation to Palm Beach and affecting to have forgotten she was a journalist. Clearly a much longer time had passed, time which Anna hadn't chosen to tape record and which explained her late arrival at my flat. Anna had said that Greer had invited her to stay for lunch at ten to one. They'd gone through to the dining-room ten minutes later and the truncated meal, every second of which was accounted for, had lasted about thirty-five minutes on the tape. The very latest Anna should have left the house was a quarter to two. On the tape she said she'd catch a taxi and she'd told me when she turned up at my flat that she'd come directly from the interview. In fact, she'd only arrived in Battersea at around five to five. Which left about two and a half hours of unaccounted-for time in Hyde Park Gate.

All this churned uncomfortably in my mind as I took a cab into work that Friday morning.

Whatever interpretation you put on it, it didn't look good. I remembered the way Anna had described Erskine Greer in the afterglow of her interview: 'I can't imagine him making a pass unless he was absolutely certain of success, but probably most women would say yes to him anyway.' Was he, I wondered, that confident of success? And was Anna 'most women'?

On the face of it, Greer was certainly her kind of man. That's if you bought the standard *Sunday Times* line about Anna having a special weakness for the super-rich. He was thirty years too old for her, of course, and the whole idea made me feel sick, but you had to allow it as a possibility.

One explanation which crossed my mind was that Anna had only done it for the story. Having blown the interview by asking about arms dealing, she'd rescued it and her trip to Palm Beach by desperate measures. She was never less than courageous when it was a question of getting access. I had this sudden picture of her lying back and thinking of *Man Alive*, but frankly it didn't make me feel any better.

At eleven o'clock I wandered down to see the editor of *Smart Living*, Meredith Carew-Jones, and found her in her office surrounded by contributing editors. Contributing editors on magazines fill a similar role to non-executive directors on boards of private companies: paid a modest honorarium and expected to roll up several times a year for meetings. Their names are listed on the masthead at the front of the magazines, and they pack a lot of social punch. At Weiss Magazines, the contributing editors are much the same species as non-execs at Sotheby's and the sitters on committees for prominent charity galas.

Meredith was a tall, energetic woman in her mid-fifties and one of the kindest people I knew. She travelled in each day from Rutland where her husband was a red-faced squire and Master of Foxhounds. She often referred to him, and deferred to him too ('Buster can't stand root vegetables so we can never have them, worst luck'), but since he seldom ventured up to London he was a shadowy off-stage presence in our lives. On Fridays, by tradition,

Meredith didn't come in but 'worked from home', a convenient fiction that enabled her to prepare the vast carnivorous meals Buster expected and so enjoyed at weekends. I'm sure he had no idea he was married to the foremost decorating guru of the age.

Her office, which she redid every spring, was a shrine to whatever was next fashionable. When I first met her, it was full of giant obelisks and miniature topiary. This year the walls were clad with weatherboards like a Cape Cod beach house, with sailcloth blinds and bleached furniture.

Today, Meredith had summoned half a dozen of her best-connected contrib eds to an emergency summit. She had a crisis on her hands: there was a famine of good English country houses to photograph.

We know from research that of all the mansions, apartments, vicarages, penthouses, schlosses, chalets, haciendas and palazzos photographed each issue, it is the four-square English country house that readers can't get enough of. And not just any old country house either; the kind they like best is Georgian with sash windows, a flagstoned entrance hall, drawing-room with an Adam fireplace and upstairs a series of mellow bedrooms overlooking parkland. That's what they expect, and if we don't deliver month after month, they're disappointed.

The problem for us is that the turnover of good Georgian and Queen Anne houses is slower than the turnover of our issues. And it isn't enough simply to locate an old one because either it's been seen before in a rival magazine, or else the place is a tip. What we need is a constant supply of 'new' old houses: houses recently bought and redecorated in an authentic way. Traditional, but full of new fabrics from our advertisers' showrooms. Readers expect to be able to look at a picture of someone's spare bedroom and discover the toile de Jouy on the bedhead is from Percheron. They like ideas to copycat.

Another problem on the English country house front is that, when English country houses do come on to the market, they're usually bought by foreigners. Americans,

Germans, Scandinavians of all sorts: they arrive in London to work for merchant banks and insurance companies, and a year or two later decide to buy an estate. So they snap them up with their two per cent company loans in dollars, Deutschmarks and kronor and then entirely miss the point. Their finished houses are wonderfully comfortable but they don't help *Smart Living*: however hard they try, they're not *English* in taste.

Meredith was looking concerned but composed when I appeared through her door.

'Oh Kit,' she said, 'we're just finishing. We've been brainstorming country houses again.'

'Any leads?'

'One or two. There's a Baring house in Hampshire we haven't done, but they're not mad for publicity at the moment. And Annabel's on to a house near Hungerford which David Mlinaric's doing.'

'Maybe you could run the Baring one without saying whom it belongs to.'

'We might have to. But it always sounds so odd, "the property of an English family near Micheldever".

'By the way,' said Meredith, 'you know all our contributing editors, don't you.' She introduced me round the room. I'd met five before but not the wife of a big-bucks National Hunt stud owner.

'What about London houses that are decorated like country houses?' I suggested. 'I always feel we can fudge it a bit and get away with it.'

'We're having a blitz on them too. Some cousins of the Aga Khan's ex-wife apparently have a very good new house in Chiswick, and there's a technology tycoon I've never heard of who's bought a huge gothic place in Regent's Park. He invented the CD-ROM or something. Nina Campbell's doing the curtains.'

'Sounds promising. Any others?'

'Well, we've been trying for Conrad Black's house in Kensington for ages. He's agreed in principle, but still no date. And Minnie thinks she can twist Erskine Greer's arm to do his house in Hyde Park Gate.'

Minnie was Minnie Vass, real name – by which I mean first married name – Charlotte Vass. Her maiden name, I'd once been told, was Sharkey. Char Sharkey. Successive marriages had made her Minnie Al-Rahman, wife of a Saudi business tyro, and Minnie Strath Brora, mistress of half of East Sutherland. But her first marriage to Johnny Vass being the smartest, and probably also the cleanest of three messy divorces, meant Vass was the surname she reverted to between times.

'I hear Erskine Greer has great paintings,' I said to Minnie Vass.

'You haven't been?' she asked, surprised. 'You must have had dinner there.'

She looked up accusingly from beneath a fringe of dyed black hair, as though I had either been to dinner and forgotten or else was telling her a fib.

'No, I never have. I heard about the art from a friend who had lunch there last week.'

'Who was that?' she asked suspiciously.

'Anna Grant.'

'Anna Grant the journalist? It can't have been her. She's dead.'

'Actually this was a week ago. Anna had lunch with Erskine Greer last Saturday.'

'Well, he didn't mention that to me,' said Minnie. 'I've seen Erskine twice this week and he never mentioned it.'

'I can assure you she did.'

This cross-questioning was beginning to annoy me. Minnie Vass was without doubt one of the most irritating women in Europe. She drove Meredith crazy too. She'd ring her several times a month, always reversing charges, from friends' houses in Nevis or Acapulco and try and bully Meredith into agreeing to photograph them, sight unseen. And there was always a problem over her expenses. From time to time she'd gather up a fistful of restaurant bills and aeroplane tickets and dump them on the managing editor's desk. Few had much relevance to her work for *Smart Living*, so most were refused. A couple of times she'd appeared in my office, complaining bitterly about our meanness and quoting rich friends who took her side. Each time we were on the point of firing her, however, she pulled off some great coup. Her contacts were incredible and, after all the aggravation, she delivered. We never would have got the Kennedy compound at Hyannis Port without Minnie's help.

'How well do you know Erskine Greer?' I asked.

'How well do I know him? Darling, Erskine and I go back *twenty years*. He's one of my oldest and dearest friends. We practically got *married* at one point.'

'Really? I didn't know that. Why didn't you go through with it, if that's not a rude question?'

'Oh darling, it was so long ago. I think because I was still married to Abdul Rahman. And Erskine had a situation in Hong Kong. It wasn't ever really going to happen. Shame really, I'd have enjoyed being Minnie Greer.'

One of the enduring mysteries of Minnie was her age. Viewed by candlelight across the width of a mahogany dining-room table, she didn't look a day older than forty-five. I had once seen her on the dance floor, rock-and-rolling with husband number three, and she moved like a twenty-year-old. And yet there were people who claim to remember her, as Char Sharkey, at parties in the very early 'fifties, which had to make her at least sixty.

'So who did Greer marry in the end?'

'Nobody, though not for lack of offers. Half my girl-friends have flung themselves at him. He's always been marvellous in bed.'

'Who's this we're talking about?' asked the stud owner's wife. 'Who are we saying's marvellous in bed here?'

'Well, not your husband for a start,' said Minnie darkly. 'Actually, darling, Erskine Greer.'

'Oh yes, I've heard he's amazing too. A neighbour of ours in Lambourn had a thing with him and she said he's into these incredible Chinese aphrodisiacs. He can keep a hard-on for over an hour which isn't bad for a man of his age.'

'I can assure you,' said Minnie, 'that in my day Erskine didn't need any extra help at all. The idea horrifies me. He kept going half the night in Gstaad. And then expected me to be out on the slopes straight after breakfast.'

'Maybe they should be writing about him in *Man Alive*, not *Smart Living*,' said Meredith. 'I'd have thought *Man Alive* would love an article about oriental aphrodisiacs.'

'As a matter of fact, *Man Alive are* doing an article about him. Or rather were. I doubt it'll happen now. Anna Grant had just interviewed him when she died.'

'Is that the same Anna Grant who writes for *In Society*?' asked the stud owner's wife. 'The one who did that big attack on Anastasia Fulger? Bruno Fulger's absolutely livid. We have five of his mares at the stud and he was telling my husband about it. He says he's going to sue.'

'Well, he hasn't so far, thank God. And, anyway, we don't think he's got any sort of case.'

'He might just for the hell of it,' said Minnie. 'The costs aren't going to be a problem, and it'd give him something to do. Bruno's such a bloody idiot sometimes. Darling Bruno, I think I'm seeing him later this week and I'll tell him not to be such a silly baby.

'As a matter of fact,' she went on, 'Bruno's one man who *does* need those Chinese pills. Let me tell you, his combined hard-ons for the whole year wouldn't last an hour.'

In the afternoon I found a backnumber of *Hello!* waiting on my desk with a yellow Post-it note from Suzy. 'See pages 42–51. No wonder she's done a runner.'

I could see her point. On first impression, this was certainly what *Hello!* had termed 'a modern fairytale'. Anastasia was effervescing out of every frame like that chorus girl in *The Boyfriend* trying to catch the eye of the big-shot director. But on close inspection Bruno came over as the husband from hell. It was evident that he wasn't just reluctant to be taking part, he was positively hostile. His eyes and the line of his mouth hinted at barely contained violence.

Suzy appeared in the office looking terrific in a bright pink suit.

'Do you like it?' she asked, twirling about. 'I've bought it for this evening.'

'This evening?'

'The Annalina Lau shop opening. They've invited me too.'

'I'd forgotten that's tonight.' Annalina Lau, the Chinese-American fashion and homeware designer, was opening a big boutique on Bond Street. Our magazines had been heralding the event for months.

'From six to nine o'clock. Apparently they're expecting a thousand people.

'Also,' said Suzy, 'I've got you this.' She handed me a long typed list of addresses. 'Computer maintenance places. Have you any idea how many there are that service AppleMacs in Central London? A hundred and nineteen. Mostly based in Wembley and Perivale but they all cover South Ken.'

'And?'

'And what?'

'And did any of them have Anna Grant's AppleMac?'

'No.'

'You're sure?'

'Kit, I've just spent three solid days talking to probably two hundred different repair men, all of them asking for the job number on the receipt *which we haven't got*. All I'm promising is I've rung every single one, generally several times since they never call back, and they all deny having it.' She glared at me.

'Thanks, Suzy. Really thanks, I mean it.' Sometimes I do this. Suzy spends days researching something for me, like where to buy a special toy I've seen for Cazzie and how to get it sent over and through customs from America, and I forget to say anything. She never sulks, but she glares. The thing to remember about Suzy is that she's invariably friendly and polite, and beloved by all levels in the company, but if she feels people are taking advantage, they encounter a freeze. Beneath the surface, there's a Cheltenham Ladies' College crispness.

Then she laughed, ruefully. 'Don't mention it. It's been very productive. Now if we ever need to service one of the office PCs, we've got a hundred useful new addresses on the rolodex.'

At half past six we strolled together up St James's and across Piccadilly into Bond Street. It was still light and very humid; you could see the diesel from taxi exhausts settling on the road, and the flowers along the pavement wilting in their concrete tubs. The art galleries had filled their windows with their most expensive paintings, to lure the tourists who poured into London for those four short weeks around Wimbledon and Ascot. The jewellers were holding special exhibitions of 'English summer season pieces': earrings and bracelets you could only imagine being worn by foreigners. Sometimes I worry about London. Sometimes we just seem to be one big offshore shopping mall.

You could tell where the Annalina Lau party was taking place from two hundred yards away. Guests were spilling on to the street while their invitations were checked, and forty or fifty photographers lined the entrance behind a rope barrier. Suddenly all the flash bulbs began going at once.

'Someone's arriving. Who's that?'

'Hugh Grant and Elizabeth Hurley it looks like,' said Suzy. 'Unless it's all for Micky Rice.'

Micky slunk inside ahead of us, behind the film stars, and we slowed down to let him increase his lead.

Entering the Lau boutique was like stepping into a kitsch Hollywood vision of cyberspace as conceived in steel by a Japanese architect.

Directly ahead, towering above the hundreds of jostling heads, was a cantilevered steel and glass staircase which wound its way around a cylindrical fish tank containing black carp. Suspended from the double-height ceiling were two enormous banks of video screens, which broadcast clips from Annalina Lau's catwalk show interspersed with glimpses of world events: the signing of the Palestine–Israel peace accord, and a long line of Rwandan refugees winding its way across the border.

We signed the visitors' book, writing our names and company as conspicuously as possible. It's an odd tradition, this signing-in at launch parties. Ostensibly for tax reasons, to establish that there really were a thousand clients through the door, it also ensures the magazines turn up. I've known PRs count the autographs afterwards by company: twenty-eight Weiss Magazines, nineteen Incorporated. Turning up shows commitment. No show, no advertisements.

Just inside the door, the designer herself waited to greet us, chaperoned by her Chinese business manager and backer, C. C. Wang. I was glad to see that both were already encircled by *Couture* staff, who were effectively making it impossible for any competitors to get near them. Leonora Lowell and her deputy editor, Tasmin Feeley, were talking animatedly to Annalina while Kevin Sky worked on C. C. Wang.

Beyond our hosts stood a phalanx of shop assistants in tailored suits with big brass buttons, and young waiters holding trays. The food, like the decor, was exclusively black and white: squares of black rye bread with mozzarella and black olive paste, mini sushi nori, trembling white squid on long black skewers and dwarf baked potatoes topped with caviar and crème fraîche.

I reached for a glass of champagne and, taking a deep breath, forged into the writhing interior of the party.

There were so many people that for every yard you pushed forwards you were swept, as though by a strong ocean current, a greater distance to the side. Backs pressed up against you, forcing you to alter direction, waiters cut you up with trays of food and champagne, guests stepped back without warning or spun round with half-empty glasses to attract the bottle, or to hiss some greeting as you passed by.

Next to a glass cabinet full of coiled leather belts, the balance of our publishers were talking to one another: Kay Lipschwitz Anderson of *In Society*, Robin Reese of *Man Alive* and Kathy Davis of *Smart Living*. It's an odd thing about launch parties: there can be a thousand people and still magazine publishers will gravitate together like seals on a rock.

'Just to warn you,' said Kay, 'Howard Trench is here and spitting blood. He's just heard we've won the Mouchette deal.'

'Great. I'll watch out for him.'

'You can't miss him,' said Kay. 'For some reason he's wearing a Chinese coolie hat. Probably in honour of Annalina Lau.'

Minnie Vass loomed towards me, accompanied by the formidable Chairwoman of the National Benevolent Society for Distressed Ballet Dancers. At least I think that's what she said. It could have been Disabled Rally Drivers. More likely the first.

'Kit darling,' shouted Minnie above the roar, 'I've been looking everywhere for you. We've had an absolute brainwave. Wouldn't it be marvellous if Weiss Magazines sponsored the Society's centenary gala in October? Wonderful publicity. Princess Michael's the guest of honour. And not expensive: £250,000 which includes a table on the night.'

The Hon. Chairwoman pressed up close. She had rock-solid hair swept up and away from her face, and a huge diamond brooch of a poodle pinned to her bosom. 'I *do* think you'd be the perfect people,' she breathed. 'We all so admire *Genteel Living*.'

'Not ours,' I replied, seizing on the get-out. '*Genteel*

*Living* belongs to that man over there in the Chinese hat. He's sure to agree.'

Tasmin Feeley hovered at my sleeve. 'Seen Yando anywhere? He's disappeared.'

'Disappeared?' For good, I hoped.

'He arrived with us in the limo but hasn't been seen since. He's sulking because we cut the Jamaica story from eighteen to sixteen pages. I'm quite concerned, because he's meant to be photographing the office suits for us tomorrow morning.'

I was edging forwards between the TV anchorbabe Tania Bryer and AIDS fundraiser Marguerite Littman when Norman Turner hove into view.

'Evening, guv,' said our circulation director. 'Quite a do this. Seen the buffet upstairs? Dickens of a spread. I should have told the wife not to bother with an evening meal when I get home.'

'I didn't know fashion was your thing, Norman,' I said, frankly astonished to find him here.

'Oh, you know me,' said Norman. 'Any excuse for a bit of a party. Can't say I think much of the clothes though, it's all long black skirts. Bring back the mini, that's what I say.'

Meredith Carew-Jones came up to tell me she thought Minnie Vass had got the Erskine Greer house. 'He's given a tentative yes.'

'That's great.'

'One thing,' said Meredith. 'Minnie's feeling a bit under-appreciated at the moment. She doesn't think we show sufficient gratitude. Anyway, she's going to ask you to sponsor some big ballet gala she's involved with. Say yes, won't you? Otherwise she might give Erskine Greer's house to *Genteel Living*.'

Just then a great commotion broke out and television arc lights illuminated the atrium. Two members of the rock group Blur were making an entrance, closely followed by Kate Moss.

As I stepped up on to the staircase for a clearer view, I

noticed something that made me feel distinctly uncomfortable: Howard Trench deep in conversation with Pierre Roux. Trench was saying something and Roux nodded his head in agreement. The confirmatory fax about Mouchette still hadn't come through, and until it did I couldn't feel relaxed.

'Kit Preston?' A girl I didn't recognise was descending the stairs behind me. She had mousy brown hair pulled back into a ponytail and a corduroy jacket of the same colour. 'You are Kit Preston, aren't you?'

'Sure.'

'I'm Carol White. We haven't met, but I'm a journalist on *The Sunday Times*.'

'Don't worry, I know.' My first reaction was to tear into her, but she looked timid and ineffectual. 'You wrote that article about my friend Anna Grant.'

'That's why I wanted to talk to you. I feel so terrible about it, after what happened, and especially since it was my name on the article.'

'What do you mean, "your name on the article"? Presumably you wrote it.'

'In a way, yes. But, well, it was one of my first pieces for the paper and it sort of got taken over.'

'How do you mean?'

'Well, they commissioned me to write it on Friday morning, when the profile of Anastasia Fulger came out in *In Society*, and at first it was meant to be a nice article. That's what I was told to write. They asked for 750 words about how Anna Grant gets so many scoops. They definitely wanted it to be nice about her because Colin Burns, the editor, was trying to headhunt her to write a column for the paper.'

'I see.' Typical Burns. Those Sunday newspaper editors are nothing but pirates. 'And then what happened?'

'Well, on Friday afternoon, after I'd handed it in, I suddenly got told the angle had been changed, and had to start again. The features editor told me to ring Micky Rice at *In Society* who had a lot to say about her. So I rang him and he was expecting the call. And then he told me all the stuff in the article. He just went on and on. All the quotes were from him, though I had to promise not to attribute them.'

'Why do you think he did it?'

'That's what I wondered. He sounded obsessed on the phone, as though he really hated her.'

'And do you think it was Micky Rice who'd contacted the paper in the first place?'

'Like what?'

'I mean, do you think Micky heard *The Sunday Times* was writing about Anna and intervened to alter the angle?'

'He must have. He'd definitely spoken to someone very senior there. I don't know who, maybe Colin Burns since it was his idea originally.'

I had more to ask her when she turned white as milk and retreated back against the balustrade. I turned to see Micky Rice advancing up the stairs with a plate of squid.

'Good evening, Micky,' I said. 'Are we covering this party for *In Society*?'

'No way,' said Micky. 'There's nobody here. And anyway, they gave the exclusive to *Couture*, more fool them.'

'By the way, do you know Carol White of *The Sunday Times*?'

Now it was Micky's turn to drain of colour.

'Hi,' he said, furtively. 'Actually Kit, I can't stop. Yando's here somewhere and I want him to work for us.'

'Remember he's under contract to *Couture*.'

'Oh, he'll dump *Couture* for us, he's desperate to. Everyone knows there's no room for creativity at *Couture* any more.'

And then, with a single hard stare of warning to Carol White, he proceeded upstairs.

# 12

The Saturdays I don't take Cazzie to the park, we go swimming. Given the choice she'd probably choose swimming every weekend, but generally I can't face it. The club where I swim midweek doesn't admit children, so we head back over the bridge to the Hammersmith & Fulham Sports Centre on the Lillie Road and take our chances with the world at large.

On my way to Clapham Common I ring Sally from the car to tell her it's swimming, which gives her time to collect together the stuff. So when I arrive Cazzie is waiting in the hall with her rolled-up towel and swimsuit, spare set of clothes, big pink comb and goggles.

'*Hooray*, it's swimming. Swimming, swimming, swimming,' sang Cazzie jumping up and down. She appeared pleased to see me. When Sally and I first split up I had this phobia that one Saturday I'd roll up and she'd look at me like a stranger, she'd have forgotten who I am. But I'm no longer worried about that. If she can remember the plot of a television programme one week to the next, why not me?

Sally came down the stairs carrying a plastic basket of laundry.

'Kit,' she said, 'I don't mind you taking her swimming but don't let her get her ears wet, please. She's got a throat infection.'

'Fine. So we'll avoid the water chute and the wave machine.'

'Aww,' moaned Cazzie. 'It's no fun without the water chute. Anyway, I can go down it without getting my ears wet, like this.' She poked her fingers into both ears, blocking them.

'I mean it, Cazzie,' said Sally. 'There's this bug going round the school, Kit. They sent a note about it. Oh and I have to ask you, you wouldn't have any objection to her learning the violin? It's an extra.'

'None whatever. What's it cost anyway? Two pounds a lesson?'

'Come off it, Kit. *Fifteen* pounds. Don't be so stingy, you can afford it.'

'Yes I can – and the answer's yes – but at fifteen pounds a pop it's a good business to be in, that's all I'm saying.

'Well, Cazzie,' I said, 'we'd better be on our way. Got everything?'

'I *think* so. Have I, Mummy? What about my California Raisins hairband?'

'I didn't put that in, darling. It's too precious, in case you lose it.'

'But I *need* it. It's by my bed.' Cazzie pounded up the stairs to her room, leaving Sally and me in the hall.

'Kit, I wasn't going to tell you this yet,' she said, suddenly serious, 'but I feel you should know. I'm seeing someone. Cazzie doesn't know about him yet. I mean, she's met him but doesn't know anything else.'

'What you're trying to say is that she doesn't know he's Mummy's boyfriend.'

'Don't use that word, it's too early.'

'Does he stay here?'

'Of course not.'

'So you go over to him.'

'Kit, with respect that is none of your bloody business. I didn't even need to tell you, I just wanted you to know. I thought you'd be pleased for me.'

'Actually I am. Sorry, it was a bit of a surprise, that's all.'

'What's a surprise? That I can find someone?'

'Of course not. You're very pretty and kind and dozens of men would be lucky to get you. Look, I regret saying anything now. I'm pleased, OK? By the way, do I know him?'

'No. He's a banker. With Flemings.'

'Rich?'

Sally blushed. 'I don't know. But yes, I think he is rather. He works very hard. He's always going to the Far East. He's there now in fact.'

It's funny, I'd thought of myself remarrying but hadn't really imagined Sally. I'd just sort of visualised her carrying on for ever in this house, bringing up Cazzie, and me one day telling her I was getting married again. Cazzie would be a bridesmaid, she'd love that. But what I hadn't reckoned on was Sally teaming up so quickly with some bonus-rich merchant banker. Where had she met him anyway? I thought she stayed home in the evenings, babysitting our daughter. But now I could see it all. The move to some big house north of the river, probably a country house too, and Cazzie evicted from the little bedroom she'd grown up in, the bedroom I'd painted for her in the house I paid for.

'So when are you getting married, then?'

'Don't be ridiculous, Kit. We've only known each other three months. Four months next weekend, to be precise. Anyway, it would be a big sacrifice for him: taking on a divorcee with a child.'

*Sacrifice*? Becoming Cazzie's stepfather. And I didn't like the expression 'taking on' either, suggesting as it did that they were a liability and I didn't pick up every last bill.

A sudden thought hit me. 'You wouldn't move to the country, would you? I have to be able to see Cazzie on Saturdays.'

'Kit, you're being absurd. This is just too premature, I wish I hadn't told you now. Paul does have a house in the country as a matter of fact, but it's only near Basingstoke. And we'd work something out about Cazzie. It wouldn't change anything, I promise you.'

We drove to the sports centre and Cazzie came with me into the men's changing room. I don't really like it, but there's no option. So we hurried past the communal showers where a dubious selection of exhibitionists were soaping their bits, and into one of the changing cubicles. Cazzie took fifteen minutes to undress, insisting on folding each piece of clothing as she took it off. They were going to get bundled into a tin locker anyway, so it was all futile. Then I helped her struggle into her swimsuit, blew up her armbands, and we dashed back past the nudists to the lockers. For once I had the correct coin to release the key, and I slipped the rubber tag around my ankle. Whenever I do this I feel like a hospital patient awaiting amputation. Then, holding Cazzie by the hand, we paddled together through the germ-busting footbath with its feeble ankle-height shower, and out into the grey light of the public pools.

As usual, the children's pool was closed for maintenance and the big pool partially roped off, but we managed to find a free lane and swam a couple of lengths together. Cazzie's swimming is getting so good. She doesn't mind her face going under and she can float on her back without anyone holding her. I wondered whether Paul the banker's house near Basingstoke had a swimming pool. Bound to, frankly. Do houses even exist in Hampshire without one? We were on our fifth length when a lifeguard in a track suit began blowing her whistle officiously and signalling us over to the side.

'Can't you read?' she asked. 'It says "No children deeper than one metre".'

'But I'm with her,' I said. 'There's no danger.'

'Either obey the rules or get out, I'm not bothered which.'

I trod water beneath her, protesting my case, knowing it was pointless.

'Listen,' I said half reasonably, half belligerently, 'the children's pool is closed. Most of this pool is off-limits too. Where do you expect us to swim?'

'If you're not satisfied, write to the Council,' she replied. 'But you can't go deeper than a metre.'

We got out and I promised Cazzie a Burger King as compensation. It really didn't matter, it was getting cold in there anyway.

We were passing the showers on the way back when I noticed two men standing under a single showerhead, taking turns to soap each other's backs. One was muscular and bald with sideburns and a black pencil moustache; the other was slim and blond. They were laughing as they washed each other, and I felt that at least part of their enjoyment lay in drawing attention publicly to their intimacy. It was only when we'd gone by that I realised the blond one was Micky Rice.

From the changing cubicle I could still hear him. In the office he keeps his campness on low-voltage, but here it was unrestrained. Their backchat echoed around the changing room.

'Hurry up, Cazzie,' I said, 'keep going. Then we can have our lovely hamburgers.'

But really I wanted to get her out before Micky and his friend had finished showering.

I'd been thinking a great deal about my conversation last night with Carol White. Everything she'd said had had the ring of truth about it. I didn't now for a moment doubt Micky had somehow intervened at the paper. His motive was clear enough too: green-eyed jealousy compounded by fear of losing his job to Anna. But that didn't explain why *The Sunday Times* would switch angles just because Micky asked them to. As far as I knew, he had no special influence at the paper. And if Colin Burns had been serious about headhunting Anna then it made it even more inexplicable.

Cazzie finished dressing and I scooped her up and headed for the exit. As we passed the locker room I caught a glimpse of Micky and his bald friend, ostentatiously towelling themselves between their legs. Did I imagine it, or did the friend really have his left hand in plaster? I didn't wait to find out.

*

156

I was more wary now. The burglary, the fight on the roof: they'd made me watchful. I tried to avoid getting home late and crossing the car park in the dark. And the lifts in the flats were starting to freak me out too: that moment when the doors jerked open on to my floor, where anyone could be lurking.

You are supposed in these situations to vary your routine. Come and go at different times by different routes. Change addresses. Jack the pattern.

But it's not that easy to do. I still needed to arrive at Park Place at seven o'clock each morning, and I'd signed a lease on the flat through till Christmas. And every Saturday afternoon, after I'd dropped Cazzie off, I invariably returned home demoralised at much the same time. These once-a-week visits, it was like dating. Collecting her from her mother, taking her out to a restaurant, the snatched kiss in the car, home by curfew. I wished she still lived with me but I'd nixed that for good the day I walked out on Sally. Only one person was going to see more of Cazzie in the future and that was the big bucks banker from Basingstoke. The friend from Flemings. That's assuming he could make the supreme sacrifice of watching my daughter grow up.

I got into the flat without incident and slipped into the kitchen to see if anyone was spying on me from the car park. It had become part of the routine of arriving home. An unmarked white transit van with darkened windows was stationed at right-angles to the gates. I watched it for a bit until it started up and drove off. Could have been a coincidence, plenty of vehicles use our car lot for a lay-over and a smoke.

Who had they been anyway, the masked men in Anna's flat? It had been nagging at me since Tuesday night. Obviously it could have been a routine break-in, there were enough of those in South Kensington. But why then were they helping themselves to Anna's papers from her desk? The answerphone I could understand, but her notes and files? And why masked? And why were they so intent on killing me?

Which brought me to another big question. When they'd broken into the flat, had they any idea I was already inside? Surely not. Otherwise they'd have searched the place. But it was strange none the less that we'd both decided to raid Anna's flat at the same time, and both gone for the answerphone.

I wanted to talk all this through with somebody and thought of Suzy. If she'd been away in Wales last weekend, chances were she'd be in London this one. She shared a flat somewhere in Pimlico with six other girls. Or at least it seemed like six, probably it was only three. They rang her up a lot in the office and the cast kept changing.

'Suzy?'

'No, it's Gemma. I'll just get her.'

I heard her call out to Suzy in the background. And then: 'He didn't say. It's a man, anyway.'

Suzy came to the phone.

Suddenly I felt slightly awkward. I'd never rung her at home on the weekend before. 'It's Kit,' I said. 'Kit from the office.'

She laughed. 'I guessed *that*. How many Kits do you think there are in my life?'

'Listen,' I said, 'I need your help. That's if you're not doing anything. You remember the stuff I told you in the Korean restaurant about my flat being watched and everything before Anna was killed? Well, quite a lot more has happened since then. And I wondered whether you're free this evening, because I very much want to discuss it with someone – with you, that is.'

'We'd been planning to see a movie later on. But we haven't done anything about it. So yes, I'd love to. If you think I can help.'

'I'll pick you up at seven o'clock.'

I arrived at Cambridge Street at five past, with the soft roof down and music blaring. It was a warm summer evening and I'd somehow guessed Suzy's flatmates would be milling about on the first floor balcony, watching her go off. Just because I was her boss it didn't mean I had to behave like one. I turned the music up as I approached the flat.

We headed for the Cromwell Road and out on to the M4, past the turning for Greenford and Harrow.

'Where are we going anyway?' asked Suzy.

'Datchet. There's a place on the river we can eat outside. I felt like getting out of London.'

I waited until we were clear of the speed cameras around Heathrow, then pressed down hard on the accelerator. People knock BMWs but they've still got a big kick when you ask for it. Suzy borrowed a pair of dark glasses as the speedometer touched a hundred and twenty. Her blonde bob was whipping about her face in the wind.

I didn't want to talk about anything important until we arrived. On the dashboard was a list I'd made of things not to forget to mention.

'What's this?' Suzy asked, picking it up. 'An agenda for conversation over supper? Very spontaneous.'

'It's a working supper. Like a working breakfast, only later. There's always an agenda, secret or otherwise.'

'All work and no play,' she said. 'Be warned.'

The Frog and Three Counties has been my favourite bolthole for as long as I've lived in London. I knew about it even before I met Sally, and in our early days we often drove down on summer evenings. When I first went it was still very much a pub: beer and cold beef salads on wooden benches overlooking the Thames. Then it was upgraded to pub-restaurant with trout and almonds and they stuck a row of umbrellas outside. These days you can get a *plat de fruits de mer* and lobster and the place gets written up every weekend in the Sunday supplements. But, amazingly, they haven't ruined it, not completely. Each time I think they will, but somehow it's still OK.

We turned off Datchet High Street past a close of modern houses and a playground, and into a lane. A real country lane. On one side a field of cows, on the other water meadows down to the river. The Frog and Three Counties lay at the end, a many-gabled building flanked by top-of-the-range company cars.

There was a Pimms bar in the saloon, serving No. 5 cup from a silver punch bowl, and we stood about under the beams with our drinks ordering dinner from the blackboard.

Then we bagged a table outside at the end of the terrace, where we could watch the skiffs and plastic gin palaces glide home along the river to their boathouses and moorings, and where we couldn't be overheard.

'OK, Kit, spill the beans,' said Suzy.

I said, 'I'll start by telling you what I know for certain. The facts. This, by the way, won't take long.

'Anna Grant,' I said, 'was strangled some time between eleven p.m. Saturday night and lunchtime Monday when she was found by Maria. Most likely before ten-thirty Sunday morning, or she'd have rung me back. To be honest, that's about all we *do* know.'

'Plus your flat was watched last Saturday afternoon,' said Suzy. 'And those men in the park. And we think whoever it was who killed Anna also stole her computer.'

'The question is, are all those events connected? I mean, the men in Battersea Park, are they the same people who strangled Anna? In which case, why would they have bothered spying on me and Cazzie? I can understand them watching the flat if they thought Anna was coming over, but not watching me without her. And there's another reason they might be a red herring.'

I told Suzy about the fight on Anna's roof on Tuesday night, and how the masked men had seemed to be of different build to the watchers in the park.

Suzy looked increasingly concerned as she listened.

'At least that explains why you've been wearing a polo-neck every day since Wednesday,' she said. 'And why you've been so tense in the office.'

'I've been tense?'

'Gibbering, actually. But don't worry about it. I thought it was to do with Anna. I didn't know about the fight.'

A waitress brought oysters on a tray of crushed ice and a cold bottle of Chablis.

'The thing we need to focus on,' I said, 'is who had the motive. Unless we believe there was no motive. Some sicko who goes round strangling women. Or a burglar interrupted who gets carried away. Personally, I don't buy either.'

'Then it must be someone with a serious grudge against Anna,' said Suzy. 'Or had some other reason for getting her out of the way.'

'Any ideas?'

'Micky Rice for a start. I told you already how jealous he was of her. His secretary says Micky's been on cloud nine all week. He's telling everyone he's mortified, but can't stop smiling.'

'But do we seriously believe he'd have been up to strangling Anna?'

'Do you mean up to it psychologically, or up to it physically?'

'Both.'

'Well, he certainly seems schizoid. I don't know enough about psychiatry to say whether he'd actually kill someone.'

'And physically?'

'Not on his own, he doesn't seem strong enough. Though they do say mad people can access enormous strength.'

I told her about seeing him that morning at the swimming pool, and how I thought the other man in the shower might have had his hand in plaster. I said it could even have been Micky and his friend on Anna's roof.

'If we only knew who the other man is we could check him out,' I said. 'Presumably he's Micky's boyfriend, they looked amorous enough.'

'That might not mean a lot. According to Delphine he changes partner every week. Faster usually.'

'This one looked rough. Bald head, maybe shaven. And built like an ox. And he had this strange pencil moustache, like an actor in an old Ealing comedy.'

'Probably picked him up at a leather club,' said Suzy. 'He does that a lot. Delphine says she can see a pattern. The more high life there is, the more he balances it with low life. For instance, if he goes to some enormous flashy launch given by Versace or someone, the next night he treks off to some S&M joint in Whitechapel.'

'Has anyone ever met his boyfriends?'

'They don't come to the office. But Delphine says they ring up and they're all types. Students. Waiters. Squaddies. Bikers. Micky isn't fussy. When they ring, he shuts the door to take the calls. Delphine says he's quite flirtatious with them, she can hear him through the wall. She says he's the girl in the relationship, not that I know much about it.'

'What I really meant was, does he go for rough trade? I was thinking about what access he might have to criminals. If his taste was pretty-boy Italian counts then he probably wouldn't. But it sounds like he'd meet everyone at these leather clubs.'

And there'd be leather masks too, I thought, no shortage of them.

'You know what I could do?' I said. 'Watch his flat. Even someone as promiscuous as Micky will probably still be with the bald one tomorrow morning. I can park across the street and take a close look at his left hand when they surface.'

'Won't Micky recognise your car?'

'That's a point. He's seen it several times. And if it was Micky and his friend I was fighting with on the roof, he'd be doubly aware of it.'

'Borrow mine,' said Suzy. 'You can't get less conspicuous than an eight-year-old Vauxhall.'

'You're sure that's OK?'

'Totally. But only if I can come too.'

'No way. Two people sitting together for hours in a car will look suspicious.'

'Not more than one person. Less suspicious, actually. We could pretend to snog.'

She smiled cryptically as the waitress cleared away the oyster shells and put down a large platter of crab and lobsters in the middle of the table.

'Leaving Micky Rice,' I said, 'there's also Bruno Fulger, of course. For my money he's got a much stronger motive and certainly the money to hire hitmen.'

'I imagine his solicitor would know where to get them. He sounds like one himself.'

'The real problem with Bruno Fulger is that I don't know much about him. Beyond the hype, I mean.'

'Do you want me to call in all the cuttings?'

'Sure. But I bet they won't be very illuminating. Just more stuff about his castle and the parties. We need to find out about his character. Specifically, is he capable of having people bumped off?'

'How do we discover that?'

'That's just it, I'm not sure. But I had one thought. If Bruno Fulger's done it for Anna, then chances are there have been other incidents too. Not murder necessarily, but other acts of revenge. Things he's done that have had to be hushed up.'

'Who'd know?'

'People he was at school with maybe. He was at Le Rosey in Switzerland. I looked him up in *International Who's Who*. If he's violent now, he was probably violent there too. I'm sure if we worked at it we could find someone at Le Rosey in 1962.

'Also,' I said, 'there must be people in Munich who know about him. That's where his headquarters is. And his castle's only about an hour outside.'

'What about that friend of yours, the one you sometimes have supper with when you're over there?'

'Nick Gruen? That's not a bad idea. He's always plugged into every scrap of gossip.'

I still looked on Nick Gruen as one of my best friends, not that we saw much of each other these days. At university we'd been as thick as thieves, had even shared a student house for a year in the New Town. But after we came down we drifted apart. Sally hadn't liked him much, which didn't help. Not that I really blamed her for that. You had to have known Nick Gruen in his heyday, aged twenty-two, to really get the point of him. These days he didn't put himself out much, especially with women. We'd had him round to supper in Clapham quite a bit, but some evenings he was so cynical and morose he infected the whole party. It was difficult to know who to seat him next to. With Sally's married girlfriends he was openly bored, with single girls he was either lecherous or hostile. One of his party pieces was asking unmarried thirty-year-olds why they'd got left on the shelf. 'Too late now,' he'd tell them. 'Hope you've got a proper pension plan, that's all.' Nick was a liability.

Then, three years ago, he'd gone to work in Munich for the European Bank for Reconstruction and Development. He was evasive about what he actually did there, but I think it involved dishing out millions of dollars to no-hope old paint factories in Eastern Germany. I can see that, for Nick, it would have its attractions: giving away other people's money to unfeasible projects. He'd enjoy the irony.

'You know what,' I said to Suzy. 'Why don't I simply go over to Munich for the day on Monday? It'd be easier than pumping Nick over the telephone. I'd see him for lunch and could call on the Müller fashion people to justify the ticket. I might take a look at Schloss Fulgerstein too.'

'If you want me to fix flights and cars I'll make some calls tomorrow,' said Suzy. 'I won't be able to get hold of Müller until Monday morning, but could confirm your appointment through to you at the airport.'

It was getting dark on the terrace and waitresses came round the tables with candles in glass bowls. We drank coffee and for a moment sat in silence, listening to the breeze in the branches. Somewhere in the water meadows a bullfrog croaked noisily. Otherwise there was peace, complete peace.

Some people live their whole lives like this. I know about it from reader research. They spend their summer evenings sitting in deckchairs in English gardens, counting their blessings and reading *Smart Living*. That's what the marketing people tell me, anyway. It never sounds very plausible. Except when I'm here.

'Is there anybody else we should be considering?' asked Suzy. 'Other than Micky and Bruno.'

'Well, the police are considering me.'

'Come off it. You were in love with Anna, weren't you?'

'Why do you say that?'

Even by the guttering candle I saw Suzy blush.

'I'm sorry,' she said. 'It was just something I thought. Not based on anything. Sorry.'

'If I was,' I said, 'it's no use now.'

I didn't want to discuss Anna with Suzy. It was too painful. And I didn't think she'd understand. I got the impression Suzy didn't really approve of Anna.

'It's good of you to declare me innocent of murder, anyway,' I said. 'I wish Inspector Barratt had your faith.'

Then I said, 'There is one other possibility I haven't told you about. Erskine Greer.'

'The Hong Kong Erskine Greer?'

'The same. He's got a motive too in a way, though not as strong as Bruno Fulger's.'

I told Suzy about Anna's profile for *Man Alive* and the outburst in his dining-room about the arms dealing.

I said, 'I suppose he could have admitted that stuff about supplying the North Vietnamese to impress her, and later regretted it. It wouldn't be good for his image if it got out he'd been so close to Hanoi. The ASEAN governments wouldn't like it, particularly Singapore where he has an office. Actually, they'd be pretty disapproving in Hong Kong too, with his airline homebased there.'

'So to stop Anna Grant writing the article, he could have had her killed.'

'Exactly. A bit farfetched, but maybe not. Again, I don't know much about him beyond our one encounter in Nassau five years ago, and what I read in the press.'

'I know plenty about Erskine Greer,' said Suzy. 'He's disgusting.'

'You do?'

'My father worked for him. Years ago, around the time I was born. If it wasn't for Erskine Greer, Dad would probably still be alive.'

'What do you mean?'

I'd never heard Suzy sound bitter before. It was a new side to her.

'Oh,' said Suzy, 'it's a bit of a long story. I'm sure you don't want to hear it.'

'I do,' I said. 'What was your father like?'

'I never really knew him,' she said. 'I mean, I can remember him being there, I've got this memory of an old man sitting in an armchair by a window, but he died when I was four. But I've got quite a clear sense of his character: conservative and honourable. Qualities nobody cares about any more. I think he might have been slightly boring and unimaginative too, to be honest. Anyway he worked for twenty years for a company called Anderson & Neame.'

'Which was later taken over by Greer, wasn't it?'

'Exactly. Dad was Managing Director when the Neames sold out. They didn't tell him until afterwards, so it came as quite a shock. Anyway, there wasn't much else on offer so he decided to make a go of it and stayed on to work for Erskine. Mum said he hated it from the start. The culture at Greer's was completely different. They kept sending people over from Hong Kong to teach Dad how to run the company, and they wanted more and more profits. And they made him do things in business he was uncomfortable about: sharp practices, Mum said.

'After a year and a half he got the feeling he was going

to be sacked. He was really worried about it. Don't forget he was fifty-two and I'd only just been born. He was an old father. And he thought if he was fired it'd be difficult to find another job. So he did a ridiculous thing. He asked Erskine to be my godfather.'

'Your *godfather*? I never knew that.'

'I know. Mummy was furious. He asked him without telling her. He sent a telex to Hong Kong inviting him, and a telex came back saying yes.'

'Whatever possessed your father to do that?'

'Oh, he had this stupid idea. He thought if Erskine could see us as a family, and come to our house and watch me being christened, he'd see Dad in a different light. He made him my godfather to save his job.'

'And did Greer show up?'

'At my christening? He certainly did. He came by helicopter. Imagine it, a helicopter in Kent in 1969. We lived in an old oast house in those days next to the church. It landed in our paddock. Mummy described the whole scene – it was the worst day of her life.

'I had three other godparents, all old friends of my parents, and everyone stood around waiting for Erskine to arrive. Eventually they heard the rotor blades in the distance which got louder and louder, and then the helicopter began circling the church spire. Apparently it took ages to land, as though they were checking out the terrain for signs of an ambush.

'When it came down, the door slid open and there was Erskine Greer. Striding across the clover of the paddock in a white suit. Seersucker.'

'How did he fit in?'

'With the other guests? Chalk and cheese, I expect. But even Mum admits he was very charming at first. He chatted everyone up. Charmed them at the font.

'Then after the service everyone went back to our house for lunch in the garden. It was a boiling hot day, and Dad took a photograph of all the godparents together on a bench, with me being held in the middle in my christening dress. I've got a copy of it somewhere, it's the oddest picture: my great-aunt Dot and a friend of Dad's from the golf club and my poor godmother Mary who never got married and Erskine Greer.

'Actually, Erskine then said he couldn't stay for lunch, he had to get back to London, but first he handed over this amazing christening present. Or rather his pilot did, it was so heavy.

'Mum unwrapped it and it was just incredible. There was masses of tissue paper, and inside was a huge silver bowl. Enormous. And solid silver, half an inch thick. He'd had it engraved "To Susannah Elizabeth Forbes. From her godfather Erskine Greer". And the date in Roman numerals. It must have cost a fortune. My other godparents, who were giving things like silver-plated napkin rings, were completely eclipsed. Dad was so touched. He couldn't believe his boss would give such a generous present.

'As I said, Erskine had to leave so everyone walked back down to the paddock to watch the helicopter take off. Dad was still thanking him as the motor was starting, so he had to shout to make himself heard.

'Dad said, "See you tomorrow at the office, Erskine," and then Erskine turned round and said, "Actually, Gerald, I think it would be best if you didn't come into the office again. We're going to let you go."

'Dad was stunned. Eventually he gasped, "What are you saying? That you're sacking me?" Erskine told him he shouldn't even collect his personal stuff, it would all be sent down to him. Then he slid the helicopter door shut and it took off into the sky. All Mum and Dad's friends stood there watching it disappear into the clouds. And Dad was fired.'

'Jesus,' I said, 'that's extraordinary. Why do you imagine he bothered?'

'The present and the firing? Sadism. Simple as that. He wanted maximum humiliation.'

'But it's odd, you've got to admit. The solid silver bowl. Why so generous?'

Suzy's mouth tightened. 'That wasn't generous. Erskine Greer's never generous. Don't you see, the bowl was symbolic: thirty pieces of silver. Betrayal. I'll tell you how generous Erskine is. Dad had worked for that company for twenty years; nineteen years for Anderson & Neame and another year after the takeover. But when it came to a pay-off, Greer gave him nothing. He said when they'd bought Anderson & Neame they'd folded it into a new offshore company, so none of Dad's earlier years counted for anything.'

'So what happened?'

'Well, Dad fought for a proper golden handshake but he never got it. Mum says he wrote about a hundred letters. Most never even got replies, or else there was a two-line brush-off from a lawyer in Hong Kong. Eventually Dad wrote to the Neames to see if they could do anything to help, but they weren't interested. They'd sold out and moved to the South of France. They didn't care.'

'Did he find another job?'

'He couldn't. He was broken by the whole thing. We had to sell the house and move to a cottage up the road. Then to another smaller cottage. Dad just sat about writing letters. In the end he more or less accepted that nothing would do any good, and he gave up and died.'

'And you. Were you OK?'

'My mother got a job in Tunbridge Wells as a secretary to an estate agent. That's why I type so well: it's hereditary.' She laughed. 'Actually, it can't always have been so easy, we were perpetually short of money, not that I noticed at first. It's later on you notice, when you're fourteen or fifteen and can't do the things your friends do. Holidays etcetera. I never left England until after I left school. One day when I was eighteen I found the silver bowl in a cupboard, still in its tissue paper. Mum had never mentioned its existence. Anyway, I sold it. In Tonbridge. Pretty stupid place to choose, I probably got ripped off. The man gave me two thousand pounds in cash.'

'What did you spend it on?'

'Going round Europe. Actually, a very odd thing happened on that trip. I was travelling by train from Rome to Florence and had run out of things to read. On the seat opposite was an Italian magazine and I picked it up and there was a photograph of Erskine Greer. I didn't really know what he looked like before. He was at a party with that woman who writes for *Smart Living*, Minnie Vass. Well, as you can imagine, I spent ages looking at it. I was fascinated to see the man who'd indirectly paid for my trip. He was sort of the devil incarnate in our house, but here I was bumming around Europe entirely courtesy of him.

'After I got to Florence an even stranger coincidence happened. I'd been looking round the Uffizi and was sitting in a pizza place in the square next door, having a coffee. Suddenly this big white open-topped car drew up and a man got out with a Chinese girl. It was Erskine, there wasn't the slightest doubt. They went into a restaurant with tinted windows to have lunch.

'The funny thing is, I didn't know what to do. Mum had always said if ever she saw him again, she'd hit him. She probably would too, she blames him for killing Dad. So I half-thought I should do it on her behalf. At the same time, I was intrigued by him. He just looked so cool getting out of that car. And the Chinese girlfriend was beautiful. I'm ashamed to admit this, considering the way he behaved to Dad, but I felt rather proud about having him as a godfather. Don't forget I was eighteen at the time and Erskine Greer was the only famous person I had any connection to.'

'So what did you do? Slug him or say hello?'

'The second, I'm afraid. I hung around outside the restaurant for about two hours. There was a doorman who kept glaring at me. No wonder: I had a backpack and hadn't had a bath for a month. In the end they came out of the restaurant, laughing. When I stopped them, Erskine looked amazed to be talking to someone who looked like me.

'I told him who I was, and that I was Gerald Forbes's daughter, and before I could say anything else he threw his arms around me and exclaimed, "My long-lost god-daughter!" He insisted on buying me a drink in a tea shop and was so charming. He asked where I was staying, and I said it was near the bus station, and he said how sad they were flying to Rome that evening or he'd have asked me to join them for dinner.

'They were so easy to talk to, so interested in my trip. Erskine made me have a bellini – peach juice and champagne – which I'd never tried before. We were chatting away when I suddenly had this vision of my mother watching me, disapproving. Like I was consorting with the enemy. The champagne probably had something to do with it too, because I said to him, "You do realise my father died thanks to you."'

'How did he react?'

'Hardly blinked. He looked at me and then said, "Susannah. Your father was an admirable man and you are lucky to have had him as a father. Nothing will ever change that. But I am a businessman. Your father wasn't. I have an obligation to run the best companies possible. And people who work for me have to perform. If they don't, or won't, or can't – and in your father's case I think it was a question of can't – then they go. It's that simple. I don't expect you to condone it, or to forgive me, but it's a fact of life. Your father couldn't handle the job. So he went. It's not personal. It shouldn't colour our relationship either. Now," he said, "if you've finished your drink, I'd like to buy you a present. Something useful for the rest of your holiday. Perhaps a pair of shoes, or a new suitcase. Florence is known for its leather."'

'Did you go?' I asked.

'No. I burst into tears. Don't ask me to explain it. It was all to do with Erskine Greer saying Dad was a failure and deserved to be sacked. He was so callous. I couldn't take it.

I felt such a traitor, drinking champagne with him and liking him so much. So I burst into tears and ran out to the street. A woman at the till by the door tried to stop me, she thought I was doing a runner without paying. But I pushed her aside and kept going all the way to the hotel. Now you know why I despise him so much.'

'Have you heard from him since then?'

'Not a word. Actually, that's not true. I think he might have sent me something once. On my twenty-first birthday a card arrived at home. It wasn't signed by anyone. Inside were ten fifty-pound notes. No message. Other than Erskine Greer, I don't know anybody who could do that.'

'What did you do with the money? Burn it?'

'Come off it. I spent it. You're not that great a payer, you know.'

We drove back along the motorway in silence. It was rather shaming that Suzy and I had worked together for three years but I still knew so little about her. On the surface she was the most straightforward of girls, she kept her disappointments well hidden. Well, I could relate to that too. I knew more than I cared to admit about money shortages. My own father spent his life racketing about between one hardship post and another, trying to grub together enough cash to keep the family solvent. Lagos, Brunei, Sharjah, wherever the oil business needed a qualified biochemist, he went. Sometimes he took us all with him to live in some ex-pat compound, sometimes we were left behind in England in a rented house to await his remittances. In the end it destroyed his marriage, as I think he always knew it would. I've got a theory my father accepted jobs in the worst places to test the strength of his marriage, in the full knowledge that eventually it would fall apart.

Suzy's head flopped against my shoulder as we re-entered London. I wasn't sure whether she was asleep or to read something more into it. Her hair smelt of baby shampoo and there was a scent I couldn't recognise too.

Something floral and old-fashioned, not one of those petro-chemical flysprays we promote in the magazines.

When we arrived at Cambridge Street I pulled up outside her house and whispered, 'Suzy?'

'Mmm.'

'We're back.'

She leant over towards me, nuzzling her face against mine.

'Wake up, Suzy,' I said softly.

She opened her eyes. I had parked under a streetlight, so I could see her clearly. She was looking at me with a kind of misty intensity.

'Will you come in?' she said.

'It's late,' I said. 'We've got an early start tomorrow if we're going over to Micky's flat.'

'I want you to stay tonight.' She kissed me on the cheek. 'Please stay.'

I put my arm around her. 'Suzy. I can't, I just can't. In some ways I'd love to, believe me, but it's too soon. After Anna and everything.'

'I knew it'd be Anna,' said Suzy sadly. 'I knew it was hopeless.'

'I'm sorry, Suzy. If Anna hadn't existed ...' I left the sentence hanging.

'You don't have to pretend anything,' said Suzy. 'I know I'm not Anna. But can't you just stay tonight? I'm sorry, but talking about Dad has made me emotional.' She sounded close to tears.

'I'm sorry, Suzy.'

I opened the car door, went round and helped her out. Then we stood together under the portico while she rummaged in a brown purse for her door key.

'Now I've gone and made a complete fool of myself,' she said.

'No, you haven't. You're just upset, that's all. It's nothing.'

'All right, it's nothing,' she said. 'Nothing, nothing.' Her bottom lip was trembling. 'Silly me thought it could be something, but it was nothing.'

I kissed her goodnight on the cheek very quickly, and then she went inside and pulled the door behind her.


'If he doesn't come out in the next half an hour, we're giving up and I'll buy you a pizza.'

It was ten past one and we'd been parked up at the top end of Nottingham Street since ten. Suzy had been right about her car being inconspicuous; in three hours no one had given us a second glance. Strewn across our knees and the floor were the Sunday newspapers. Suzy was reading aloud from the problem page of the *News of the World*. 'They cheer me up, the problems,' she said lightly. 'Keeps things in proportion.' After last night, she found it difficult to look me in the eye.

Although the address of Micky's mansion flat was Marylebone High Street, the entrance to his block was round the side in Nottingham Street. The numbers were painted in a glass fanlight above the porch: 96–136. Micky's flat was number 116. The block had five storeys which meant eight flats on each floor, so Micky would be on the second. There was nothing about the curtains to indicate which was his.

We'd considered ringing the flat from a payphone to see if anyone answered and hanging up if they did, but I'd said no. 'We mustn't do anything to make Micky jumpy. If they've murdered Anna they're going to be nervous as hell already without adding to it.'

So we sat there, watching the entrance and stiffening each time it opened. At a quarter past ten two old ladies in hats hobbled out, apparently on their way to church. At eleven a whole family of Arabs – the women wearing yashmaks, the men in shellsuits – emerged and sat outside on a low wall before going back inside. At eleven fifteen Suzy went off in search of snacks and returned with a kofta kebab and pitta bread in greaseproof paper, which stank out the car. Then she put on a cassette called *Now That's What I Call Music 15* until it drove us both crazy.

'Haven't you got anything else?' I asked Suzy.

She scrabbled about in a glove compartment full of empty Perspex tape boxes. 'They must be under the seat somewhere. This car's a black hole for cassettes, they vanish.'

'You know what,' I said, 'I've got Anna Grant's answerphone tape with me.' I had on the jacket I'd worn that night to Harrington Gardens. 'Any objection if I put it on? There were some calls from someone I don't recognise I'd like to relisten to.'

So we rewound the tape and for the second time Kim on the *Man Alive* picture desk was asking Anna to ring her.

When Erskine Greer's voice came on, Suzy grimaced. 'He's just too smooth. "If you forget your jewellery, I can buy you some out there." *Yuk*. What is he? Her lover?' Then she reddened. 'Sorry,' she said. 'I didn't mean that.'

We listened to the menacing message from Rudolph Gombricht and then the succession of embarrassing calls from me, and finally Peter. 'Hi, sweetheart,' he said. 'I'm at the river lodge for twenty-four hours. The story's really hotting up and I wonder how you're getting on your end.'

'Beats me,' I said. 'I just don't get what that's about, or who Peter is.'

'Sounds like a journalist,' said Suzy. 'Did Anna know any war correspondents? The connection suggests he was ringing from somewhere like Cambodia.'

The second Peter message came on. 'It's now four o'clock in the afternoon which I guess makes it seven your time ...'

'That rules out Cambodia,' I said. 'Wrong direction: Cambodia's ahead, not behind.'

'I'm still at the lodge,' said Peter, 'but only until tomorrow morning. So ring me tonight, it doesn't matter how late, I've got to speak to you ... Bye, sweetheart.'

'If he's three hours behind that makes wherever he was ringing from two hours closer than New York. New York's five behind London. Three could be Greenland,' I said doubtfully.

'Or Newfoundland,' said Suzy. 'That's three hours. So is most of South America, come to that. Argentina's three behind, I think. So's Uruguay and Brazil. Great: we've narrowed it down to half the world.'

'As for Peter,' I said, 'that's not much help either. There must be several million Peters.'

But how many of them called Anna 'sweetheart'?

'This waiting's getting boring,' said Suzy. 'What if Micky's shacked up for the rest of the weekend at his place? And I'm starving.'

Just then the door of the flats swung open and out came two men.

It was them.

They were a hundred yards away from us on the opposite side of the road, walking towards Marylebone High Street.

'Keep absolutely still,' I said to Suzy. 'And whatever you do, no eye contact. Pretend you're reading the paper.'

Micky was half a step ahead of the bald one, making it difficult to get a clear view of his hand.

They passed us without seeing us and turned at the corner into the High Street.

Suzy started the car and pulled out. We edged up to the junction and looked right. There was no sign of them. We could see only three pedestrians and none of them was Micky Rice.

'Pull over to the kerb and wait. They can't just have disappeared.'

A minute later they stepped out of a newsagent's, almost on top of us, clutching a heap of papers. Or rather Micky was holding the newspapers. The bald-headed ox kept his hands in the pockets of a leather jerkin. We allowed them a hundred yards lead before pulling out again.

At the junction with Blandford Street they turned right

and by the time we reached the corner we'd lost them again.

Blandford Street is lined on both sides with restaurants and spaghetti houses.

'Shall I park or drive on?' asked Suzy.

'Drive on. But slowly. I want to see if I can spot them in any of these places.'

It wasn't hard. They were sitting at a window table in a restaurant called Stephen Bull. Named after a celebrity chef, I'd read about it often enough on Micky's expenses.

It was a table for three with Micky sitting in the middle. A waitress was standing over them, taking orders for drinks. On one side of Micky was the bald ox. And on the other side sat Colin Burns, the editor of *The Sunday Times*.

After Suzy dropped me home I spent the remainder of the afternoon pretending to work. Next week were the quarterly editorial review meetings, when the editors, publishers and I compared the performance of our titles against the competitors.

There was a tendency for these meetings to drift into blind self-congratulation. We would kick off by paging our way through our own recent issues, while the editor commended particular scoops: film stars who had turned down a cover for *Town Talk* but had agreed to appear in *In Society*. That sort of stuff.

Then we'd switch our attention to the opposition, examining their front covers, features and fashion pages. Here the tone changed to one of withering mockery.

'I can't *believe* it,' the editor would exclaim. 'An interview with Courtney Love. We did her six issues ago.'

Or, 'I don't know why they've done Ralph Fiennes now. The movie's not even released for another two months.'

My role in the proceedings was devil's advocate, pointing out unpopular home truths. Such as *Town Talk* had had nine big sellers in succession (only Anastasia Fulger had dented their stellar circulation graph) and were now fewer than eleven weeks away from passing us.

My first editor, in one of his favourite philosophical pronouncements about magazines, liked to adapt the old cliché about success having many parents but failure being an orphan. 'When it's going well,' he'd say, 'we all take the credit: editor, publisher, circulation people, printer. You can't see the stage for people bowing. But the moment it turns sour, it's everyone else. Editor blames the circulation director. Circulation blame the front covers. Publisher says he can't sell adverts against a falling readership and someone's got to go. Usually we settle on the art director. Less messy than an editor. But I'll tell you one thing,' he said, 'switching the typefaces about never did the trick yet. Not on its own.'

I had invented a system for tracking how well or badly our magazines were performing editorially. There was nothing scientific about it, just an exercise in advanced personal prejudice.

It worked like this. First I'd take two competing titles, one ours, one theirs. I'd make a long list of the fifteen principal articles and fashion stories in both. Then I'd award marks out of five. How sincerely do people want to read this stuff? A five means they'd lap it up, probably read it at the bookstall. A four means pretty exciting and good. And so on down to one which indicates they'd finish it only if stuck on the Moscow–Tehran Mail with a week to kill and nothing else available.

Then, on top of that, there was a second scorecard for general excellence: marks for slickness, charm and above all for surprise. A reader's relationship with his magazines is less straightforward than people think. It's like marriage. He chooses a particular magazine because it's a mirror to himself. It likes the same people he does. But after ten faithful years a mistress comes along: younger, sexier, with a new circle of friends. The reader walks out with barely a twinge of guilt. The mistress title invigorates him. What can the wife do? Rouge her cheeks and prance about in Lycra? Or wait patiently at the hearth until her reader slinks back home?

Safest is never to let him wander at all. The magazines I like best are utterly predictable but every third issue the wife answers the doorbell in the nude.

I spent an hour comparing and contrasting *Smart Living* with *Genteel Homes*. Which one had produced the better supplement on bathrooms? Sometimes there's too much excitement in this job. Then I went through the same exercise for *In Society* and *Town Talk*. Micky was running a six-page profile this week on the Dutch royal family followed by an essay on the history of royal mistresses from Nell Gwynn to Mrs Parker-Bowles. *Town Talk* had exclusive pictures of Johnny Depp and Kate Moss's new apartment in Manhattan plus an article about Salman Rushdie's twenty favourite dancing partners. Thirty-love to *Town Talk* I felt, irritably.

The telephone rang and it was a crisp-sounding older woman. It took me a moment or two to place her as Bridget Grant.

'Forgive me for ringing out of the blue,' she said, 'and particularly at the weekend.'

'That's fine,' I said. 'It's good to hear from you. In fact, I was meaning to write to you anyway, to say how well I thought Anna's funeral had gone. It was a nice oration by the vicar.'

'It was about Anna I wanted to talk,' said Mrs Grant. 'You said something to me when you were leaving the church. I don't know whether you meant it or were just being kind, about Anna being an exceptional young writer.'

'I certainly did mean it.'

'You may think this is completely inappropriate, but I was wondering whether some sort of memorial prize might be established for her. It's just an idea, and I haven't really thought it through. But maybe there could be an annual award for young journalists who write in the same sort of way as Anna did, if you feel there'd be any interest.'

'My immediate reaction,' I said, 'is yes. Obviously I'd

like to consider it for a bit. But yes. The Anna Grant Award. It should be restricted to profile writing. You know what,' I said, 'if I speak to our owner, Barney Weiss, he might agree to fund it: that's if you'd like me to.'

'I hadn't thought so far ahead,' said Mrs Grant. 'That would be an extraordinary kindness. My first step was simply to ask if you agreed with the idea and, if you did, whether you'd be prepared to advise me. The only other person I've mentioned this to is Peter.'

'Peter?'

'My son Peter. Anna's brother. He lives in Brazil. Sadly, he couldn't fly back for the funeral, the place he lives is just too far from anywhere.'

The mystery solved. I felt an unexpected wave of relief. 'Sweetheart' was what Peter called his sister.

'You know one thing I'd like to do,' I said to Mrs Grant. 'I'd like to talk it through with Peter too, if that's OK with you. Anna often used to mention him. She had a lot of respect for him.'

'That's nice to hear,' said Mrs Grant, sounding slightly surprised. 'At one point they fought like cat and dog. Peter's so much more serious than Anna. He used to accuse her of writing trivia, which so enraged her. You know how seriously Anna took her journalism, deep down. But I'm glad to hear you say she respected him. I think she did come to find Peter's work quite interesting as she got older. At Christmas, when Peter was last home, they agreed they were *both* anthropologists in their different spheres.'

Bridget Grant gave me a telephone number for somewhere called the River Mocó Lodge, which she said was eight hundred kilometres west of Manaus. 'Peter's there about half the time,' she said. 'Otherwise he's camping out in the forest. But you can always leave a message. He's good about ringing back.'

I wrote down the number and then asked, 'Is there any news, incidentally, from the police? I wondered if they were any closer to finding whoever did it?'

Bridget Grant didn't answer straight away, as though she were weighing up how much to tell me.

'I don't know,' she said. 'The Superintendent in charge has rung several times, but I'm not really qualified to assess what actual progress they're making. They asked me a lot of questions about Anna's friends, including you actually, but as I've told them I'm only her old mother, they can't expect me to know all that much.'

She fell silent for a moment, and then continued, pointedly.

'The Superintendent seemed to be very interested in Anna's boyfriends and whether anybody might be jealous of anybody else.'

Was she trying to warn me about something?

Mrs Grant said, 'He suggested there could have been a quarrel which turned nasty. As far as I can tell, the police seem to believe Anna was killed by someone she knew rather than by a stranger.'

After we'd said goodbye I stood by the window for a bit and watched the river flowing sluggishly past down below. The water level had dropped in the last few weeks. Another month like this and the houseboats moored on the opposite bank would be resting on mud flats.

So the police suspected one of Anna's boyfriends. Well, good luck to them. I imagined there'd been quite a few over the years, not that it was something I'd ever cared to focus on. Simon Beriot the photographer was one, if Micky could be believed. Who else? Erskine Greer? Depends how you define boyfriend.

I dialled the number Bridget Grant had given me and after a lot of clicking heard a distant ringing tone.

'Mocó Lodge,' a voice answered. It was very faint.

'Can I please speak to Peter Grant?' I could hear my own voice echoing down the line.

'Peter's out of station right now. He'll be back Wednesday or Thursday. Can I leave him a message?'

'Just say Kit Preston,' I shouted. 'It won't mean

anything. But tell him I called and I'll ring him next week.'

Some time around eight o'clock the telephone rang again. I cursed. My mother always maintained it's inconsiderate to ring anyone on Sunday evening, and I've never entirely shaken off her prejudice.

'Mr Preston?' It was a male voice with a North Country accent. 'Sergeant Crow from Chelsea CID.'

'Good evening,' I said. 'Any news?'

'Well, we were wondering if you could come down to the station this evening, sir.'

'What, now?'

'If that's convenient. Superintendent Barratt has requested to see you.'

'Er, OK. This won't take long, will it? Where do I come?'

'Chelsea police station at 2, Lucan Place,' said Sergeant Crow. 'Entrance on the corner. When you get here, ask the desk sergeant to ring me, Sergeant Crow, in the major incident suite. I'll collect you at the desk.'

'Got that. I'll be there in half an hour.'

'If it would help, we could pick you up in a patrol car.'

'No, I'll be fine, thank you. I'll make my own way.' Frankly, I thought I'd pass on a white and orange panda, all sirens blaring, turning up at the flats.

I threw on some clothes – jeans, jacket, shirt and tie – and with mild irritation drove across the bridge. I'd planned on having a quiet Sunday evening getting a deep-pan pizza sent over, and generally slobbing out in front of the television. But it probably wasn't a bad thing to get my two ha'penceworth out of the way before next week got too heavy at the office. With luck I'd be able to brief them about Anna and still be home before the Sunday night film.

I circled Sloane Avenue and Draycott Avenue looking for a parking place. The restaurants and bars were full to the gills, the streets almost impassable with double-parked cars. Still, I felt it wouldn't look too good to park mine illegally outside a police station.

Sergeant Crow met me at the desk and introduced himself as the office manager of the inquiry.

'What's that mean exactly?' I asked.

'Means I do all the work,' he replied. 'No, just kidding. I take care of procedure for the investigating officer. In this case Superintendent Barratt.'

He led me along a warren of passages to a staircase. On our way we passed a self-service canteen full of policemen eating omelettes and chips, and rows of offices with internal glass windows overlooking the corridor. Every twenty yards was a firedoor with posters stuck on advertising careers in the police force. Bit of a case of preaching to the converted, or the unconvertible, I felt. As we went deeper into the station, I began to feel unaccountably guilty, like walking past the headmaster's office at school. Apparently it's perfectly normal: a well-documented phenomenon.

Sergeant Crow was a burly, dark-haired man in his early forties, with a suntan.

'Been away?' I asked.

I wasn't certain of the protocol about asking personal questions of police officers, but it didn't seem to bother him.

'Corfu,' he said. 'Ten days with the kids.'

'Enjoy it?'

'Week would have been long enough, to be truthful,' he said. 'Kids at that age.' Then he said, 'Here we are,' and led me into a room containing four desks, three large personal computers with women logging in data, a coffee machine and a water dispenser with disposable plastic cups.

At one end of the room was a partitioned-off section and inside, sitting behind a desk, I saw Superintendent Barratt.

He offered me tea which he made himself, dunking a teabag into a cup of hot water by its string and squeezing out a cloud of brown tannin with a spoon. 'You'll need a second cup round it for protection,' he said. 'Otherwise it's too hot to hold.'

'A lot of people you've got working here on a Sunday night,' I said. 'I'm impressed.'

'Not sure they are though,' said Barratt. He smiled ruefully. 'Though the overtime's welcome.

'Actually,' he said, 'it's important they finish getting all this on to the computers. Five days of house-to-house and interviews with Anna Grant's relatives and neighbours.'

'These look like powerful machines.' I suppose I was making all this conversation out of nervousness. I'm no computer buff.

'They are. Though standard now for this kind of investigation. We call them Holmes: that's Home Office large major enquiry system. For cross-referencing, you can't beat them. But you know what they say about computers, you can only get out what you first put in.'

When I'd met Superintendent Barratt in Anna's flat on the afternoon they found her, I confess he hadn't made much of an impression on me. There were so many authority-figures about, they blurred into each other. Tonight I sized him up properly. I put his age at thirty-seven, which seemed young for a Superintendent though I'm told it's normal these days. There must still be professions out there where you can't get to the top before the age of fifty, but I can't think of any offhand, other than High Court judge. He looked fit and keen and in the best sense competent. If you asked me to make a guess about his life outside the force, I'd say he read geography at university and that his hobby is bungee-jumping.

I followed him into the inner sanctum, trying not to spill my tea, and sat down on a chair across the desk.

'Smoke?' He offered me a cigarette. I shook my head.

'Mind if I do?'

'Go ahead.'

Pinned to a cork board behind Barratt's shoulder was a photograph of an attractive woman with orange hair and three small children. All boys. They looked nine and seven and five: all gingertops.

'Let me begin, Mr Preston,' he said, 'by thanking you for coming in on a Sunday evening. I'm aware you're a busy man, and leisure time's precious. But I wanted to have a quiet off-the-record talk about Miss Grant. I should stress there's nothing official about this. It's totally informal. You haven't been brought in.' He smiled reassuringly.

'No, of course not.' I smiled confidently back. But it struck me as an odd thing to say: 'You haven't been brought in.' I should think not.

'Tell me your feelings about Anna Grant,' he said. 'No need to think too deeply. There's no right or wrong answer here. Just whatever comes into your head.'

'Well,' I said, 'I first met Anna about four years ago. At a polo match of all places, in Windsor Great Park. It was an event sponsored by one of our advertisers, and they'd invited a couple of hundred people to lunch in a tent. Anna was at the same table.'

'And your first impressions of her?'

'That she was very attractive and amusing. Actually, I already knew who she was before we met, from her writing. She'd contributed a couple of short pieces to newspapers, which I'd noticed and admired.'

'And in your judgement the feeling was reciprocated?'

'How do you mean? I don't write articles myself, so Anna certainly couldn't have admired them.'

'I mean your general impression: amusing and attractive.'

The question surprised me. 'I very much doubt it. The day was a bit of a chore actually. I'm not sure I was particularly amusing.'

'And after your meeting at the polo, you next saw Anna?'

'Oh, not for ages. Five or six months. Her newspaper journalism got better and better so, when a job came up

185

on our magazine *In Society*, I encouraged the editor to take her on.'

'And how did the editor feel about that?'

'Fine, I think. I seem to remember we hired Anna together. In the bar of the Stafford hotel.'

'You didn't feel your motives might have been open to criticism?'

'I'm sorry, I'm not sure what you mean.'

'Let me put it another way. I understand the job you gave her is regarded as an important one.'

'It certainly is. To be senior features writer is a great job. On a weekly magazine, you're contracted to write sixteen to twenty major pieces a year, plus a quota of shorter articles.'

'So it's a job that would attract any number of professional journalists.'

'Very much so.' What the hell was he driving at?

'Forgive me, Mr Preston,' said the Superintendent, 'but if this job as – what was it again – senior features writer is so highly sought after, why would you give it to a writer with almost no track record? That's what I meant by motives being subject to question.'

'You're asking why we employed Anna? Because of her talent. Simple as that.'

Superintendent Barratt made some notes on a pad and I watched his pen moving across the paper. For some reason I was reminded of a visit to the doctor, watching him write out a prescription.

'This word "talent".' He enunciated it as though, as a concept, it was something foreign and suspect and he was picking it up with a pair of tongs. 'Not an easy thing to define, is it? Subjective. Particularly in your business, I'd have thought.'

'Sometimes, yes, certainly. But with Anna Grant it was pretty easy. I should explain that there are really two separate skills you need to be a good features writer. Three actually. You have to be able to choose good subjects, which can sometimes be done for you, but Anna invariably came up with her own. And then – very important – you have to get people to agree to be interviewed. And then of course, most important of all, you have to be a natural journalist: make it come alive on the page. Anna was great at all three.'

'And this last skill you've mentioned, the writing part. Would you really categorise Anna Grant as a top-flight writer?'

'Definitely.'

'The reason I ask,' he said, 'is that this isn't what I've heard. It's been mentioned to us in the course of the investigation that Miss Grant sometimes had to redo her work. Rewrite it.'

'That's total rubbish.' I suddenly felt quite angry. Who the hell had been feeding him this stuff? Of course: Micky Rice.

I said, 'I can only imagine you got that from Micky Rice, her editor at *In Society*, whose opinion on just about everything is fundamentally warped.'

'I'm afraid we can't disclose how we come by any particular piece of information. I can only say that over the last few days we've interviewed a number of different people.'

'Look,' I said, 'I'm not stupid and I think I can see where this line of questioning is taking us, so let's just cut straight to the quick. No, I did not give Anna Grant her job because I fancied her. And no, she didn't retain it because of my patronage. She worked for us because she was a bloody impressive journalist. And her contract wasn't just with *In Society* either, she wrote for *Man Alive*. So you can ask her editor there, Spike Steel, about her talent.' I was really boiling now.

'Easy, Mr Preston. Calm down now. Remember what I told you at the beginning: this isn't an official interview. It's just a nice, quiet, informal chat.' Superintendent Barratt waited patiently until he thought I'd cooled off a bit. The look on his face said 'your reaction is quite understandable and we have all the time in the world'. No doubt it was a technique he'd picked up on some strategic leadership course at Bramshill police college. It was uniquely infuriating.

After the requisite hiatus, Barratt set off again: 'It was you who raised the subject, not me, Mr Preston, but let me ask you about your affair with Anna Grant.'

'My *affair*? I didn't have an affair with Anna Grant.'

'Again, that's not the information we have.'

'Then perhaps you'd better share this amazing information. Then I can put you straight.'

'According to our sources, you and Miss Grant conducted an affair over several years.'

'Categorically untrue.'

'So it wouldn't be accurate to say you left your wife for her?'

'No, it damn well wouldn't.' I could hear myself starting to shout.

'Keep calm, Mr Preston. I don't want to have to tell you that again.' He waited for half a minute. I was really furious now. I just couldn't believe I was sitting here listening to this stuff. The police should have been out arresting Micky Rice or Bruno Fulger or someone, not raking over a load of gossip about me and Anna. And the line about me leaving Sally for her really pissed me off. I'd gone out of my way, when our marriage hit the rocks, not to have another woman cited. And I'd done it the only sure way possible: by not having one.

'Let's get this completely straight, shall we?' said Barratt. 'Just so there are no crossed wires later on. You're saying that at no time did you have an affair with Anna Grant.'

'Exactly that.'

'And you won't have any objection if we ask your permission to take a mouth swab.'

'None at all. Anyway, what do you need it for?'

'DNA. If you'd prefer, we could take a blood test.'

'No, a mouth swab is fine. What are you hoping to prove?'

'Not proving anything as a matter of fact. It's just a routine test. The idea here is to eliminate not incriminate.'

'Eliminate what?'

'Actually, Mr Preston, the swab may enable us to confirm what you said about not having sexual relations with Miss Grant. It's very straightforward. The standard gynaecological examination as part of the post-mortem revealed traces of semen. We can compare the DNA with the mouth swab.'

'Well, you'll find it's positive.'

'Positive? Are you now telling me that you and Miss Grant *were* sexually active?'

'In fact, we made love for the first time ever at about half past five on the Saturday evening before she was killed. At my flat in Battersea.'

'I see.'

'And then a second time about an hour or so later.'

'I see.'

Superintendent Barratt looked at me, unblinking. It was a look that said, 'OK, now we're finally levelling with each other.'

'Listen,' I said, 'everything I've told you is true. Every word. I didn't have an affair with Anna Grant. Never. The one and only time we went to bed together was that afternoon. Before then, our relationship simply wasn't like that.'

Barratt said nothing. He just looked at me.

'Quite a coincidence, wouldn't you agree? The one time you sleep together is the one time we can prove that you did.'

'I can see it might look that way to you.'

'Thank you for that, Mr Preston. And now, if you're still willing for us to proceed with the mouth swab, I'd like to get that out of the way.'

Someone calling himself the exhibits officer invited me to lean back and open wide, and then scraped away some mucus from the roof of my mouth with a plastic spatula like an ice-cream spoon. 'There, all over now.' It was a surprisingly easy and painless procedure. Nothing to it.

While he was sealing the swab in a sterile container, I had time to marshal my thoughts.

'Can I please ask a question? Because I think I must have missed some vital step in your logic here. As it happens I was in love with Anna Grant. The sex bit was a new development – truly – and if she hadn't died we probably would have had a future together. So, why on earth would I want to strangle her?'

'Whoever suggested that?' said Barratt at once. 'I certainly didn't.'

'Well, it seemed to be where we were heading.'

'Not unless you say so, Mr Preston.'

'This whole thing's unbelievable,' I said. 'You've gone off on a tangent. There are endless other people you should be investigating, with real motives. Micky Rice. Bruno Fulger: Anna wrote that article about his wife and he's crying out for revenge. Erskine Greer the tycoon.'

'Who said we're not investigating them, Mr Preston? At this stage of the inquiry we've eliminated nothing and no one.'

'It just doesn't look that way to me, that's all.'

'Before you go,' said Barratt, 'one final question. Would you say your character is obsessive in any respect? I'm not saying that it is. I want your own assessment.'

'Obsessive?' I considered all the nuances here before answering. 'It depends, doesn't it, what you mean by obsessive. I'm probably quite obsessive at work. I like to do things well. And I'm obsessive about the magazines performing well, and looking good. And I prefer them to win. Is that obsessive?'

'I was thinking more about your personal relations.'

'No, I wouldn't say so, then. I don't think of myself as obsessive. Why do you ask?'

'Just something that was said, a passing remark.'

Then Barratt stood up and walked me back down the

long corridor to the main hall. When we reached the entrance, he followed me outside on to the steps and we stood together in the warm summer night.

'As I say, it was good to have an opportunity for a bit of a chat there. I think it clarified things a bit.'

'Sure.' It had actually been the most bemusing fifty minutes of my life.

'If anything else comes up, we can get hold of you on the numbers we've got.'

'Sure.'

'And if anything occurs to you, anything you want to tell me, Sergeant Crow can always get hold of me.

'While I remember,' he added, 'you're not planning on going away anywhere in the near future? No holidays scheduled?'

'I'm off to Germany tomorrow morning, but that's work. Only for the day.'

He looked dubious and for one mad moment I thought he was going to confiscate my passport.

But he said, 'No problem. Just let us know if you're leaving the country for any length of time, won't you?'

Then he shook my hand and headed back inside the station.

# 13

Munich's new state-of-design airport, the Franz Josef
Strauss, has added an hour each way to the journey into
the city; but for a visit to Müller, the Bavarian fashion
giant, it is strangely convenient. Barely fifteen minutes
from the European terminal, their headquarters is plonked
in an industrial park overlooking a manmade lake.

My visit was a courtesy, but then no account needed
more courtesy than Müller. As fashion advertisers went,
Müller were significant. Not quite in the Chanel or Ralph
Lauren league, but certainly high in the second division.
Last year, across the group, Weiss Magazines took gross
revenues of £473,416 from Müller and it could be higher
still if *Couture* wasn't so sniffy about them.

The problem for Müller was the same as for many
German fashion houses: they were German. And for
fashion editors a German label carries the mark of Cain. A
garment has only to derive from Paris, Milan, Tokyo, New
York, even Belgium, to command instant admiration. Let
the same garment originate in Munich or Düsseldorf and
it is greeted with suspicion and disdain. To get our editors
to take German fashion seriously required coercion: even
to get a junior editor to cover the Düsseldorf collections
was a triumph, let alone to put a Müller suit into the
pages of the magazine. Much of Kevin Sky's time was
spent soothing hurt feelings in the Rhineland while
cajoling Leonora Lowell and Tasmin Feeley in Park Place.

Heiner Stüben, *obergruppenführer* of Müller Verlag
*GmbH*, was a tall, fifty-year-old Berliner who had lived in
Munich for most of his life. Like other Germans I had met,
he was ostensibly an ascetic Lutheran, who had banned

alcohol from the Müller plant and oversaw an administration of fearsome precision. After work, however, another more boisterous side came to the fore. One evening, after an epic three-hour exposition of Müller's marketing strategy, Heiner had taken me to a beer house underneath the town hall, the *Ratskeller*, where he proceeded to get rapidly and violently ratted. At midnight we were still there. After four hours of *bier* and *rotwein*, and several saucers of soused herring and onion, Heiner was telling me his life story.

His father had been killed aged twenty-two in the final days of the war, leaving behind the pregnant wife he had married less than a year earlier. His mother had moved in with a reluctant aunt in Nürnberg and given birth to her son four months later. But the aunt complained she couldn't support the three of them, so Heiner and his mother had drifted south to the flattened city of Munich, where she'd found work as a chambermaid in one of the first hotels to reopen. Mother and son had lived on the premises in a tiny room under the roof. 'We lived like *gastarbeiters*,' Heiner had said bitterly. 'Guest workers. Like Turkish *gastarbeiters*.' We had ended the evening swearing undying friendship, toasting the European Community, toasting Mrs Thatcher, toasting the newly reunified Germany, toasting Müller and Weiss Magazines which together would rule the world. As we climbed the wooden stairs up to the street, Heiner had rather unsteadily offered me a woman. 'Good German fräulein,' he'd promised. 'Bitch from Mannheim.' His driver had happily appeared at this point and helped him into the back of a black Audi.

When I had seen Heiner Stüben the next morning he made no reference to our evening out and had talked earnestly about currency exchange.

'So, Kit,' said Heiner today, rising from behind his desk, 'and how is publishing in the UK?'

We talked about the escalating price of paper, and how England was emerging from recession faster than France and Germany. 'First in, first out,' said Heiner. 'In Germany soon it will improve too. With the former DDR included, we are once again the largest nation in Europe.'

Upside-down on his desk I spotted a record of the editorial credits for Müller in our magazines, or rather the lack of them. The memo began: Chanel 63, Armani 61, Müller 2, Donna Karan 31.

The only means of defence was attack.

'The reason I've come to see you,' I said, 'is that I urgently want to invite you to come over to London for the day. Our editors are desperate to meet you personally. They feel that, as a company, Müller is rather remote and hard to deal with, which is leading to fewer editorial credits than would otherwise be the case.'

Heiner Stüben looked alarmed. The implied criticism that he was being insufficiently proactive was a grave one.

'What I mean,' I went on, 'is that, compared to companies like Calvin Klein and Christian Lacroix, we just see far less of the Müller bosses. Which I fear is militating against the brand.'

'But this is a bad situation,' intoned Heiner. 'This bad attitude of ours must be rectified.' He shook his head. 'Kit,' he said, 'I must thank you for coming to tell me this. A visit to London has become a priority for me now.'

Goodness knows what I'd tell them in Park Place: a lunch with Heiner Stüben wasn't going to set the joint jumping. But I'd worry about that later.

'You are in Munich long?' asked Heiner. 'I would like to offer you dinner at the *Ratskeller*.'

'Unfortunately, I'm only here for the day. And this afternoon I was thinking of driving out to Starnberger to take a look at Schloss Fulgerstein.'

'Bruno Fulger's place? It isn't opened for the public, you know that.'

'I do know. But I believe you can see it from across the lake. I'm told it's very impressive.'

'Impressive, yes. Fulgerstein is the jewel of Bavaria. But it is also a happy family home.'

'Bruno and his wife have recently split up, haven't they?'

Heiner shrugged. 'This I cannot tell you. Bruno Fulger is my age, or one year younger. But our circumstances are very different.'

'What is his family history?'

'His father, Dietrich Fulger, was a great patriot,' said Heiner evenly. He paused. 'His grandfather had been close to the Kaiser. Then, after the formation of the FDR, Dietrich once again made an important friend in Konrad Adenauer. When the concessions to reindustrialise the Ruhr were being awarded, Dietrich Fulger obtained many important ones for steel and coal. He invested millions of Deutschmarks in modernising these industries which quickly became highly profitable. By the time Dietrich died, some time in the 'sixties, he left more than one billion Deutschmarks.'

'And what about his son Bruno? Is he still heavily involved in the steel industry?'

'Less so, I think. But he has many other important businesses here in Munich. Insurance, pharmaceuticals. And he is fond of hunting.'

'Wild boar?'

'Also wolves. Each winter he enjoys to hunt wolves in the old DDR. This sport is very popular in Germany. All the industrialists must enjoy this activity.'

Nick Gruen had suggested we meet at the restaurant. With Nick you always met at the restaurant. It was years since anyone had seen the inside of his various flats. Naturally, theories abounded, such as he had installed a Haitian girlfriend, or even that he'd moved in with a boy. Personally, I never put much store by them. Nick just preferred to keep a little distance.

'London still hell, I trust?' said Nick, pouring saki. We were in a Japanese restaurant somewhere off Klenze-strasse, where he said he ate most lunchtimes. 'Sorry not to offer you *bratwurst*,' he'd said on the telephone, 'but I'm only paid to assimilate Hun culture during office hours.'

He'd looked the same as he had for ten years: tall, dark and guarded. I knew Nick as well as anyone, but there were areas of his character and life I couldn't begin to fathom. Such as how he passed his time, and what if anything he enjoyed doing, and whether he saw any point to it all. Life, I mean. With Nick, the big questions were always barging their way to the fore. I suppose it was the natural consequence of having nothing more trivial to dissect.

'It's great you could make lunch at such short notice,' I said. 'I was afraid you'd be tied up inspecting one of your born-again Communist workhouses.'

'No danger of that these days,' said Nick. 'They're all belly-up. Totally predictable, of course. If you put a bunch of ex-Stasi secret police in charge of a nineteen-fifties car production line, what do you expect? They siphon off half the capital and mismanage what's left.'

'So what happens now?'

'Oh, more of the same. The Central Banks are divvying up another four billion and we're busy scouring the East for lost causes. There's a bottling plant near Potsdam it might look good to privatise. That's providing nobody actually goes to see it.'

'I'll tell you who I want to ask you about,' I said. 'Bruno Fulger. Has he entered your life at all?'

'Not directly. But you can't live in Munich without being aware of him. Why?'

'It's just that we published an interview with his wife recently and he hated it. It sounds like he's going to sue.'

'If he does you'll sure as hell know about it,' said Nick. 'He's highly litigious for obvious reasons. I'd almost call him a serial litigant.'

'Why obvious reasons?'

'Oh, classic guilty conscience. Because of the war and everything. You can't directly blame Bruno, it was his father they say was the real shit, but Bruno's certainly done nothing to atone for it.'

'Atone for what?'

'Colluding with the Nazis. It's not something people will talk about much round here, but Dietrich Fulger was almost the first of the old German aristocrats to embrace Adolf Hitler when he came to power. He was a real Nazi stool pigeon. If you ever go to the Eagle's Nest at Berchtesgaden, there's a very telling group photograph on the wall taken at Hitler's *Berghof*. The Führer, Goebbels, Hess, the whole lot of them having tea together, and in the middle of the picture Dietrich Fulger. I'm surprised Bruno hasn't had it removed, actually.'

'Creepy. And you're right about people not mentioning it. I had a meeting this morning with a German industrial-ist and he only said Dietrich Fulger had been in with Adenauer.'

'That's true too. But the Fulgers were dyed-in-the-wool Nazis during the Reich. But nobody remembers that: they're scared shitless of Bruno.'

'Why? What can he do to them?'

'What can't he do? If you haven't noticed already, Munich is just an overgrown market town. Berliners call it the *Millionendorf*: big provincial village. And Fulger abso-lutely calls the shots here. With the exception of BMW, he has a finger in just about every important business in the whole place. And he's very in with the police too: he subscribes a fortune every Christmas to some fund for police widows and orphans. If he doesn't like something, you know about it, because he's got a filthy temper and he's a bully.'

'This afternoon I'm going to take a look at his schloss. The outside. I'm aware you can't look round inside it.'

'You certainly can't,' said Nick. 'It's like a fortress. He daren't risk anyone getting past the front door in case they see the wrong paintings.'

'Which paintings?'

'Corots. Cézannes. A whole bunch of Impressionists.

197

He'd never admit to owning them, but I'm assured they're there. The trusted few occasionally get to see them. All looted from Jews during the war. Not directly of course: bought by Dietrich from the Gestapo. It comes to much the same thing.'

'And they've never been claimed back?'

'That's why the schloss is kept private: no one really knows what's there. Apparently, in the last months of the war Dietrich had all the pictures boxed up and shipped to a bank vault in Switzerland. Bruno sneaked them back in some time in the 'seventies. That's what people say anyway.' Nick tipped more saki into my cup, then added, 'Those that dare say anything.'

'Which brings me rather neatly to the other thing I wanted to ask you: is Bruno capable of violence? Not necessarily himself, but is he capable of commissioning it?'

Nick considered the question for a moment.

'Yes,' he replied. 'I'd say, unequivocally, yes.'

'Why so sure?'

'Things I've picked up. Nothing concrete. There was a story doing the rounds about an Italian businessman who might have had a thing going with Bruno's wife. He was some super-smooth super-rich textiles man from Como. They'd met somewhere and he'd invited Anastasia down on to his yacht. The only thing was, she didn't mention it to Bruno. Not before, not afterwards. When he found out, he went mad. A fortnight later the Italian was killed by a hit-and-run driver. A car drove up on to the pavement and ran him down. That was in Milan. Nobody could ever make the connection stick, but it made quite an impression round here. The message came over. Loud and clear.'

'How did Anastasia take it?'

'Badly, apparently. But of course she was in an impossible position. Having insisted to Bruno that nothing had been going on with the Italian, she couldn't crack up when he was "taken out" as they put it in American pulp movies.'

'So she carried on as before?'

'Doubtless blew a few million Deutschmarks on new clothes to get back at Bruno. But I'm not the expert on women's fashion. That's your bag.'

A half-German half-Japanese waitress brought slices of melon in blue china bowls. She had oriental eyes and black hair but broad Teutonic shoulders. Protruding from underneath her kimono you could see leather trousers.

'By the way,' asked Nick, 'who was the author of your libellous Anastasia Fulger article?'

'Anna Grant. One of our contract writers.'

'I know Anna,' said Nick. 'Not that I've seen her for ages. She used to be God's gift at screwing.'

'How do you know?' I said coldly.

'Who didn't? She went like an absolute train. Our first time was in a bathroom during a party. We had to do it diagonally, to fit our heads between the loo and the side of the bath.'

I hated this. 'How long were you together?'

'That fuck or our relationship? Both were regrettably brief. She went off with some rock star I'd never heard of, who she'd met when interviewing him. Such a scrubber.'

Anger was welling up inside me again. After last night it was pretty close to the surface anyway. I couldn't listen to this about Anna, it was unbearable. My knuckles were clenched white beneath the table.

'Look, fuck off, won't you, Nick. I know Anna and she's not like that at all.'

Nick looked at me quizzically, and then he sniggered. 'I don't believe this. Not you as well?'

I glared at him.

'That girl's incredible,' he said. 'It's a virus.'

'I said just fuck off about her, Nick. OK?'

He was still pretending to be amazed. 'She's like a chain letter. Goes round and round.'

I stood up, knocking back my chair, and tossed a fistful of Deutschmarks on to the table.

'I'm sorry, Nick, but I can't talk to you when you're like this. See you some time in London.'

And I stormed out into Klenzestrasse.

Still fuming, I picked up my hire car and headed for autobahn 95 and Starnberger. It was a journey of little more than thirty kilometres, and forty minutes later I was parking my rented Volkswagen in a car park next to the lake.

Nick's outburst about Anna was typical Gruen: unsettling, misogynistic and no doubt grossly exaggerated. I tried to put it out of my head, but wasn't completely successful. The image of Nick and Anna humping in the bathroom hung about. Anyway, I wasn't under any illusions about Anna, she'd been thirty-one for God's sake. You expect footprints in the sand. But it still niggled as I left the car park.

To the best of my knowledge, Bruno Fulger was still in St Moritz, but for some reason I felt apprehensive. It was illogical, but true. Bruno Fulger remained my principal suspect for arranging Anna's murder, and there was something slightly creepy about arriving in his ancestral *heimat*.

I walked along the shore to a place I was told had the best view of the schloss. It was a beautiful afternoon with a slight breeze coming off the water, and some of the cleanest air I'd ever breathed. I began to calm down. After the flight to Munich and then the drive, it was good to stretch my legs. On the lake, people were windsurfing and water-skiing, and half the Müncheners on the shore-path were riding bicycles. I wished I'd brought my rollerblades to put in a little practice.

The first thing you noticed were the white turrets, which soared like a thicket of space rockets above the fir trees. Then, arriving at a special vantage point provided with benches and picnic tables, I could see the whole castle across the lake: a fairytale concoction of drawbridges and towers and gothic buttresses. If you've watched the Disney version of *Snow White*, and can remember the Wicked Queen's palace at the beginning, then you've got the general idea. I bought a guidebook from a man wearing lederhosen, who served me from inside a kiosk like a scaled-up cuckoo clock, and here I read: 'The Schloss Fulgerstein, rebuilt in the 1870s on the ruins of a twelfth-century castle on the same site, was intended by its creator, Heinrich Fulger, to rival both the neighbouring schloss of Ludwig of Bavaria, Neuschwanstein, and that of Ludwig's father, Maximilian II, Hohenschwangau. Fulgerstein, which took eighteen years to complete, contains numerous wood-panelled chambers (it took twenty woodcarvers more than a decade to complete Heinrich's bedchamber) as well as part of the library of Bismarck and original scores by Richard Wagner. The collection of paintings includes works by Dürer and Grünewald. The Schloss is still in the possession of descendants of its founder, and since 1962 has been the home of Herr Bruno Fulger. The Schloss is not open to the public.'

I returned to the kiosk and bought a bottle of the only soft drink on offer, a vile-tasting cherry fruit juice.

While I was waiting for my change, I flicked through a rack of postcards on the counter. They were mostly views of the schloss, but there were some family shots too: Bruno and Anastasia posing happily on a flight of marble stairs – the photograph looked ten years old – and a more recent one of Bruno fishing from a boat on the lake with his daughter Natascha in pigtails.

'You need postcards too?' asked the shopkeeper.

'Not really. I'm just looking. Is this Bruno Fulger?'

The shopkeeper beamed. '*Ja*, that's Fulger.'

'And this is Anastasia Fulger?'

Now he darkened. '*Ja*, that's Frau Fulger.'

'She's very beautiful.'

'Beautiful maybe,' he spat back, 'but *sauerbraten*.'

'What's that?'

He looked at me suspiciously. 'What are you, a yellow press journalist?'

'No. A tourist. I'm walking around Bavaria.'

He seemed reassured by this. 'Frau Fulger has said bad things against her husband. I have read them myself. They were printed in a magazine in England, and these words were repeated in every German newspaper.'

'Was Bruno Fulger angry with his wife?'

'Of course. He made her leave the schloss. No second chances.' The shopkeeper in his lederhosen smiled his approval. 'With the Fulgers there is only ever one chance. She should know that already.'

I drained my cherry *saft* with a shudder and walked back to the car. Then, before heading back into Munich, I decided to drive round the lake past the main gates of Fulgerstein. I found them easily enough, flanked by a pair of thatched lodges, each one like Hansel and Gretel's cottage in the forest. I slowed down to take a look and immediately an armed security guard carrying a walkie-talkie emerged from inside one of the lodges, and gesticulated at me to move on.

I was about to do so when the guard was diverted by an impatient hooting from behind him inside the drive. A long black Mercedes was waiting for the gates to be opened.

He hurried off, and I heard a chauffeur curse him for keeping them waiting.

A moment later the Mercedes swept past in the direction of the autobahn. In the front seat I could see the chauffeur wearing a cap with the scarlet Fulger plume. And in the back, unfolding a copy of the *International Herald Tribune*, I recognised Bruno Fulger.

The road followed the estate wall uphill for three kilometres before branching off at a second set of gates. These were more modest than the first and led into a farmyard. I could see a half-timbered Bavarian barn and a granary. Beyond the farmyard was a road heading towards the middle of the estate.

On impulse, I turned through the open gates and drove straight on through the farmyard. Nobody was about. A minute later I was sufficiently far up the back drive to be shielded from view by a copse of pines.

I continued driving to the crest of a hill and stopped to take my bearings. On one side of the road were fields of corn, glowing golden in the sunshine. On the other, parkland. About three quarters of a mile to my left, at the bottom of a gently sloping valley, lay Fulgerstein.

Don't even ask what I thought I was doing. Maybe from the moment I left Munich, maybe from the moment I thought of hiring a car, I'd envisaged this. Sometimes these things are unconscious. And the sight of Bruno in the back of his car had made me furious for Anna. Seeing him there, untouchable, so confident he'd got away with it, made me realise he had every right to feel that way: if he'd arranged for Anna to be bumped off, then he *had* got away with it. It was all very well me strolling around his lake and gossiping with shopkeepers in lederhosen, but the fact was I was getting nowhere. The British police, let alone the German, barely rated Fulger as a suspect. As far as I knew they had only one serious candidate as Anna's murderer: and that candidate was me.

It was a quarter to four and I didn't need to set off back to the airport for a couple of hours. I decided to spend it nosing about the Fulger estate. As a strategy for solving a murder it wasn't faultless, but it beat hanging around the departure lounge.

I backed the car off the road, clear of the skyline, and set off on foot in the direction of the schloss. I walked for forty minutes. By keeping to the high ground on the rim of the valley, it was possible to get quite close without ever coming into view of the castle. About fifty yards above me on the hill was a monument to Kaiser Wilhelm II, and down below I could see a stone horseshoe staircase leading from the back of the schloss into terraced formal gardens with an Italianate grotto.

It occurred to me that if I edged my way another two hundred yards round the side of the valley, I could enter the gardens through the grotto.

I was within twenty yards of the boundary wall when I saw the cameras. The red light caught my eye as the heat-sensitive surveillance equipment locked on. The box was attached to the trunk of a tree. The lens swivelled in my direction and transmitted its silent alarm.

My first reaction was to turn and run. But then I thought there was a reasonable chance that no one would be monitoring the screens. It happens. The day a sneak-thief got in at Weiss Magazines and stole a bunch of handbags, the commissionnaires never noticed a damn thing. So I turned slowly on my heels, and began to make my way up the valley. If they'd seen me, and I didn't panic, they might think I had some legitimate reason for being there: a guest or a forestry expert.

I had covered another twenty yards when the sirens went off. A succession of loud, flat blasts like a tug boat: they must have been audible a mile away.

Then I spotted the security guards.

There were two of them, racing around the side of the schloss from the direction of the kitchens.

They were shouting at me to stop and looked like they meant business. I began to run.

The gradient of the hill was steeper than it had seemed on the downward journey, and my shoes were a liability. The last time I ran in loafers on grass was the fathers' race at Cazzie's sports day. I hoped my performance would be better this time. The sun was glaring directly into my eyes as I pounded up the slope, and I was soon sweating profusely.

The car was still a quarter of a mile ahead and the men, I estimated, were three hundred yards behind me. As I ran I fished in my pocket for the car key. If I could make it to the car, I'd be away.

I glanced back over my shoulder and saw they were closer than I'd realised. They were dressed in jeans and trainers and black leather bomber jackets, buttoned up to the neck, and neither could have been much older than twenty-five. They looked fit. And they were gaining on me.

I could see them both quite clearly now. One was a classic Aryan stormtrooper type, with short blond hair; the other wore a moustache and was dark and swarthy and looked Middle Eastern. His face was oddly familiar. Then I remembered: he was the second man in the car park who'd been watching my flat.

I could see the Volkswagen now. The white metal of the bonnet was glinting in the sun. Another hundred and fifty yards and I'd be there. The men were still gaining on me, but I thought I could make it providing the engine started first time. The muscles in my stomach and around my heart felt ready to spasm. At least the car was pointing in the right direction for a quick getaway.

Distantly in my right ear I could hear a motor and then a new voice ordering me to stop. Fifty yards away a red jeep was bouncing towards me across the park. Three men were inside, one driving, another brandishing a revolver. In the back sat an older man in a tweed suit, with an Alsatian dog.

The jeep cut across my path, blocking my route to the car. It pulled to a halt and the guard with the revolver sprang out and pushed me roughly to the ground. Then he kicked me hard in the ribs with the top of his boot.

I lay there, winded, with my face pressed into the grass, while my pockets and armpits were frisked for firearms.

Satisfied I was unarmed, an older man said, 'You may get up now, Mr Preston.'

I raised my head a few inches and found myself eyeballing a pair of brown suede shoes. Their owner was looking down on me, smiling.

It was Rudolph Gombricht.

'One thing I will say for you, Mr Preston,' he said, 'is that you know how to keep the legal profession busy. At lunchtime I took instructions from my client on suing your magazine for libel. No doubt I shall now have to sue you for trespass as well.'

'I don't know what you mean,' I said. 'I was simply taking a walk in the German countryside when I was attacked without provocation by these men. Is there a law against walking in Bavaria? I thought walking was your national pastime.'

'Please, Mr Preston,' said Gombricht, 'spare us your pathetic excuses. They may impress the local magistrate when you see him in three or four days' time, but don't insult me with them. We're all perfectly aware what you're doing here.'

'Which is what?'

'Spying on Bruno Fulger and his family. No doubt you're sufficiently gratified by the outcome of your first unwarranted attack on Mrs Fulger that you intend to follow it up with a second instalment.'

Rudolph Gombricht's face turned suddenly vicious. 'Don't try and deny it, Mr Preston. We know more than you think. Herr Weser who has the gift shop across the lake has already reported your gutter-grubbing about Mrs Fulger. Does that surprise you? The local people round here have an old-fashioned belief in other people's privacy.'

'Does that extend,' I asked, 'to spying on other people's property?' I pointed at the dark-skinned guard who was now sitting on the jump-seat of the jeep. 'That man spent last weekend parked outside my flat in London.'

'And why, please enlighten us, would he have wished to do that?'

'Because of Anna Grant, who you arranged to have murdered.' I was suddenly furious and my back was throbbing from the kick. 'This man followed her on your orders – or Bruno Fulger's orders – and later broke into her flat and strangled her.'

'That, Mr Preston,' said Rudolph Gombricht steadily, 'is the most serious example of slander I've heard in my long career. You will please retract it.'

'I will not retract it. Because it happens to be true.'

'You will retract it, Mr Preston.'

The four security men had dismounted the jeep. One of them was restraining the Alsatian on a short chain.

'I will not retract it. In fact, as soon as I get the chance, I will report everything I know to the police.'

'Mr Preston,' said Gombricht. 'When we were first introduced in London I took you to be a capable, if somewhat arrogant, young man. Clearly, I was misled in the first part by the apparent responsibilities of your job. Now I can see you are both foolish and hysterical.'

He said something to Security and two of the men advanced on me and held me in an arm lock. Then they lifted me into the jeep, squashing me between them on the bench. Gombricht and the Alsatian climbed up behind, and sat across on the jump-seats. The driver started the engine and we set off in the direction of Fulgerstein.

'Why are you taking me?' I said.

'Why? I would have thought that was obvious: to cool off. This is for your own good, Mr Preston. At the moment the only person who has witnessed your slanders is me.' He glanced at the guards. 'They don't count. For them, words mean nothing.

'But were you to repeat those slanders to the police,' he said, 'that would be a different matter. That could cause trouble for Mr Fulger. It would be an inconvenience for him. And one of my responsibilities in this household is to contain as far as humanly possible all inconveniences.'

'You're saying your job is to cover up murders?'

'That remark you will regret, Mr Preston,' he replied.

The jeep arrived at the side of the schloss and I was led inside through an entrance at basement level. We walked along a series of stone passageways with a guard on each side of me, and Gombricht and the dog following. Through open doors I could see coldrooms hung with meat and a stillroom with kegs of beer. Then we headed upstairs into a grander part of the castle. There was a dark panelled hall full of religious paintings including, I thought, a Dürer, and another wall covered with tapestries. We passed the marble staircase as seen on the postcard and an enormous spray of scarlet flowers in an urn. Eventually, I was taken into a small, simply furnished room without a window.

'This is the head housekeeper's pantry,' said Gombricht. 'I strongly advise you to sit down and regain your composure. I have asked them to bring you up a cup of tea. You have plenty of time. Mr Fulger returns from St Moritz tomorrow evening, and you will see him then. Frankly, Mr Preston, this whole matter has got out of hand and Mr Fulger will need to decide himself what action to take.'

'Why don't you just call the police as I asked you, and let them decide?'

Rudolph Gombricht leant against a slate counter and regarded me for a moment.

'Allow me to tell you a little story, Mr Preston,' he said. 'And unless you are an even more foolish young man than I take you to be, you'll pay good attention and learn from it. You are not the first journalist to take on Bruno Fulger. You may imagine yourself to be, but you are not. Believe me, when you are as successful and powerful as Mr Fulger, there will always be white knights – because that's how they see themselves, however ludicrously, as white knights – who wish to take a tilt at you. It is the method, is it not, for journalists to make a name for themselves? You take a tilt at a powerful man and a little of his aura rubs off on your lance.'

'If you are referring to our interview with Anastasia Fulger, all this is preposterous. Mrs Fulger gave an interview to one of our journalists, Anna Grant. It was entirely voluntary. There's no conspiracy.'

'You may care to present it that way,' said Gombricht. 'But let me finish my story. The last journalist to try and make his name at the expense of Mr Fulger was a man called Heine. Karl Heine. The name may mean something to you. For several years he was considered a rising journalist with the weekly news magazines here in Germany. His speciality was pricking the reputations of men more successful than himself. There were a number of examples. Then one day he had the idea of attacking Mr Fulger. That was what he decided and he proposed this to his editor, and the editor said yes, go ahead. So for four months he did nothing except ask questions. Every employee of Mr Fulger, past and present, he tried to interview. And he attempted to obtain papers – confidential papers – from Mr Fulger's private businesses too. He would even pay money for them. All this in an effort to make mud stick on Bruno Fulger.

'During this time I made many overtures to dissuade him from this course. But Karl Heine wouldn't listen. He was too arrogant, you see, too keen to build up his own name. He even began questioning people about certain activities of Mr Fulger's father during the Nazi period, all baseless. One week before Herr Heine was due to complete his article, I wrote to him at the magazine a final time. I offered to read it in advance of publication – for no fee – and identify any inaccuracies that might have crept into the research. My intention was not, I emphasise, to censor this man's work: only to correct falsehoods. But he did not even give me the courtesy of a reply.

'On the morning of publication I was fortunate in obtaining an early copy of the magazine. I say fortunate because it was full of inaccuracies from start to finish. I believe that eventually we identified twenty-three separate libels or gross errors of fact. Within one hour we had injuncted the publication and had all copies removed from the kiosks. So at least the damage on that occasion was contained. Eventually the copies were all burned.

'But, you see,' said Gombricht, 'there remained one problem. Some copies had been read, and some even still existed. In the hour before the injunction was granted we estimate fifteen thousand copies passed into circulation. So all those readers have had their minds poisoned against Mr Fulger. Who can quantify the possible ramifications? Years later, they will still remember those libels. So we were left with no option but to sue Karl Heine. Not the magazine, you notice, but Herr Heine personally. And we pointed out to the owners of the publication that we had warned Heine of the high likelihood of libel, and of our offer to read the article for accuracy, which he had rejected. And I am sorry to say the publisher took the view that, by not alerting them to these risks, Herr Heine had forfeited his right to have his costs indemnified. So when we took him to court, it was Heine himself who had to pay out of his own pocket. It was a chastening experience for him.' Gombricht laughed. 'Very chastening. Our costs alone came to three hundred thousand Deutschmarks. And the damages awarded by the judges totalled four hundred thousand Deutschmarks. When Heine heard it, he collapsed in the courthouse. Of course he had no chance to pay that money. Even after he sold his house, he couldn't pay. It was a bad time for him, I think. Nobody wanted to employ him any longer, not after an award so large. No publisher would permit him to work for their organisation. Even the pretty girlfriend who had come each day into the courthouse deserted him. So now we don't read many articles by Karl Heine any more.'

Gombricht and Security left the room and I heard the key turn in the lock. After their footsteps died away in the passage, I tried the door. It was immovable.

I sat on a bentwood chair and considered the bleakness of my position. In ninety minutes' time my flight left Munich airport and my chances of being aboard seemed less than zero. Even assuming I could somehow get out, the hire car was parked up on the back drive an hour's walk away. And, worst of all, Bruno Fulger was scheduled to see me tomorrow evening. I didn't have the slightest doubt now that he lay behind Anna's murder. The fact of his security guard watching my flat had confirmed that, not to mention Nick Gruen's assessment of his character – and Gombricht's, come to that. When Fulger realised how much I knew, he might feel he had only one option: to dispose of me too. It wouldn't be difficult. Any one of his goons would do it for him without a moment's regret and

I didn't suppose they'd have much trouble getting shot of a body. It would be easy enough to hide my car. They would probably arrange to have it smashed up on the autobahn, with me inside. I didn't put anything past Fulger and Gombricht.

Who knew I was here anyway? Suzy. Or rather she knew I'd considered driving down to the schloss, but nothing more. Nick Gruen and Heiner Stüben. I'd mentioned Fulgerstein to them both. That was a bonus. And yet neither knew I'd arrived. The only person who'd positively seen me in the area was the cherry *saft* salesman, and he was a Fulger nark.

Where I felt so stupid was in coming here at all. What the hell had I thought I was up to? Now, if I disappeared, they'd never catch Anna's killer. Either they'd find my body as the centrepiece of a Bavarian car accident, in which case the whole inquiry would eventually peter out, or else I'd be made to disappear altogether and Superintendent Barratt would conclude I'd made a dash for it.

And Bruno Fulger would have triumphed yet again. Before I knew it, my own life story would be featuring in one of Rudolph Gombricht's homilies about what happens to interfering idiots who mess with his boss. And he'd have a point too: I was an idiot.

Outside in the corridor I heard the tread of approaching footsteps and the rattle of china. Someone was coming with the tea.

If I had any chance at all of escaping from the schloss alive, surely this was it.

The door was unlocked and the blond-haired guard – the stormtrooper – edged into the room with a tray of tea in a bone china cup. Presumably, they owned nothing more suitable for a prisoner at Fulgerstein.

I remained seated until he was standing directly above me, then kneed the tray hard up into his face. The hot tea shot out of the cup into his eyes, and he let the tray drop. It was silver and heavy and engraved with the Fulger coat-of-arms.

I lifted it above my head and cracked it down on the top of his skull. He keeled over and fell motionless on to the pantry floor.

Turning the key in the lock behind me, I crept out into the corridor. The place was deserted. I edged past a salon with a grand piano inside, and another room – a library – full of Impressionist paintings. Ahead of me I could see the entrance hall and the front door beyond.

There was still no one about so I tried the door. It opened. Outside lay a courtyard with several cars parked, and some way to the right an archway leading to a stable yard.

I slunk across the courtyard to the arch, at each moment expecting to be challenged. There must have been a hundred windows overlooking the front of the schloss.

One side of the stable yard comprised a series of open garages, housing Bruno's collection of coaches and landaus. On the other side I could see a display of armour including mounted waxworks of knights brandishing halberds.

And then I spotted the motorbike.

It was a Kawasaki ZZR 1100. Black and monstrously powerful. We'd once organised a readers' day for Kawasaki with *Man Alive*, and I'd given one a spin round the park at Stowe. One serious machine.

And then came my first decent break of the afternoon: the key was in the ignition.

I climbed on board and switched it on. The engine roared beneath me. I kicked the bike off its stand and accelerated across the cobbles. As I approached the gate, a bald-headed man in a mattress-ticking jacket – probably a cook – shouted at me to stop, and took a swipe at me with his fist.

I roared past him, across the drawbridge and out on to the drive.

It was a quarter of a mile to the gates and they were open. A delivery man had his head stuck through the driver's window of his van, in conversation with the gateman. I saw the guard turn at the sound of the engine, but it was too late, I hit two hundred kph and swung out into the road.

I considered swapping into the hire car, but fuck that. Suzy could square it with Avis tomorrow.

In ten minutes I was racing, helmetless, up the autobahn in the direction of Munich airport.

I made it in fifty minutes, moments before they closed the flight. Even as I boarded, I was half-expecting to be hauled back off.

The plane cruised to the top of the runway, turned and then I heard the engines roar as we readied for take-off.

Only when we'd cleared German airspace did I feel able to accept a drink.

# 14

I dragged myself into the office in the morning to find Suzy already there.

'You want the good news or the bad news?' I asked, dumping my briefcase on to her desk.

'Strangely enough,' she said, 'that's exactly the choice I was about to offer *you*: good or bad news.'

Suzy looked terrific today in a fringed cowboy jacket I hadn't seen before, but she seemed anxious. I had a premonition her bad news was going to overshadow the good.

'I'll shoot first, then,' I said. 'The good news is: I'm still alive.' I gave her a bullet-point account of my afternoon at Schloss Fulgerstein.

She listened, increasingly horrified. 'And the bad news? I hardly dare ask.'

'The bad news is: you remember that Volkswagen you booked for me in Munich, the one I had to return to Avis at the airport? Well, it's parked in some bushes about half a mile up Bruno Fulger's back drive. Oh, and these are the car keys.

'Also,' I said, 'I've got a set of motorcycle keys here which need couriering round to Rudolph Gombricht's office in Broadgate. With a note telling him they'll find the bike outside the Lufthansa terminal.'

'Anything else to declare while I'm about it?' said Suzy. 'Any boat keys in your pockets? Lear jet's?' She laughed hollowly. 'On the subject of Rudolph Gombricht, this came during the night. I just found it on the fax.'

It was the bad news. Two typed sheets of it, double-spaced. I don't pretend to be a lawyer but I've seen some heavy solicitors' letters in my time, and this was the worst. The words that leapt first off the page were 'flagrant and wilful misrepresentation', 'defamation', 'prominent retraction' and 'substantial damages'. It was one of those legal missives that are so generally scary you can barely steel yourself to read them in one go, and that need to be broached clause by clause between shots of pure alcohol.

'My God,' I said when I'd finished reading. 'This is World War Three. I feel I've been napalmed.'

'But surely there's nothing they can get us on?' said Suzy. 'It was a straight interview.'

'Gombricht's claiming Anna quoted Anastasia Fulger selectively. "To the extent of material misrepresentation" is what it says here.'

'Didn't Anna Grant always tape her interviews? I'm sure she did.'

'Blast,' I exclaimed. 'Blast and shit. Anna's tape. I bet you anything you like it was inside her bag when it was stolen from my flat. That's what Fulger's men were doing there; that one I saw yesterday at the schloss. Waiting for a chance to steal the tape. And they've probably got it too.'

'But what good can it do them?' said Suzy. 'Anna wouldn't have misquoted her. Bruno Fulger couldn't get the tape doctored, could he?'

'Quite probably, but don't you see? Without the tape it's our word against theirs: worse than that actually, because Anastasia can make a tearful appearance in court and Anna's dead. I'm fairly certain Anna told me the interview was one-on-one, just her and Anastasia in the room. But the Fulgers can pretend the housekeeper was listening in too now, and have her say Anna made it all up. With no Anna and no tape, we're on thin ice.'

'Why are you so certain the tape was in Anna's bag, anyway?' asked Suzy.

'Good point.' For the briefest of moments I saw a reprieve. Then I groaned. 'In fact, it probably *wasn't* there, which is why they were searching Anna's flat that night. They must have played back the cassettes from the bag by then and discovered they were the wrong ones. Which meant breaking into Harrington Gardens. That's what they were doing with the dustbin liner. Clearing the place of all the old tapes.'

For the second time in as many minutes I felt deflated. Bugger Gombricht. No wonder he'd waited ten days before issuing the writ. Coming after all his threats, I'd thought it out of character for a Swiss-German to stall on the paperwork. But now I understood it. Gombricht was strengthening his hand. First remove our only witness, then the taped evidence. It was galling to have to admit it, but he was outmanoeuvring me.

I reread the whole letter, spotting two vicious refinements I'd missed first time through.

Rather than serving it on Weiss Magazines, Gombricht had turned the writ into a Cecil B. de Mille spectacular. Anna Grant was named personally (not that that would do them much good now). So was I. Barney Weiss was enjoined as proprietor. Kay Lipschwitz Anderson as publisher. Printer, distributors and retailers: we were all on there. Everyone, in fact, except Micky Rice who had mysteriously been excluded. This struck me as sinister and probably indicated they intended summoning him as a witness for their side.

Was it feasible Micky might appear in a witness box testifying against me and his own magazine? I didn't see how he could and keep his job. Maybe the Fulgers simply planned to buy him out. I wondered what it would cost them, to indemnify Micky's editorship.

My first reaction to the serial writs was exasperation. If you want to provoke maximum disruption and timewasting, this is the way to do it, as Rudolph Gombricht knew perfectly well. Presumably, all writs had been faxed simultaneously, which meant they'd be landing on desks and causing consternation everywhere right now. I'd ring the managing directors of the retail newsagents first, I thought, then the distributors and printer. They'd all need briefing and they'd all expect us to cover their legal costs. By serving so many separate writs, Gombricht had ensured these would be astronomical. What was it Anastasia Fulger had said to Anna about lawyers in the famous interview? 'It's a game for Bruno. He has all the money, he couldn't spend what he has.'

Then I thought of Barney Weiss. The time-received data on the top of my fax showed it had arrived at Park Place at eleven p.m. last night, sent from Gombricht's London office. I guess he'd drafted the thing at the schloss and dictated it over the telephone. His secretaries must have stayed late to send them all through. But with the time change to Chicago, Barney's copy could have arrived before he left his office yesterday. I didn't imagine he'd been over-amused to get it. Barney hated libel actions on the magazines. Probably he'd seen more than enough of lawyers and attorneys over his various divorces. 'What beats me,' he once said, 'is why you guys feel you need to attract litigation anyway. They're lifestyle books, not Woodward and Bernstein stuff.'

It was still too early to ring Barney, but I'd put in a call as soon as America woke up.

The other refinement was chiefly interesting because it showed Gombricht opening up a second front. He was proposing to sue us for invasion of privacy over the cover photograph. He'd come up with a lot of stuff about the picture having been taken on private property, which even I knew would never stand up in court. I wondered why he'd bothered.

Then it hit me.

Gombricht was employing the bogus privacy argument as a pretext for summoning Simon Beriot, the photographer, as a witness. Then he meant to shift the focus of the case on to whether or not we'd published a stolen picture. Which of course we had. The jury might feel this discredited our whole defence. How would you feel, ladies and gentlemen of the jury, if you saw a photograph of yourself falling out of a swimsuit on the front cover of a popular magazine? And you hadn't even been asked your permission? And you knew it was stolen property?

Do I hear half a million pounds plus costs?

'Suzy,' I called, 'I want you to try and get a photographer called Simon Beriot on the line. He works for *Man Alive*, but there won't be anyone on their picture desk yet: it's too early. He may be listed in the phone book.'

I could have kicked myself now for not following up on Beriot after Anna's funeral. He'd mentioned Gombricht was on his case. I should have discovered what it was all about. One consideration that held me back, I expect, was the knowledge he'd been out with Anna. If indeed he really had. There was only Micky's word for it.

A minute later Suzy buzzed through. 'There's an S. Beriot in the Harrow Road. Shall I try it for you?'

'If it's him, find out whether he can drop by my office any time today. Tell him it's important. Or else I could meet him at his studio, if he's got one.'

Before long, Suzy reappeared in my office. 'He was asleep. And less than pleased about being woken. Quite a sexy telephone voice though.'

'Don't get too excited. He's forty-something.'

'So are you, aren't you?' said Suzy. 'Good as.'

I glared at her. 'What time's Beriot coming in here anyway?'

'Tomorrow morning. He said he's photographing diving watches for *Man Alive* all day, and can't be interrupted. But there's a *Man Alive* editorial meeting he's attending at eleven tomorrow. I said you'd drop by and see him at that.'

'By the way,' I said. 'What about this good news you mentioned? If there really is some, now's the moment to share it.'

'Well, the Magazine Society rang yesterday afternoon, to confirm you were still going tonight and to check which table you'd be sitting at.'

'Going to what?'

'The awards.'

'Jesus, those aren't tonight, are they?' I rolled my eyes. The annual Magazine Society awards ceremony at the Grosvenor House hotel ranks amongst my least favourite fixtures of the year. It's gruelling enough at the best of times, and I was knackered. 'That's *good* news?'

'You don't get it, do you? If they've asked which table you're at, it probably means you've won something. They need to know to put a spotlight on you when you go up to collect the prize.'

'Pull the other one,' I said. 'I'm not even eligible for a prize. Prizes are for editors.'

'Then why ask where you're sitting?'

'Probably to hand me the bar bill.' The prospect of a long, late night in black tie left me cold. 'Anyway, remind me who's going from here?'

'All the editors and publishers for a start. Their deputies. Various contributors. Norman Turner, of course.'

'Why of course?'

'He's shortlisted for some circulation category. Also Megan Whiley's going, representing the production department, and Ellen Durlacher for corporate PR. And don't forget,' Suzy added, 'you included me too.'

Just then the telephone rang on my desk. It was eight forty-five: from here on the day would start in earnest.

'Kit? If you've got two minutes, I'd like a quick word on the phone.' It was Robin Reese, the publisher of *Man Alive*.

'Sure. What's up?'

'Well, you know the Mouchette deal you struck in Paris last week? It's rather strange. We've been trying to get signed orders and copy from the agency and they're not coming through. You haven't heard anything, have you?'

'Nothing at all. As far as I'm concerned it's a done deal, though they've never officially confirmed. Tell you what, if this doesn't sort itself out by lunchtime, I'll put in a call to Jean-Marc LeNoy.'

No sooner had I replaced the receiver than Kay Lipschwitz Anderson came on the line.

'You know, Kit,' she said, 'this is the darndest thing but we can't get copy out of Mouchette. The issue's printing Friday and there's nothing. They've optioned sites for Mesdames de la Nuit and the skin renovator and I don't know what's happening.'

At that moment Kevin Sky appeared at my door.

'Let me guess,' I said. 'A problem with Mouchette.'

'Potentially a very damaging one too,' said Kevin. 'I've just dropped by the women-in-sportswear breakfast at Selfridge's and bumped into that girl from DDHD who does Mouchette's planning.'

Dern DeLuca Hideki Dern was Mouchette's London advertising agency. Policy on the account was handled out of France, but DDHD did the donkeywork and cracked the whip on positioning.

'What Jackie said – that's her name by the way – is they've had a complete stop put on advertising in Weiss Magazines. Directive came from Paris yesterday lunchtime. Jackie said they couldn't understand it because on Thursday they were told we'd won favoured-publisher status and should be given everything. Now that's all changed.'

'Christ, what the hell's happened?' I reached for the telephone.

'Before you do anything,' said Kevin, 'there's worse to come. According to Jackie, they're switching the whole account into Incorporated.'

'It's not possible.'

'That's what she says.'

'But why the fuck ...?'

'Apparently, Pierre Roux, who I always said was the loose cannon in this, saw Howard Trench at that Annalina Lau shop opening. He's always favoured Incorporated's stable anyway. His wife likes the chicken recipes or something. Anyway Trench gave him a hard time and Roux admitted the deal wasn't signed yet, and he could still be in with a chance. So Trench flew out to Paris on Sunday night for a breakfast meeting yesterday morning.

Jackie says he made them a counter offer they couldn't refuse.'

'What offer?'

'Mind blowing. Free pages. Free scent strips. Dozens of them. An impregnated scratch-and-sniff front cover on every single magazine, which Incorporated are paying for themselves.'

'*Every* magazine? What'll they do on *Genteel Living*: scratch-and-sniff cooker and hob?'

But I didn't feel like laughing. It was a catastrophe.

'There's only one thing for it,' I said. 'Fabrice Mouchette. The big boss. We need to start cashing in our favours now if it's not already too late. I'll go and see him in Paris this afternoon.'

It would mean missing the awards evening. But if ever there was a right time for a selfless sacrifice, this was it.

I asked Suzy to get me Fabrice Mouchette on the line without delay.

What I was going to say to him, I wasn't sure. The fact was, we'd only ever spoken two or three times and I couldn't count on him remembering me. He had once given me a lift in his car, a wonderful 1930 Hispano Suiza coupé, to a race day Mouchette were sponsoring at Chantilly. That was two years ago. Fabrice had insisted on taking the wheel himself while his chauffeur sat in the back. He had struck me as an elegant old goat, much smarter in every way than the people who worked for him. In fact, he'd made me laugh by describing his new separate personal headquarters: 'Just for me and my *secrétaire* and my chauffeur. It is situated in the far – no, the farth*est* – *arrondissement* from Mouchette's main offices. Otherwise I would be driven half-mad by those people, expecting me to do all their jobs for them.'

'Bad news,' said Suzy. 'Monsieur Mouchette's away in New York until the end of the week. His secretary says she'll be speaking to him in a couple of hours though, so she'll tell him you called.'

'Blast.' As days go, this one was panning out rather

badly. 'Then perhaps I'd better crack on with ringing all these newsagents about the libel writ.'

I spent a couple of hours reassuring the distributors and then a further hour on the telephone to our lawyer. That conversation, at least, was more encouraging. We have a new lawyer, Joanne Pratchett, who also does a lot of work for the trades union movement: safety in the workplace, unfair dismissal and so forth. Bit of a culture shock for her representing our particular magazines, but she seems to enjoy it. I think she's one of those utopian socialists who believes every worker should one day own a Tiffany keyring.

By the time Joanne and I spoke, Suzy had already faxed through the writ and Anna's original article so she was fully up to speed.

'You know, Kit,' she said, 'I've read this thing and it really is a heap of shit. You know why? The entire premise. When I tell you there are people in this country with genuine grievances – single mothers harassed from their homes by unscrupulous landlords, race discrimination cases that would make your hair stand on end – and they can't get court time. And now these horrible-sounding Fulgers want to hijack our whole legal system for some facile little quarrel about who said what in a social magazine.'

That's what I enjoy about Joanne Pratchett: she has this great sense of natural justice, and she never pussy-foots.

'So you think we'd win, then?'

'Not necessarily. I said the writ was a heap of shit, which isn't the same thing at all. Get real: this is the British justice system we're talking about here.'

'So what's the next step?'

'I write them a stalling letter, acknowledging receipt of the writ. Then we meet and decide what you want to do. Either fight it, or else you might want to propose a compromise.'

'What sort of compromise?'

'For instance,' said Joanne. 'You're not going to like this, Kit, I know, but it's one possibility: a token apology in the magazine in exchange for Fulger dropping the damages.'

'Out of the question. Not now Anna's dead. It would be like selling out her reputation the minute she's not here to defend herself.'

Joanne chuckled down the line. 'OK, I get it.' Then she said, 'Let's get one thing straight, Kit, my role's simply to give you all the options, not tell you what to do. And if you want to fight them all the way to the High Court, I'm right behind you. But before you get entrenched, you will think seriously about the cost implications, won't you? I mean it. This would be a big commitment.'

'Like how much?'

'Costs could reach four or five hundred thousand pounds easily. I'm assuming Bruno Fulger would hire a raft of QCs. And even if you win, which I hope and expect you would, there's no guarantee you'd be awarded your own costs.'

For the third time that morning I felt nauseous. To pledge that kind of money to litigation, I'd have to clear it first with Barney Weiss. And there wasn't a hope in hell he'd sanction it.

The only alternative was a public grovel to the Fulgers, which I was damned if I was going to do.

I was fixing a strategy meeting with Joanne for later in the week when Suzy began signalling at me through the door. 'I've got Barney Weiss holding on line two,' she said. 'He says he's ringing from a private jet.'

I apologised to Joanne for cutting her short and cleared the decks for the great proprietor.

'Barney?' There was a noise like a turbo jet engine in the background and rushing wind. Where on earth was he sitting: outside on the wing?

'Kit? Is that you?' Then he hollered, 'Lola, switch that damn machine off, won't you, I can't hear a thing back here. Excuse me for that, Kit,' said Barney at normal volume, 'Lola's blow-drying her hair in the cabin.'

'Where are you anyway? I gather you're in an aeroplane.'

'And not just any plane either: *my* plane. My new Gulfstream. Go on, guess where we are now. Three chances.'

'Er, Florida?'

'Nowhere near. Further north-west.'

'Alaska?'

'Alaska? Hey, don't bullshit, you're throwing guesses there.' He sounded quite annoyed. 'Final clue now: think Caesar's Palace.'

'Nevada?'

'Right third time. We're thirty thousand feet above the Nevadan desert. No, hang on, my pilot's telling me I'm mistaken here. What's that? We've crossed the state line already. You heard that, Kit? Sorry, you were wrong, sucker. We're overflying Utah.'

'I'm glad you've rung me,' I said, 'I was about to call you anyway. Have you received the writ?'

'No idea what you're talking about,' said Barney. 'If you faxed me something yesterday, I won't have seen it. I've been trying to buy a valet-parking business in Vegas.'

'Sounds interesting,' I said, I hope not too insincerely.

'You bet. Nineteen-million-dollar revenues and no capital investment. Margins of sixty per cent. You should do a story about it: Who valet-parks which filmstars.'

Then Barney said, 'Reason I'm calling you, Kit, is that I want you to come over and meet with me in New York. There's something I need to talk over with you.'

'Sure. When were you thinking of?'

'How about tomorrow? If you come in on the evening flight, we can have lunch together Thursday. You're familiar I'm sure with Smith & Wollensky's, the steak restaurant in midtown? I'll have them reserve us a table for twelve-thirty. Captain's name is Paolo if you have any problems.'

I called Suzy in and told her the latest change of plan.

'New York. Try and get me on to an early afternoon flight. The slower the better, so I can crash out on board.'

'On the subject of New York,' said Suzy, 'while you were talking to Mr Weiss, Fabrice Mouchette's secretary rang back. He's decided to extend his trip and stay in America over the weekend. But he sends you his best wishes, and says he hopes you haven't forgotten your drive in his Hispano Suiza.'

'You know what,' I said, 'if I'm going to be in Manhattan, I should see him there instead. Suzy, could you ring his office again and explain everything's changed. Say I'd like to invite him for a drink at the Pierre while I'm in town.'

Half an hour later, Suzy reappeared looking pleased with herself.

'Guess what?' she said. 'Fabrice Mouchette's asked you to a dinner party at his apartment on Park Avenue. You won't be too tired will you? It's tomorrow night.'

'Tired? Me? Heavens no. This is *brilliant* timing, couldn't be better.' I was so happy, I felt like cheering.

'You realise something, Suzy,' I said. 'This could be just the break we need. Howard Trench may think he's so damn smart having breakfast with Pierre Roux, but he sure as hell won't be having dinner with Fabrice Mouchette.'

Suddenly I felt elated. I had this very strong feeling I was about to snatch back the Mouchette advertising from out of the jaws of disaster.


There were twelve hundred people pressing up against the mezzanine bar of the Grosvenor House hotel, and the four Italian bar stewards were doing their unsuccessful best to serve them all. Looking around the room at my fellow magazine workers – the men in dinner jackets and the women with their eye-boggling necklines and tottering stilettos – I found I recognised about a quarter of them. All our competitors were out tonight in force, plus large and excitable delegations from publications I hardly knew existed. Reading down the list on the table plan, I noticed cat and dog lovers' magazines, acid house and hip-hop, amateur shrub plantsmen, magazines for croupiers, hunt saboteurs and hotel caterers, on-line information and reinsurance publications; the grisly-sounding roster went on and on.

I craned my neck for any sign of our party, and spotted Spike Steel from *Man Alive* across the bar clustered with Leonora Lowell and Tasmin Feeley from *Couture*. None of them looked as if they were enjoying themselves much, which they probably weren't. Our editors hate awards. When Billy Heathcote owned the company he didn't make them compete, claiming it was sullying for his titles to be judged against rubbish, though I think the cost of entering may have been a factor for him too. These days we're less snobbish about it, not that it does us much good. Last year *Couture* was beaten into second place by a magazine called *Better Breads & Pastries*. Leonora burst into tears and had to be sent home in a cab.

From the balcony I could see the whole of the Great Room extending beneath me, with a hundred and twenty tables laid ready for dinner. A phalanx of young Calabrian waiters was gathered outside the kitchens listening to a final briefing from the banqueting manager, while sommeliers plunged hundreds of bottles of white wine into steel pails filled with melting ice. Across the room, close to the stage, I could see Suzy circling our tables with placecards. I hoped she wouldn't put me too near to Micky Rice. Knowing Suzy, she'd have thought of that already.

'Hi, Kit.' I spun round to find Micky standing at my shoulder. I can best describe his appearance as subtly startling. While technically still respecting the black-tie dress code, his trousers were black leather and so was his bow tie.

'I've been trying to see you all day,' he said, 'but your secretary said you were unavailable.'

He looked at me bug-eyed and accusingly, as though I'd been intentionally avoiding him.

'I'm afraid it's been one of those days, Micky. Some commercial problems and, oh yes, Bruno Fulger sent a writ.'

'That's partly what I wanted to talk to you about,' said Micky. 'Well, about Anna Grant anyway.'

'Yes?'

'I was curious to know how you got on at the police station the other evening.'

How the hell did he know about that? But then of course he would. If he'd shopped them all that rubbish in the first place, they probably kept in touch.

'Fine,' I said. 'I filled them in about Anna's star status in the company and they seemed grateful. I don't think they'd realised quite how crucial she was to magazines like *In Society*.'

Micky darkened. 'How do you mean, crucial?'

'Like I told them, I've always reckoned Anna's articles were worth twenty thousand copies on the circulation.'

'As a matter of fact,' he said huffily, 'losing Anna won't have any impact at all. Some of her profiles were beginning to seem quite dated.'

As he spoke, Kay Lipschwitz Anderson joined us on the balcony. She looked stunning that night, with her shiny black hair drawn into a chignon, and blood-red lipstick. Around her neck was an enormous piece of Mayan gold jewellery, like doubloons strung on a chain.

'We were just saying what a blow it's going to be to the magazine, losing Anna,' I said.

'Devastating,' said Kay. 'People really took notice of her stuff. You remember her interview with Pamela Harriman? Hilarious.

'Incidentally,' said Kay, 'have you heard any progress on the police front? I hate the idea of Anna's killer being still on the loose.'

Micky looked at me pointedly, and I stared him out.

'Apparently, they've narrowed the field quite a bit,' I

said. 'And they've come up with a psychological profile. They believe the murderer was someone who knew her, possibly even worked with her, and who had some strong professional reason to be jealous of her.'

Micky glowered furiously.

At that moment, preceded by a salvo of ear-splitting bangs with his gavel, the toastmaster announced that dinner was served, and the twelve hundred guests began pushing and stumbling their way down the horseshoe staircase. As I crossed the banqueting room floor, I indiscriminately glad-handed anyone whose face I recognised. I've always reckoned half the value to these industry jamborees lies in pressing the flesh of suppliers you didn't want to waste time on anywhere else.

Suzy had solved the placement problem deftly. The editors and publishers were shared out equally across our three tables, and so were our shortlisted contributors. I would defy anyone to scrutinise those placements and tell me which was the A table. My own neighbours for the evening were to be Ellen Durlacher and Minnie Vass. Micky, I was pleased to see, was on the furthest possible seat from my own.

All around us, guests were still streaming by searching for their places. Several looked already the worse for drink. A woman in gold slingbacks and a diamanté boob tube lurched on to the chair next to mine, before being helped away by her deputy on a finger-food partwork.

The toastmaster in his red tails made increasingly agitated pleas for guests to take their places. 'Your Chairman is waiting to say grace,' he kept intoning, as though this provided some special incentive to hurry up. 'Your Chairman is waiting to say grace.'

Minnie, who had been watching the proceedings with the leaden enthusiasm of one who had forgone dinner with Princess Firyal of Jordan to be here, began unwrapping the complimentary package of scent on her sideplate.

'Gracious,' she said archly when it was revealed to

contain a miniature bottle of Mouchette's Aurora. '*Horrible* smell: so sickly-sweet. Ah well, it might do for a maid's birthday present.' And she let it drop into her capacious Lacroix evening bag.

Rather to my annoyance, I saw that Incorporated's tables had been placed adjacent to our own, and my view of the stage was partly obstructed by Howard Trench's bearded profile. And then, even more annoying, I saw something else: sitting on Trench's right as guest of honour was Pierre Roux.

It was the first time I'd seen him without his silk giraffe tie, and I can't say he looked any better in evening dress. Trench was making an enormous fuss over him, introducing him around the table to all his editors. On Roux's other side they'd put the sex columnist from *Girls on Top*. I wondered whether they'd given her any special instructions.

Trench looked so thoroughly smug and self-satisfied at it all that I had an overwhelming desire to go over and tip a drink over him. He was wearing a white tuxedo with a winged stiff collar, and a pre-tied bow tie which reminded me of a pier-end windmill on a stick.

'Pierre, may I present the editor of *Ladies' Home Cookery*, one of our biggest brands?' I heard him say. 'Stephanie's readers spend an astounding three hundred million pounds a year on looking good.'

In two days' time, I thought, Howard and Pierre would be looking rather less good themselves. Because by then I'd have swung the whole Mouchette campaign back to us.

Our Chairman for the evening – some venerable old geezer from a yachting magazine – welcomed us to the industry's premier awards and threw in a few platitudes about what a wonderful industry it was. Then the waiters swarmed out of the kitchens like bees from a hive, bearing trays of cut-crystal schooners containing melon balls in kirsch.

'You know what's so weird about Howard Trench?' said Ellen. She'd been watching him at the next table.

'Tell me: what *isn't* weird about Howard Trench?' I laughed. I'd had a couple of glasses of wine now and was feeling less misanthropic.

'I guess he must be effective in that job, or he wouldn't keep it,' said Ellen. 'But I simply can't imagine him reading his magazines. I can't visualise what he'd look like, reading those articles they have on oral sex and painful periods.'

'I don't suppose he does,' I said. 'Any more than the head of a package holiday company spends much time buying wicker donkeys on the Costa Brava. Trench sees himself as a quintessential marketing man. Don't forget he started life in Newcastle at Procter & Gamble. It doesn't make any difference whether he's selling household bleach or magazines.'

'But how's he tell if they're any good?'

'He can't. If the circulation goes up, it's good. If it drops, he puts in a new editor. If it still drops, he puts in another new editor. And so on. If nothing works, he closes it down and blames market forces.'

'But isn't it a big disadvantage, not knowing?'

'Not really. Could make it easier. At least he isn't backseat driving.'

The waiters reappeared with the main courses under a thousand silver cloches, which at a given signal they unveiled with a flourish. Ellen, having carved off a morsel of meat with her knife, declared it to be veal. I, on the other hand, was convinced it was roast duck.

We appealed to Minnie to arbitrate. 'Goodness,' she said, smacking her lips appreciatively. 'I haven't eaten lamb like that since we stayed with Abdul's mother in Dhahran.'

There was a fanfare of bugles as the Chairman of the Magazine Society reappeared at the rostrum, escorted by a detachment from the massed pipes and drums of the

Grenadier Guards. The National Anthem was played, and then the Chairman proposed the Loyal Toast.

'The Queen,' responded the guests, with varying degrees of conviction.

'Ladies and gentlemen,' announced the toastmaster portentously. 'Following the Loyal Toast, you now have your Chairman's permission to smoke.' Minnie, who'd been puffing away since the melon balls, gave a hollow cheer.

'The awards will commence in five minutes,' declared the toastmaster. 'Your Chairman has asked me to remind you that those guests desiring brandies, liqueurs or cigars should place their orders directly.'

As had been predicted, success for Weiss Magazines during the first section of the prizegiving was entirely elusive. In the photography category, Yando's revolutionary fashion pictures of rubber dresses, taken aboard the Tokyo–Kyoto bullet train, were beaten by a charming study of a kitten playing with a ball of wool. In the circulation category, Norman Turner was gutted when the prize went instead to a nursing journal which had targeted subscriptions at longterm residential patients. Minnie, who regarded victory in the lifestyle category as a foregone conclusion, was furious to watch it go instead to an article about decorative bird tables.

All in all, we were a despondent party by the halfway mark, and I knew I was taking flak for forcing them to come at all.

In the second section, however, things looked up. Spike picked up an award for *Man Alive* for general excellence in feature journalism, and *Smart Living* was runner-up in the typography category for its elegant seriphs. The fact that the winner was a football fanzine induced tears of laughter in Minnie.

Next came the major award for profile writing.

'This year,' read the Chairman from his teleprompt, 'we received a record number of entries: 347. And many of them, reported the judges, of a very high standard indeed.

231

But one entrant in their opinion stood out from the crowd. The judges commended her for her depth of research and her ability to condense large amounts of information into thoroughly readable pieces of journalism. And above all, they praised her work for its wit and, it says here, her ability at interviewing the great and good without coming over either as sycophantic or censorious.'

I felt my heart lurch. There was only one person he could be referring to, surely.

'This year's winner,' he said, 'tragically cannot be with us tonight to collect her prize. As many of you will know, Anna Grant from Weiss Magazines died a little over a week ago. So tonight, in her place, I invite her editor at *In Society*, Micky Rice, to come to the rostrum and receive it on her behalf.'

Micky rose to his feet and in a blaze of circling spotlights made his way up to the stage. I could see Suzy across the table looking aghast. I caught her eye and we stared at each other in disbelief. Suzy was the only person in the room who knew how I was feeling just then.

Micky shook hands with the Chairman, posed triumphantly with the framed citation for the photographers, and then I watched with horror as he asked permission to make a short speech from the rostrum.

'Ladies and gentlemen,' he began. 'I am proud to accept this award on behalf of all of us at *In Society*. As many of you on the editorial side here tonight are aware, awards of this nature, while gratifying to receive, can also be invidious. Why invidious? Because however talented the journalist being honoured may be, it is so often the backroom people who really deserve the prize.'

I saw Micky cast a look in the direction of the Weiss Magazines tables, and recoil at my steely glare.

'When I first had the idea of hiring Anna Grant,' he went on, 'I knew I was taking a big risk. But that's what editors should do more often: employ young untried writers and train them up. It takes longer of course, and requires more effort on your part, and you have to have the patience to oversee any number of rewrites. But it can be done. After three or four years of holding her hand and exposing her to my best contacts, I had created a highly serviceable young staff writer. Which is how we at *In Society* all regarded Anna Grant.

'So, in recognition of all our commissioning editors and unsung sub-editors who worked alongside me on Anna Grant's raw copy, I gladly collect this trophy.'

He left the stage and prudently headed straight for the exit. I say prudently, because I wouldn't have given high odds on his chances of remaining alive if he'd come anywhere near me just then. As a proxy acceptance speech, I'd class Micky's as just about the most self-serving and treacherous ever given. There and then, I made a promise to myself which I had no intention of breaking. The minute I got this American trip out of the way, I was firing Micky Rice.

There was still one prize to go. Frankly, I was so mad at Micky I had pretty well tuned out of the whole thing, and it was only Ellen clutching at my arm that brought me back on line.

The Chairman was saying something about one company maintaining consistently high standards of presentation and content across all its titles, and suddenly everyone at our tables was rising spontaneously to their feet and the spotlight was seeking me out like an escaped prisoner around Colditz.

Weiss Magazines had won the Chairman's Award for Publishing Excellence.

I felt myself walking up to the stage in a trance, inexplicably moved. All I could see was Suzy whooping with joy as I passed her seat, and Leonora and Tasmin fanning themselves with their programmes against all the attention. Megan Whiley was standing on her chair, toasting the world at large with Metaxa.

The Chairman was waiting for me at the rostrum, holding the ugliest trophy I've seen in my life. It was a cut-crystal sculpture of a flamingo, specially made at some famous glassworks in Hungary.

He guided me by the arm towards a microphone, and it became clear I was expected to say something. But I was so choked with emotion, I wasn't sure I could manage it.

In the end I just said, 'On behalf of all my colleagues in Park Place, thank you very much indeed.' And then I added, 'We're all particularly sad Anna Grant isn't able to be with us on this great night. Anna was our most talented writer, one of the few I've ever worked with who didn't need any editing. So you're included in this prize too, Anna. You'll never be forgotten.'

And then I burst into tears.

# 15

I woke up on Wednesday morning with a major league hangover, so I had the taxi drop me off at Buckingham Gate and walked into work across the park while the cab went on ahead with my luggage for New York. I arrived to find Suzy waiting with a carton of Solpadeine and a dry bagel.

'For you,' she said. 'You'll need them. You don't want to fly cold turkey.'

'On the other hand, a hangover will double my street cred at the *Man Alive* meeting.'

I spent a couple of hours gathering together my papers for the trip, including the latest profit and circulation forecasts for the magazines and a load of stuff about print and paper costs. Barney Weiss had an awkward habit of asking for the one statistic you didn't file in your head, so now I took a slim pocket digest of the key facts with me which fitted inside my wallet.

At ten to eleven Suzy reminded me the *Man Alive* meeting was about to begin, so I staggered upstairs to their offices at the back of the building, ready to intercept Simon Beriot.

The editorial offices of *Man Alive* are spiritually as far removed from those of *Couture* and *Smart Living* as it's possible to be. They're perhaps best described as a cross between a Wall Street dealing room and the back room of a pub.

As I opened the door, something whistled past my ear, followed by a dull thud as a dart impaled itself in a girlie calendar on the wall.

'Christ – fuck, sorry about that, mate,' said Dean

Dwight, Spike Steel's deputy. Then he added, 'We're researching a story on new lad culture. We've called in forty sets of darts and all these garage calendars.'

One entire wall of *Man Alive*'s open-plan newsroom was now plastered with topless redheads, blondes and brunettes, each ostensibly promoting sparkplugs and dipsticks. Another wall was similarly covered by football posters.

Spike was sitting at a computer terminal in his glass editor's office, drinking from a bottle of Red Rock cider. He was an angular former war correspondent in a Paul Smith suit, whose twin passions were smart weapons and smart tailoring. Until I hired him last year to edit *Man Alive*, Spike had reported the Bosnian war and styled catalogues for Katharine Hamnett.

'Hey, Kit,' he said when he saw me. 'So it turned out OK last night in the end.'

'The awards? Sure. Well done for your prize. You deserve it.'

'Pity Anna Grant wasn't able to collect hers, though,' said Spike. 'She was a neat writer as well as a complete babe.'

I laughed. I'd never thought of Anna as a babe, but it suited her rather well. One facet of her.

'Anyway, take a look at this,' said Spike. 'I promise you: it'll turn your stomach.'

He hammered away at the keyboard, hitting the return button and skating across the screen with his mouse. I could see we were heading into the Internet. We progressed along a main thoroughfare of the superhighway, then turned off down an electronic sliproad, then another, until we fetched up at some wretched back alley. It was an area of the web I never even knew existed.

'Here you go,' said Spike triumphantly, logging on to the final blue lintel, and slipping inside. 'Bet you haven't seen this before. Japanese cyberporn. I knew it was in here somewhere. It's just taken a bit of finding.'

He scrolled through the offerings of this obscure red-light ryokan.

'Originates somewhere in Okayama. They keep the site secret, it's not published anywhere.'

I watched as Spike flipped me through a freak show of dismembered Japanese schoolgirls and manacled burikos.

'It's a problem the images are so fuzzy,' said Spike, 'because we're trying to photograph them straight off the screen.'

'For a story? Isn't this rather sick?'

'Sick? Sure it's sick. It's great. We're going to expose this whole Japanese electronic porn trade. Investigative journalism. It's the way to go.'

Spike's office began to fill with contributors who sat along the windowsill and on the edge of desks. Most were got up for the meeting in black Helmut Lang or Hugo Boss suits, with narrow black ties; the rest seemed to have come straight on from a softball league in sweatpants, or else the mailroom, which in fact they very possibly had. Spike was always refreshing his editorial talent from the mailroom. Of Simon Beriot there was still no sign.

Spike kicked off the meeting by reviewing where we were with the October issue.

'The story on sex change surgery is now in,' he said, 'and is waiting on artwork. Any progress on that, Russ?'

Russell Hall, *Man Alive*'s art director, looked up from his laptop. 'Yeah,' he said. 'I spoke to Yando's agent last night and he's agreed to shoot something early next week in LA. He wants to get a kind of *Psycho* feel to it.'

'Does that involve hiring a motel room?' asked Dean anxiously, who doubled as managing editor responsible for budgets.

'Yando's demanded a suite at the Château Marmont, as a matter of fact,' said Russ Hall.

'Moving right on,' said Spike, avoiding my eye, 'the rest of the main features are beginning to take shape. Drugs cartels in San Salvador is in, portable CD players is in, Las

Vegas gambling rings is in, and the Axel Rose profile. What else is ready?'

'Most of the fashion and front-of-book,' said Dean. 'The chinos story's ready to be laid out now. So are the overcoats and gangland violence in Newcastle. And the results of the circumcision poll.'

'You know what we're missing?' said Spike. 'Humour. There's just nothing funny in the issue. We need a funny spread.'

'There's still time,' said Dean, consulting his schedule. 'Just about. Providing it's clear of the office by next Tuesday.'

'I suppose we could revive the old Dickheads concept,' said Spike, 'if everyone worked on it. "Are you a Hothead, a Meathead or a Dickhead?" Lists of celebrities and bigshots. Anyone got any nominations? Don't worry which category they fit into. We'll decide that later.'

The contributing editors began spieling out suggestions.

'Jarvis Cocker?'

'Keanu Reeves?'

'Michael Schumacher.'

'We must include Pete Sampras – he's a classic.'

'Robert Dole or Martin Amis?'

'How about that German industrialist Bruno Fulger?'

'Not Bruno Fulger, if you don't mind,' I put in sharply. 'We've already got one writ from him this week. I couldn't cope with another.'

Just then I noticed Simon Beriot. He had slipped in at the back and was squatting against the glass partition. He looked strained. I wasn't surprised: a twice-daily telephone grilling by Rudolph Gombricht would take its toll.

I caught Beriot's eye and motioned him to follow me outside. Reluctantly, he stood up and joined me.

We sat on chairs between empty desks in the middle of the newsroom. Through the glass walls of Spike's office we could see the backs of the contributors still in the meeting.

'Sorry to drag you out,' I said, 'but we need to talk.

About Bruno Fulger and your photograph. You heard me say we've received a writ.'

'I told you that was coming,' said Beriot. 'I warned you about it.'

'I should have rung you after the funeral. When you said Rudolph Gombricht was giving you a hard time.'

'You should, yeah. You've really dropped me in this. Gombricht says he can force me to give evidence in court. He says I've no choice.'

'I'm afraid he's right. If they subpoena you, you have to turn up. But what's he want you to say? Has he told you?'

'That Anna Grant stole that picture from my studio. To begin with, he asked me to sue Anna myself and was going to cover all my costs. I said no, but he wouldn't let go. He said he'd pay me too. When he told me how much I almost fucking fainted. But then Anna was murdered so there wasn't much point any more.'

'But Gombricht still rang you.'

'Yeah. Now he wants me to give evidence saying the magazine told Anna to steal the picture.'

'Which we didn't.'

'I wouldn't know.' He looked at me meaningfully. 'I just wouldn't know that.'

'Look, are you trying to tell me something?' I said. 'Why don't you just come right out with it?'

'I'm not saying anything at all,' said Beriot. 'But you might think about it from my angle. Like, at the moment, I get about six magazine assignments a year from *Man Alive* and you pay a couple of hundred pounds a page. Work it out. It's not a lot of money. And now this solicitor's come along and is offering ten times that to help him out in court. So you see: I'm not asking for anything, just reviewing the options.'

He took out a cigarette and lit it, and smirked.

'What is this?' I said. 'It sounds like blackmail to me.'

Simon Beriot's face darkened. 'Watch it, mate,' he said angrily. 'Don't you ever use that word to me again, OK?

All I'm saying is that other photographers in this company have contracts. I know that. Monthly retainers. And guarantees of a certain level of work. I'd like to be given fashion stories. Ten-, twelve-page fashion stories.'

He stood up. 'I leave it to you, mate. It doesn't bother me what you do. It's you people who got me into this shit, and you can get me out. If you want to call me with a proposition, you've got my number.'

And then he walked back into Spike's office and sat down at the side of the meeting.

I had a business-class ticket on the two o'clock flight from Heathrow to JFK and was standing in line to check in. Check-in queues always remind me of flu inoculation drill at school: you edge forward, uneasily waiting your turn, while the man at the front shoots the catches on his briefcase – *plok* – before striding off, relieved it's all over, with a nothing-to-it expression.

There was a commotion somewhere to my left and I saw, beyond a red rope on a narrow strip of red carpet, Yando and three obnoxious young men surrounded by a mountain of metal suitcases containing camera equipment. They were remonstrating with the girl behind the first-class desk.

'I'm sorry, gentlemen,' the check-in girl was saying, 'but there really isn't any more I can do. You have two first-class tickets here and two economy tickets. It's not possible to upgrade you all to first.'

'Listen, this must be a misunderstanding, right?' Yando's third assistant whined back. 'Yando's whole entourage always flies first. It's contractual, right? I don't know what the fuck's gone wrong at Weiss Magazines.'

Yando was dressed head to toe in black, the hems of his parachute trousers tucked into black motorcycle boots and his long ginger hair tied into a ponytail. He regarded the check-in girl through half-closed eyes and yawned, as though nothing in the world counted for quite so little as the obstructive functionary before him.

'What you want to do, Yando?' asked the third assistant. 'Jack the whole trip?'

'Put the upgrades on my Amex for now,' said Yando. 'Either the magazine reimburses us or we don't release the pictures.'

As soon as we took off I began drinking red wine. Three airline mini-bottles combined with the altitude always has the same good effect: fifteen minutes of pure optimism followed by deep sleep. I love that rather public sense of privacy air travel produces: the certainty you won't be telephoned or interrupted for the duration of the flight. At some point between the first and second bottle, while scanning the *Wall Street Journal*, my eye was caught by an item about Erskine Greer. The headline read, 'Greer Corp tipped to buy Federated Aviation.' It went on to say that Greer Aerospace, a subsidiary of the Hong Kong-based conglomerate, is viewed as the most likely of five suitors to take over America's troubled aviation spare-parts company. Houston-based Federated, with a capitalisation of $2.3 billion, is the third largest US manufacturer in this sector. Privately held Greer Corporation, still controlled by its founder, Erskine Greer, sixty-three, also comprises Trans-Asia Airways, Greer Assurance and Mutual Life, the Greer Star line of container freighters and a chain of business-oriented hotels around the Pacific Rim, Inns of Happiness. Stock which had been trading Monday on Wall Street at $6.40 had already risen to $6.90 in anticipation of a bid from Greer Corp of around $7.25.

What a pity, I thought, before drifting into oblivion, that Anna's profile of Greer wasn't about to come out. There'd be a lot of interest in him now, and we'd have ridden it right on the crest of the wave. Even for Greer this was a major acquisition and he was largely unknown in the States. We could have syndicated our piece half a dozen times.

I slept with my head in my arms on the plastic table and didn't stir until we were about to land. The fact was, I was shattered. The escape from Schloss Fulgerstein, the writ, the magazine awards had caught up on me. As we circled for our approach over Queens, I stared down dully from the window on to the gas refineries and blocks of suburban rooftops. If I eked it out carefully, I thought I had enough energy left to recapture the Mouchette advertising. But only just. And I wondered too what it was Barney Weiss needed to see me about so urgently. He'd sounded jovial enough on the telephone, but it made me uneasy.

Altogether, it was with a certain sense of foreboding that I passed through customs and immigration into the land of the free.

I joined a line for yellow cabs outside the terminal and rattled into Manhattan behind a Gujarati cab driver who was listening to some Brooklyn-Hindi radio station. When I told him my destination – the Pierre hotel – he just nodded and released the trunk so I could load my own suitcase. The back seat of the cab seemed to have been the victim of a recent knife attack, and was bleeding chunks of foam, partly stemmed by strips of black electrical tape.

Shortly before we reached the toll booth on to the Triboro Bridge, we were overtaken on the inside lane by a long white limousine. Inside, I could see Yando and his assistants knocking back highballs from the in-car bar. The petulant assistant from the check-in was talking on the telephone. We might have screwed up on the first-class flights, but at least we'd delivered on the contractual limo.

Each time I'm in New York on business I stay some place different. The Plaza, the Carlyle, the Mark, the Four Seasons, the Plaza Athenée, the Ritz-Carlton ... put me down in any Manhattan hotel room and I'll tell you where I am: a Manhattan hotel room. I defy anyone to tell them apart. The bedcovers, marble-floored bathrooms, lamps, mini-bars, shopping channels, framed architectural prints, breakfast orders to hang on the door knob; there must be some central depot where they pick up the whole kit. Not that I'm complaining. I've always preferred big anonymous hotels where no one gives a damn who you are so long as you can produce a valid credit card. My idea of a nightmare is a boutique hotel where they greet you by name. The moment anyone says, 'Have a nice day, Mr Preston,' I check out.

My room at the Pierre was on the fifteenth floor and suitably anonymous. The bellboy lingered about the place, demonstrating how to use the television and turning on and off bathtaps until I bought my privacy with a five-dollar tip.

I lay down on the bedcover and wondered who to telephone. When Sally and I were together, I always rang her the moment I arrived anywhere, it was automatic. Now there wasn't anyone. Anna, if you could only know how much I'm missing you.

Fabrice Mouchette's apartment was on the fourth floor of a quiet building near the junction of Park and 72nd. There was a canopy outside on to the sidewalk, a porter and an Adam-style fireplace in the lobby with a club fender. The porter had a typed list of guests for the dinner and checked my name before ringing up to announce me. 'Mr Preston on his way up now.'

I tried to read who else was coming, but he gave me a sour look. From the list's length, it was a big dinner.

The door to the apartment was already open and a butler in a white jacket waiting inside with a tray of drinks. Beyond him in the drawing-room I could see about thirty people standing about in small groups, and a black maid passing a tray of smoked salmon squares on rye.

The first person I saw as I came in was Minnie Vass. I don't know which of us was more surprised. She was talking to a tall debonair Venezuelan whom she introduced as Reinaldo Herrera.

'Who else is here?' I asked Minnie. 'You always know everybody.'

'Darling,' she said, 'just the same people you meet everywhere.' She pointed out Princess Lee Radziwill,

Jackie Onassis's sister, Reinaldo's wife Carolina, the dress designer, and a bunch of steel-haired businessmen who ran various investment funds.

'The Dutch model over there you know, of course. Tigra. She's never out of *Couture*.' She pointed out the new Mouchette 'face', a seven-foot blonde glamazon who had rolled up for the dinner in a floor-length diaphanous evening dress with trainers.

'And over there by the fireplace, talking to Fabrice, is Anastasia Fulger.'

Christ, I thought, thank goodness she warned me. I made a mental note to spend the rest of the evening keeping as far away from Anastasia as possible.

'Tell me what you're doing here,' said Minnie, 'and I'll tell you what I'm doing here.'

I explained I was in town for lunch with Barney and hoped to talk business with Fabrice for a few minutes later on. 'And you?'

'Look around you,' said Minnie. 'This apartment is a *fossil*. Old gold curtains. Fiddly French furniture. All this wood panelling. Hasn't been *touched* for twenty-five years since Angelique died. She was Fabrice's wife. It's all her taste from the 'seventies and Fabrice won't change it, sentimental old dog. But don't you worry, I've got my plans.'

'I didn't realise you were a decorator too.'

'Strictly speaking, I'm not. I put people together. For a fee.'

Fabrice came over and greeted me, steering me by the arm around the room and introducing me to his other guests. When we came uncomfortably close to Anastasia, I extracted myself by launching into an enthusiastic conversation with a banker's wife about Fabrice's Chagall, which hung above the mantelpiece.

Dinner was announced and we went through into a panelled dining-room, where three round tables had been set for twelve people each. At the centre of each table

stood an elaborate silver candelabrum, flanked by miniature silver replicas of Napoleonic cannons. One wall of the
room was entirely covered by a patchwork of Cubist and
Surrealist paintings, each individually lit.

We circled the tables seeking out our name cards and,
to my horror, I found I'd been given Anastasia Fulger on
my right. It was too late now to switch the placement so,
seconds before she arrived, I flipped over my own card so
she couldn't read it.

'Good evening,' said Anastasia. Her accent was stronger
than I'd imagined. 'I am Anastasia Fulger.'

'Christopher,' I replied. It was years since I'd used my
unabbreviated first name. I'd been Kit since kindergarten.

She was even thinner than her photographs, or maybe
she'd lost weight since the separation. Her waist, accentu-
ated by a fitted aquamarine jacket, was impossibly tiny.
Her lapels and sleeves were embroidered with pink raffia
flowers, and she was wearing the enormous Kutchinsky
diamond earrings from the *In Society* photo session.

I succeeded in avoiding her for the whole first course,
concentrating on the woman on my other side. She was
French and tedious, with a pneumatic wrinkled cleavage
and big gold earrings which had elongated her lobes. Her
husband, she said, was the General Manager of Mouchette
for South America. They lived in Rio de Janeiro and she
came up to New York each month to shop.

With Anastasia, I resolved to know nothing. When I
turned to speak to her, I asked, 'Are you a New Yorker?'

'Actually,' she replied, 'we have seven homes but
recently, you know, I am spending a lot of time in this
city.'

'Why's that?'

And suddenly she was off. I didn't need to ask her
another question for forty minutes. Out it all came: her
marriage to Bruno, her separation, how he'd treated her,
his meanness with money ('He has more than one billion
dollars and he behaves like he's broke, I'm telling you'),
his affairs ('Any little hooker who bats her eyes at him,

245

with Bruno it's that easy, you know'). I got the feeling she'd told the same story a hundred times before. There was no sense that some special rapport between us had made her decide to confide in me. I was simply the man who happened to be sitting on her left in a dark suit.

'This divorce has been terrible for me, just terrible,' she said. 'Each day, lawyers, lawyers.' Two little frown lines appeared between her eyebrows, and her eyes began to flick nervously back and forth. 'It's OK for Bruno, he has all the money. It's a game for Bruno. It's not even like I'm asking for half his money. I ask only ten per cent for my daughter's sake. I am a very simple person, you can see that.'

I nodded dumbly.

'Believe me,' she said, 'when this whole divorce thing is over, I won't miss Bruno's world at all. I will buy a few simple pieces each season, nothing ostentatious. Who needs it? Beauty is from within.

'The thing that is so hard,' she went on, 'is all the attention. The newspapers, magazines, I am so shy, so private, I never speak to them. So they make it up. I promise you, it happens.' She stared at me suddenly. 'Where is it you said you live?'

'Er, London.'

'Then maybe you read this terrible article. They put me in this magazine, without my permission, and told terrible lies about me. About my divorce, everything. You know this magazine *In Society*?'

It was all becoming uncomfortably close to home. I didn't want to lie, but I wasn't about to unveil myself as the puppet-master either.

'*In Society*?' I said airily. 'Not many people buy that one in England' (true enough, unfortunately), 'but tell me, where do you head to at weekends from the city?'

Just then I was saved by the arrival at the table of a mousse au trois chocolats. Anastasia helped herself and then switched with Teutonic efficiency to the man on her right.

The French woman with the cleavage seemed less than

overjoyed at seeing me again when I swung round, and frankly the feeling was mutual, but we were stuck with each other and at least she wasn't Anastasia. We lumbered on. I praised the chocolate mousse and so did she. I asked her about the cosmetics scene in South America and she said it was a problem.

'For Henri, my husband, it is not so easy at the moment. It's a huge market one day but there's so much inflation, the sales girls must change the prices each morning. And the Indians are driving Henri mad too.'

'Why's that? Surely they don't wear Mouchette cosmetics?'

She glared, wondering whether I was a fool or merely teasing her.

'Of course not,' she said sharply, 'they just cause problems at the research station. Whenever Henri's scientists choose to use this new plant or flower, the Indians say it is sacred for the tribe. They're ridiculous, worse than the animal rights people who picket our laboratories in France.'

Luckily, we had coffee in the drawing-room and I was able to position myself next to Fabrice – and a safe distance from Anastasia – on a sofa. I prayed that Minnie, whom I could see talking to Anastasia across the room, wasn't about to blow my cover.

I apologised to Fabrice for talking business at his party, and then proceeded to do just that. In three minutes I'd encapsulated the advertising problem, and how it had been switched away from us at the eleventh hour. Fabrice listened carefully, without interrupting, his shrewd old eyes never leaving my face. When I'd finished, they snapped shut for a moment, as though he was deciding how much he could tell me.

'You know the best advice I can give you?' he said after a bit. 'Don't worry, and do absolutely nothing. For the present I can't explain this, but before too long you'll understand. Our two companies can only benefit from being closer.'

247

'But seriously,' I said, 'we have nothing booked for the autumn at all. It's unprecedented. Even the promise of some interim space would make the publishers feel better about it. I'd be grateful if you could spare me an hour tomorrow morning to discuss it further.'

Outwardly, I was calm and discursive, but inside I was starting to panic. I hadn't really expected to fix the problem over coffee, but nor had I envisaged Fabrice's mysterious pronouncements.

He looked at me meaningfully, and I sensed he was trying to establish how much, if anything, I already knew.

'Have you spoken with Barney Weiss lately?' he asked.

'Not in detail, but I'm having lunch with him tomorrow.'

'Well, maybe at lunch ...' He trailed off. 'Now, tell me, how did you like my granddaughter when she was working with you last summer?'

Just then Minnie Vass swooped down on us and said, 'Fabrice, darling, I haven't properly introduced you to my hot date for this evening, Christophe Culper.' Fabrice eyed him suspiciously. He was blond, thirty years younger than Minnie and transparently homosexual. 'He's just finished decorating Yando's place on Long Island,' said Minnie, 'and he just *loves* your Chagall.'

I was woken by the doorbell of my room and stumbled to open it with a towel wrapped round my loins. Outside stood a waiter wheeling a steel breakfast trolley, laid up with a tablecloth, china and a red rose in a champagne flute.

'Room 1547? Your breakfast order for seven-fifteen.'

He kicked open the door with his foot and trundled the widebodied wagon into the room.

'You prefer breakfast here or here, sir?' He pointed to a space between the windows or the foot of the bed.

'Er, by the bed please.'

I'd forgotten what madness had possessed me last night to sign up for the full American breakfast. The waiter raised the side flaps of the trolley and then, with a great deal of clattering, opened the steel hatch to the hot box and produced a plate of fried food. On it sat two congealed eggs over easy, two slices of griddled ham, a maple waffle with syrup running into the ham and a blueberry muffin. Plonked dead centre between the eggs lay half a strawberry.

'You have everything you need now, sir?' wheedled the waiter in his white and gold livery, as I signed the bill. 'Coffee, hot water, milk, two eggs over easy ...'

I palmed over another five dollars of Barney Weiss's money and, having rebought my solitude, took a long hot shower.

While I picked at my food I dragged over the telephone to the extent of its cord, balanced it on the breakfast wagon and dialled Cazzie. It would be half past twelve in London and I had a decent chance of catching her. Even a year ago it never really worked, trying to have a telephone conversation with Cazzie: she stiffened up and just replied yes or no or grinned silently. Recently, however, she'd got the knack and chatted away as naturally as if we were in the same room.

I heard the number ringing far away in Clapham and wondered whether it would be Cazzie herself who answered: she's started doing that lately too.

'Hello?'

It was a man's voice.

'Er, hello. I'd like to speak to Cazzie please. Who's that?'

'It's Paul. Who shall I say's calling?'

'Her father, actually.'

'Ah, yes.' I could hear his awkwardness down the line. 'I'll just fetch her for you.'

In the background I could hear Paul calling out into the garden. 'Cazzie. Your father's on the telephone.' Then he said, 'Yes, Sally, it's Kit for Cazzie.' And then, 'I don't know. I just answered the telephone. Yes, of course I said who I was, I could hardly not, he *asked*.'

There was a pitter-patter of feet and Cazzie picked up the receiver.

'Hello, Daddy.'

'Hi, darling. Guess what, I'm ringing you all the way from America. It's still breakfast time here, that's funny isn't it?'

'Are you going to bring me back a present from America?'

'Really, Cazzie,' I said, pretending to be shocked. 'You shouldn't *ask* people for presents or they don't happen.'

'But I asked Paul for a present and it happened. He's been to Hong Kong, we went to meet him at the airport before breakfast. And he's brought me this huge Chinese dragon made of paper for my wall. *And* he brought me the little salt and peppers from the aeroplane. *And* a special little towel thing in a packet which is already wet for when your fingers are very sticky.'

'I see,' I said. 'And is there anything in particular you'd like Daddy to get you in America?'

'Well,' said Cazzie. 'Um, um, what I'd like, Daddy, is those little jams or little knives and forks on the aeroplane. Paul says they do have them. Then I could keep them with the salt and pepper and have a whole picnic set.'

'OK, darling,' I said, 'I'll do my best. Be good. And can I talk to Mummy now?'

Sally was already hovering over the telephone and came straight on.

'Hello, Kit,' she said. She sounded apprehensive.

'Could you please explain to me what the hell that man is doing in my house on a Thursday lunchtime?'

'Oh, grow up, Kit,' she said. 'You heard Cazzie. Paul's just back from three weeks in Hong Kong.'

'And he comes straight round to Clapham, does he, even before he goes home? Or is my house home to him too now?'

'Look, I'm not going to talk to you if you're like this. It's a waste of energy. And anyway, I wish you'd stop referring to this house as "your" house all the time.'

'Well, it *is*, isn't it, now you mention it? I don't remember you paying for it.'

'This isn't the time,' said Sally, 'and you're evidently in a foul mood, but when you're back in England I wouldn't mind sitting down with you and Paul and discussing everything properly.'

'Paul too: what's he got to do with it? Your financial advisor?'

'As a matter of fact, Kit, he'd like to buy your share of this house off you. I thought you'd be pleased.'

I spent the morning pacing Fifth Avenue, feeling troubled and despondent. It sounded like Paul and Sally were serious and I wasn't sure I was mentally ready to relinquish the house. Of course I could see it made sense. The money I'd release would enable me to buy a proper flat instead of renting. But there was something so final about it. When I went round on Saturdays to collect Cazzie I wouldn't be the landlord any more, I'd be a visitor. Another thought occurred to me too. Buying out my equity could be part of a plot by Sally and Paul to leave London. They'd be free to move to Basingstoke, or even Hong Kong. Then I'd never see Cazzie. She'd be Paul's daughter.

I reflected, too, on my conversation last night with Fabrice Mouchette. It was nonsensical. What did he mean 'Our two companies can only benefit from being closer'? Of course they could. The whole point was that, of this minute, our two companies had no relationship at all. There was something here I didn't understand, and I didn't like it.

I headed downtown to 49th Street and on the stroke of twelve-thirty reached Smith & Wollensky's. It was a big, clubby steakhouse evidently patronised by red-toothed businessmen, exactly the kind of place Barney liked. The walls were hung with ornithological prints and duck decoys, and there was a pervading smell of grilled meat. I could see Barney across a large dining-room, already deep in conversation with the head waiter.

'Hi, Kit,' said Barney when I joined him. 'I'm just debating with the Captain here whether I'd prefer the sirloin or the lobster.'

'Why not have both, Mr Weiss,' said the waiter. 'I can ask chef to do you a lovely big lobster, fresh in today, and the steak blue, just as you like it.'

'OK. Sold,' said Barney. 'And just bring me a side order of onion rings and fried zucchini. And what about you, Kit? Same again?'

'Just the lobster for me.'

'Aw, come on. This place is famous for its steaks, isn't that right, Paolo? Bring Mr Preston the same as me – and a bottle of French wine and some iced water.

'Tell me, Kit,' said Barney when Paolo had departed. 'You came over on the Concorde?'

'No, a 747 actually.'

'That surprises me. I'm surprised you could spare the time. That's what I tell people. If you can't make a couple of thousand bucks in the time you save flying the Concorde, you shouldn't be travelling at all.'

'How's the valet parking going?' I asked, switching the subject.

'Terrific business. Vegas is only the beginning. Everywhere needs custom parking. Indianapolis, St Louis ...'

He gave me a little homily on margins in the parking industry, which certainly sounded lavish next to publishing, and questioned me about the prospects for expansion into England. For a moment I thought he was going to suggest turning Park Place into a car park.

A waiter appeared with our lunch. The steaks flopped like pink hot water bottles over the rim of the plates, with two bright pink lobsters sitting up top.

'Won't you just look at the size of those claws?' exclaimed Barney. 'A pound of flesh inside of each one, I reckon.'

I told him how the magazines were faring, giving it the best possible topspin without actually perjuring myself, but he seemed strangely disengaged. Only when I mentioned our continuing problem with Mouchette did he wake up and take notice.

'The oddest thing,' I said, 'was a conversation I had last night with Fabrice Mouchette, who, as you know, owns the company. He seemed to be inferring something big is about to happen, but I don't know what.'

Barney looked agitated. 'What exactly was it Fabrice said to you?'

'Well, it was all rather oblique. Something about our two companies becoming closer, but he couldn't explain why.'

'He had no business saying that. That's privileged information.'

'How do you mean?'

'Aw, what the hell. It's being announced Monday in any case. The Bourse has kissed the deal off now.'

I looked at him across the steaks, uncomprehending.

'Listen, I've been picking up stock in Mouchette for three months now. As of today, I have eleven per cent of the company. But Fabrice and I have been negotiating for some time. He wants out, and has accepted my private offer for his remaining forty-five per cent. Which gives me fifty-six and control.'

So that's what Fabrice had been hinting at. No wonder he'd advised me to relax and do nothing. Both companies would shortly belong to Barney Weiss. My first thought was how this development would affect our advertising pages. Surely Barney wouldn't allow the budget to stay with Incorporated now. And presumably he'd fire Roux and LeNoy. That would be my advice. And what about Howard Trench? I couldn't wait to see his face when he heard Mouchette had become another subsidiary of LoCo Inc.

On the other hand, I wondered how L'Oréal and Estée Lauder would react to the news that we had a rival beauty company as first cousin. They might not like it, and we'd have to be careful not to be over-partisan in our coverage of their products.

On balance, though, I loved it, and told Barney I was sure we could make it work to our advantage.

He looked round the restaurant uneasily and poured us both another glass of wine.

'Let me level with you, Kit,' he said. 'There's something I need to tell you. It's the reason I requested you come over.'

Something in his tone made me wary. I looked at him but he wouldn't meet my eye.

'This Mouchette acquisition,' he said. 'It's costing a heap of money. I'm not kidding, it's one big deal.' He took another mouthful of claret. 'In order to finance this one, I need to divest a few properties too. For cashflow.'

I kept looking at him, saying nothing, waiting for him to say it. I felt sick and cold.

He said it.

'So I've put the magazines on the block. That's just the way it goes.'

'You mean they're already for sale?'

'Have been for a month. Ansbacher's handling the offering. There's been quite a degree of interest shown.'

'Great,' I said flatly. 'Thanks for taking me into your confidence so early.' I was furious with Barney. For a whole month a firm of media brokers had been hawking my future all over town, and I'm not even told about it.

'Don't you think it would have been courteous to mention this before?' I said. 'Like at dinner two weeks ago, for instance?'

'Listen, Kit,' said Barney, suddenly angry. 'This is a business matter. I'm the vendor. You're the property for sale. No potential purchaser needs a building full of opinionated journalists making conditions or trying to find themselves new jobs. I'm selling the company as a going concern.'

'Nevertheless ...'

'This isn't negotiable, Kit.' Barney hated being defied. But I was damned, especially now he was no longer going to be my boss, if I'd leave it there.

'Might I at least know who our new owners might be?'

'That's confidential.'

'I just thought it might be helpful to tell the editors, before they read it in the newspapers. That's all.'

Barney replied, 'Fuck the editors. Who gives a fuck what they think? It's just piss and wind. Magazines are terrible business. Sooner I'm shot of them the happier I'll be.'

The waiter reappeared with maple-pecan pie, but Barney waved him away.

'The deal's going through later today, anyway,' he said. 'The attorneys are engrossing the final draft. So you'll know soon enough.'

'Wonderful,' I said icily. 'Perhaps you can have your office send me a press release, if that's not too much trouble.'

'And fuck you too,' said Barney. 'You never delivered. Listen, call the office in Chicago twelve o'clock London time tomorrow morning and I'll tell you who your new owner is. Then you can pass on the glad tidings to who the hell you please.'

Barney pushed back the table and, seizing a lobster claw, strode off across the restaurant. I watched him until he disappeared from sight and out on to the sidewalk.

I wasn't due back at the airport for another seven hours, so I persevered with the hall-full bottle and ruminated on my prospects. Objectively, they didn't look good. In fact, they were disastrous. God knows what it would all mean for me personally. I resented being a chattel, to be sold at will to whomever Barney pleased. And the new owners, whoever they turned out to be, would be sure to put their own man in, or else absorb us into their existing structure. An appalling scenario presented itself: what if we were bought by Incorporated? It wasn't impossible. They were a quoted company without much debt.

The spectre of Howard Trench as my new boss didn't even bear contemplation.

# 16

I went straight from Heathrow to Park Place and, all things considered, felt surprisingly good. I'd slept for most of the flight and awoken with renewed optimism. Probably putting the width of the Atlantic between me and Barney was a factor. And no more Thursday evening conferences on the world-phone: there were certainly going to be compensations in a change of ownership.

I made a list in the taxi of all the potential purchasers I could think of. Apart from Incorporated there were two British magazine publishers who might be in the frame, and two German. And there was Kerry Packer's Australian Consolidated Press. And the obvious American houses. On the other hand, the possibilities weren't restricted to publishers. There were telephone and software companies that might be interested, and several conglomerates. Now the company was profitable, there would be a lot more suitors than in Billy Heathcote's day.

As soon as I got in, I asked Suzy to gather heads of departments for half past twelve. Whatever the outcome of my midday conversation, it was better they knew as early as possible. If one of the big boys had bought us, it could be all over the *Evening Standard* business pages by three o'clock.

Suzy said, 'Kit, are you worried about it?'

'A bit. Actually, a lot. It could be great or terrible. All depends.'

'You shouldn't be pessimistic. Seriously. Whoever buys us will see what a good job you've done. The results speak for themselves.'

'Comparatively, I agree. That's judging us against

Billy's regime. But we don't know what criteria the new owners are used to. If they expect twenty per cent profit margins, I'm finished.'

'Think positive,' said Suzy. 'The new owners will need you, they'll recognise that. In fact they're probably figuring out right now how to keep you with a huge pay rise. You'll see.'

'Thanks, Suzy.' I stood up and kissed her on the cheek. 'Pity *you're* not buying us.

'Now,' I said, 'it's one minute to twelve. Perhaps you could get Barney on the line for the last time.'

A minute later, Suzy buzzed through.

'It's Gloria.'

Gloria was Barney's secretary in Chicago. Rumour had it she'd held the fort sexually in the hiatus between Bonnie and Lola, which was why Barney kept her on. There was certainly no other obvious explanation.

'Kit?' she said. 'I'm afraid Mr Weiss is out of town right now, but he's asked me to pass you a message.'

'Fine.'

I could hear her scrabbling about in her in-tray, and muttering.

'OK, here it is,' she said at last. 'It was clipped to another sheet.'

In the background I could hear Barney's raised voice on another call. He was saying, 'I'm sorry, Lola, no way does your sister use my plane. She flies commercial.'

Gloria said, 'This release is embargoed until seven a.m. East Coast time, so I guess it's OK to read it now.

'It says, "LoCo Inc. to sell the Weiss Magazine Company Limited." It's long, maybe I should fax it through to you?'

'No, read it. Please.'

Gloria sighed.

'OK,' she said irritably. 'It says, "Mr Barney S. Weiss, Chairman and President of LoCo Inc., today announced the successful divestment of the company's British publishing subsidiary Weiss Magazines. The magazines, which include fashion book *Couture* and shelter book

*Smart Living*, were acquired by the group four years ago.

'"The purchaser, which paid $140 million in cash, is the privately-held Munich-based insurance-to-pharmaceuticals company Fulger AG."'

I felt my stomach contract as though I'd been punched. Fulger. Bruno bloody Fulger. Anna's murderer. It was all over.

Gloria was still reading. '"Mr Weiss commented on the transaction: 'Bruno Fulger is a long-standing close personal friend of mine, and I know these high-class publishing properties will be in safe hands.'"'

The hell they would. Smarmy bastard.

'"Mr Fulger, Chairman of Fulger AG, added, 'The acquisition of these new businesses goes some way towards fulfilling our stated ambition of becoming a fully diversified international conglomerate. Intellectual properties such as these are particularly valuable in this emerging age of on-line and information technology.'"'

I was so furious with Barney I began to shake. I was seething. I'd kept him informed at every stage about our problems with the Fulgers, and all the time he'd been negotiating with Bruno. If he'd arranged to have me taken outside and shot against the wall, he couldn't have finished me off more effectively.

Gloria was asking, 'Shall I have this release faxed through to your office now?'

'Why not?' I said. 'And you can tell Barney, who I'm perfectly aware is skulking right there behind you, that he's a complete and utter shit.'

'I'll pass on your comments to Mr Weiss when he returns,' said Gloria tartly as I slammed the telephone down on her.

Ten minutes later, the department heads began trickling into my office. General announcements are quite rare, so they knew something was up. 'Not 'til everyone's here,' I told Meredith Carew-Jones. 'I want you all to hear this at the same time.'

The others arrived and stood around the walls. Micky,

Leonora, Tasmin, Spike. Kevin, Kathy, Kay. Robin Reese clutching the new copy of *Man Alive*, straight off the press. Megan looked a bit unsteady: I guessed she'd had another heavy night. Norman Turner with the sheaf of circulation figures he was hoping to discuss with me after the meeting. Ellen had her notepad and pen at the ready in case a release was needed for the press. She didn't know it yet, but Ellen was going to be kept busy all weekend.

'Quiet, everyone,' I said. 'I've got an important press release to read out to you. I should tell you that the first I knew about all this myself was ten minutes ago. So it's as big a shock to me as it will be to you.'

I read the release without comment. Suzy, who was watching everyone's faces, told me afterwards she'd never seen such bewilderment. They stood there open mouthed.

After I'd finished there was a long silence.

Ellen spoke first. 'When does this all go through?'

'It already has. The Fulgers own us now.'

Then Leonora. 'Will they keep all the magazines going?'

'I expect so. Otherwise why spend $140 million?'

Even as I said that, a thought hit me. Could Bruno have bought us simply to close us down? As an act of revenge? Not even he would do that, surely.

'Will there be changes?' asked Tasmin.

'Too early to say. I expect so eventually. But I wouldn't worry about it. You're probably pretty safe.'

'I'll go quietly if they want me to,' said Meredith. 'Buster's always grumbling I'm not at home to cook his lunch.'

The telephone rang in the outer office and Suzy slipped out to answer it. Seconds later she was signalling at me through the door.

'It's Rudolph Gombricht. He needs to speak to you.'

'I'll take it at your desk, Suzy.'

Gombricht was restrained and matter-of-fact. Whatever feelings of triumph he was experiencing at this conversation, he kept them well disguised. There would be time enough to gloat, no doubt, later on.

'This is a fortuitous moment for your company, Mr Preston,' he said, 'as you have doubtless already observed. Ownership by Fulger AG confers both security and investment in the product.'

'I've just broken the news to the senior staff,' I said.

'And their reaction?'

'Amazement mostly. They had no idea.'

'With transactions of this nature,' said Gombricht pointedly, 'it is always best to proceed on a need-to-know basis.

'Mr Fulger, I should inform you, is already in London,' he went on. 'He flew in this morning from Geneva with the intention of inspecting his new properties without delay. You have no objection?'

'I can hardly object if he owns them, can I?'

'Quite. Mr Fulger and I will arrive at your offices at four o'clock. We would be obliged if you would be waiting for us downstairs in the front lobby, and then escort us around the building. Mr Fulger would like to be introduced to all the executives in their own offices. He has suggested we later celebrate his acquisition with a small reception in an appropriate office. I leave the number and criteria of the guest list to you.'

At four o'clock I was standing in the lobby and watched a long red Maserati pull up at the kerb. There was something so surreal about this whole business, of waiting to welcome the man who'd had Anna killed, I felt I might as well see it through to the bitter end.

Bruno was taller than I'd expected, well over six feet, dressed in an open-necked blue shirt with the two arms of a green cashmere pullover tied loosely across his shoulders. Gombricht hurried behind him in a dark suit, tie and stiff white collar.

Gombricht presented me to Fulger, who regarded me noncommittally with bleak, rich man's eyes. You got the impression that he'd seen and experienced everything that is expensive and luxurious in the world, but none of it had really impressed him.

'I thought we'd start at the bottom and work our way up through the building, if that's OK,' I said.

I was conscious of the large number of my colleagues who'd somehow contrived to be hanging about the lobby to coincide with Bruno's arrival.

We got in the lift and shot up to the first floor. On the way, Bruno said, 'Mr Gombricht tells me you are fond of walking in the German countryside.'

Before I could reply, the doors opened and we were outside Norman Turner's office.

'Welcome, welcome to my humble abode,' said Norman, leaping up to greet his new guvnor. 'I believe you'll find that, where circulation matters are concerned, Norman Turner knows the game better than most.'

'That's good to know,' replied Bruno flatly. He glanced cursorily around Norman's little office, with its coloured graphs and invitations to news-trade functions.

'Have you any circulation experience yourself, sir, if you don't mind my asking?' said Norman.

'Regrettably not,' said Bruno, evidently already impatient to move on.

'I've taken the liberty of preparing a little dog and pony show as we call it,' said Norman. 'It won't take fifteen minutes. I've obtained some competitive data through my industry sources that I believe you'll find interesting.'

'Not this afternoon, thank you,' said Bruno sharply, 'we have a lot of people to meet.'

'Of course,' said Norman. 'But any time you need anything in the circulation line, you just ask for me.

'By the way,' added Norman, 'I nearly forgot. I wanted to tell you how brilliantly that issue sold with your wife on the cover. Went like a bloody train. The minute I saw it I knew we had a sell-out on our hands. Bloody marvellous.'

I hustled Bruno out into the corridor where the first person we met was Minnie Vass.

'Bruno!' she said, throwing her arms around him.

'Darling Bruno. I've just heard the good news. It's going to be just too wonderful having you here. You know, Barney never really understood these magazines culturally. Not like you.'

'You are generous, Minnie,' said Bruno stiffly.

'Listen, darling,' she said. 'How long are you in town for? I need to talk to you about a gala I'm organising for Distressed Ballet Dancers. Princess Michael's coming. It's a wonderful opportunity for the magazines to get involved.'

I walked Bruno through the editorial floors, followed by advertising. Everywhere we went, Bruno greeted the staff with the same bloodless formality, giving nothing away. Spike offered him a Red Rock cider which he declined, and Leonora said how nice it would be if Anastasia could become a contributing editor to *Couture*. Leonora has never been a great one for following current affairs, of either variety.

By the time we arrived at *In Society*, Micky was looking white. His office, I noticed, had been tidied up and the front cover of Anastasia removed from his wall display.

'I wonder if I can have a word with you in private,' he said as we trooped in.

'Sure,' said Bruno unenthusiastically. 'If you'd like to.'

Gombricht and I stepped outside the glass office while Micky talked earnestly to Bruno. I could see Micky's eyes practically bursting out of their sockets in his efforts at being agreeable.

'Problem?' asked Gombricht when Bruno re-emerged.

'No problem,' said Bruno. 'He was assuring me he'd been away on holiday when they published that article about Anastasia. Apparently, it was taken out of his hands.'

The tour complete, we headed for my office. Suzy had laid out a tray of glasses and half a dozen bottles of champagne. I can't say I've ever felt less like a party, but I set to work popping corks and handed a glass each to Fulger and Gombricht.

When everyone was assembled, Bruno clapped his hands for silence.

'Excuse me,' he said. 'I am not much of a man for making speeches, but I wish to say welcome to you all and let us make a toast to much success.'

'Much success,' we all intoned. It seemed harmless enough as toasts went.

'Now,' said Bruno, 'I must hand over to Mr Rudolph Gombricht, who I think most of you have just met. Mr Gombricht for many years has been looking after all kinds of matters in this country for our companies, which he will of course continue to do.'

'Thank you,' said Gombricht, drawing from his inside pocket a narrow strip of card. 'I, too, am not given to long speeches, but you see I come prepared.' He laughed tepidly. 'I have now to tell you two things of great importance for the development of these magazines. The first is that Mr Kit Preston is with immediate effect resigning from his position and from the company.'

I felt the eyes of the whole room boring into my back.

'Oh God,' I heard Ellen say. 'Why resign? Can't he at least give it a try?'

'Don't be naive,' Meredith hissed at her. 'He's been booted.'

Afterwards, I knew exactly what I should have done: dashed my full glass of champagne into Gombricht's face. But I remained absolutely rigid.

'At the same time,' said Gombricht, 'I am delighted to announce the appointment of a new managing director.'

There was a flurry of renewed interest, and glances exchanged as though one of the group was about to be revealed as my surprise successor.

'The new managing director is a man of unrivalled publishing experience, familiar with all aspects of the business,' said Gombricht. 'For the past eight years he has held an equivalent position with Incorporated Periodicals.'

Jesus! It wasn't possible. Howard Trench.

Gombricht paused theatrically. 'It is with great pleasure

I announce that Mr Howard Trench has accepted Mr Fulger's offer, and will be joining you here on Monday morning.'

I can remember almost nothing of the next couple of hours. Suzy cried, I do know that, and so did Ellen, and Meredith pounded down to her office and presented me with a bag of Rutland vanilla fudge. Fulger and Gombricht hung about for a bit, ingratiating themselves, but only Norman had the stomach for them just then. I overheard him attempting to explain to Bruno the wholesale distribution system, and some small refinements he was hoping to put in place. Bruno looked stony. If Norman didn't shut up, I didn't rate his life expectancy either.

The editors and publishers were kinder than I'd any reason to expect. I can be tricky sometimes at work, especially when I'm tired, and they might have been glad to see the back of me. But they rallied around, doing their best to cheer me up and expressing derision at the appointment of Trench. 'If you've got to be fired in life,' said Megan philosophically, 'there's at least some compensation in being replaced by a lesser man.'

'Shit happens,' said Spike. 'It's too bad.' And he punched me hard on the shoulder as a gesture of friendship.

'You'll be missed,' said Leonora. 'I really mean it. Even though you never saw the point of Yando.'

The only person who made no effort to say anything was Micky, who slipped away at the same time as Fulger.

'I suppose I should start packing my stuff,' I said to Suzy as the party began breaking up.

'No, I'll do all that. I've ordered you a taxi, it'll be here in a minute. You go home.'

'Thanks. I think I probably should.'

I took a long last look at my office – the glass desk, the leather sofa I never sat on – and gathered up the pictures of Cazzie along the bookshelf. I wondered how many hours I'd spent in that office in the last four years. Ten thousand? Well, it was all over in ten minutes.

I walked along the corridor in a kind of trance. Waiting by the lifts were a couple of junior sub-editors from *Smart Living*, who must have heard the news by now and tried not to look at me.

On the way down we stood in awkward silence, so I said, 'This is my last day. Isn't that great? Free at last.' But the words choked in my throat, and when the lift doors opened, they bolted.

The taxi must have taken me home, though I've no memory of it, nor of how long I sat by a window of my flat staring at the Thames. It had to have been a considerable time because when the entryphone buzzed, it was already dark.

I stumbled into the kitchen. 'Hello?'

'It's me, Suzy.'

'Er, sure, come on up.'

I opened the door to a pile of boxes and carrier bags. Suzy had her foot jammed against the doors of the lift, unloading the last of my stuff.

'It seemed best to clear it all now,' she said. 'We can't have Howard Trench contaminating your personal things.'

'Don't get into a habit of slagging him off,' I said. 'Not if you want to keep your job.'

'I'm resigning on Monday. I've decided.'

'I wouldn't. Wait 'til you find something first. You've got rent to pay.'

'But Kit, after that disgusting speech by Rudolph Gombricht announcing you'd resigned, how could I possibly stay? I can't work for people I don't respect.'

'For a few weeks you can, when you need the money.'

'What about you?' asked Suzy softly. We were sitting on the carpet in darkness, the river down below twinkling from the reflected lights of the bridge.

'Me? God only knows. I notice no mention was made of any severance package.'

'That's automatic though, isn't it? It's in your contract.'

'I suppose. I'll have to look it up. It was more of a letter than an actual contract. From Barney.'

'Anyway, you'll easily get another job.'

'Maybe. I'd like to take a bit of a break first before rushing into the next thing. A month, anyway. That's assuming the redundancy comes through.'

Suzy went into the kitchen and returned with a bottle of wine and two glasses.

'My advice to you,' she said, 'is spend the whole of this weekend in the park. Forget Bruno Fulger. Forget Barney. Forget all of them. They don't matter any more. Take Cazzie off to a funfair or somewhere. And tomorrow night I'm coming round to make you supper. Don't try and stop me. Because, as Barney would say, it's not negotiable.'

Just then the entryphone rang again.

'Who the hell's that at half past nine?'

It was a man's voice. 'Mr Preston?'

'Yes.'

'Sergeant Crow from Chelsea CID. I'd like to come up, please.'

I buzzed him in. A minute later he appeared in the flat, accompanied by two other officers.

'We were just having a glass of wine,' I said. 'This is Suzy Forbes who works with me.' Strictly speaking, it was *worked* with me now.

'Mr Preston,' said Crow. 'I must ask you to accompany me to the station. You are under arrest on suspicion of having murdered Anna Elizabeth Grant of 195E Harrington Gardens. You do not have to say anything, but it may harm your defence if you do not mention, when questioned, something which you later rely on in court. Anything you do say may be given in evidence.'

'Come off it,' I said. 'This is ridiculous. I'm the last person who'd have killed Anna.' The whole thing was so corny, it was beyond belief.

'I'm sorry, Mr Preston, but you are under arrest. If you don't come quietly I shall be obliged to handcuff you.'

'I'll come quietly.'

Suzy, protesting there was some mistake, tried to follow us into the lift but Sergeant Crow blocked her way.

'Listen, Suzy,' I shouted to her as the doors slid shut, 'don't worry about me. It's just another police fuck-up, that's all. I'll be home in an hour or two.'

'I'll wait for you,' Suzy called back. I liked that. It's what they all say, isn't it, criminals' molls? 'I'll wait for you.' Only they seldom do.

We drove across town with me wedged in the back seat between Crow and another policeman. At each set of traffic lights I half-expected to see someone I knew. Maybe I should have asked them to pull a blanket over my head, like they do on the television news.

When we arrived at the station I was wheeled into an interview room. A character called the custody officer played receptionist with the paperwork and informed me I was allowed to make one telephone call.

'Depends how long you think this'll take,' I said. 'I'm due to collect my daughter tomorrow morning, but I'd prefer not to ring my ex-wife from here unless I have to.'

'Couldn't say,' said the custody officer. 'Have you got a lawyer? Otherwise you have the right to be allocated one through legal aid.'

'She's called Joanne Pratchett. Her office is in Holborn. But I doubt she's there this late.'

'We'll get her a message. There'll be a referral number.'

Superintendent Barratt joined us in the interview room. There was no denying the balance of power had shifted somewhat since our last encounter. This time there was no mention of quiet, informal chats. Instead, he told me our conversation would be recorded – the room, he explained, was wired centrally for sound, to prevent anyone tampering with the tape. The implication was that I might otherwise lunge at the cassette, and destroy some crucial admission of guilt.

'Let me take you back to your relationship with Anna Grant,' he began. 'Last time we spoke, you first denied there was a physical dimension, but later admitted there was.'

'As I told you, we made love for the first and only time on the Saturday afternoon before she was murdered.'

'But you'd have liked to, wouldn't you, for a considerable period before that?'

'Have an affair with Anna, you mean? That's a difficult one. You see, it simply wasn't a factor. Looking back now, with hindsight, I guess the answer's yes. I regret we didn't make love years ago. There's a lot of things I regret, actually. I regret not marrying her. Then she wouldn't have been living on her own in that flat, and would probably still be alive.'

'What I was getting at, is the considerable sexual frustration you must have been experiencing.'

'Truly, there wasn't any. As I've explained, Anna and I were friends. Sexual attraction, while it was doubtless always present, wasn't the mainspring.'

'I have to tell you,' said Barratt, 'that we've been informed that you and Miss Grant had quite a tempestuous relationship. Violent.'

'How do you mean, violent?'

'When Anna Grant declined your sexual overtures, you became abusive, sometimes extending to actual physical violence.'

'I deny that categorically. It's simply untrue.'

'Let me sketch you a scenario,' said Barratt. 'Four years ago, at a polo contest, as I remember, you meet a very attractive young lady. She has aspirations to be a journalist, and you have the wherewithal to make it happen. So you fix her up with a nice job on a magazine, and no doubt she's very grateful to you. But the only problem is, you want the relationship to go beyond the strictly professional. You want Anna Grant as your girlfriend. And she doesn't go along with it.'

'This is balls. Total balls.'

'If you'll allow me to finish, Mr Preston. For almost four years you treat her to regular lunches, dinners, press your attentions. And this leaves Miss Grant in an awkward predicament. She feels obliged to accept the meals, but doesn't want it to go any further. Is this beginning to ring bells? Now all the time you're becoming progressively angry. It's understandable. You're the boss and this pretty young girl owes you her job. And it doesn't seem right, does it? She keeps leading you on and then rebuffing you. So you're frustrated. More than once it all boils over, and you give her a good hiding. Isn't that what used to happen, Mr Preston, you'd give her a good smack round the face?'

'That's outrageous. Did you make this up yourself, or is it someone else's invention?'

'Let's just leave it as a well-placed source. Obviously, I can't be more specific.'

'But it's a complete travesty.'

'All I can say is, our source is a good one.'

We went on like this for another hour, round and round, with Barratt citing his anonymous source and browbeating me about Anna. He didn't seem to have much to add in the way of evidence. His whole scenario depended on my supposed unrequited passion, which led eventually to my strangling her. The discovery of my semen in Anna's body, far from undermining his theory, actually endorsed it. Although Barratt didn't mention the word rape, I could tell it wasn't far from his mind. In his version of events, I was supposed to have gone round to the flat some time during Sunday, overpowered her, penetrated and then killed her.

At some point after midnight the interview was suspended until Saturday morning and I was transferred down to a cell to sleep.

Before they took me away, I asked Barratt when he thought this would all be over and I could go home.

His reply was not reassuring. 'We can detain you for sixteen hours under the Police and Criminal Evidence Act of 1982, but I expect we'll be requesting an extension.'

'What about my lawyer? Did you get hold of her?'

'I understand a message was left with her answering service, but so far she hasn't made contact.'

I think it was the moment when the cell door slammed shut behind me and I heard the bolt slide, that the full hopelessness of my predicament came home to me. Jailed for murder. That would be my epitaph. In the end, all our lives can be distilled into one glib label. Mine would be 'murderer'.

Shortly afterwards, a policeman came into the cell and took away my watch, tie and wallet, giving me a receipt in exchange. I lay down on the bench, covering my face with a thin grey blanket to shut out the overhead light. The blanket smelt of urine and stale sweat. Although I hadn't slept at full stretch since checking out of the Pierre in New York more than thirty hours earlier, and I was tired beyond belief, I couldn't drop off. Somewhere way above me, at street level, people were still pouring out of the Chelsea restaurants, laughing and slamming car doors.

I cried that night as I've never cried before. I cried for everything: for the loss of my job, for the way Barney had betrayed me, for the disintegration of my marriage and the prospect of losing Cazzie. I cried for the shame of being locked up in this cell under Lucan Place, and the sheer unfairness of it all. But most of all I cried for Anna. Because I loved her so much and I'd failed her. I hadn't protected her then, and I couldn't avenge her now. One thing Superintendent Barratt had said was true: I *had* encouraged her as a journalist. And I *had* egged her on to write more ambitiously and more dangerously. And now, thanks to me, she was dead.

And there wasn't one damn thing I could do about it.

# PART II

7 July – 15 July

# 17

It took Joanne Pratchett eleven hours to extricate me from that cell, and a further seven before they let me leave the police station. But just having her there, on my side, made all the difference.

'For heaven's sake, Kit,' she'd exclaimed when she'd finally been tracked down on Saturday morning. 'You're meant to be my one respectable client. I only took you on as a change from sweatshop bullies.'

I laughed, something I'd thought I might never do again. It was great to see Joanne. She wore jeans and a bomber jacket but there was no mistaking her gravitas when she locked horns with Barratt.

'Two options,' she said. 'You can either charge my client properly or let him go. And since it's perfectly clear to me you're not in a position to do the former, you'd better wind this charade up right now.'

I asked Joanne to ring Sally, and tell her I'd have to skip my visit to Cazzie. She must have done a great job because she'd managed to persuade Sally to give me a Sunday slot instead. I'd never have achieved that myself.

'You didn't mention ...'

'... you're a jailbird? No, I said your flat's been broken into, and I was a woman police officer.'

'Thanks, Joanne. And thanks too for fixing Sunday with Cazzie. Assuming I'm out by then.'

'Count on it. Even if it means dragging the Home Secretary from his bed.'

'By the way, there's something I should have mentioned earlier. I'm not with the magazines any more. I was fired last night. So you'll have to send your bill for all this direct to me.'

'Don't even think about it,' said Joanne. 'I'll lose it with the Fulger libel stuff. And I hope they gave you a mighty pay-off too.'

'Actually, it wasn't mentioned.'

Joanne rolled her eyes. 'You people,' she said. 'You're meant to be the fat cats. Even my Cypriot pieceworkers up in Kentish Town know their rights better than that. You'd better come and see me in my office first thing Monday.'

Barratt and Crow resumed their interrogation for three more hours, but with Joanne sitting in I felt less intimidated and less exasperated.

Their questioning again focused on my thwarted sexual ambitions leading to violence. They asked me about my other affairs since splitting with Sally and found it difficult to believe there hadn't been any.

'Are you really telling me,' said Superintendent Barratt, 'that a man of your age and health can forgo intercourse for weeks at a time?'

Joanne, who had hitherto sat in silence, broke in, 'Surely, Superintendent, you manage it yourself all the time.'

Barratt looked affronted. 'Actually, Miss Pratchett, I'm the married father of three young children.'

'My point exactly,' said Joanne dryly.

At some point during the interview Barratt told me they'd obtained a search warrant for my flat, and would I object if they let themselves in using my keys. 'The alternative is breaking down the front door,' he said.

At four o'clock in the afternoon, Barratt summoned us back to the interview room.

'It's all over,' Joanne said. 'You'll see. You're on your way out.'

Barratt and Crow were waiting.

'I'd like you to explain these,' said Barratt. 'We found them in your flat.'

Anna's spare set of keys. The ones I'd taken from Harrington Gardens.

'How do you mean, explain them?'

'How you came by them.'

'They're Anna's spare keys. I looked after them for her. I was her keyholder.'

Barratt looked sceptical. 'Doesn't really add up, does it? A keyholder who lives on the other side of the river?'

'As you well know, we were friends.'

'But convenient, you'll admit. To be able to come and go as you please. Makes things easy.'

'Don't you think,' said Joanne, 'the time has come for you guys to either put up or shut up? Question. Are you charging my client or aren't you?'

Barratt faced her evenly. 'For now,' he said, 'we won't be pressing charges.'

'Thank you,' said Joanne. 'So he's free to leave.'

'For the time being, yes, he's free to leave.'

'Thank you, Superintendent. Then perhaps you might tell Mr Preston where he can collect his personal effects. I'm sure he's anxious to head home now for a hot bath.'

The first thing I did when I arrived back at the flat was strip off all my clothes and dump them in a heap on the kitchen floor. Then I wandered naked towards the bathroom for a shower.

On the sofa, something moved. 'Who's that?' asked a yawning voice, and Suzy sat bolt upright wrapped in a duvet.

'Kit!' I don't know whether she was more surprised to see me naked, or see me at all.

'I've tunnelled out,' I said, dodging into the bathroom. 'Actually, they let me go.'

'I've been so worried,' Suzy called out as I turned on the taps. 'I stayed awake most of the night, waiting for you to come home. They wouldn't tell me anything at the police station when I rang. In fact, they were quite rude.'

'They were quite rude to me too,' I shouted, above the noise of the shower.

'Incredible. When you think we pay for them with our taxes.'

Ten minutes later, I slipped on a dressing gown and poured two large whiskies for myself and a glass of wine for Suzy.

'You know the police came round this afternoon?' she said. 'They turned the place upside-down. It took hours putting everything back. That's why I was having a little nap just now.'

'We need to talk through this whole thing,' I said. 'But not here in the flat. Somewhere outside.'

'You don't think we're being ...' Suzy mouthed the rest of the sentence.

'It's possible. Someone's certainly out to get me, that's obvious now. It's a precaution.'

I threw on some clothes and we strolled up to the deli near the corner with Battersea Park Road. We bought prosciutto and melon and tomatoes and ripe Camembert and a stick of French bread, and carried them into the park. It was six o'clock and the place was still packed with people enjoying the late afternoon sun. There were several cricket matches in progress, and American students playing softball and sinister old men flying radio-controlled model aeroplanes. In places the grass had been burned almost brown by the sun, or had been rubbed away altogether around the cricket stumps, exposing patches of acrid London dust. The whole scene, suffused with evening sunlight, was so tranquil and quintessentially English, it was hard to believe that only two hours earlier I'd been incarcerated for murder.

We found a quiet spot under the spreading branches of a lime tree, and laid out our picnic.

'You know the most frightening thing, Suzy. It's knowing someone's out to get you, and you don't know who it is. In the police station last night, someone had been feeding them really vicious stuff. I'm not joking. Someone's out to fix me up.'

'But who'd do that?'

'We always come back to the same people, don't we? Micky or Bruno. Or Micky *and* Bruno. They left together after my firing party. Maybe they're working in concert.'

'It doesn't really make sense though, does it? It's Micky that Bruno should be persecuting, not you. He's the editor who commissioned the article about Anastasia.'

'Maybe Micky's somehow shifted the blame. I think I told you he insisted on a private audience with Bruno when I was giving the royal tour.'

'But why go on and on? Bruno's had his revenge now. Anna Grant's been murdered and you've been sacked. Isn't that enough? Why bother to frame you too?'

'Finish me off good and proper, I suppose. Make sure I never work again. Even if the police don't charge me with murder, it's damaging enough to have been the prime suspect. I can easily imagine Gombricht letting every potential employer know I was hauled in several times for questioning and held overnight. It doesn't take much. Who wants to take a punt on a suspected murderer? There's plenty of other good people out there to choose from.

'Another thing,' I said. 'This line about me being violent with women. That's almost as damaging as murder these days. Think of all the jobs I could conceivably do. They'll all involve working with an office full of women. One telephone call is all it would take: "This is off the record, of course, but Kit Preston has a problem with women. If he can't fuck them, he hits them." Over and out.'

'Are Bruno and Gombricht really that vindictive?'

'I told you about Munich, didn't I? Nick Gruen's story about how they had Anastasia's boyfriend knocked off a pavement. I wouldn't put anything past them.'

Suzy was lying on her back on the grass, bathing her face in the sun's last weak rays.

'All these people,' she said. 'All the ones you put in the

magazines, who readers are meant to look up to and admire. Don't you find that, the more you get to know about them, the nastier they actually turn out to be in real life?'

'Not always. But often. I suppose it's just the shits that make most effort. To achieve anything at all, you have to be at least a bit single-minded, selfish, even.'

'But I thought you liked those sort of people. You're always having lunch or dinner with them. They're your friends.'

'With friends like these. You know the saying. You're quite right in a way,' I said. 'I do spend too much time with people I'm ambivalent about. But that's work. Or rather it *was*. I won't need to now. And they sure as hell won't want to see me, not without my job. And once Gombricht starts broadcasting the murder rap, I'm going to be the sparest man in town.'

'So what are you going to do about it?'

'Not a lot I *can* do. Ride it out. Hope there's someone out there who doesn't believe I'm a psychopath. Oh, Suzy,' I said. 'Right now I'm just so fucking tired, I don't know what I'm going to do. I can't think straight. Maybe I'll buy a cheap ticket to Goa and live in a hut for six months on Arambol beach. I used to daydream about doing that sometimes in the office. I worked it out: two pounds a day is all I'd need to live on.'

'Sorry, Kit, you'd be bored to death in a week. You'd be pacing up and down the beach.'

'And anyway, there's Cazzie. I can hardly commute between India and Clapham every weekend. Basically I'm stuffed. That's the truth. From the moment we published that article, it was all inexorably over. My own fault. Serves me right for messing with someone like Bruno Fulger. One talks grandly about the power of the press, but the press doesn't have any power. Some big exposé in the *Financial Times* could make a difference, I suppose. But not the journalism Anna wrote. The best it can do is change the way a few hundred thousand people regard a particular celebrity. But that doesn't last long. Only until the next article. How many people can remember now what Anna said about Bruno and Anastasia? And that was only two weeks ago. Nothing makes any difference. Bruno goes on exactly as before. Actually, I was forgetting, there *is* a difference: Bruno owns the magazines now so that's one irritation for him out of the way. And I'm unemployed, so that's another. And Anna's dead, so that's another. Bruno Fulger triumphs again. He must be laughing, him and Gombricht. They'll know I spent last night in jail. They're probably sitting right now in the Connaught Grill, celebrating. And shaking their heads at stupid, arrogant Kit Preston who had the temerity to take on the mighty Bruno Fulger. And who never had a hope.'

'If you've quite finished,' said Suzy, 'I hope you don't mind if I get a word in edgeways.'

'Sorry. I was on a roll.'

'Yes, you were. And self-pity doesn't suit you. Not your style. Now you're no longer my boss, I can say this. It won't do any good ranting against Bruno Fulger. If he had Anna murdered, prove it. That's the only way to clear your name. Find out how he did it.'

'That's easy enough to say. But how? All we do is go round in circles.'

'You can do it. Remember how we trailed Micky's boyfriend to see if his hand was in plaster.'

'We failed, that I do remember. His hand was inside his jacket pocket.'

'But we solved the mystery of the *Sunday Times* article about Anna. If we hadn't followed them, we'd never have discovered Micky was such close friends with Colin Burns.'

'It didn't prove anything.'

'For God's sake, don't be so negative, Kit. Think. There must be a pattern in all this. Bruno. Micky. The vilification of first Anna, then you. It's all connected.'

I lay on the grass with my eyes shut, saying nothing. In the distance we could hear the park police vans beginning their rounds, their tannoys announcing the park would soon be closing for the night.

'I'll tell you what I'll do,' I said. 'I'm going to spend tomorrow doing absolutely nothing except seeing Cazzie. Then, on Monday morning, I'm snapping out of this. No more self-pity. You're right, it doesn't suit me. And I'll devote one hundred per cent of my energy to clearing my name. I've got a date with Joanne at her office about my pay-off, but apart from that, it's a clear diary. One month, flat out. That's what I'll give it. My best crack. If I haven't made any progress by then, I'll think again. That's unless they've locked me up by then.'

It was with a renewed sense of purpose that we walked back through the dusk along Prince of Wales Drive. I'm always happiest when I have a proper plan.

Suzy hailed a taxi by the bridge and I watched it until it disappeared over the brow in the direction of the Embankment. I began to miss her even before she was out of sight.

Sally was in the back garden reading Sunday newspapers while Cazzie arranged her in-flight picnic set on the lawn.

'Daddy's here, Daddy's here,' sang Cazzie when she saw me. 'Come and sit down on this rug, Daddy, we're having a picnic.'

'Mmm, those look good,' I said. 'Are they jam tarts? Can I have one?'

'Don't be silly, Daddy. They're just pretendy. People can't *eat* them.' She sighed. 'Look, Mummy, he thought the Duplo was jam tarts, and wanted to eat them *all up*.'

Sally came over and kissed me on the cheek. 'I'm so sorry, Kit, about your job. I know how it mattered to you.'

'You heard already? Bad news always did travel fast.'

'It's in the papers. I just read it.'

I picked up *The Sunday Times* and saw a photograph of Howard Trench at the foot of the business section. He was posing in the lobby of Park Place, giving a thumbs-up sign in front of a display of our magazines. The item was headed, 'Trench replaces Preston in High-gloss Shake-out'. It continued: 'The febrile world of glossy magazines was rocked yesterday by the news that Howard Trench, 52, has succeeded Kit Preston, 39, as boss of Britain's most prestigious magazine publisher, whose titles include *Couture*, *Smart Living* and upper-class bible *In Society*.

'Marketing expert Trench, previously Managing Director of arch-rival Incorporated Publications, is understood to have been personally headhunted by incoming proprietor Bruno Fulger, the billionaire German industrialist who on Friday purchased the magazines from American plastics-to-valet-parking mogul Barney Weiss for $140 million.

'One media analyst commented, "Howard Trench's arrival at Park Place will re-energise their sales and marketing strategy, which has lagged behind Incorporated. Trench will bring a fresh approach and new thinking."

'Trench last night told *The Sunday Times*, "There is a lot of work to be done, but I am immensely looking forward to my new challenge. These are world-class brands, with enormous potential for bilateral marketing initiatives and brand extensions. I hope, within a matter of months, to be able to offer advertisers and readers alike a total integrated package of communications."

'Kit Preston,' the article concluded, 'is understood to have left the company to pursue his own interests.'

So, that was that: I had left to pursue my own interests. I hoped Bruno Fulger realised the principal interest I'd be pursuing from now on was him.

'Kit, when did this happen?' Sally's concern seemed genuine enough.

'Friday. Friday afternoon.'

'And you had no idea it was coming?'

'None. A new owner and then, a few hours later, I'm out.

'I probably should warn you,' I said, 'that I'm not sure what'll happen now about maintenance. I mean, I'll pay everything I can, but until I get a new job it might be difficult.'

Sally took my arm. 'I'm not thinking about that, Kit. I'm more worried now about *you*. Are you feeling terrible?'

'Funnily enough, not really. Not yet. Maybe I'm still in shock. Everything's happened so quickly.'

'Take some holiday. You need a break.'

'Everyone seems to want me to take a holiday.'

'Well, you should. Look, I hope you won't think this is too interfering, but there's a cottage in Hampshire you can use if you like. It's empty. If you ever want to get out of London, the key's under the stone by the back door. Here, put this in your pocket, I've written directions.'

'This isn't Paul's cottage, is it?'

'Not where he lives. It's a farm cottage, two miles from his house. One day he's going to rent it out, but it needs doing up first.'

I took the paper and slipped it inside my wallet. I didn't envisage becoming Paul's tenant in a hurry, but didn't feel like rebuffing Sally just then either. The argument on the telephone from New York was still too fresh.

'Does this mean you won't have to see all those grisly ragtrade people any more?' asked Sally.

'For a bit, anyway.'

'That's something.'

I've always thought half the reason Sally and I split up was the endless succession of business dinners we had to go to. Sally never really saw the point of them. She found them overlong and artificial, and would rather we'd stayed at home with Cazzie. In the end I think she could no longer distinguish between the tedium of the dinners and her husband who inflicted them on her.

'Drink?' said Sally.

'You're sure?' It was the first drink she'd offered since I walked out.

She reappeared with a lacquered bamboo bottle carrier, with special compartments for plastic jugs and glasses.

'Heavens,' I said, 'where on earth's that from?'

'Somewhere in the Far East. Rather flashy, I know, but fun for the garden.'

'Will this cottage you're lending me in Hampshire be full of amazing contraptions like that?'

'Don't tease me,' said Sally. 'It's just something to carry drinks about in. That's all.'

The sun came out from behind a tatter of London cloud, illuminating the backs of the houses and narrow strips of garden. Someone, I noticed, had recently mown Sally's lawn in perfect vertical stripes. The purple buddleia I'd planted six years ago, when she first became pregnant with Cazzie, had flourished and was alive with white, darting butterflies.

'This probably won't come as much of a surprise,' said Sally. 'But I'd like you to know first. Paul has asked me to marry him.'

'Sally, I'm so pleased. That's great news.' I walked over to her deckchair and kissed her. 'I hope you'll be very happy.'

Both of us, I think, felt rather awkward at that moment. Seven years ago, in a medieval church at Beaulieu near Sally's mother's house in the New Forest, we had made solemn and public vows to stick together until death did us part. And now, here I was, congratulating her on lining up my successor before our own marriage was officially dismantled.

'When?' I asked.

'When what? The date is partly up to you, depending how quickly the divorce goes through. If you mean "When did he ask me?", it was on Thursday. The day he got back from Hong Kong.'

'Has he given you a ring yet?'

Sally coloured. 'Yes, actually. In fact it's here.' She delved in her pocket and produced a giant blood-orange ruby, cut into a lozenge, in a setting of cultured pearls. To me it said just two things: expensive and ugly.

'Paul got it made in Singapore. He designed it himself.'

I wondered which of her two engagement rings Sally genuinely preferred. Maybe, first time round, she had been secretly hankering after something like this from the Lucky Plaza gem emporium. If so, then our marriage had been doomed from the start. I could see anyway that deep down we'd never had much in common. But how was I to know that then? Getting married had just seemed the obvious next step. We'd been going out for fifteen months, were the right age, and Sally was my first serious relationship with PWM: Potential Wife Material. Attractive but not tarty, stable, liked children, she was the kind of girl men do marry. If I hadn't asked soon, there were plenty of others who'd willingly have stepped into the vacuum. So I lined her up in a French restaurant with a track record for proposals, popped the question, and there we were: blissfully engaged, like all our friends.

'Does Cazzie know about all this?' I asked.

'No, you're the first. We haven't even told my mother. Kit, you may think this is an odd idea, and won't want to, but we wondered whether *you* might tell Cazzie. I've been thinking: it would make it less divisive, somehow, if it was her father who broke the news. It would show her we are both relaxed about it.'

I wasn't sure relaxed was a word that particularly applied to me just then, but I agreed to tell Cazzie and we went outside to transfer the child seat from Sally's car into mine. The BMW, I reflected, would have to be turned in soon. It wasn't my own, it belonged to the office.

We drove across the bridge to an Italian restaurant off the King's Road where they like children, and ordered spaghetti and breadsticks and Coca-Cola.

'Cazzie,' I said, choosing my moment carefully. 'Cazzie, you know Paul who's Mummy's friend?'

Cazzie stiffened and became suddenly grave. Despite my best efforts, she somehow sensed that what I was about to say was important.

'Do you like Paul?' I asked her.

She thought about it before replying. 'I do *like* him, yes,

Daddy. Usually he's nice but sometimes he gets cross. Frinstance, in the mornings, when I go downstairs to get in Mummy's bed, sometimes Paul's there already, and then Mummy says, "Go away, Cazzie, it's too early," and Paul says, "Yes, it's *too early*, go back to bed at once."'

'I see.'

'So then Paul said, you know that little television at home in the kitchen, the one Mummy watches when she's doing the ironing. Paul said, "Let's move that little television upstairs into Cazzie's bedroom." So now, in the mornings, I can turn it on *all by myself* and watch *Power Rangers* until the big hand on my clock points to twelve and the little hand points to eight. And then I'm allowed to go to Mummy and Paul's room.'

'What would you think, Cazzie, if Paul and Mummy got married?'

'But they *can't*.' Cazzie laughed. 'You and Mummy are married already.'

'You see, we're thinking of stopping being married, and then Mummy can get married to Paul.'

'But ... she *can't*. Because then *you* wouldn't be married to anyone. You'd be lonely.'

'I know, darling. But maybe one day I might get married again too.'

'Yes. To me, Daddy. One day we can get married.'

'I don't think so. People can't marry their own daughters.'

'I don't see why. Then you can come home and live in our house again. And we could live upstairs in my room, and Paul could live in Mummy's room. That's a good idea, isn't it?'

# 18

At six o'clock I got out of bed and made a pot of strong coffee. I'd lain awake for much of the night anyway, wrestling with my grand plan. Or, more accurately, wondering how to constuct one.

Some time around three or four o'clock I'd been seized with pessimism about my prospects of nailing the killer. Whatever my prejudices against Superintendent Barratt, he was methodical and backed up by a stack of officers and forensic pathologists. My own attempts at detective work had not, to date, been conspicuously successful. The stake-out at Micky's flat in Nottingham Street was inconclusive, and the detour to Schloss Fulgerstein resulted only in my being locked up.

With the dawn, however, came new resolve. I had promised Suzy to give it my best shot for a month, and she was right. Unless I could galvanise myself into action, and establish who really strangled Anna, I was in deep trouble. The way things were going, the police were either going to fix me up as the murderer, or leave the inquiry permanently unresolved. And from my position, the second option was hardly preferable to the first. If I didn't find the killer, I'd never work again.

And there was another spur too. I was angry. The knowledge that Anna's murderer – whoever he was – was walking free, made me furious. Who was thinking of Anna in all this? Who was going to avenge her? The one person who genuinely cared about Anna Grant, aside from her mother, was me, the prime suspect.

I've always been objective. I think even my detractors would allow me that. At Park Place, I wasn't one of those people who over-reacted to each new situation, which is rare in a magazine house. For twenty years I worked in an environment where every eventuality inhabits a narrow vortex between triumph and disaster. Each day was like conducting an orchestra in which only the deepest bass and shrillest high notes appeared on the score.

My objectivity extends to my own capabilities. I acknowledge my faults. Believe me, I know them. But I know my strengths too. I can solve problems: painstakingly, rigorously. That's what I'm trained to do. Tip a heap of conflicting data on to my desk, and I'll analyse it and draw conclusions, and present them in the Queen's English. When Dad was in the oil business and we were living on a compound in Sharjah, he showed me how to do it with a bunch of R&D reports from geologists and their Arab backers. I must have been about eleven at the time. Dad ploughed through the whole stack in an hour, marking the margins with a variety of coloured codes. Red meant exaggeration, blue implausible, yellow sceptical and so on. 'In every written report there's a hidden agenda, keeping you at arm's length from the truth,' Dad said. 'Locate and destroy. Then decide for yourself.'

I dragged a table into the centre of the room, swept it clear of everything, opened a notebook and marked down two names: Bruno Fulger and Micky Rice. Then I added a third: Erskine Greer. The suspects. I wrote:

BRUNO FULGER, 49. German industrialist, Fulger AG. Lives: Schloss Fulgerstein, Munich. Also Paris, St Moritz, Cap d'Antibes, Manhattan, Newport, Barbados. Parentage and background: father – Dietrich Fulger, steel and coal, Nazi sympathiser; mother – Renata, nothing known. Marital status: separated from wife of twelve years Anastasia, socialite, neurotic. Resources: substantial; private company, heavy industry, insurance, pharmaceuticals, publishing. Character: ruthless (NB. Nick Gruen story about textiles man in Como/ Gombricht's German journalist homily), considers himself untouchable (at least in Munich), adulterer – but impotent? (cf. Minnie Vass on Bruno's erections.)

Motive for killing Anna: hurt pride. Anna has exposed him to the world as uncouth in bed, frequenter of hookers, unwilling or incapable of sexually satisfying young beautiful wife, bullying tactics with lawyers, suggestion of perversion of justice through intimidation of witnesses. NB. Important not to underestimate significance of sense of personal esteem to super rich.

Opportunity for murder: in London Friday morning before murder (cf. photographed outside the Connaught on morning of publication of Anna's article). Checked out some time Sunday evening for St Moritz, having apparently spent whole weekend in London.

Likelihood of having committed murder himself: Feasible, but improbable. Rich enough to delegate ('He has all the money' – Anastasia).

Access to criminal elements: high. Rudolph Gombricht on site as middleman. Also security people from Fulgerstein. One of the men watching me in Battersea Park and outside my flat on day before murder *definitely* part of Fulger's retinue.

Completing Fulger, I decided to crack straight on with the other suspects. I wanted to evaluate and compare their motives and psychographic profiles.

MICKY RICE, 43. Ed.-in-chief, *In Society*. Lives: rent-controlled flat, Marylebone. Parentage and background: unknown (father rumoured to be smalltime 'fifties bandleader?). Marital status: single, homosexual. Resources: none apart from salary and expenses. Character: bright, jealous, untrustworthy, social climbing, possibly vindictive (instinctive buck-passing to subordinates).

Motive for killing Anna: jealousy of her reputation, star status etc. Anxiety she might replace him as next editor. Also, through hard-hitting Anastasia profile and publication of cover picture, Anna has screwed up Micky's access to rich Eurotrash. Hatred of Anna well established (cf. Carol White on

M feeding negative quotes to *Sunday Times*. 'Obsessed'). Opportunity for murder: lives in London, seldom leaves it. Of the three suspects could most credibly have dropped round to visit Anna without arousing suspicion.

Likelihood of having committed murder himself: possible, more so with accomplice. NB. If there'd been a second person on the scene, wouldn't police forensic officers have picked up on this? If so, then why still pursue *me*? Physical power: could Micky strangle Anna? (cf. Suzy's observation about mad people accessing enormous strength.)

Access to criminal elements: high. Homosexual underworld; wide exposure to marginalised groups, S&M, leather clubs etc. (NB. Was Micky one of my two assailants in the fight on the roof?)

## And finally:

ERSKINE GREER, 63. Tycoon. Chairman, CEO, Greer Corporation. Lives: Hong Kong, London (Hyde Park Gate), Bahamas (Nassau, Lyford Cay). Parentage and background: father – senior manager with Jardine Matheson Company, Hong Kong; mother – Elspeth, elder daughter of Assam tea planter. Marital status: single, active heterosexual. Resources: considerable; airline, shipping, hotels, financial services, Pacific Rim.

Character: charming, mercurial, womaniser (cf. Anna 'Probably most women would say yes to him anyway'), probably amoral. NB. The firing of Suzy's father at her christening, refusal to pay severance. Disquiet at 'sharp practices' inside Greer companies.

Motive for killing Anna: curtailment of profile about him, and publication of damaging (if historic) revelations about arms deals. Alternative possible theory: sexual encounter with Anna (unwilling on her part?) turns nasty, leading to accidental strangulation?

Opportunity for murder: definitely in London until after four p.m. Saturday. Also for much of following week (cf. Minnie Vass – saw him twice). After that, presumably flew off to watch polo in Palm Beach as planned.

Likelihood of having committed murder himself: unlikely unless during sexual encounter. Would contract out dirty work. Access to criminal elements: not known.

Once I'd set it all down, I reread the three résumés several times. Apart from Micky, whose public persona I knew all too well from the office, the others remained frustratingly opaque. All had a motive, the wherewithal and opportunity. Of the three, Bruno still struck me as the most likely, but I'd already mentioned him to Barratt without arousing much interest. And, to be honest, I had nothing to add since then.

What I needed was glaringly obvious: deeper background, and specific details of their respective movements that Sunday morning. Right now I knew next to nothing. The last I'd seen of Micky was Friday evening at celebration drinks in my office. I hadn't a clue where he'd been all weekend. With Bruno it was equally sketchy: a suite at the Connaught. As for Erskine, he could have spent the remainder of that Saturday and the whole of Sunday in Hyde Park Gate, or driven out to stay somewhere in the country. If his only alibi was the midget Filipino housekeeper, I wouldn't get anywhere.

At ten o'clock I hit the telephone, starting with the Tasiemka Archives in Golders Green, one of the few agencies that will fax through a stack of newspaper cuttings on account. I requested everything they had on Fulger, Rice and Greer, going back fifteen years.

Twenty minutes later the cover sheet started coming through. It read; 'Page 1 of 137'. They never let you down at Tasiemka. I watched as the first cutting fed out of the machine: 'Fulger heir to wed house model Anastasia', dated April 1983. Seeing Anastasia as a gamine nineteen-year-old posing in Christian Dior's atelier, gave me an idea. If Bruno had really arranged for her boyfriend – the textiles man – to be driven off a pavement in Milan, other people would surely know about it. They must have suspected Bruno of being behind it, otherwise it wouldn't have reached Nick Gruen. Maybe there was a widow. At the very least someone would have taken over the textiles business, and they'd be able to tell me something.

If I could somehow connect Bruno with the hit-and-run, it would take the heat off me with the police. Better still, it might be possible to discredit him publicly.

Nick Gruen was out of the office for the day, but his secretary agreed with ill grace to give me a contact number in Leipzig.

'Nick? It's Kit.'

'Don't tell me,' said Nick, 'you left too much money on the table when you stormed out, and want some back.'

'In fact, I need your help.'

'Let me guess: the telephone number of a good clap doctor. I told you Anna Grant was trouble.'

'Bugger off, Nick. You remember at lunch you said something about Anastasia Fulger's Italian lover, who Bruno Fulger had run off a pavement? Can you remember where you heard that? Also, any leads on who the bloke was?'

Nick sounded uncharacteristically furtive. 'Not a great time to talk, actually. I'm in a room full of people. We're brokering a joint venture between an old DDR paint factory and the private sector. Fulger AG, as it happens.'

'Answer without being specific, then.'

'Well, the first thing you mentioned, it's just common knowledge. Can't remember precisely who first told me. The second bit, the identity, I also can't help you with. Sorry. Probably best to speak to someone in Italian fashion. You of all people should be able to do that.'

'Thanks, anyway,' I said. But he was already off the line.

I put in a call to Loella Renouff-Jones at *Couture*, and felt awkward as the switchboard patched me through. I wondered whether the telephonists still remembered my voice after one day. I'd always rated the telephonists.

Loella's assistant said she was in a meeting, but five minutes later Loella herself rang back.

'Sorry I wasn't here when you called, Kit, but we were summoned upstairs for a pep-talk. Howard Trench has been lecturing us for almost an hour. He says there's nothing in *Couture* for his wife to wear.'

'Listen, Loella, you know everything about the Italian fashion business. I need you to find something out for me. Do you remember, some time last year, a big textiles manufacturer was killed by a hit-and-run driver in Milan? I need to know his name, and the name of his company. He lived in Como.'

'It does ring a slight bell,' said Loella. 'They were talking about it one lunchtime at Bice, during the collections. How urgent is this?'

'Very. But only if you can fit it in.'

'Trust me. You're at home? I'll ring you in an hour.

'By the way,' said Loella, 'what's this for? You're not moving into the fashion biz, are you?'

I laughed. 'That's how rumours start.'

'OK, be mysterious. Talk later.'

The remainder of the cuttings had spewed through by now, unravelling like a thick roll of kitchen towel across the floor. As I gathered them up, I noticed several photographs of Micky that were new to me, dressed from head to toe in chains and leather. The great thing about Tasiemka is that it clips *everything*. These had apparently appeared in a small publication called *Blowtorch*, which circulates in London's clubland. In one picture Micky was joined at the hip with a young, hairless Japanese boy. The caption said they were at 'The Ice House on Thursdays at Light Fantastic'. Micky, as editor of *In Society*, was evidently reckoned to be a minor celebrity. In the copy, it said he was a regular at the club.

It was in the fourth photograph that I recognised him. He was unmistakable: the bald head, sideburns and pencil moustache. The man from the swimming-pool shower was pictured standing next to Micky, his well-developed pectoral muscles and a thatch of underarm hair bursting from a sleeveless leather vest.

Underneath was a caption: '*In Society*'s Micky Rice with Jackson Chalk'.

I studied the picture for several minutes. The longer I looked, the more feasible it seemed that Jackson Chalk was the second man on the roof. The build was certainly similar. Perhaps I was too much influenced by the proximity of Micky and Jackson to an array of leather-wear. In the background of the picture, its clarity not enhanced by being faxed, were several young men dancing in leather masks and dog leashes.

The London telephone directory lists one hundred and eighteen Chalks. Fifteen bear the initial J. Of these, five were in when I called but weren't named Jackson. Nor had they heard of a Jackson Chalk. One was an answer-phone but was a woman. That left nine, and there didn't seem more I could achieve until they returned home after work.

Had any of them admitted to being Jackson Chalk, I'd planned on saying I was from the local council, updating the electoral roll of registered voters. In any case, my plan wasn't to talk to him. I wanted his address.

The problem with Micky and Jackson was puzzling out a motive for their return to Harrington Gardens two days after the murder. Supposing Micky, either on his own or with Jackson, had gone round to Anna's flat on Sunday morning and strangled her. It was easy to imagine him in a frenzy, convinced that with the circulation on the slide, his job was being touted around town. Losing it, he'd believe, would finish him not just socially, but sexually too. Those star-buggers in *Blowtorch* surely weren't enam-oured of Micky just for himself. And I could understand why, in his demented state, Anna might become the focus of his paranoia.

But having successfully dispatched her from the scene without detection, why risk everything by going back?

The two men had been clearing Anna's desk of papers. What was it that was so important that they'd return to the scene of the murder? Was it possible Anna was collecting information for some exposé on Micky? Unlikely. Nothing Micky got up to would surprise anyone very much, and anyway it wasn't Anna's style; she was no homophobe.

Another scenario suggested itself. Suppose Micky really was by then working in collusion with the Fulgers. Bruno or Gombricht could have rung him at home some time on Saturday, the day after the profile came out, frightened the shit out of him, and warned him something bad would happen if he didn't play along. Then Micky either helped Bruno's henchmen get into Harrington Gardens – Micky could easily have buzzed up on the entryphone – and left the dirty work to them – or even undertaken it himself. Gombricht, having first had my place done over to no avail, would quickly have realised the tapes of the Anastasia interview must still be inside Anna's flat. Without them, he couldn't sue me. So he'd have told Micky and Jackson to go fetch.

It was plausible. Though it still didn't explain why Anna's AppleMac was missing by the afternoon following her murder.

Whatever it was they'd taken from Harrington Gardens might still be retrievable. Not the interview tape: Gombricht would have locked that away in a safe somewhere. But the rest of the stuff in the black dustbin liners. It ought to have been destroyed, but something told me Micky hoarded everything; his desk at work was a repository of old memos and newspapers. If so, where would it be? His flat in Marylebone? Possible. Though Micky must realise he's a potential suspect, and he's not stupid. More likely they'd have dumped the bags in Jackson's place. Nobody, so far as Micky was aware, even knew of Jackson's existence in his life. It was only my chance sighting at the pool and the picture in *Blowtorch* that forged the connection.

There was no doubt about it: I needed to track down Jackson Chalk.

The telephone rang. It was Loella.

'Kit? I've got that information you wanted. The man's name was Alessandro Mazzelli. He ran a company called GTM – Gruppo Tessuto Mazzelli. Quite big, apparently. They manufacture some of the cloth for Ferre and Cerruti. Anyway, Alessandro was killed in November some time. A car drove up on to the pavement, hit him full force, and accelerated off. No one I spoke to knew why it happened. The police never arrested anyone. Could have been Mafia.'

'And the company? Who got that?'

'His daughter Maruccia. She worked with her father before. She's taken over. I've got a number for her if you need it.'

'Thanks, Loella.'

I dialled the number in Como and spoke to Maruccia Mazzelli's office. She was in Milan for the day and would be returning late that evening. I left my name and number but no message, and said I'd ring back tomorrow.

It was half past twelve and I was hungry. And after six hours of fax and telephone my head was spinning. I threw on some clothes and walked to a pub, the Prince Albert, on the corner of Parkgate Road, picking up a *Financial Times* en route. Above me was another cloudless blue sky and already the pavements felt hot underfoot. Along Hester Road, a young mother and her children were watering a windowbox outside their house. It felt strange to be walking about in weekend clothes on a Monday.

I was paying for my beer and sandwich when the name caught my eye on the daily front page digest of financial news. 'Greer Corp closer to Federated takeover. Page 12.'

The article inside said the Greer Corporation had 'reached agreement in principle' for taking a controlling position in £1.5 billion ($2.3 billion) Federated Aviation. 'We are confident of a sufficiently large number of stockholders accepting our revised offer of $7.10 a share to give us control,' a spokesman for Greer Aerospace was quoted as saying. The article concluded that it didn't expect the Greer Corporation to be unduly troubled by regulatory hurdles.

Only then did it dawn on me. The takeover of Federated. *Of course* Erskine Greer didn't want Anna's revelations about his arms dealing coming out in *Man Alive*, the timing would have been fatal. It could have scuppered the whole deal. Once it was known he'd sold rocket launchers to the Vietcong, there wasn't a cat in hell's chance of any American administration clearing him to buy Federated. There'd be editorials in the *New York Times*, demonstrations outside Federated's headquarters in Houston and at the Washington Monument. Questions asked by Congress. Federated Aviation might not exactly be the Ford Motor Company or Coca-Cola, but in its way it was as inherently American. Sell it to a Gook-lover? They'd be more likely to arraign him and then hit him with a multi-billion-dollar suit from the parents of dead servicemen.

For Erskine Greer this was the pivotal deal of his career, his chance to buy into the big craps game in the U S of A. He'd sewn up the Far East. And he was sixty-three. This was his opportunity to go global.

I could see it all now. Anna had somehow bamboozled Erskine into co-operating with an interview. She'd gone round to his house in Hyde Park Gate that Saturday morning and he'd been smitten by her. She'd flattered and coaxed him with her questions. He'd wanted to live up to the swashbuckling image she had concocted, didn't want to disappoint her. Then, right out of left field, she'd asked him about arms dealing. Direct question. 'Did you sell armaments to the Vietcong during the Vietnam war?' He should have denied it flat. And then had his lawyers send a gagging writ, threatening to injunct if there was any reference to the rumour in her piece. But, instead, his vanity took over. He tacitly admitted it. She had it on tape. Erskine Greer supplied rocket launchers to the Vietcong. It was a compromising enough confession in normal circumstances. But for a man who wanted to take over a quoted American company, it was dynamite.

Erskine's motive was at least as strong as Bruno's and Micky's. It might even be stronger. To proceed this far in an acquisition of this size, the Greer Corporation must have invested millions of dollars in discovery and lawyers' fees. It could all have been undone by the publication of that one admission. Within hours of *Man Alive* coming out, the quotes would have been wired around the world, picked up and amplified by the American, British and Hong Kong press.

The motive was clear enough. What I didn't know was anything about Erskine Greer's capability for murder. His companies, so far as I was aware, were respectable. Several of my more conventional contemporaries at university had ended up working for them in Hong Kong; there was a graduate entry scheme. Back at the flat, I read through the Greer cuttings from Tasiemka. There was a lot of stuff about the takeover, six years earlier, of the Inns of Happiness hotel chain from a group of Thai investors; none of it very enlightening. In 1982 the Greer Star line of container freighters had been among the first to establish permanent offices in both Shanghai and Taiwan. Earlier still, in the late 'seventies, his Trans-Asia Airways had beaten Cathay Pacific and British Caledonian to various hotly contested South-east Asian routes, prompting the *South China Morning Post* to comment on Greer's unprecedented level of lobbying. One item did catch my attention. In an otherwise bland business profile in the *Far Eastern Economic Review*, the journalist referred obliquely to gossip stories about Greer in the local Chinese-language press, without giving any clue to their nature.

I noted down the journalist's name – Bruce McFall – and rang international directory inquiries. I requested two numbers: the magazine and B. McFall, residential. Hong Kong is eight hours ahead of London; it would be ten p.m. there already, and I doubted the *Review* would still be open. If McFall was still working in Hong Kong, it was worth a shot trying him at home.

Three minutes later, I could hear a number ringing at an address in Deep Water Bay.

'Hello?' He sounded slurred, and Australian.

'Bruce McFall?'

'Who wants him? Friend or foe?' He bellowed with laughter.

'My name's Kit Preston. I'm ringing from London and am researching an article about Erskine Greer. I came across a piece by you in the cuts. I wondered if I could pump you for some background, off the record of course.'

'Believe me, mate,' said Bruce, dropping any pretence he might not be himself, 'you can quote me on the record, off the record or tattoo it across yer bloody arse. There's plenty on Greer, none of it printable on this island, that's for sure.'

'Really? Like what?'

Bruce suddenly became guarded. 'What did you say was the name of yer publication again?'

'Er, *Man Alive*. It's a British men's magazine.'

'I've seen it. Load of bloody cobblers. Do they pay well?'

'So so.'

'Maybe I can file you some crap myself some time. I assume you accept contributions from pissed old hacks.'

'Er, yes. Very much so. You were telling me about Erskine Greer,' I reminded him wearily. I wasn't optimistic about learning anything useful.

'Greer? Yeah, so I was. Well, what can I tell ya, mate, apart from his fondness for yellow pussy? Not that there's anything wrong with it. Good luck to him. Prefer mine white and tight, but they do say Chinese girls try harder.'

'Any particular girl he sees?' I expected him to name an expensive mistress, installed in some high-rise apartment in Midlevels.

'Used to be,' said Bruce. I could hear him down the line cracking a fresh beer. 'Whole line of them. I had all their names for that piece for the *Review*, but they wouldn't touch it. No one'll print anything lively about Greer out here. No jism. Apart from the Chinese papers, that is. They know all about him. All the paydirt.'

'What dirt?'

'Listen, mate,' said Bruce. 'You may have all night but I

haven't. Best thing to do if you want to write an exposé of Erskine Greer is get over here. Do some legwork. No use talking to guilos either, they don't know anything. Ask the Chinese. If you can find any that'll talk to you, that is.'

'Talk about what exactly?'

'Greer's other businesses. The ones you won't read about in the *Far Eastern Economic* bloody *Review*. Does that answer your question, mate?' And then he rang off.

Joanne's offices in High Holborn don't look like legal offices at all. Initially, when we hired her, this had disappointed me. I had expected Dickensian chambers with a mile of wood panelling and tin deed boxes. Instead I got plastic modular partitions and Scandinavian furniture. I told Joanne it looked more like a citizens' advice bureau than a leading firm of solicitors.

'I take that as a compliment,' Joanne had said. 'That's how our offices *should* look. We're into problem solving round here, not intimidation.'

Joanne was in her plastic sheep pen finishing an Emmenthal and tomato sandwich.

'Behold the old lag,' she said, leaping to her feet to greet me. 'Let's take a look at you. Yes, definitely rosier after a proper night's sleep. You know something, Kit, I don't think the slammer's really your style.'

'Tell that to Superintendent Barratt.'

'Don't worry, I have. In no uncertain terms. I'm not promising they won't rearrest you, but next time it'll be by the book, and I'll be right there holding your hand.'

'I've been thinking,' I said. 'Are you really allowed to represent me? I mean, you're retained by the magazines. Isn't there a conflict of interest?'

'I've thought of that too. And there is. But only with your severance. With the murder rap, it's not a problem. So if this is OK with you, I'll hand you over to one of my colleagues, Robert Ostler, to handle the pay-off. Don't worry, he's good. If I'm honest, he's the best.'

'That's fine by me. Thanks.'

'In practice, however, we can work on it together. So long as Bob's name goes on the letters and Bob makes the calls, there won't be a problem. After all, we don't yet know whether the new regime at Park Place will continue to retain us.'

Bob Ostler joined us in Joanne's office and copies were made of my original letter of employment from Barney Weiss. I had eventually located it in the kitchen drawer, tucked into a stack of guarantees for the cooker and fridge-freezer.

The letter was four lines long, typed on Barney's LoCo Inc. paper, confirming my job title, salary and one year's rolling contract either way.

'On the face of it,' said Bob, 'this is clear enough. The one advantage of brevity is it allows less leeway for semantics.'

I had instinctively liked Bob Ostler. Physically, he was reassuringly bovine in a grey chalkstripe suit, but his manner was light and mischievous. He was in his early forties, with a shock of prematurely grey hair, razored short around the ears.

'Our only potential hazard here is whether Fulger AG is honouring all prior contractual obligations. One assumes so. It's difficult to see how they could get out of them.'

'Will you write to Fulger for clarification?' I asked.

'Why write?' said Joanne. 'They invented the telephone. Let's use it.'

Bob dragged Joanne's conference phone across the desk and pressed for a line. The dialling tone broadcast around the room.

'Number?' he asked.

I spieled the familiar digits for Park Place.

'And the name of the man who's replaced you?'

'Howard Trench.'

'Please put me through to Howard Trench.'

I heard Suzy pick up the phone. 'Howard Trench's office.' From her tone, you knew she resented saying it.

'Can I please speak to Mr Trench? This is Robert Ostler from the solicitors Pratchett & Co.'

'Mr Trench is in a meeting, I'm afraid. Can I take a number and ask him to ring you back later?'

'I'm afraid not. This is a legal matter.'

'Just a minute. I'll see if I can put you through.'

Forty seconds later, an irritated-sounding Trench came on to the line. 'Good afternoon. I understand you have something so important to tell me that it can't wait. You should know this is my first day in a new challenge.'

'I'm perfectly aware of your new job, Mr Trench,' said Bob. 'That's why I'm acting with some urgency. You realise, of course, that technically you are breaking the law in being there at all. Our client, Mr Kit Preston, has yet to receive a formal letter of dismissal or any indication of his terms of severance. Legally he remains Managing Director.'

Trench was temporarily lost for words. 'I am informed,' he said at last, 'that Mr Preston's contract is a private matter between Kit Preston and Barney Weiss, from whom our company recently acquired the magazine properties. Mr Preston has at no time been an employee of Fulger AG.'

'Come off it, Mr Trench. You know that doesn't stack up and so do I. Mr Preston is entitled to a full year's severance and you can either honour it now or face legal action with concomitant costs and bad publicity.'

'As a matter of fact,' said Trench, 'it is your client who faces legal action. I understand he has been personally named in a serious defamation suit by Mr Fulger. Proceedings are already in train, and Mr Fulger has expressed no intention of letting the matter drop. Under the circumstances, any talk of large severance packages is misplaced.'

'I hear what you say,' said Bob, 'though we are both aware it's simple dissembling. Tell me, would you prefer to accept service of the writ at your office address, your home or have you a lawyer to accept it on your behalf?'

We listened as Trench gave the name and Broadgate address of Rudolph Gombricht.

'So,' said Joanne after Bob had rung off. 'They want to play hardball.' Her eyes were sparkling. 'Then we'll give them hardball.' She buzzed her secretary who entered with a pad, and Joanne dictated one of the stroppiest, most caustic missives I've ever heard. I can't remember whether it actually threatened Trench with jail, but it might have done.

'The only problem for you, Kit,' she said, 'is it looks like you won't get your money for a while. Can you wait?'

'I think so. For a bit, anyway.'

'Don't worry, this won't drag on, I promise you. Before long they'll be on their knees begging to be allowed to send you your cheque.'

Suzy rang me after work from a pay phone.

'It's me,' she hissed. I could hear traffic in the background.

'Where are you?'

'Dover Street. Can I come round? There's lots to tell you. And sorry about the callbox. We're banned from talking to you.'

She arrived by cab, glistening with indignation. 'You've no idea. I don't even know where to start.'

'Drink? Wine?'

'We've spent the entire day in meetings, being lectured. Everything's got to change. Meredith Carew-Jones was fired, by the way. She went at lunchtime.'

'Replaced by?'

'You won't believe it. That peculiar-looking woman from *Genteel Living*. Trench wants to take *Smart Living* downmarket.'

'I wonder why.'

'He says nobody's interested in Georgian houses any more. It's not relevant. He wants more jacuzzis for the advertising.'

'Anything else?' I felt peculiarly distanced from it all, as

302

though nothing Suzy might say would either surprise or dismay me very much. When it's over, it's over.

'*Couture*'s going to have six pages every month on clothes for fat women. And they're banned from using expensive supermodels unless the cosmetics company supplies them, like Tigra for Mouchette.'

'Quite a day.'

'You haven't even heard half. At lunchtime Ellen Durlacher was hauled in and told she was being made redundant. Guess who's replacing her?'

'Not a clue.'

'Pierre Roux.'

'Jesus.'

'He's being named "Group Executive Communications and Marketing Director". I had to type the press release. It was totally illiterate. I just left the mistakes in. Full of jargon about Pierre's important strategic contribution at Mouchette and how he was going to oversee a ...'

'Don't tell me, a "total integrated package of communications".'

Suzy looked amazed. 'How did you know that? It's meant to be embargoed until tomorrow morning.'

'Pure guesswork. Well, I'm sorry for Ellen. As for Roux, he and Trench deserve each other.'

'Anyway, the *pièce de résistance* came at four o'clock. Everyone was summoned down to the lobby, which is the only place big enough to fit the whole company. Howard Trench stood on the reception desk. He looked so serious, I thought he was about to announce an execution: we were going to be fired en masse. Even the mailroom boys looked nervous. Then Howard launched into this great speech about working towards the new millennium, all in gibberish, and no one understood a word. Finally he talked about you. By the way, did you ring Loella Renouff-Jones this morning?'

'Yes.'

'I thought so. Howard had ordered the telephonists to inform him if you rang into the building. Said they'd be fired if they didn't report it. So when you called Loella, they did. In his speech, Howard said nobody's allowed to make any contact with you. Not even socially. If they do, they're out.'

'Does that include you?'

'Especially me. I was given my own personal lecture. Not that I care. I'm not staying, even if he wanted to keep me, which I doubt. I'm looking about.'

'It's weird, isn't it? Why's he doing this?'

'Fulger's orders, I expect. Relayed by Gombricht. Who rang at least six times today, by the way.'

'And Micky? How's Micky Rice shaping up to the new regime?'

'Haven't seen him all day. Except at Howard's speech. He looked apprehensive.'

'Suzy,' I said, 'I'll tell you what would be helpful. Though I don't want to get you into trouble, so say no if this is difficult.'

'If I can, I'll try.'

'Just keep a sharp ear open for everything involving Fulger, Gombricht and Micky Rice. How close *are* they? Does Gombricht ever ring Micky direct? That sort of thing.'

'Easy. I can ask Delphine too.'

'Don't blow it. This has got to be totally subtle.'

'I hope,' said Suzy archly, 'you can delegate to me with confidence by now.'

After she'd gone I resumed ringing J. Chalks. Evenings proved more fruitful for response. Of the nine outstanding Chalks, six were now at home.

And the sixth one was Jackson.

He had a slight North Country accent and sounded unphased receiving a call from a clerk of the electoral roll.

He confirmed his name as Jackson Raymond Chalk and his address as 617A Finborough Road, SW10. He said he was pleased to be added to the register of voters, having

304

moved into this flat eighteen months ago and done nothing about it.

I decided to chance a supplementary question, and asked for his place of work, 'in case we ever need to contact you during office hours'.

He named a discount wine warehouse in Fulham Broadway. The place opened at ten a.m., he volunteered, and stayed open until nine every evening, Monday through Saturday.

Finborough Road was less than twenty minutes by car across the river. If anything of Anna's was stored in Jackson's flat, I'd find it tomorrow, while he was out at work.

# 19

Tuesday dawned to the drumming of raindrops against the bedroom window. I drew back the curtains. For the first time in two months the river below was choppy with steel-grey waves, and the sky overcast. The hot spell had broken.

The clock on my table showed ten to nine. Normally I'd have been at my desk for two hours already. I stretched out in bed and yawned. Getting fired did have its upside.

The telephone rang. It could only be Suzy with news of some fresh outrage.

But the voice was Italian, speaking heavily accented English: Maruccia Mazzelli.

'Kit Preston? I found a message you rang yesterday to Como.' She sounded uncertain.

I was fully awake now, sitting on the edge of the bed.

'Thanks for getting back. Listen, the reason I rang you, this could sound rather strange. But I might have information about who killed your father.'

I could hear Maruccia breathing hard at the other end. Her tension was palpable.

'This isn't a joke, is it? If it is, please tell me now.'

'It's no joke. Seriously. We need to talk, but not on the telephone. Can we meet in Milan?'

Maruccia sounded doubtful. 'It is eight months ago now since it happened. The pain for me was very great. I have tried to put all this behind me.'

'Maruccia, we haven't ever met but I promise you I won't upset you needlessly. This could be important. I can't explain now, but something similar happened to me. Another death. They could be connected.'

Maruccia was weighing my words, evaluating their sincerity.

'OK,' she said at last. 'But not in Milan. Tomorrow I will anyway be coming to London. Some meeting about business. That is at three o'clock in Great Titchfield Street. My flight arrives into Heathrow around one o'clock I think. Maybe we could meet for a few minutes, if you really ...'

'I'll meet you in the arrivals hall. At the barrier. I can drive you into London. Which airline are you flying?'

She said Alitalia and gave me a flight number.

'Terminal Two, then. I'll be there. *Ciao*.'

I took a hot shower and examined my neck in the bathroom mirror. The scar, now a fortnight old, was almost healed up. Afterwards, I went into the kitchen and began preparing a major fry-up: the full works. If I was ransacking Jackson's flat, I'd prefer to do it on a full stomach.

I was frying bacon when I thought of him, and cursed. Peter Grant. It was more than a week since I'd tried contacting him in Brazil. Between trips to Germany and America, it had slipped my mind.

It was a little after one o'clock here, which made it ten a.m. at River Mocó Lodge. Perfectly respectable, I reckoned, to ring a jungle camp.

The familiar clicking preceded the distant ringing tone.

'Mocó Lodge.'

'Can I please speak to Peter Grant?'

There was a long silence. 'Who is this speaking, please?'

'Kit Preston.'

'I'm sorry, I don't think I recognise the name. Are you one of Peter's family?' It was a male voice, distracted and shaken.

'No. A friend of his sister's from London.'

A further long silence. 'I thought maybe you were with his mother. Do you happen to know whether she's got our messages at all?'

'I'm sorry, I don't know about any messages.'

'We've been trying to contact her for two hours. Since they found Peter's body. But there's no answer from her flat. We've left messages on her machine.'

'What do you mean, "found Peter's body"? He's not dead, is he?'

The voice, so absorbed in the unfolding drama which to him already felt old, sounded almost surprised I didn't know.

'We're all in a state of shock here. They found him last night, ten miles upriver near the tented camp. News only reached the lodge this morning.'

'How did he die?'

'Snake bite. A fer-de-lance. At least he must have died quickly.'

I didn't know what to say. I know nothing about venomous snakes, and felt awkward at the idea of commiserating with a stranger about Anna's brother, whom I knew only vicariously. My thoughts flew to Bridget Grant. It didn't bear thinking about, that she'd lost both her children within the space of a month.

I heard myself asking, 'Would it help if I broke it to Mrs Grant? I think I know where to find her. She'll be at the school.' Even as I spoke, I was regretting it.

'If you're a friend of the family, sure, why not?' He sounded relieved at the chance to offload the responsibility.

'I expect she'll ring you herself later on.'

'Sure.' Then he said, 'He was a great guy, Pete. One of the heroes.' He sounded close to the edge. 'They're fetching his body down to the lodge this morning.'

Hamilton Hall, private school for the sons and daughters of the North London professional classes, occupies a gabled palazzo near the junction of Hamilton Terrace and St John's Wood Road. From the tiled hall, a stone staircase curls impressively through five floors to a stained-glass skylight. Strung across the stairwell was a web of iron netting, augmented by fiercely worded notices cautioning pupils to 'on *no account* climb up on to the banisters'. From somewhere above me I could hear someone practising the bassoon, and a classroom of children chanting in French.

I had made no appointment to see Bridget Grant. Somehow it had seemed simpler just to turn up.

Along a corridor I found an office with frosted-glass windows marked 'School Secretary'. A woman with her hair in a bun and a powdered face was working at an electric typewriter.

I asked for Bridget Grant and she consulted a timetable.

'Mrs Grant is teaching at the moment. Musical appreciation. But after that she has a free period. Will you wait?'

She showed me into a wood-panelled staff room and left me to pour myself a cup of coffee. A percolator stood on a refectory table, with a plate of biscuits and a tray of china mugs. There were sofas and armchairs in unmatching loose covers, and a noticeboard pinned with information about holiday projects and flat-shares.

In ten minutes a bell, followed by a pounding of feet on the stone staircase. Staff began appearing in the room, dumping text books and fetching coffee.

Bridget Grant entered the staff room carrying a carousel of slides. In her schoolday uniform of pleated skirt and loose tweed jacket, she looked composed and handsome; only a certain distance in her expression, a weariness about the eyes, hinted at recent tragedy. Watching her across the room I was struck by her resemblance to Anna: a particular grace of movement as she stooped to put down the slides, the neatness of her ankles.

'Mrs Grant.'

She looked up, startled. 'Kit?'

'Sorry just to appear like this. But I need to have a word with you. Is there somewhere private we can talk?'

'How about over there?' She indicated a bay window with Venetian entablature. 'Otherwise there are various Quiet Rooms down the corridor. They should be free at this time.'

We found a Quiet Room, recently vacated. Stackable

metal chairs were arranged in a semicircle, and on a blackboard someone had written 'All religions are equally valid. Discuss.' Underneath, in the same hand: 'I don't believe in Jesus ... I just believe in me – John Lennon (1940–80).'

We sat, one space apart, in the arc of chairs. 'Mrs Grant,' I began.

'Kit, do call me Bridget, won't you? We may be in a school, but I still can't be doing with it.'

'Bridget. I don't even know how to begin to break this to you.'

I told her about the telephone conversation, the snake bite, Peter's body being brought to Mocó Lodge.

She heard me out in silence, her face impassive, steeling herself against the finality of the news. Until I mentioned the removal of the body, I think she was still clinging to the hope that he might pull through, that there might be some serum or antidote.

Then, taking my hand, she began silently to weep.

'Tell me it isn't true, Kit,' she said. 'It can't happen twice, it *can't*. Peter was all I had left. Please tell me it hasn't happened. Why are you telling me this when it can't be true?'

A second bell sounded and a class of pupils, holding brightly coloured folders and box files, burst into the room. Finding us already there, they called, 'Sorry, Mrs Grant,' and backed out to wait noisily in the passage.

'Is there someone I can ring?' I asked. 'Someone you'd like me to get hold of?'

'No,' she said hopelessly. 'There isn't anyone now. Nobody's left. All my family is gone.'

'Would you like me to take you home, then? My car's right outside.'

She collected her bag and we drove together to Belsize Park, Bridget directing me through the back ways. The limited concentration this involved seemed to buck her. We reached the flat where I made tea and lit the gas fire. Then I rang the lodge in Brazil and watched over Bridget while she spoke with the project leader. For the duration of the telephone call she was magnificent. I listened as she asked crisply about death certificates and Brazilian formalities over the release and repatriation of corpses of foreign nationals. She made it clear that she would prefer Peter's body to be flown home, and buried alongside Anna.

Afterwards, she crumpled. She caved into the oatmeal depths of her armchair, the same chair where I had found her correcting schoolwork to Mozart the night Anna took me to meet her. For more than an hour her whole body shuddered in her misery. At first I felt my presence must be intrusive, but was uncomfortable at the idea of abandoning her alone to her grief. I didn't know what to do or say. In the tiny, old-fashioned fridge I found potted shrimps and an egg, and made her a snack. Astonishingly, she ate it.

'Kit,' she said, 'over there on top of the bookcase, there's a photograph album. Bring it to me, would you?'

The book looked new, with peel-back self-adhesive pages.

'I only finished at the weekend,' she said. 'Anna was really the spur. There were so many loose ones tucked away in drawers around the flat, I wanted to collect them all together.'

She began turning over pages, eyes barely focusing, lost in her own thoughts.

To lose a child; I needed only to think of Cazzie. For some reason I had a vision of her in the Italian restaurant, so grave across the pink tablecloth. Her worried little face telling me I'd be lonely. I had a sudden twinge of guilt that Sally and I hadn't worked harder at our marriage. When Cazzie was three, for reasons I still can't adequately explain, I simply withdrew myself. First emotionally, then physically. There was no great showdown. I just backed away, like a latecomer to a full elevator, shrugging nonchalantly. Now, in Bridget's flat, I felt remorse. Because in leaving Sally I had also left Cazzie. To have a living, breathing daughter, and by my own choice walk out on her. When Bridget, having diligently raised both her children herself, has them dashed from her; first one, then the other.

Anna had only once spoken of her childhood. We had stopped at a pub in the Gloucester Road after one of our rollerblading sessions, and were sitting at a wooden table outside on the pavement. I took the confidence, as I think it was intended, as an honour; a little piece of her private self, imparted to betoken some new level in our friendship.

Anna was always reticent about her life before magazines. She would refer warmly to her mother, but never in my hearing to her father or adolescence. Because she had never said otherwise, I'd assumed she grew up in Belsize Park. But that evening in the pub she told me about a maisonette in a crescent in Hove, where you could almost see the sea from the top-floor bedrooms, and her mother driving an old Austin Morris each morning to teach at a girls' boarding school on the cliffs. She had talked about the local High School for Girls in Hove, and as a fifteen-year-old travelling into Brighton by bus on a Saturday afternoon to hang about the pier and the antiques stalls of The Lanes.

'And where was your father in all this?' I asked.

'Nowhere,' she'd replied, quite airily but in a tone that discouraged further inquiry. 'Australia. Dead.'

'Look at this one of Peter,' Bridget said. 'He must have been about six. Such a shy boy then.' The photograph was of a small boy in a woollen balaclava, sitting in a mechanical car, the sort you put money in and it vibrates. He was peeping at the camera through a cat's cradle of fingers. 'At the time I thought it was Peter who'd taken Maurice's departure most badly. Maurice was their father. When he walked out, Peter wouldn't acknowledge it. He just never mentioned his name again. I ended up taking him to see a psychiatrist in London, we went several times. I couldn't tell you whether it was worthwhile.' Bridget spoke calmly and deliberately, though I didn't feel her words were particularly addressed to me. She was

312

speaking out loud to herself. 'Later, I wondered whether it wasn't Anna who'd taken it the hardest. At the time it didn't show. She hardly seemed to notice. She was such a pretty little girl, though a mother shouldn't really say that about her own daughter. Blonde hair in those days, look.' She showed me a picture of Anna standing in a church porch, wearing dungarees. 'She was four then. It didn't begin to turn dark until later.

'Four's a difficult age to lose a father,' she said, 'and I think it's worse when they walk out on the family, worse than dying in a car crash actually. You can't explain it to a child. Death you can: "Daddy died and went up to Heaven and lives with the angels." They can picture that. With Maurice, he more or less disappeared overnight. He'd met the girl at an hotel somewhere, Kent, I think. He travelled for a firm of publishers, was away on the road two or three nights a week. Didn't breathe a word about her, though it must have been going on for quite a long time. One evening he told me he wanted to move out. He'd already packed two big suitcases. A week later I received a letter, saying they'd left for Australia. That was the only time he referred to the other woman. Sandra, her name was. He promised to send money for the children, but he never did, not more than once or twice. That's when I took up teaching.'

'And you say it hit Anna harder than Peter?'

'In the long run, yes, I do think that. I'm sure she told you about the troubles of her teens. That must have been a reaction to having no father: her fascination with unreliable men. It was such a worrying time. I used to lie awake at night fretting. Such dreadful men. Horrible men, one after the other. She'd disappear, sometimes for days. Didn't telephone, I was desperate. I had no idea where she was, though I knew it was often London. We had such terrible arguments, we couldn't be in the same room for ten minutes. Nothing I said made any difference. She said she was eighteen and could do as she pleased. And then she became pregnant. I don't know why I'm telling you all this. I think part of me just feels so angry with her for dying, almost as angry as I felt then. She never told me who the father was. She was ten weeks pregnant before she even mentioned it. Peter had just gone up to Manchester University for his first term. I remember ringing him, quite desperate, and he drove down on his motorcycle overnight, all the way without stopping. That scared me too. Mercifully, Anna lost the baby. It happened naturally. And then she was ill for three months, which was a good thing really, though it didn't seem it at the time. She was so ill: we wondered if she'd even pull through. But it meant I could get her back home, and look after her, and it broke the spell. After that, it got better. Her whole personality changed. Dr Austin, our GP, said it was probably to do with coming so close to dying. It made her look at herself.'

'Was that when she started writing?'

'Around then. Though she had a job down here for a year first, helping at the theatre on the organisation side. She loved the actors. I don't need to tell you how Anna enjoyed well-known people. Peter used to tease her about that. He called her "Little Miss Guess-who-I-met-today?"'

'I think you once told me they didn't get on very well then?'

'They had so little in common, or thought they did. Peter was so sweetly serious, always ringing me to make sure I was all right. He had his whole life mapped out; he was set on being an accountant. He regarded Anna as trouble and irresponsible, was blind to her good side. It's funny, isn't it, how life turns out? In a way, they passed each other going in different directions. Peter's seriousness took a different turn, and he became absorbed in all his ecological things. Anna, who started out rejecting everything conventional, ended up knowing all those glamorous Establishment people you read about.'

'Anna certainly respected Peter, I do know that. She used to call him "my bearded brother in the jungle", but it was affectionate.'

'Peter became such a passionate person. That's what I mean about it being funny how life turns out. You can't tell. At school, he wouldn't say boo to a goose. Never questioned anything. Never went through a tricky phase. I can say, as a teacher, he must have been rather a frustrating pupil: you want a bit of healthy scepticism in the classroom. Anyway he sailed through economics at Manchester. Always found himself jobs in accountancy firms for the long vacation. He had a very sweet girlfriend, a nurse called Kirsty, whom he met in Manchester, whom I hoped he'd end up marrying. Sorry, I don't know why I'm rambling on like this. But then he threw it all in. He became interested in green politics, and that was that. It worried me at first, throwing up a good career, but he was so determined there was no stopping him.'

'Did Peter work for one particular group?'

'They call themselves AF: Action First. There's an office in Kennington, near the Oval cricket ground. That's where they do their fundraising. Peter worked for them all over the place: first up in Greenland, keeping a watch on Japanese whaling boats. Then with the Kurds out in Turkey, researching a paper on genocide and germ warfare: so tragic all that. And for this last year in South America, where they've got a project going to do with the rainforests.'

'You must have missed him, being so much abroad.'

Bridget smiled bleakly, her eyes rimmed with tears. 'He was very good about keeping in touch. Wherever he was, he'd always telephone if he could. Anna was the same. They were thoughtful children like that. And since Anna ... since Anna was killed, Peter's rung me twice a week, like clockwork.' She started to break down. 'I'm going to miss those calls, Kit. They kept me going. They were something to look forward to.'

'I'm so sorry,' I said again, emptily, hopelessly. 'It's so terrible all this, I'm just so sorry.'

'Leave me now,' she said. 'Go on, I mean it. There's no more you can do. You've been very kind and I'm grateful, but I'd sooner be alone now. Don't worry,' she said, patting my hand, 'I've become accustomed to tragedy, I've seen so much. I'm not inured to it, you never are that, but I know how to cope. The Grants are resilient, you know.'

'I do know.' I had a sudden vision of Anna, her head cloudy with flu and running a high temperature, pounding away at her typewriter against a deadline. 'I've known that for a long, long time.'

I drove back across London to Fulham Broadway and cruised about until I located the discount wine warehouse: Benjy's Bin-ends. There was a blackboard on the pavement advertising Liebfraumilch and Becks at rockbottom prices, and windows plastered with special offers. I had to drive past three times before I spotted Jackson Chalk behind the counter.

Reassured he wasn't at home, I headed for Finborough Road and parked a safe distance from number 617. Finborough Road is among the longest residential streets in London, and one of the most anonymous, running from Gunter Grove in Chelsea all the way up to Earls Court; a mile of grimy brick houses converted into flats, hotels and student hostels. It is also a main thoroughfare for lorries cutting north on to the Cromwell Road, and as I walked towards the flat with my bag of tricks I was buffeted by tailwinds.

617A turned out to be the basement. There was a wonky iron gate at street level and then steep steps down to the front door. I walked confidently down to a concrete area, shielded from the street. There were flowerpots on a windowsill, full of dry earth and dead ferns, and, piled outside the door, damp cardboard boxes.

For a couple of minutes I stood motionless. I was listening, above the traffic, for a sound of approaching footsteps. I could hear nothing. Moving to the window, I tried to raise the bottom sash, but it wouldn't budge. Inside, I could see a bedroom with an unmade futon. The window was bolted top and bottom, and painted over where it joined the sill. Evidently Jackson Chalk never opened it.

The front door seemed a better bet. It looked flimsy, with a rose-shaped pane set into a panel. I tapped close to the lock and it felt hollow: a couple of sheets of plywood packed with sawdust and foam.

Into a leather rucksack, I'd stuffed a pair of gloves and various tools from the flat, including a serious screwdriver. This I inserted into the jamb, close to the lock, and wrenched it back, hearing the wood splinter against the flat edge of the metal. After ten minutes of levering, I'd gouged deep enough into the wood to partially uncover the latch. From my wallet I extracted a slim plastic Telecom card, which I slipped inside the enlarged crack. It was surprisingly easy to do. I had no idea how simple it is to break into a strange house, or how little it would trouble me, ethically. I ran the card up and down the jamb, until it retracted the latch. A moment later, the door swung open.

Jackson's flat consisted of three rooms and a wide central corridor which also functioned as a kitchen. As well as the bedroom, which overlooked the area steps, there was a dark, barred sitting-room with views across Brompton Cemetery, and a small bathroom. In the passageway stood an oven, an old Benelux fridge and a metal sink filled with cold water, bacon rind and dirty crockery. The flat's compactness was an advantage: I didn't imagine there'd be that many places to hide Anna's stuff.

I began in the bedroom. The futon was covered by a heap of blankets and black sheets, which gave off a slight smell of damp and armpits. A half-full glass of water and a pile of magazines lay on the floor next to it. Around the walls were several large pieces of 'fifties furniture in light-coloured wood: dressing table, wardrobe and armchair. I think the style in question is Festival of Britain. This was overwhelmed, however, by an array of kitsch memorabilia on the dressing table and along the mantelpiece: china statuettes of the Madonna and Child, Highland terriers, commemorative mugs for the Duke and Duchess of York's wedding, porcelain girls on swings, crooning piccaninnies, devotional figurines and souvenirs of Blackpool and Ayr. There must have been eighty pieces, covering every surface.

I rummaged through the drawers and wardrobe but found nothing of Anna's, just piles of folded clothes. My hopes rose with the discovery of a leather trunk on top of the wardrobe, but it contained only pornography and dildoes.

The bathroom and kitchen-corridor took no time. The oven was empty and the bathroom cupboard packed with junk, none recognisably Anna's. That left the sitting-room. So far I had spent six minutes in the flat, and I wanted to be out in less than ten.

The sitting-room, as elsewhere, was decorated with thrift-shop furniture, but here were strong paintings too: a large canvas by Duggie Fields of an amputee sailor, and two framed posters by Gilbert and George. There was a chest of drawers full of papers, a desk and a teak music centre with a pile of records, predominantly South American salsa.

If Anna's tapes and research were anywhere, I guessed they'd be here in this room.

I began at the chest of drawers, frisking through piles of papers. Most were to do with Jackson's job at the warehouse; he was clearly serious about wine, there were catalogues and invitations to tastings. There were handbills for London clubs, and consecutive backnumbers of *In Society*. If these were an indication of the longevity of his relationship with Micky, they'd been together since last November. Near the bottom of the second drawer were the deeds to the Finborough Road flat and a framed photograph of two old people standing on the banks of a canal, presumably Jackson's parents. In the bottom drawer, stuffed into a buff envelope, I found more photographs. I recognised Micky at once: lounging on

Jackson's futon, stark naked apart from a mink stole thrown around his bony shoulders. Next to him, wearing only a leather posing pouch, was Colin Burns. No wonder he'd allowed his newspaper to promote Micky's line on Anna. There were other pictures too: Micky in a bath, Micky dancing naked in Jackson's sitting-room, his face partly obscured by a leather mask.

I studied the mask carefully. It looked similar to the masks on Anna's roof, though this one only covered his eyes and forehead.

But it was at the desk that I struck lucky. Jackson had a wooden letter-tidy, shaped like a toast rack, in which he filed unsubmitted cheques and unpaid bills. In the middle slot I found a cheque from Micky Rice. It was made out to Jackson for four thousand pounds.

Now why on earth would Micky need to give him that much money? It could have been a loan, of course. There were any number of explanations. One in particular suggested itself. If Micky had been paid by Bruno and Gombricht to go over Anna's flat, this could be Jackson's share of the bounty.

When I'd entered the basement, I'd pulled the front door to behind me, so that it remained fractionally ajar but from the street would give the impression of being closed. Now, to my horror, I heard someone calling.

'Excuse me?' It was a man's voice. 'Excuse me? Anyone there?'

It could be Jackson. Maybe his shift had finished early. I was frozen to the spot, my heart racing. The sitting-room windows, which gave on to the cemetery, were barred by security gates. Why the hell hadn't I found the key, and opened them up when I first arrived?

'Excuse me? Is anyone at home?'

Surely Jackson wouldn't ask that. I decided to chance it.

'Hello. Who is that?' I shouted down the corridor. So long as they didn't see my face.

'Postman,' the voice called back. 'Did you realise you've left your front door open?'

'Sorry,' I shouted back. 'Shut it for me, will you?'

I heard him pull the door but fail to close it. It was dragging on the carpet. In forcing the lock, I must have skewed the hinges too. Any moment now the postman would see it had been forced. I heard him try again, grabbing the door by the knocker and wrenching it hard. This time it slammed shut. Then I heard him push a pile of post through the letterbox, which clattered on to the mat.

I waited five minutes, giving him time to work his way down the street.

Then I scraped open the door again, slipped outside, slammed it behind me and edged up the area steps.

There was no sign of anyone. I crossed the road between slow-moving traffic and walked along Finborough Road on the opposite side from my car.

Only when I was convinced I wasn't being observed did I recross the street and head for home.

I arrived to find a little pile of post on my own doormat too. There was a note from Bob Ostler at Pratchett & Co., formally confirming his status as my solicitor for the unfair dismissal suit and copying me on a suitably terse opening letter to Rudolph Gombricht. The rest of the post looked less official, being hand-addressed, so I ran a hot bath and saved it to read in that. I was keen to soak away the stench of Jackson's flat.

There were three letters. The first, postmarked Uppingham, was from Meredith Carew-Jones. It said,

My dear Kit,

No doubt you've heard about my reversal of fortune by now. It didn't take the new broom five minutes to sweep out an old cobweb like me. Buster's over the moon, of course, anticipating game pie for lunch midweek at last. Can't pretend I'm too heartbroken myself. My God, your successor's an unsavoury-looking fellow. Reminds me of a butler who used to work for an aunt of mine up in Shropshire. Fearsomely efficient, but used to creep past the bedroom doors at night hoping to catch a glimpse of someone getting changed – man *or* woman. Well, *que sera sera*. It was fun working for you, I did want to say that. Never could understand how you could bear to do the job you did. Ghastly! So no doubt you're only too pleased to be shot of it. If you're ever up in this neck of the woods, we're eight miles south of Oakham.

Best wishes. Meredith.

The second letter came from an address I didn't recognise in Kensington. But I knew the handwriting: Ellen's. Aside from the humiliation of being replaced by Pierre Roux, Ellen sounded OK. She asked for a reference, and said she was thinking of doing PR for either George Soros, the financier, or Euro-Style TV, the cable channel. If I knew Ellen, she'd have a new job inside a month.

The final letter was from Suzy. Her writing on the envelope was unmistakable. I noticed, however, there was no stamp; it must have been biked round.

Inside was a typewritten letter from Trench. I read,

Dear Kit Preston,

Since you are no longer employed by this organisation, I must require you to return your company BMW, three series, four door, navy blue which as you are aware is now the property of Fulger AG, following our purchase of the Weiss Magazine Company Limited. Could I therefore ask you to return the car at your earliest convenience, anyway within the next twenty-four hours, to our registered offices at 32 Park Place, W1. The car keys, and any spare sets in your possession, should be remitted to the lobby receptionist.

Yours faithfully,
Howard Trench.

Thanks, Howard, I thought. I particularly liked the touch about returning the car at my earliest convenience, so long as it was within twenty-four hours. Inside the flap of the envelope Suzy had scrawled, 'Sorry about this, Kit. He insisted.'

At that moment there was only one thing in the world I was quite certain about: that this time tomorrow my car would be anywhere but Park Place.

# 20

Wilson Bramble, Chief Executive of AF: Action First, occupied a modest second-floor office in a converted rectory on Kennington Park Road. AF, it transpired, had colonised the whole of the second floor, while the first and ground floors were given over to separate, but compatible, community projects and pressure groups. In the tiled Victorian entrance hall, an enlarged colour photograph of Peter Grant had been erected on an easel with the dates '1961–96' stencilled underneath. Peter was standing next to a jeep on a mountain pass. I guessed it had been taken in Eastern Turkey, near the border with Iraq.

When I visited Wilson that Wednesday morning, I explained that I was an old friend of the Grant family who had broken the tragic news to Peter's mother on behalf of AF.

He thanked me and poured coffee. He was a professional administrator of environmental charities in his mid-forties with a thin, intelligent face, somewhat malnourished, and deeply sunken eyes. But I was impressed by his sense of energy. He'd been at AF, he said, for almost a year; before that, he'd done a similar, though less plural, job as community liaison for Friends of the Earth, protecting heathland and mud flats against fringe development, 'or anyway trying to'.

'How well did you know Peter?' I asked.

'Scarcely at all, regrettably, though there are several others in the group here who did know him. He was a very popular guy. People here are really shaken, the whole office. You just don't expect something like this.'

'Do we know exactly what happened yet?'

'Only what our people at the lodge have told us. It's hearsay really. Peter was up at the jungle camp – a small research facility we've established ten miles upriver. He was found about a mile from there on the jungle path. One of our Indian guides discovered him. He'd been expected back at camp the previous evening, but hadn't shown up. Our other researcher on the spot, a Dutchman, decided to wait until morning to search for him; completely correctly, by the way, you can't see ten yards ahead in the jungle at night. The Indian found him at first light, but by then Peter had been dead for several hours.'

'And it was definitely a snake bite?'

'Oh yes, no doubt about that. Fer-de-lance is unmistakable. Rather gruesome, but instantaneous.'

'Presumably he stepped on it by accident, in the dark.'

'That was our initial assumption, but apparently not. The bite was on his hand.' Wilson looked troubled. 'Forgive me, but how much do you know about the fer-de-lance?'

'Practically nothing, to be truthful.'

'Then let me explain. They rank among the most poisonous snakes anywhere. Eight feet long when full-grown, though equally deadly at half the size, diamond-patterned back, a species of nocturnal pit viper. Known locally as the "tres minutos": three minutes. That's how long it takes for the venom to take effect. You find them across most of South America, all the way from Belize and Guatemala to the Amazon.'

'And they kill a lot of people every year?'

'So I'm told. Indians mostly, which is why you don't read about it in the British newspapers. If you're interested, I'll ask Jim Herman to pop in and join us. He's been out to Manaus and knows everything there is to know about snakes, tarantulas, you name it. Jim and Peter were good friends, incidentally. Excuse me a moment, I'll go and find him.'

Wilson left me in his office and I drank my coffee and absorbed the surroundings. One wall was taken up by bookshelves crammed with leaflets and boxes of AF badges; the other with posters confronting the erosion of the rainforests and the Yanamami Indians. He returned with Jim, a handsome activist in his early thirties in jeans.

We exchanged condolences about Peter, and Jim poured more coffee.

'Wilson says you're interested in the tres minutos,' he said. 'The fer-de-lance, that is.'

'I'm just astonished it can kill a human so quickly.'

'Three minutes is all you get, four maximum. That's no exaggeration. When Peter and I were at the lodge we used to collect horror stories about it. All the guides had their own: a friend of their sister who found one down her bed, that kind of thing. Or they swam up a toilet. You could scare yourself thinking about it. But at least it made you careful. That's why I'm quite surprised Peter disturbed one after dark, he knew the dangers.'

'Couldn't you carry some antidote with you?'

'For the fer-de-lance? There isn't one. Listen, let me tell you a story that demonstrates how lethal this venom is. We heard this one from an Indian boatman, Peter and I, and it really gave us the creeps. The guy swears it's true too. Well, a friend of his from his village was cutting wood in the forest, when a fer-de-lance shot out of the undergrowth and bit him on the thumb. The thing about this snake is its two retractable fangs, both very long, which sink into you, and the Indian knew he was done for if he didn't act fast. So he picked up his machete and lopped off his own thumb, and raced back to the village to have the stump bound up. Amazingly, it worked. The venom didn't get into the bloodstream and the Indian was saved. Now, here comes the revolting bit. Two weeks later, with his hand still bandaged up, the Indian went back to the same bit of forest to collect more firewood. On the ground he spotted this big brown fungus thing, like a toadstool, except it wasn't a toadstool, it had a thumbnail on the end. It was his thumb, infused with venom and blown up to the size of a fist. He was pretty sickened but

325

also intrigued. So he picked up a stick, knelt down and prodded it. Immediately the thumb exploded, spattering his face and eyes with poison. Within three minutes he was dead.'

'Jesus.'

'I know. It's a vile story. I can tell you, we didn't wander round the campsite in bare feet after that.' Jim laughed. 'Peter used to joke that we were saving the rainforest as the historic habitat of the fer-de-lance. Save the fer-de-lance. Hasn't got quite the same ring as the panda or rhino, has it?'

'By the way, what exactly is it AF are doing in the rainforest?'

'I'll answer that one, if you like,' said Wilson. 'It's quite complex. We have set ourselves a number of specific goals, some short-term, others long-term. In no particular order: an end to deforestation, demarcation of tribal lands, affirmative action against dam-building in certain areas, influencing public opinion against mineral exploitation and the removal of scarce indigenous plants and herbs, violation of nomadic tribes. As Peter would have told you, there's a hundred years of work to be done and a decade at the outside in which to do it. After that, it'll be too late.'

'And Peter's particular role in all this?'

'He was working on various related projects to do with tribal lands and rights. You have to understand that even in this relatively remote part of the country, there's encroachment by outside agencies. Peter's job was to limit this as far as possible and, where the national government has made concessions for development, ensure the terms of the contract aren't overstepped. That's so often the problem with so-called strategic development: how to monitor it. A company gets permission to do a certain job, but they exceed it. They're thousands of miles into the jungle, and who's to know?'

'What sort of companies are moving in?'

'Right across the spectrum. Mineral extractors, logging,

of course, Jim would know the details better than me. Who else is out there, Jim?'

'Let's just say that if you take a stroll down Main Street Manaus, you'll see the nameplates of half the multinationals. They're all there in one guise or another. Energy companies, timber, rubber. Increasingly, the pharmaceutical and cosmetics companies are showing an interest in native medicine from jungle plants and flowers.'

'That sounds positive,' I said. 'I'm rather in favour of natural remedies rather than endless chemicals.'

'You're right in one way,' said Jim. 'The longer I spend with the native population, the more impressed I am by their knowledge. But in another way it's terribly destructive. With some of these plants, it simply isn't sustainable. Once they use them in full production, they can strip the forest bare in a few years.'

'This may seem an odd question,' I said, 'but could Peter have had any enemies in the area? I mean, is it possible his death wasn't an accident?'

Wilson and Jim exchanged glances. 'Do you have a particular reason for asking that?' said Wilson noncommittally.

'Nothing concrete. It's just that Peter's sister, Anna, was murdered a month ago. It crossed my mind she could have told him something before she died, or vice versa, and the two deaths are somehow connected.'

Wilson chose his words carefully.

'I confess,' he said, 'that when we first heard about it, there were some aspects of Peter's death that surprised us. You heard Jim say how conscious Peter was about the dangers of the fer-de-lance. Why, then, was he apparently walking alone in the jungle at night? He never did that. None of our people do that. Secondly, it was surprising the snake bite was to his hand. One would have expected it on the ankle. The fer-de-lance will coil and spring, but not generally high into the air. Which suggests Peter was stooping or reaching towards it, a highly risky thing to do. But in answer to your question "Did Peter have any enemies?", my response is a definite "no". None that we've heard about anyway. And no enemies inside AF either. As I've told you, he was a popular guy. Very well liked. No rivalries we know about, and I think we *would* have known: Mocó Lodge has a total headcount of fewer than twenty people, six overseas aid workers and a dozen or so Brazilians.'

'So you've concluded it was an accident?'

Wilson looked at me steadily. 'That *is* what we've concluded, yes. But I'd be misleading you if I said we felt absolutely secure in that conclusion. There was – how shall I put this? – an uncomfortable element of doubt. Having said that, we've got no evidence it was anything but an accident. And what more can we do? What's to be gained, particularly in an organisation like this one dependent upon charitable donations, by speculation? Peter's dead. The staff are devastated. What I need to do here now is allow a decent period of grieving and then remotivate the team. We need to move on. Peter would be the first to see that. We don't have infinite time. That's the difference between Action First and a normal business. The clock's ticking away. In twenty years there'll be no need for an organisation like ours. Either we'll have achieved our aims, or else it'll be too late.'

Maruccia Mazzelli was the first off the plane through customs. I was waiting behind the barrier like a chauffeur, holding a cardboard sign: MAZZELLI. But it wasn't necessary. As soon as I saw her, I knew it was Maruccia. She looked thirty-five, with shiny conker-brown hair held back from her face by a velvet hairband, a well-cut acid-green suit and contemporary costume jewellery. She was conspicuously Italian and defiantly attractive.

'Maruccia?'

'Kit Preston?' She looked apprehensive. I think she'd half-hoped I wouldn't show.

She followed me into the multi-storey car park and we circled the ramps in the BMW down to the barrier. Only when we'd cleared the airport tunnel and hit the M4 into London did I broach the subject.

'Thanks for agreeing to meet me,' I said. 'It may turn out to be nothing, but I needed to talk to you.'

Maruccia frowned. 'Since we spoke yesterday on the telephone, so many feelings have come back to me. I believed I had got over it, but now, all over again ...'

'I promise you, it's just questions. That's all.'

'OK. If it's so important, you can ask.'

'Does the name Bruno Fulger mean anything to you?'

Maruccia smiled warily. Then she said, 'What's the point of pretending? Yes, of course, Bruno Fulger. My father – I can say this – was the lover of Bruno's wife.'

'Was that widely known at the time?'

'No, not widely. The affair was kept secret, it was necessary, but for my father not usual.'

'How do you mean?'

Maruccia laughed. We were driving along the raised section of the motorway past the Alfa Laval building. 'I must tell you about my father,' she said. 'He was a wonderful man. A wonderful father and a wonderful husband too, I think. But he was a true Italian man of his age. My mother understood that. She did not approve, of course, but she understood. Papa always had women. They were part of his life. He would never have left Mamma and his family, but they were always there. He would go away on trips for business, take this woman or that. For us it was normal.'

'And Anastasia Fulger was one of his women?'

'Sure, but this time was different. From the beginning Papa knew it was a dangerous situation.'

'Why dangerous?'

'Because of the husband. Bruno Fulger, you know his reputation.'

'So they met secretly?'

'Always secretly. Never in places where they might be recognised.'

'He took her on his boat.'

329

Maruccia looked surprised. 'You know that?'

'I heard it in Germany.'

'Nothing can be truly secret. I warned Papa about that. But he needed to be with her so much. I believe he was a little in love with her, it meant more to him than a normal affair. That made me nervous.'

'So what happened?'

'They met secretly in Sardinia. Papa had the crew sail his yacht from Porto Ercole. Anastasia flew from Germany, Papa from Milan. The crew had instructions to say nothing. They spent a week together on the yacht sailing around the island. When he returned to Como, Papa was in such a good mood. You did not need to ask about the holiday, his happiness was evident on his face. I think they had a plan to meet again in a few weeks. He told me he would soon be going away on business. I was sure he meant to be with Anastasia.'

'But instead ...'

'He was killed. It was quite sudden. He had driven into Milan to visit some fashion companies. As he was crossing the Via Manzoni, a car drove up on to the pavement and ran him down. A white Mercedes with Roman number-plates. That is all that was known.'

'What do the police think happened?'

'To be honest, they don't know. They had some theories, but after some time the investigation ended.'

'Did you mention Bruno Fulger to them?'

'Yes, but it was awkward, you can understand. I needed to protect Mamma. You see, she loved her husband, and it would have hurt her so much if his death had been connected with one of his love affairs.'

'Did the police ever question Bruno?'

'I don't know. My impression is not. Or if they did, nothing came from it.'

'And what's your own opinion on what happened?'

'You mean who do I believe had Papa killed?'

'Exactly.'

'Of course, Bruno Fulger.'

'Why so sure?'

'Just a feeling. Also something that happened later.'

'Which was?'

'Well, for two months afterwards we could do nothing, make no decisions, nothing. Every day we cried. The factory was forgotten. But then we had to choose what to do next, and I decided to take over the running myself. It is a good business, and either we must sell or I must do it. Already I had been working there five years, so I moved into Papa's office and called the managers together and told them I was now in charge. They were so kind: they gave a little cheer. I think they believed we would sell out to some other group. Anyway, a few weeks later, a German – or Swiss, maybe – came to see me, sent from Bruno Fulger.'

'Was he called Gombricht, by the way?'

'Yes, I think that's correct. A lawyer. Very cold, he made me shiver.'

'And what did he want?'

'He said Bruno Fulger's company wanted to buy the business.'

'Did he explain why?'

'He just said they'd heard it might be for sale. And he named a price: very high, much higher than it's worth.'

'Why'd he do that? Fulger isn't famous for overpaying.'

'I wondered that too. And I think I know the reason. He wanted to buy our silence, and maybe test my reaction to the name Bruno Fulger – to judge how much I knew.'

'So what did you reply?'

'I was very polite, I can say that. I listened to everything he proposed, and then I said no, so sorry, not for sale.'

'And how did you react to this idea of Bruno taking over the family business?'

'In front of the lawyer, I disclosed nothing. It was as though his name meant nothing to me.'

'So Gombricht went away satisfied. If his intention was to sound you out, you passed the test.'

'When he was leaving he said one thing which shocked

me very much. It was a kind of threat, though I only recognised this later. We were standing outside the factory in the car park, and he warned me to beware of Italian drivers, they were so dangerous. I asked him why he said that. He looked at me, so coldly, and said, "The Roman drivers are the worst. They drive so fast in their large white cars, every pedestrian is in danger for her life." Those were his exact words. It was only after he'd gone I realised their significance. You see, no newspaper had ever mentioned the Roman numberplates. That wasn't reported. So there were only two ways he could have found out: either from the police or from the driver of the car itself.'

'So what did you do? Tell the police?'

'I know I should have done. It makes me ashamed to say it, but I did nothing. Maybe I was a little afraid. There was something about the lawyer's eyes, they scared me. And, anyway, what could I tell them? I had no proof.'

'That's the whole trouble with Bruno Fulger: there's *never* any proof. You can't make the connection.'

We had arrived in Great Titchfield Street and pulled up outside a wholesale fashion shop. The window was full of headless mannequins in beige blouses. Maruccia sat in the car, staring down at her shoes.

'Excuse me,' she said, 'but I need some time to calm myself. Before I go inside for my meeting. When I think about Bruno Fulger, it still makes me so mad. People like Bruno are evil but you can't do anything. Nothing can touch them. In the end, people don't even try any more.'

'I'm trying.'

'I know. That's what makes me feel so sad. Because whatever you do, it will achieve nothing. Bruno knows that. Even you know that in your heart, I think.'

And then she climbed out of the car and, without looking back, disappeared inside the shop.

My first thought was to drive to Chelsea police station and

repeat my whole conversation with Maruccia. She might be afraid of involving the police, but I wasn't.

The more I could incriminate Bruno, the better it would be for me. And Maruccia's story about Gombricht's threat, and all that stuff about the Roman numberplate, would surely impress Superintendent Barratt. Bruno Fulger had a history of strong-arm tactics.

I was halfway to Lucan Place when I lost my nerve. The more I thought about it, the more circumstantial it all seemed. What was I really saying? That Fulger's lawyer had made an oblique remark in an Italian car park, which in all probability had been misconstrued. They were hardly going to send the Black Maria for Bruno on the strength of that.

And I had a second motive for avoiding Lucan Place. I had an uneasy feeling that, given half a chance, they'd redetain me. I was pretty certain I was still Barratt's number one nap, and it would require more than unsubstantiated hearsay for Bruno to be taken seriously as a suspect. Maruccia was right: nothing *could* touch people like Bruno Fulger.

I arrived back at my flat to find the telephone ringing. I considered ignoring it. It could be Howard Trench asking for the BMW back.

It continued ringing, so gingerly I picked it up.

'Is that you, Kit?' It was Sally. She sounded hysterical.

'Sally? What's happened?' My thoughts flew immediately to Cazzie.

'Something terrible. I've found this envelope on the mat, addressed to Cazzie. Someone had pushed it through the door.'

She could hardly get the words out.

'Calm down, Sally. Take it slowly. Is Cazzie OK?'

'She's fine, she's right here next to me, thank God. But Kit, this envelope. It was one of those children's party ones with balloons and animals on the front. I thought it was an invitation to a birthday party.'

'Yes?'

'When we opened it, there was a message inside, with words cut out and stuck on to the card.'

'What does it say?'

'I'll read it. It only came an hour ago, I've been trying to find you everywhere.' She was right on the edge.

'What does it *say*, Sally? Just read it out to me as calmly as you can.'

'It says, "To Cazzie. Your father is asking too many questions. We know who he's spoken to. Tell him to stop or something bad will happen to you. Tell nobody about this." It isn't signed. Kit, what the hell's all this about? What are these questions you're asking? And what's it mean, "something bad will happen" to Cazzie? I just can't bear it.'

'Listen, Sally, I can't explain now but I'm coming right over. I'll be there in fifteen minutes. In the meantime, don't leave the house and don't open the door to anyone. *Anyone*. Just me. OK?'

I bolted down the stairs and out into the car park. If something happened to Cazzie I'd never forgive myself. I accelerated up Prince of Wales Drive, overtaking a bus on a blind corner and jumping the lights. How dare anybody drag Cazzie into this? How *dare* they? My hands were gripping the steering wheel so hard, my knuckles were white. I had tried to calm Sally, but I didn't feel calm myself. I knew the lengths these people would go to. They'd murdered twice, probably three times, already: Anna, Alessandro Mazzelli and Peter. And they'd have killed me that evening on Anna's roof, I was sure. Now they had Cazzie in their sights.

I pulled up outside the house and could see Sally watching out for me through the sitting-room window. Cazzie was with her, standing on the arm of the sofa. She waved as I came up the path, and I lip-read 'Hello, Daddy'.

Sally unbolted the front door and I went inside. The threatening letter and envelope were lying on the hall table. I examined them while trying not to finger them too much, though they were probably already smeared with prints.

The message had been formed from letters and words cut out from different magazines. I could identify some, but not all, of the typefaces: it was a jumble. But the message itself was chillingly lucid. *Your father is asking too many questions. We know who he's spoken to ...*

We went into the kitchen and Sally tried to shoo Cazzie out into the back garden so we could talk. But then I saw her hesitate. 'Will she be OK, Kit, outside on her own?'

Jesus, not even in her own back garden. 'Probably best if you play in your bedroom for a bit, Cazzie,' I said. 'Mummy and I need to talk.'

'Awww, but there's nothing to *do* upstairs all by myself.'

'Go and see what's on television. I'll come up soon and watch it with you.'

'And will you bath me tonight too, Daddy? You *never* bath me any more.'

'Maybe, darling. Now hurry upstairs, Mummy and I need to be grown up.'

Cazzie trailed upstairs and Sally boiled the kettle and made tea.

'I'm not just over-reacting, am I?' she said. 'That letter isn't a hoax.'

'It's not a hoax. At least, I don't think so. I'm afraid it's probably all too serious.'

'But what's it all *mean*? That's what I want to know. Who sent it, and how do they even know about Cazzie?'

'It's a complicated story. But the short answer is I believe it was sent by a German billionaire called Bruno Fulger. Or rather by a member of his staff. Fulger's suing the magazines because of a story we published about his ex-wife. He's dangerous and used to getting his own way. He's trying to scare me – scare *us* – by threatening Cazzie.'

'Shouldn't we tell the police?'

'Definitely. But not right now. I'm not sure that's enough. We need to get Cazzie out of London, hide her somewhere until this blows over. Sally, you're just going to have to trust me on this.'

Sally was drinking from a big spongeware teacup, and looked at me over the brim.

'You know what makes me so angry?' she said. 'It's the way that, once again, your work is screwing up this family. When we were married ...'

'Which we still are, don't forget.'

'OK, if you must be pedantic, before we *separated* it was always your work which came first in our lives. If I wanted to go away at the weekend, there was always something else, some bloody work thing. Sponsored polo or a fashion show or a design fair. Every weekend. Now, once again thanks to your work, there's a big problem for Cazzie – and this time it's scary. I just hate the way it keeps happening. This is *our daughter*, Kit. When you were living here you hardly ever saw her, you were always out, and now you've left us, your work still spoils everything. I just want you to know how I feel about it, that's all.'

'Look, I understand that, Sally, your whole outburst. I don't deny a single thing you've said. All the same, for one last time, you've just got to trust me. Cazzie's got to get out of London – and I don't mean tomorrow, I mean *tonight. Now.*'

'Where do you expect me to take her?'

'I don't expect you to take her anywhere. That would blow it. You must stay here in the house and carry on as usual. Make them believe she's still at home. *I'll* take Cazzie. What about that cottage you mentioned? The one you said is empty, near Paul's house. How many people know about that?'

'Apart from Paul – and me – nobody in London.'

'That's where I'll take her, then. Even if it's only for a couple of nights. And tell absolutely *nobody*, not the police, no one. I'm serious, we should leave now, pack Cazzie's things and go.'

Sally still looked unconvinced, so I said, 'Truly, Sally. I

haven't always been right in the past, I freely admit that. But I *am* right this time.' I was imploring her.

'OK,' she said at last. 'One last chance. You can take her. But if anything goes wrong, if Cazzie gets hurt ...'

'You'll what? Divorce me?'

'I'll never forgive you. And you'll never see Cazzie on your own again, I'll make sure of that, believe me.'

'I believe you. Now let's get moving.'

We both raced up to Cazzie's bedroom where I told her she was coming on an adventure with me. 'Just you and Daddy.'

'What? Not even Mummy?'

'Just us. You're going to have to look after me. So, quickly, collect together your things and help us get you packed.'

Sally was folding nightdresses and stuffing jerseys into a canvas holdall. I wouldn't have any luggage myself, I decided. No way was I going anywhere near my own flat with Cazzie. I'd just have to manage. Anyway, I could buy wash things at a service station on the way.

But first we needed to transfer Cazzie into the car without being seen. If, as seemed all too possible, the house was being watched, I needed to get away without being followed.

'Have you got any really *big* canvas bags?' I asked Sally.

She produced a couple of square-sided nylon jobs, which Paul apparently used when travelling: compact enough to fit in an overhead locker, but just roomy enough inside for Cazzie.

'This is a game,' I told her. 'I want you to really squeeze up tiny, and then stay still, like a statue.'

Then, as nonchalantly as possible, I heaved the bag out to the car and on to the floor by the back seat. 'Don't move a muscle, darling,' I whispered. 'The game isn't over yet.'

Sally was right behind me with the second bag. Inside was the car seat. I made an elaborate show of calling goodbye to Cazzie in the house, and then cut across

Wandsworth towards the motorway. Once I'd satisfied myself no one was trailing us, I pulled over, released Cazzie and strapped her into her chair.

'Was that fun?' I asked her.

Cazzie wrinkled her nose. 'It was *quite* fun. But my legs are all tingly with pins and needles.'

Sally's directions lay on the passenger seat: from the Basingstoke exit of the M3 we'd head towards Axford, then a succession of small lanes from Preston Candover, culminating in a half-mile track to the cottage. Not even Gombricht, I reckoned, could find us there.

Somewhere near Chertsey we stopped for petrol and crisps, and I bought toothpaste, shaving tackle, bread and some cans of soup. There's virtually no traffic at five o'clock on a Wednesday evening so we were making good time. Cazzie was singing a little song she'd learnt at school about a crocodile swallowing a fish, when the carphone began ringing.

Instinctively, I picked it up.

'Hello, is that Kit Preston?'

It was a man's voice, all too familiar: Howard Trench.

I could think of nothing constructive to say to him, so didn't answer.

'Excuse me,' said Trench. 'I believe I'm ringing the Vodafone number of a fleet car belonging to the Fulger Magazine Company. Could whoever is driving please reply? This is the Managing Director speaking.'

I held the telephone away from my face, so he couldn't hear me breathing.

In the back, Cazzie was singing loudly and tunelessly.

'*A crocodile swam in the wa-ter*

'*His jaws were o-pen wide,*

'*A little fish swam in the wa-ter*

'*And he swam right inside.*'

'Who is that?' I heard Trench shouting down the line. 'Is that you singing, Kit? Stop fooling about when I'm speaking to you.'

*'The crocodile's jaws shut tight – SNAP!'* sang Cazzie. *'The little fish slept inside all night ...'*

'Let me say formally,' said Trench, 'that unless that car is returned to Park Place by noon tomorrow, I'm informing the police. Do you hear me?'

*'The crocodile yawned in the mor-ning*

*'And the fish swam away out of sight.'*

I cut Trench short with the 'end' button and drove at full pelt until we neared our exit. Even the sound of his voice unnerved me. I was certain he meant it too about the police, which would further complicate things. Inspector Barratt would be only too delighted for a pretext on which to haul me in.

We left the motorway and climbed a winding hill lined with beech trees whose long shadows fell like dark fingers across the cornfields. Each time we reached a new crest, evening sunlight streamed into the car, making us squint. We passed a church with a Norman tower and a village green with a midweek cricket match in progress. It's strange but, living in London, months can go by and I never give one passing thought to the English countryside. But on a glorious evening like this, I'm astonished I choose to live anywhere else.

Shortly before we reached the turning for the cottage, I dialled Suzy at the office. When the switchboard answered, I asked for her in a Midlands accent.

'Suzy? It's Kit.'

She sounded nervous. 'Didn't the switchboard ...?'

'Don't worry, I disguised my voice. Like this.' I gave her a taster of my best Brummie.

'Great Scottish accent,' said Suzy. 'Sounds like you never left Aberdeen.'

'Listen,' I said, 'I can't talk long, but I've taken Cazzie out of London. She's been sent a threatening letter, all to do with the Anna thing. Sally's boyfriend's lending us a farm cottage near Axford, in Hampshire, but that's a secret. Even if the police ask where we are, say nothing. In fact *especially* the police. The reason I'm telling you is there isn't a telephone in the cottage. The only way of contacting me is the carphone, and I'm not going to ring you again. Too risky. But I want you to ring me every day at noon, I'll be waiting in the car for the call, in case you need to pass me a message. If noon's no good because you're tied up with Trench, I'll just keep waiting until you do ring. Have you got all that?'

'Sure. So we'll talk tomorrow at twelve. Got to go now, I'm being buzzed.'

High Coppice Cottage was a low-slung, gabled farmhouse next to a modern corrugated-metal barn. The two buildings stood together on the side of an exposed hill, with a view of rolling countryside and accessible only by a long mud-and-flint track. The whole place seemed deserted, but I hid my car in the barn. Then I unstrapped Cazzie and we walked together round to the back of the house. There was a small garden with a stone bench, covered in lichen, and an orchard of quince trees. We found the key underneath a stone and unlocked the back door. Inside, it smelt stale and there was a scattering of dead bluebottles on the windowsill. Evidently no one had aired the place for several weeks. Good, I thought, the fewer people who knew we were there, the better.

We hurried through the rooms, pushing open doors and searching for the immersion heater and airing cupboard. It was a bigger cottage than I'd expected: four bedrooms, a large sitting-room with worn chintz sofas and a flagstoned kitchen. It needed a lick of paint and some work on the bathrooms, but Paul would have no trouble renting it. Cazzie pulled open all the kitchen cupboards and was rewarded by finding a dead mouse, squashed flat in an antique spring trap.

We found sheets and made up our beds and then, when the water had heated up, Cazzie had a bath. I sat on a chair by the bathside, talking to her, while the mirror steamed up over the basin. Afterwards, she put on her dressing gown and we heated a pan of tomato soup and drank it from mugs on a sofa in the sitting-room. Cazzie had brought a reading book and word card from school, and read me a whole story about a fox and a duck. I half-suspect she'd learnt the story by heart, and wasn't reading at all, but it was still impressive. It was the first evening I'd spent with her since I walked out, and I hadn't realised how much I'd missed it. The whole scene was so peaceful and natural, it made me question whether I'd been paranoid in leaving London in such a hurry. Either way, I was enjoying life for the first time in weeks.

After Cazzie had gone to bed, I sat up alone listening to the silence. In a sideboard in the dining-room I found a dusty half-full bottle of Bells, and poured a large measure of whisky with tapwater. There was so much to think about, but tonight I felt like deferring the moment. Through the undrawn curtains I watched the top branches of a towering beech tree swaying gently in the breeze. Silence like this was something unfamiliar. Not for a long, long time had I experienced it. My working life unfolded against a background clamour of metropolitan muzak and tinny cocktail laughter. Silence was something I associated only with childhood and my father. Dad loved silence, especially the vast leaden silence of the desert. Once, when I was ten or eleven years old and we were living in some expat enclave of Sharjah, he took me camping in the Empty Quarter. At least that's what he called it: in fact it was the first decent stretch of sand off the main highway to Dubai. I think it must have been a spur-of-the-moment idea, because we drove into the dunes and put up our tent in the dark. Before we turned in, Dad made me sit with him outside the tent, absorbing the absolute silence. I remember him saying, 'Listen to it, Kit, just listen to it.' And me replying, 'What am I meant to be listening *to*? I'm listening as hard as I can and I can't *hear* anything.' It became a great family joke, me saying that. But for Dad it was therapy, the silence. Whenever there were frustrations in his work, he'd drive out into the dunes and just listen. Listen to nothing.

When was it that my father and I had begun to drift

apart? It was difficult to pinpoint. It was like that saloon-bar philosopher's riddle, 'How exactly was it that you went bankrupt?' and its reply, 'First gradually, then suddenly.' That's how it was with Dad and me. Even when I was at university he came up to visit me several times, as late on as that. So it can't simply have been the final split with Mum, since that happened earlier when I was seventeen. I think the rot set in when I moved to London and began working. Dad still lived in London himself then, he didn't move out to the country until after he retired, but we just didn't get it together to see each other, or only very infrequently. When I was in the mood for family life, it was to my mother's I headed round for supper. Dad could be prickly. He had a gift for inferring that whatever I achieved at work wasn't really worthy of me. I don't believe he consciously meant it to show, but when I got my first job as a commission rep, his disappointment was tangible. And later, when the scope became more interesting and demanding, he seemed to resent that too. By the time Mum died, he already occupied a marginal role in my life. Maybe I was over-sensitive but, one way or another, Dad and I felt more comfortable rationing our encounters to once or twice a year.

He changed addresses often and I hadn't even visited his present one, though I knew it couldn't be all that far from Paul's cottage. Near Alton: he'd sent me a card informing me of his latest move. On the bottom he'd written in turquoise ink, 'I have found a garden flat within walking distance of everything I need – pub, shops, etc – in preparation for growing old. Don't trouble yourself to alter the mailing address on the magazine subscription you kindly sent me for my last birthday. The *Man Alive* really isn't my bag, too many advertisements and photographs of poofs. Sorry not to be more positive when it's your livelihood. Dad.'

I went out to the car and obtained his number from directory inquiries. He was in, answering at the first ring.

He sounded cautiously pleased to hear from me, 'though I know exactly why you're ringing,' he said.

'You do?'

'You've lost your job, I read it in the newspaper. Didn't I always tell you it was a crazy line of work to go into? Now I suppose you need money.'

'Actually that's *not* why I'm ringing.'

'Just as well. Because I haven't any spare. Keep having to send off great wads to the government.'

'I'm staying nearby with Cazzie and thought we might come over. You haven't seen your granddaughter for a couple of years.'

'Longer. She was a baby.' He sounded censorious.

'You're right, it's been too long. My fault, probably.'

'I rather think it is,' said Dad. 'You get your priorities wrong. I've noticed that about you.'

It was agreed that we would come over for lunch the next day and I took directions. 'Don't expect anything elaborate,' said Dad. 'Soup and cheese do me very well in the middle of the day.'

'That's fine. Cazzie lives on cheese. See you tomorrow.'

After the call I felt unexpectedly depressed. What other expectations had I harboured for the conversation anyway? Had it ever been any other way? And of course there was enough substance to Dad's accusation of neglect to chasten me with guilt. Someone once explained, in all seriousness, that there's a finite supply of guilt in the world which passes round from person to person, and when you get landed with a great dollop of it, your natural instinct for self-preservation leads you to pass it on, before it has a chance to contaminate and corrode. Except, with me, the flow of guilt has always been exclusively incoming. Lately, I seemed to have been turning into some kind of repository for the stuff. First Anna, now my father and daughter. What was it Sally had said? *It's the way that, once again, your work is screwing up this family.* And her barb about Cazzie: *When you were living here, you hardly ever saw her.* There was something, it was true, in both these charges. Looking back from my fresh vantage point of unemployment, it astonished me how much effort I had put into the propagation of business relationships that counted for so little, even at the time.

On my way up to bed, I tiptoed into Cazzie's bedroom and tucked the blankets tightly around her. She was sleeping on her back and smiling enigmatically, with her arms ramrod-straight by her side. Through her open curtains, I could see a capricious wind snapping at the branches of the trees and beating against the tin roof of the barn. It looked as if we were in for a storm.

I was drawing the curtains when I noticed the lights a quarter of a mile away up the track: *car headlamps making their way towards the cottage.* The twin beams were dipped and the car was approaching slowly, as though its occupants didn't want to be heard. How the hell had they found us in the middle of nowhere? A charge of real fear shot through my body, temporarily paralysing me. The car was still creeping towards us along the brow of the hill. It was dark in Cazzie's room, so I risked opening the window a few inches for a clearer view. I could hear the wheels now, throwing small stones up against the chassis. In less than a minute they'd be outside.

Cazzie was breathing softly in her bed. There was only one thing for it: I'd have to scoop her up in her pyjamas and escape through the back door. I hadn't explored to the end of the orchard, but there must be a gate into the fields. Then we'd hide in the coppice until they'd gone. It was a desperate plan, but it was the only one I'd got.

I slipped my arms under Cazzie's warm back and gently lifted her up. She yawned and half-opened her eyes. 'Shhh, Cazzie. No need to wake up. It's not morning yet.'

I raced downstairs into the hall. The car's headlights lit up the whole place as it came to a halt in front of the cottage. Had they seen us crossing the hall? I couldn't be sure.

I unlocked the back door and raced outside into the

orchard. The long grass underfoot was already wet with dew. Cazzie began to stir in the cold night air. 'Shhh, Cazzie darling, shhh. Everything's all right.' I heard the car door slam shut, and cautious footsteps approaching round the side of the cottage.

I backed through the orchard inch by inch, testing each footfall. Cazzie was becoming heavy and I worried about slipping on the wet grass.

They were at the back door now, I could hear them rattling the handle.

Just then Cazzie started to cry. It began as an isolated whimper. 'Shhh, Cazzie, quiet.' I froze against the end wall, peering into the darkness for a way into the fields. Then she opened her lungs and bellowed. 'Cazzie – *shush. Right now.*' My sharpness only frightened her, increasing the volume.

I ran, stumbling through the grass, searching for the gate. I was clutching Cazzie to me, at any moment expecting to be pulled down. What would they do to us when they caught us? *Something bad will happen to you.* I was about to discover exactly what that meant.

'Can that really be Cazzie in the garden?' Somebody was calling to us. And I recognised the voice: *Suzy.*

'What the hell are *you* doing here?'

'I might ask the same of you. Shouldn't Cazzie be in bed by now, not playing outside? It's almost eleven o'clock.'

'She *was* in bed, sound asleep, until you turned up and scared the shit. I thought you were Bruno Fulger's hit squad.'

'Lucky I'm not, isn't it, the way Cazzie's screeching. Go on, hand her over. There there, Cazzie. No need to cry.' In a few seconds, infuriatingly, she calmed down. In another minute, she was asleep in Suzy's arms.

We took Cazzie back to bed and left her snoring contentedly. Then we went down to the sitting-room for a nightcap.

'Do you mind telling me how you found this place?' It

rather annoyed me the way she'd blown in, unannounced, to my safe house.

'Easy. I asked in the pub. You told me it was near Axford. I said I was a friend of Sally's. Everyone in the pub knew Sally and Paul. The landlord has a bit of a crush on her, by the way. So they gave me directions.'

'Fantastic. I find that very reassuring. What are you doing here anyway?'

'I thought you'd like to know the police turned up at the office looking for you. Two of them: a sergeant called Crow and a constable. Howard Trench explained you'd been sacked and didn't work there any longer. They said they already knew that, but wanted to question the staff about "your possible whereabouts", as they phrased it. Howard wasn't at all keen, but they insisted. They must have stayed an hour, questioning everyone.'

'Did they say what was so urgent?'

'Only that they'd driven round to your flat and you weren't in, and then to Sally's house and you weren't there either.'

'And Sally didn't let on?'

'Presumably not.' Well done, Sally. She trusted me.

'What about you? Were you questioned?'

'You bet. Howard made sure of that. He can't prove anything, but he suspects we keep in touch.'

'And you played dumb too?'

'Of course. I tried to pump them on why they wanted you, but they wouldn't be drawn.'

'So then what happened?'

'That's just it. That's why I drove straight down here to warn you. Howard told them about the BMW which he hyped up as "stolen property". Sergeant Crow said they'd issue a general alert. Every police force in the country will be looking for it now.'

Thanks, Trench, I groaned. That's really helpful of you. Outside it was pelting with rain, and the windowpanes rattled in their casements.

'The other thing,' said Suzy, 'is they're going to put a

trace on the carphone. So if you use it, they'll track you down through the airwaves or something.'

'So when you rang me tomorrow at noon ...'

'They'd have nailed you in ten minutes. Or tried to.'

'This is a complete nightmare. Bit by bit they're immobilising me. I was going to take Cazzie over to my father's tomorrow, but now I guess they'd spot the car.'

'You can borrow mine. As I've told you before, nobody but nobody notices an eight-year-old Vauxhall.'

'Generous offer, but your car won't still be here, will it? Haven't you got to get back to work?'

'Never again. I've finally summoned up the guts to resign.'

'You have? How did Trench take it?'

'He doesn't know yet. I've left an envelope on his desk which he'll find tomorrow morning when he gets in. Inside I've just put "Sorry, but you're much too boring to work for. From Suzy."'

'Very elegant. How close did I come to finding one of those myself?'

'Extremely close, actually, once or twice. But I always relented and tore it up.'

I was lying stretched out on the sofa and watched Suzy across the room as she lit a cigarette. Now we no longer worked together, she looked different somehow, or perhaps it was just me looking at her in a different way. She looked tired, but very pretty.

'I didn't know you smoked.'

'I don't. Only when I'm depressed or elated.'

'And which are you now?'

'Elated. Leaving Trench, it feels like I've peeled off a particularly fetid old coat and dumped it in the bin. Freedom.'

'Talking of old coats, I don't suppose you've brought any clothes with you.'

'Nothing at all. Not even a toothbrush.'

'A toothbrush is about all I *have* got. But I've noticed rather a nice old flannel dressing gown hanging on the back of the bathroom door. You can borrow that if you like.'

We went upstairs and fetched more sheets from the airing cupboard and I helped Suzy make her bed. Her bedroom had green trellis wallpaper with a pattern of red fuchsia, and a 'thirties button-backed bedhead. We stood on opposite sides of the wide mattress, flapping open the linen.

'Sure you'll be all right on your own in here?' I asked lightly, kissing her goodnight.

'Quite sure,' she said. 'If I'm cold or lonely, I'll move in with Cazzie. Goodnight, Kit.'

# 21

Cazzie woke at half past six and crept into my room. She always wakes early the first night in a strange bed. It didn't particularly bother me. After the anxiety of last night, it was good to curl up with her and her dreaded word cards.

I drew back the curtains and was hit between the eyes by a perfect sunrise. The storm had blown itself out during the night. Beneath the window, Suzy's Vauxhall was parked where she'd left it; this morning it looked conspicuously small and unthreatening. I searched the larder and found a box of stale camomile teabags and several tins of anchovies. So for breakfast we had anchovies on toast and a choice of tisanes or tinned oxtail soup.

Suzy, woken by the clattering, made an appearance in the kitchen in the flannel dressing gown.

'It's eight-fifteen,' she said with satisfaction. 'Any second now, Trench is going to open the envelope.'

Afterwards, we borrowed boots and sunhats from the cloakroom and set off across the fields for a long walk. It was another perfect English summer's day, the hedgerows verdant with wild flowers and berries. We walked up a steep valley, with the woods on one side and a long view behind us all the way to Preston Candover. Cazzie ran on in front, returning with fistfuls of dandelions that she'd torn off at the head. For an hour and a half we didn't set eyes on another human being, just hares that tore off when we were almost on top of them, zig-zagging through the clumps of nettles, and paunchy cock pheasants that strutted and fluttered on the boundary of the coppice.

'You know,' I said to Suzy when Cazzie was out of

earshot, 'I've been thinking more about that threatening letter yesterday. There's one aspect that's only just occurred to me. The bit where it says "Your father is asking too many questions. We know who he's spoken to". Well, *how* do they know?'

Suzy furrowed her brow. 'I suppose someone just told them.'

'You mean one of the people I've talked to tipped them off?'

'Presumably.'

'Well, that's just it. Who would have done that? I mean, assuming we still consider Bruno Fulger the most likely suspect. Who've I seen who could have alerted him?'

Suzy thought. 'That Italian woman, Maruccia?'

'But for what earthly motive? He killed her father. She told me she hated Fulger.'

'I can't think of a motive. Unless she's just terrified of him, which she anyway told you she was. Maybe he threatened to kill her if she didn't tell him everything. Like if anyone started snooping about.'

We had reached the head of the valley and rested against the broad, ridged trunk of an elm tree. Cazzie's legs were tired; it had been a good long walk for a five-year-old.

Suzy and I bathed our faces in the warm sun, while Cazzie prodded at a rabbit hole with a piece of stick.

'It doesn't work,' I said suddenly. 'The Maruccia theory. It doesn't work timewise, it can't have been her. Think: even supposing she'd gone straight into that shop in Great Titchfield Street and asked to use the telephone, and reported everything to Fulger or Gombricht, there wouldn't have been time for them to make the card and deliver it through the door in Clapham. Don't forget Sally rang me the minute I got home, and she'd been trying to track me down for ages already.'

'Maybe Maruccia rang them earlier. From Milan. After you spoke Tuesday morning.'

'Also possible. But it doesn't ring true.'

'Then who else have you spoken to about Bruno Fulger?'

'That's just it, hardly anyone. Simon Beriot the photographer. I don't trust him an inch. He could easily have passed on our conversation. But I haven't seen him for eight days. Who else? Heiner Stüben in Munich. Nick Gruen. That's about it.'

'What about Heiner, then?'

'I doubt it. I was so circumspect, it was just background probing.'

'Nick Gruen?'

'Impossible. He's my oldest friend.' But, there again, was it so impossible? When I'd rung him on Monday in Leipzig to ask about Alessandro Mazzelli being knocked off the sidewalk, he'd been furtive and bloody unhelpful. And he had been selling a paint factory to Bruno's company. I could just imagine him, over lunch, telling one of Fulger's executives about me, and how I was about to expose their boss for a hit-and-run murder. It would all have been wonderfully sardonic and worldly. Nick was good at that.

'What about if they've simply bugged your flat?' said Suzy. 'Or your car. Or both. Then they'd know everything.'

My heart sank. 'You're quite right. It could be that simple.' Why the hell hadn't I thought of that myself? Gombricht could have heard everything, every telephone call, every damn word.

And then another thought hit me. I'd rung Suzy on the carphone, telling her about the cottage and the nearest village. If Suzy had been able to find us from Axford, then so could they. Fulger's men could already be on their way. In fact, they could be there now, searching for us.

We retraced our steps down the valley but this time, before we reached the orchard wall, Suzy led Cazzie by the hand and told her to talk only in whispers. Then we climbed to the high ground round the edge of the woods, circling the cottage until we had an unobstructed view of the front. Everything appeared undisturbed. No new cars were visible, the front door remained shut. We squatted on the grass, watching silently. We trained our eyes on each window, alert for any movement inside.

After ten minutes we felt confident enough to make our way down. But somehow, even once we knew we were alone, the cottage had lost some of its feeling of refuge; we had violated it with our own fear.

I said, 'Let's grab our stuff and get the hell out of here. It won't take long, I didn't unpack for Cazzie last night.'

Fifteen minutes later we were driving through Axford in the Vauxhall in the direction of Alton. Until we left the track from the cottage, I don't think either of us felt relaxed. At any moment we expected to be driven off the road by a carload of hoods.

'Traditionally,' said Suzy as we hit the dual-carriage-way, 'you at this point ask me to send keys back to Rudolph Gombricht. Shall I for the BMW, or are you proposing to keep it a bit longer?'

'Let's just concede gracefully. Mail them to Trench, and tell him the car's parked in a barn up a half-mile, potholed track. No need to be too specific.'

In an hour we arrived at Alton and drove along the half-timbered High Street, following Dad's directions. Turn right at Boots the Chemist, then right again at the Texaco station. We were waiting at traffic lights when a police panda car drew up alongside us. I pretended not to notice, looking straight ahead. Suzy said softly, 'I think he's suspicious. He keeps staring at you and Cazzie.'

The lights changed and we headed off. The police car was right behind. It seemed to be following us. I tried to see in the mirror whether he was talking on his shortwave radio. Any moment now he'd flag us down.

We reached the corner of Dad's road and I indicated to turn left. Now would be the moment he'd tell us to pull over. I turned off and the panda continued straight on past. Suzy and I chorused a sigh of relief. My heart was pounding and my shirt was covered in sweat.

Dad's flat was halfway down the street in a small

courtyard behind a pub. You went past the wooden tables occupied by lunchtime drinkers, through an archway, and his front door was a few yards beyond. When he'd mentioned he lived within walking distance of the pub, he hadn't been exaggerating. I lifted Cazzie up so she could press the doorbell.

'Do you think your father will mind an extra person for lunch?' said Suzy.

'I probably should have rung him from a callbox. But it's only going to be cheese and soup, so there shouldn't be a problem.'

Dad opened the door looking older than I remembered him. It must have been at least a year, but he'd deteriorated five. The last of his hair had turned grey, and his chin was covered with coarse grey stubble.

'Cazzie, you remember Grandpa,' I said. 'Kiss Grandpa hello.'

She advanced self-consciously, giving his cheek a cursory brush with her lips.

'Yuk,' she said. 'That man's face is all prickles.'

'Don't call him "that man",' I said quickly. 'Call him Grandpa or Grandfather.'

'Is he really my grandpa?'

'*Of course* he is. He's Daddy's daddy.'

'Has he got a present for me, then? He must have if he's my real grandpa.'

'Sorry about all that, Dad,' I said. 'Just ignore her. And this, by the way, is Suzy Forbes. I hope you don't mind her coming along too, but she's driving us around. Suzy and I used to work together at the magazine company.'

'I see,' said Dad, scrutinising her fiercely. 'And has she been sacked too?'

'Actually, Mr Preston,' said Suzy cheerfully, 'I resigned my job last night. It wasn't any fun after Kit left.'

'Probably too *much* fun before. That's why they turfed him out, I daresay.'

We followed Dad along a dark passage into his sitting-room, which looked like every other sitting-room he'd occupied in the last twenty years. I recognised every stick of furniture and every knick-knack. There was a set of prints of the creek at Dubai, and other mementoes too: a Nigerian wooden salad bowl with giant wooden spoons, which lived permanently on the sideboard, and a framed photograph of the petrochemical department on some works outing in the Emirates. One wall of the room had french windows on to a small garden, with a lawn leading down to a brook. Beyond the brook was the car park for a supermarket, in which shoppers permanently loaded up the boots of their cars.

'Can you imagine anything more convenient?' said Dad. 'Boozer one side, supermarket the other.' If some irony was latent in this statement, then I missed it.

Dad offered us, without much enthusiasm, a choice of gin or bottled beer, and tonic water for Cazzie which she drank from a fearsomely unsuitable cut-glass sherry schooner.

We sat about making wooden conversation about wooden salad spoons. Even Suzy was getting rather dragged down by it all. Of lunch, there was neither sign nor mention.

'Seeing we're now so many in number,' Dad said at last, nodding meaningfully at Suzy, as though her presence had fundamentally altered the composition of the party, 'I thought we might go next door to eat. You probably noticed the Queen's Head round the corner. They do bar snacks, ploughman's and so forth.'

Dad was greeted warmly by the landlord and several regulars at the bar. Evidently he was a fixture there. He introduced me to his friends as 'My son Kit, who's just had the old heave-ho from his job.'

'Join the club,' said one of them. 'Everyone's had the shove round here. Blame the government.'

We sat at a table on the pavement, eating scampi and chips in a basket.

'Food OK for you, Kit?' asked Dad. 'Not up to your

usual standard, I imagine, restaurants every day. Your *former* standard, I should say. You'll miss that.'

'Actually, I love scampi. So does Cazzie.'

'Not bad, the bar food here. I eat here most lunchtimes, tend to. Evenings as well sometimes. Nice crowd.'

Then Dad said, 'How's your wife, or rather ex-wife?'

'Sally's fine. We're not divorced yet, it'll go through some time next year. She's got a new man in her life, which I think's a good thing.'

'Poor bugger,' said Dad. He turned to Suzy. 'Ever meet Sally? Pretty enough girl but personally I wouldn't have picked her. Told Kit that. Highly strung.'

I began to protest, but Suzy got in first. 'Sally's all right. She's very good with your granddaughter anyway.'

'I'll give her that,' said Dad. 'A natural mother: bossy. But not to marry. Too much of a scold.'

One of the exasperating things about my father is the way he's judgemental in all matters except himself. God knows his own marriage was no role model, but he is always the first to dish out pearls of wisdom. Career advice, investment, property, child rearing: there is no subject on which Dad, divorcee, absentee father, virtual bankrupt, doesn't have the inside rap. His lack of discrimination oppressed me. His friends seemed to be for the most part acquired at random: the work colleague, chance shipmate, crony from the country club, saloon bar. He seemed equally pleased by the company of anyone at all. Although on certain subjects, such as the primacy of university education, he could be austerely high minded, in his choice of drinking companions he was uncritical. There was an egalitarian side to him that bridled at any form of social selection. He once railed at me about the party pictures in *In Society* which he claimed to find 'morally repugnant. By what *right*,' he asked, 'can one human being play God over another, deciding who's "good enough" to have their picture published and who isn't?'

I explained that this really isn't how the choices are

made, 'or at least only partly. It's usually just a question of who's wearing the best hat.'

Dad was unconvinced. 'It reminds me of the old slave auctions. Or St Peter at the Gates of Paradise. This one can come in, this one can't. Obscene job.'

He'd once met Anna, quite by accident, at a restaurant in Shepherd Market. Anna and I were eating outdoors at a Lebanese *mezze* place, discussing some article about Meg Ryan for *In Society*. That, anyway, was the pretext. Suddenly a voice was asking, 'Isn't that my long-lost son, Kit?' And there was Dad, ridiculously overdressed for a summer's day in a herringbone overcoat.

He joined us for coffee and a drink, and I introduced him to Anna. It must have been quite soon after Sally and I split, because you could see Dad trying to puzzle it out: was Anna my new girl? Well, it was a valid question. But it would take a thesis to answer.

They'd hit it off, or more precisely Dad had taken an instant shine to Anna. I never asked her for her view; frankly, I doubt she was particularly interested, there's no mileage in Dad. But she flattered him with questions and listened attentively enough to his replies. Dad loves an audience. He treated us to an impromptu little diatribe on the decline of the British theatre, during which he confused the National with the Royal Shakespeare Company. Anna didn't bat an eyelid, though I could tell she'd noticed. 'Thing is,' said Dad, 'audiences don't dress up for the theatre any longer. It's lost its sense of occasion. Put that right and you'd have full houses overnight. You ask any American tourist.'

It was a damn silly theory, but he appeared to believe in it at the time.

'You're quite right,' Anna had replied, radiating enthusiasm and sincerity. 'Men should be required to wear dinner jackets and women long dresses.'

Dad wasn't accustomed to unqualified approval for his crackpot opinions, and he gazed at Anna with something approaching admiration.

The encounter had left me feeling irritable, but it was difficult to define why. Dad had made an idiot of himself, but that was nothing new so why should it bother me? Did I imagine Anna would think less of me, because my father espoused some half-witted theory? I had never made any pretence about him. Anna knew everything about my upbringing; far more than I knew about hers, in point of fact. Maybe it was really Anna I'd felt angry with: the way she'd implicitly ridiculed Dad by leading him on. It was her disingenuous interview technique. Well, Dad wasn't profile fodder, to be bamboozled into indiscretions. He was my father.

The next time I'd spoken to Dad, he'd asked, 'How's that lovely lady friend of yours, the one I caught you with at the restaurant?'

'Anna Grant, you mean? Fine, I think. She's one of our journalists.'

'Original mind,' he said. 'I'd like to get together with her some time, she was interested by some of my ideas.'

Looking at Dad today, I wondered what he made of Suzy. And Cazzie too, come to that. He was odd about Cazzie. If I didn't bring her to see him, he complained. But when I did bring her, he seemed curiously uninterested in his granddaughter. What he wanted to do was tell his own stories and broadcast his own theories, without interruptions from a five-year-old.

Suzy was telling him she had no idea what she'd do next, but thought she'd try and find something similar in magazines.

'Shouldn't if I were you,' said Dad, shaking his head sagely. 'Magazines are dinosaurs now. Whole lot will be down the tubes in five years. We'll be getting all our entertainment along a fibre-optic line, whatever you want, press a button, bingo.'

'I'm sure you're right,' said Suzy diplomatically. 'But won't it be rather sad? I mean, magazines are so lovely to hold and flick through. It's tactile. You don't get that feeling with a screen.'

But Dad would have none of it. God knows where he'd picked up all this superhighway stuff in Alton, but he was an evangelist.

'Another couple of years,' he said, 'whatever you want, picture of the latest hairdo, latest lipstick, press the button and there it is, all at your fingertips. Think about it: they can already store all the magazines ever printed on a micro dot the size of a flea's eyebrow. Who's going to buy new ones when they can graze an archive like that?'

'Well, I might for one,' said Suzy. 'I'd rather read the latest issue than an old one.'

'But not printed on dead tree. You'll read a virtual magazine. Read it anywhere too: on a laptop, down a cable, digital, you name it. And no need to restrict yourself to what the *editor* wants you to read. You'll select from a database and simply download your choice of contents on to your PC.'

'Isn't that more or less what one does already, Dad?' I said. 'We call it the contents page.'

'Now you're being a perfect ass.' Dad looked piqued: he hated anyone pouring cold water on his Delphic visions.

The landlord came over, carrying a copy of the *Daily Telegraph* quick crossword, seeking Dad's help with a clue. Dad got out his spectacles and adjusted them on the bridge of his nose to read the small type.

'You won't have to bother with this in a couple more years, will you, Dad?' I said, suddenly angry. 'There'll be a modem on every table in the Queen's Head, and the crossword will be on the Internet.' Sometimes Dad antagonised me so much. I'd drive miles to see him and no sooner had I arrived than I wanted to get away again.

Dad glowered and Suzy gently shook her head at me. Don't bait him, it warned. Suzy has always been good at steering me away from trouble. More than once, when I was coping with an obnoxious contributor or advertiser on the telephone, and was coming close to providing a douche of icy realism, Suzy would glide into my office and announce, 'Urgent call from Barney Weiss. He's holding for you from his plane.' At the time it always irritated; but the next day I was grateful.

Dad was explaining to Suzy the theory of global warming, and Cazzie had wandered into the bar to watch transfixed while a youth fed a flashing, grinding slot machine with pound coins. The *Daily Telegraph* lay on the table between the scampi baskets. I paged through as far as the business section, and stopped at a large photograph of Erskine Greer. He was standing in a garden, at the end of a long, smooth lawn, and in the background was some kind of pavilion: a Chinese summer house. The caption read: 'Greer Corporation Chairman Erskine Greer, at home yesterday on the Peak in Hong Kong, says talks with Federated Aviation are at a critical final stage.' The article itself didn't have much new to add. Institutional stockholders appeared to be welcoming Greer's revised offer and the takeover was now a formality.

It was four days since I'd spoken to Bruce McFall in Hong Kong. What was it he'd said? *All the paydirt on Greer's other businesses: the ones you won't read about out here.*

Cazzie returned from the slots, begging for money. 'Just two one-pound coins, *pleeeese*. Pleeeese, kind generous Daddy. It's only borrowing, I'll give them back, promise. You can get lots of money out of this machine, the man just did, it pours into this special tray at the bottom.'

I fished in my pocket for two pounds and handed them firmly to my father. 'Grandpa, you take her. It's nice for Cazzie to bond with you on her own.' Dad left reluctantly, Cazzie yanking at his hand.

'Suzy!' I said when they'd gone. 'Suzy, will you come to Hong Kong with me?'

'Hong Kong?' She looked incredulous. 'Why Hong Kong?'

'Erskine Greer. Look, there's more about him in the papers today. I think I've been stupid. I've been putting all this effort into Bruno Fulger when it could just as easily be

Greer. I mean – why not? He's got a strong enough motive.'

'But surely he doesn't fit in with the stuff you were saying on our walk this morning. The bit in the letter about "we know who he's spoken to". Well, you *haven't* spoken with anyone about Erskine Greer, so it doesn't make sense.'

'You're right, I've done less work on him than Bruno Fulger. Probably because Hong Kong's further away than Munich. But I haven't done nothing. I rang that Australian journalist, remember?'

'But he was the one who tipped you off about the sleazy side of Greer's business. He'd hardly ring him up and warn him.'

'You never know. It's possible. Some journalists do that. They have this strange relationship with particular tycoons: part protector, part tormentor. It mostly happens when they write a lot about the same one. Then they hate it when another journalist trespasses on their patch. So they warn their pet tycoon that their rival is preparing a hatchet job: "Don't speak to him. Don't give him any access. Warn your friends not to talk." Bruce McFall might have done that with Erskine about me, just to keep in with him. I'm serious.'

'So what would have happened?'

'Bruce could have rung Greer to say this journalist from *Man Alive* was asking questions. He'd probably hype it up too: say I was asking about his Chinese girls and dodgy businesses. Make out I was planning a demolition job.'

'But would Erskine Greer recognise your name?' asked Suzy.

'Maybe, maybe not. But he'd recognise *Man Alive* because of Anna Grant's interview. After she was killed he presumably thought that was the end of the profile. It wouldn't happen. He was safe. So when this second journalist from *Man Alive* moves on to the case, he's nervous. He probably suspects I've heard Anna's tape and know all about the Vietcong connection.'

'Which you do. Where *is* that tape, by the way?'

'Still at my flat in Anna's tape recorder. Blast! I should have put it in a strongbox in the bank.

'But wait,' I said, 'I want to think this through a bit more. Imagine I'm Erskine Greer. I've given this compromising interview to Anna which could fuck up the biggest business deal of my life. Somehow or other, I arrange to have her killed. Then, a few days later, I remember the tape of the interview, and have her flat broken into.' I was becoming excited as I saw the pieces form in a fresh configuration. 'In fact, the men in Harrington Gardens needn't have been Fulger's at all – they could have been working for Greer, searching for the other tape. Don't you see, it needn't have been the Anastasia interview they wanted, it was the Erskine one.'

'And they didn't find it. So why didn't they search *your* flat, then?'

'Because they already had. Only they missed the tape recorder under the sofa.' But then my heart fell. 'On the other hand,' I admitted wearily, 'the man in the car outside my flat that Saturday was definitely working for Fulger. I saw him at the schloss. Oh, bugger the whole thing, I don't get it. Nothing ties in.'

'It almost does,' said Suzy. 'Forget Fulger for a moment. I think you're right to concentrate on Greer. Keep it simple. Go on assuming he murdered Anna Grant and had her flat done over. Then what?'

'Then nothing. He'd keep his fingers crossed the tape didn't turn up, and carry on as normal, taking over Federated Aviation. If you think about it, Anna interviewed him on Saturday and was dead on Sunday. Erskine would reckon she didn't have much opportunity to tell anyone about his indiscretion.'

I also thought: Anna was in bed with Greer half the afternoon. But I didn't mention that part to Suzy. I still felt too sensitive about it.

Anyway, what *were* my feelings now about Anna, three weeks on from that fateful weekend? That was a question

I'd been doing my best to dodge. Anna, the one true love of my life, with her glossy hair and racehorse legs. The opportunities I wasted, those inconclusive lunches, when all the time we should have been together. Did I mind about her other lovers? When a collector falls for a great painting – some matchless Matisse – he doesn't mind that it comes with a provenance; even if it has been temporarily possessed by some short-fingered Wall Street arbitrageur or Chechen Mafia don.

But of course I minded. I minded so much, it ached. Anna, Anna, everything I'm doing, I'm doing it for you.

'Now let's follow it right through,' I went on. 'Three weeks go by and nothing leaks out. Anna's buried. Greer goes to Houston, back to Hong Kong, working on the deal. He's pretty certain by now he's safe and it'll go through. Then he gets this call from Bruce McFall. Everything's compromised again. Obviously Bruce doesn't realise the impact his warning's going to make. *Man Alive* haven't let the story drop after all and are sending a writer out to Hong Kong. What does Erskine Greer do next? Well, obviously he first finds out who Kit Preston is. That would be easy enough. He'll discover I've been fired, which will puzzle him. Would I still be writing for *Man Alive* in those circumstances? Possibly. Spike Steel might have assigned me the story.

'Depends how much depth he's got in his research,' I went on. 'If his people have really asked around, they might have discovered I was close to Anna. There were rumours about that, weren't there?'

'Certainly were. I was always being asked whether you were bonking her.'

'Jesus,' I laughed hollowly. 'If only they knew.' Then I said, 'OK, so Greer thinks I'm an ex-boyfriend of Anna's. That would worry him even more. He'll think Anna told me about his confession on tape and I know all about the arms dealing. I mean, if she told anyone, it would be me, right? You'd tell your boyfriend or someone in your family.'

We both said it together: 'Peter.' She could have told Peter. And now Peter was dead.

'You know something, Suzy,' I said. 'I don't want to be melodramatic, but the more we talk about it, the more the Erskine Greer theory stands up. It works timewise too. I rang Bruce on Monday evening – Hong Kong time – so he'd probably have contacted Greer some time on Tuesday. Which would have allowed about thirty-six hours to make and deliver the threat to Cazzie. And don't forget something else too. Although, to us, the wording is oblique – "Your father is asking too many questions" – it wouldn't look that way to Erskine. As far as he's aware, he's the *only* suspect. He doesn't know about Bruno or Micky. He murdered Anna to shut her up and let's assume he had Peter Grant killed too: that snake bite always sounded fishy. But why kill Peter? Presumably because he contacted Erskine in Hong Kong – or Houston – and let him know Anna had told him something. From everything I've been told, Peter was incredibly high minded and persistent. Even if he didn't realise Erskine had anything to do with Anna's death, he'd be keen to publicise the arms dealing. Anna told me her brother had a huge contempt for capitalists. He thought they were all hypocrites – and here was proof. He'd have seen himself continuing Anna's work and keeping alive the sacred flame. Anyway, whatever was said, Erskine must have seen Peter as a threat and a loose cannon ...'

'... and had him bumped off,' said Suzy. She stared at me across the pub table. 'And now a third person seems to know all about it too: you, Kit.'

'Four, actually: you as well.'

'But they don't know about me. It's you I'm scared for.'

'Then let's be doubly careful. I'm sorry to have to say this about your spiritual guardian, Suzy, but it's beginning to look like your godfather is a serial killer.'

Dad returned with Cazzie from the slots having lost my two pounds and four more of his own.

'Can't imagine why you encourage the girl to gamble,'

he grumbled. 'Might just as well make a bonfire of your money and set it alight.'

Cazzie, undespondent, hopped from foot to foot. 'Only one more horseshoe, that's all we needed for the jackpot. It's *so close*. Just one more pound, pleeeese, Daddy, that's all I need.'

'Sorry, darling, no more money, it's time to go now. Say goodbye to Grandpa and see you soon.'

'Off up to London?' asked Dad. 'Or back to this cottage you've borrowed?'

Suzy and I exchanged glances. Where the hell *were* we going? Where *could* we go?

'First packing, then off,' I replied airily. 'Best to beat the traffic.' Then we made our farewells and headed back towards the centre of Alton.

'I enjoyed meeting your father,' said Suzy bravely, when we'd put several roundabouts between ourselves and him. 'There's quite a family resemblance.'

'Don't feel you have to say anything, Suzy. Probably better if you don't. You don't choose your parents: they just are.'

'All I'm saying is that behind that gruff exterior he's interesting and quite well informed. Like you. How old is he? Sixty-five? I haven't met many sixty-five-year-olds who know about the Internet.'

'That's just it. He doesn't *know* about the Internet. He's just heard of it. It's not the same thing. He's a prize bullshitter.'

'Well, so are you. You've told me that yourself. You know just enough on every subject to get by. You pride yourself on that.'

'At least I don't lay down the law like he does.'

'Yes, you do. I'm not criticising you, but you do like to give the impression of knowing everything.'

Cazzie, strapped into her seat in the back, suddenly joined in. 'You *do* know everything anyway, Daddy. You said you did. You said you know every single thing in the whole world. Even in Australia. Even in America. Don't you, Daddy?'

I laughed. 'Seems I'm outnumbered here.' Then I said to Suzy, 'Here's one big gap in my knowledge for a start. There's a junction coming up. Where the hell are we heading for, anyway?'

'The airport?'

'What, now?'

'Why not? Drop Cazzie back with her mother – if you think it's safe to do that – and catch the evening flight to Hong Kong. I'm fairly certain they go at lunchtime and around nine p.m. If we can get seats.'

We found a callbox half a mile up the road, next to a bus stop, and Suzy got out to ring the airlines.

Ten minutes later she put her head through the car window. 'British Airways and Cathay Pacific are both full. We're on the wait list for both, but it doesn't sound promising. There are two business-class seats on Trans-Asia at ten o'clock, if you've no objection to flying with them.'

'Erskine Greer's airline? Jesus: *dare* we?'

'It's a scheduled flight via Dubai. I can't believe they'd push us out in mid-air.'

'You're right, I'm just feeling paranoid about everything, that's all. OK, let's reserve them. And then I'm going to call Sally.'

Sally answered at the second ring sounding tense.

'Thank God you've rung, Kit. I've just been sitting by this telephone, praying for it to be you.'

'Gracious, Sally, it sounds like the old days.'

'Don't joke, I've been so worried, I couldn't sleep all night. Is Cazzie safe?'

'She's fine. She's right outside in the car.'

'You mean you've *left* her? All alone in the car? Is the car locked?'

'No, but Suzy's with her, it's fine. I can see her from here.'

'Who's Suzy? You mean you took a *girl* with you to Paul's cottage?'

'Honestly, Sally, you remember Suzy. Suzy my secretary. There's nothing suspicious about it.'

Sally sounded unconvinced. Through the glass wall of the telephone box, I could see Suzy in the car, tickling Cazzie and laughing. She wasn't beautiful like Anna, but she was remarkably pretty. I loved the way her blonde hair flicked into a duck's tail at the nape of her neck.

'You know the police came round here asking for you?' said Sally. 'I've had to lie for you. They asked if I knew where you were, and when had I last seen you.'

'What did you say?'

'I said Sunday, when you came to visit Cazzie.'

'Did they believe you?'

'I'm not sure. I think so. But when I mentioned Cazzie they asked where she was.'

'And?'

'I said she'd gone out to tea with a friend, but I don't know how convincing it was. It's awful to lie to the police, I felt like a criminal. I asked them what you're supposed to have done, but they won't say.'

'And presumably you're wondering that now.'

Sally sounded exhausted. 'Kit, I don't know what I'm meant to think. This terrible card arrives, threatening Cazzie, and I want to call the police but you tell me not to. You told me to trust you, which I did, God knows why. And then the police turn up at the house like they want to arrest you or something, and I haven't a clue what's going on, not a clue. And you've got Cazzie. Oh Kit, I hate all this. I want Cazzie back, and I want you to talk to the police: surely you can just explain to them what's actually happened. *Please* do it. I'm *frightened*, Kit.'

Outside the callbox, a woman in a shellsuit with a schnauzer on a lead was gesticulating about needing to make an urgent call.

'Sally, I just beg you not to tell the police. Not yet. I promise I'll explain everything when I can, but this isn't the right time. Now listen, I'm bringing Cazzie back to you, but I daren't come near the house in case it's being watched. And, anyway, it's too dangerous for you to stay there with Cazzie. You've got to keep her out of London.'

'The cottage?'

'I'm afraid not. They may know about it now, and that goes for Paul's own house too. If they've found Axford, they'll have found both places.'

'Maybe my mother's? If I ask her, she'll say yes. She'll pretend it's very inconvenient of course, at such short notice, but she won't be doing anything else. And she dotes on Cazzie.'

That was a great idea. Sally's mother lived on the very edge of the New Forest, in a tile-slung farmhouse surrounded by conifers. Cazzie had always loved going there. You could feed sugar lumps to wild ponies from the palm of your hand, and for all her preciseness, and insistence on tidiness and good manners, Granny-in-the-Forest was a favourite.

The woman with the schnauzer was clicking her tongue as I looked through her, pretending not to notice.

'Sally, if you'll do this for me – one last thing – I want you to meet us at Heathrow in three hours' time in the multi-storey car park at Terminal Three. Let's say Level B. And I want you to be packed – for yourself and Cazzie – and then drive straight to your mother's, without telling anyone where you're going. Have you got that?'

'Kit,' Sally said, 'yesterday when you asked me to trust you, I said it was the last time. Now you're asking me again. Well, this really *is* the last time. And I mean it. You bully me into doing these things, and I say yes, and then I regret it.'

'Point taken, Sally. But you'll be at the airport?'

She hesitated. *Please say yes.* Unless Sally agreed to take Cazzie into hiding, I couldn't fly to Hong Kong. And if I couldn't expose Erskine – and fast – it was all over.

'I'll be there. But I'll tell you one thing, Kit. These last two days have reminded me exactly why we had to split up, and why we were mad to have got married in the first place.'

We reached London in ninety minutes and parked around the corner from Suzy's flat in Lupus Street. My own passport lives permanently inside my wallet, but Suzy needed to collect hers. She also wanted to pick up some clothes.

Cazzie and I sat in the Vauxhall, singing the song about the crocodile and the little fish. We'd sung it for three car journeys and were word-perfect. Cazzie loves the bit that goes: '*The crocodile's jaws shut tight – SNAP!*' It's the cue for biting me on the arm.

Suzy returned with a small suitcase, looking alarmed.

'We'd better get out of here fast,' she said. 'The police have been round at my flat too, looking for us. They were there an hour ago.'

'I just don't believe this. You'd think it was the only case in Britain.'

'Apparently Howard Trench has got them all revved up about the stolen BMW. He thinks I'm your accomplice. Gemma, my flatmate, was there; she's taken a day off work. She's supposed to tell the police if I show up, but she's not going to, of course.'

'Well done, Gemma.'

'Actually she's done a rather sneaky thing to help. The police kept asking where we might have gone, and Gemma told them I've always wanted to visit the vineyards of the Loire, and how I talk about it all the time, and that we've probably driven down there in the BMW.'

'Great. Let's hope Barratt and Crow waste a fortnight touring the châteaux. We need time.'

Then a horrible thought hit me, and I groaned. 'Passport Control! Won't they have given our names to Emigration? Isn't that what the police do automatically? So when we show up at the airport, they'll arrest us.'

'That is possible,' said Suzy. She looked thoughtful. 'But from what Gemma was saying, I don't think it's quite reached that stage. They might do it in the next couple of days, but I imagine it's quite a performance, alerting all the airports and ferry ports. We should still be OK.'

'In any case, I don't see there's much alternative. We've just got to risk it. We've nowhere else to go, and we've got to keep up momentum.'

Sally was waiting in the multi-storey, stony faced. She glared at Suzy, and refused to speak to either of us as I transferred the car seat. Instead, she addressed all her remarks to Cazzie, asking her if she had had a nice time, and expressing surprise that she was wearing the same jersey two days running. I know Sally in these moods, and it's best to steer clear.

I began to say something about not telling anyone where they were going, and Sally snapped, 'I did *hear* your instructions. There's no need to repeat everything twenty times like I'm half-witted. That may be your opinion of me, but there's no need to rub it in.' Then she said, 'My mother says it couldn't be more inconvenient having us to stay. She's got the carpet cleaners coming in, and a Neighbourhood Watch committee, endless things. But *very kindly* she's agreed to have us for three or four days.' Then her voice softened. 'Won't it be *fun*, Cazzie, seeing Granny-in-the-Forest? She's so excited you're coming. She's getting your bedroom ready and tomorrow you're going to feed the ponies.'

After they'd driven off, Suzy and I fetched a trolley and pushed our luggage inside the terminal. I bought our tickets and gulped at the price. Business-class tickets seem inordinately expensive when you're paying with your own money. At this rate I'd be broke in a couple of weeks.

Before we checked in, we decided to separate. 'Until we've cleared the airport – that's if we even get that far – best not to speak. We're travelling separately. We're strangers, OK?'

I allowed Suzy to check in three places ahead of me at the Trans-Asia desk. She looked completely unruffled. She was issued a boarding card and, without catching my eye, walked through to Departures.

I reached the front of the queue and handed over my passport and ticket. The Trans-Asia girl in her lilac and grey uniform glanced cursorily at them and tapped into her computer.

'It's the last aisle seat, Mr Preston.'

'Is the flight full?'

'Completely full tonight, sir.' And she handed me my boarding card.

I passed through Departures and could see Suzy ahead, queuing for Security. She placed her suitcase on the belt and walked through the metal detector. Just ahead lay Passport Control. Any second now she'd show them her passport. And then we'd know.

I was sweating as she approached the middle booth. She'd chosen a young man, he looked about twenty-five. The correct choice, I thought. The older man and young girl in the adjacent booths both looked more rigorous.

Suzy held up her passport and, with barely a second glance, he nodded her through.

I sighed with relief, but now it was my turn. And this might not be so easy: after all, my name was more likely to have been posted than Suzy's.

I also made for the middle booth. I held up my passport, with my photograph visible, and continued walking. If you look purposeful and unbothered, they never stop you.

'One moment, sir.'

The young man was calling me back.

'May I take a look at your passport a moment, sir?'

He began flicking through the maroon booklet, scrutinising old visas.

'And your most recent trip out of the UK was to?'

'Er, New York. I got back about a week ago. A week today, in fact.'

Was that really all it was? One week? It felt like a month.

'Thank you very much, sir.' He returned the passport with a nod. 'Have a pleasant trip.'

Suzy was waiting just beyond the barrier, and beckoned

me to follow her down a duty-free mall. 'What on earth did *he* want? I thought he was arresting you.'

'Me too. But it was just routine. I *think*.'

Forty minutes later we were shuffling, separately, down a jetty to board the plane. Suzy was chatting up a Chinese man in the queue who was wearing a track suit. Travellers boarding night flights always look like refugees anyway; a sad line of displaced people inching their way along geometric-patterned carpet.

I found my seat, which was next to Suzy's. She looked up blankly, pretending not to recognise me. But after the plane took off, and the stewardess had trundled round the drinks wagon, we decided to introduce ourselves and were soon chatting away amiably enough, strangers on a long haul.

Later, I picked up the in-flight magazine, and flicked through the photographs of 747s with their lilac and grey livery, and route maps and pictures of duty-free scent bottles. I had no idea Trans-Asia flew to so many places these days. They'd even scheduled three flights a week to Brasilia. Maybe Peter's murderer flew Trans-Asia.

At the front of the magazine I found a letter from the Chairman, welcoming us aboard and commending Greer Corp's myriad sister operations: the hotels across Southeast Asia and a new golf and condominium complex north of Seoul. There was a photograph of Erskine Greer, silver-haired and fit, sitting behind a large teak desk and signing a document with a gold pen. It was all rather disheartening: to expose Greer seemed, just then, an impossible task.

The cabin lights were dimming for the start of the film, and Suzy was swaddling herself in lilac and grey blankets for the night. Somewhere, way below us, lay Kazakhstan. On the movie screen in the chairback in front of me, Michele Pfeiffer was swaying into a hotel suite on a pair of gold mules.

I leant over to kiss Suzy goodnight and, with the lightest of touch, she directed my lips towards her own, and we kissed properly for the first time. The passion of the moment surged through me like an electric charge.

Afterwards, neither of us said anything. What was there to say, anyway?

I watched the film for a bit, while Suzy dozed beside me with her head pressed against my shoulder and, outside, the light at the end of the wing pulsed like a heartbeat in the darkness.

By the time I awoke we were already over China.

# 22

The Kowloon Inn of Happiness, forty storeys of concrete and glass with a dragon temple in the atrium housing the reception desk and cashier, is the third-tallest new hotel in Tsim-Sha-Tsui. It towers above the Shangri-La and Royal Garden hotels on either side, and from our room on the thirty-second floor we could see right across the harbour to Wanchai and Causeway Bay, and the Peak of Hong Kong island beyond.

The Chinese bellboy had delivered our solitary piece of luggage to the room, and Suzy was already in the bathroom taking a shower. The first thing I was going to do, when I'd showered myself and had breakfast, was buy some clothes. After a night on the plane, my one shirt was an offence.

I undressed and padded into the marble-floored bathroom. Suzy was standing beneath the wide jet of hot water, washing her hair, and bubbles of lather were trickling down her back. The hot water thundered on to the enamel of the bathtub as I stepped in. Suzy saw me and smiled sweetly, as though it was the most normal thing in the world, and then directed her face back towards the showerhead. I unwrapped a mini bar of hotel soap and began washing her back, very gently, and she arched her spine with pleasure. She had a wonderful curvy figure that was somehow more wholesome than Anna's had been. I stood behind her, pressing up close, and began soaping her soft stomach. She trembled, and rolled back her head so it pressed into my shoulder, and I could smell the lemon of her shampoo very close. Suzy took my hands and slowly slid them up to her breasts. I caressed them, feeling the hardening of her nipples, as the highly pressured hot water pounded on to our heads. She was leaning back against me, so every inch of our bodies was touching: I could feel the softness of her thighs against mine and the vertebrae of her spine against my chest. Then Suzy turned to face me, and we kissed, as she removed the fast-diminishing bar of soap from my hand and took it into her own.

'Put me inside you, Suzy. Put me inside you now.'

Her skin was smooth and warm against my own, and I felt the surprising strength of her arms as she wrapped herself around me. That expression 'blind with passion' or 'blind with desire': I'd never really experienced it until that Saturday morning at the Inn of Happiness. I actually felt my peripheral vision diminish when Suzy and I made it together that first time. *Man Alive* once ran a health article on the phenomenon – 'sexual tunnel vision', brought on by a massive rush of testosterone to the penis which short-circuits the pituitary gland and optic nerve – but frankly I'd been sceptical. Our health editor had to whip up these quasi-medical sexual phenomena every month. But now I verified it at first hand.

It wasn't the longest bonk I've ever had, but it was certainly the most intense; we were oblivious to everything. Afterwards, as we lay on the bathroom floor panting, Suzy asked, 'Would you say that was a spur-of-the-moment aberration that we're never ever going to refer to again, or something more, er ...' She cast about for the right word.

'*Seminal* is the one you're after here, I think. Or *anticipated*. And I'd say it was both, actually.'

We lay entwined for almost an hour, then fetched chocolate from the mini bar which we ate in the bath while waiting for breakfast. Then we put on the white towelling dressing gowns hanging on the back of the bathroom door and, clearing the desk of its promotional clutter ('Happy Hour at the Tiger's Eye Bar', 'Visit the Greer shopping emporium at Sha Tin'), prepared for work.

From our window we could see the Star Ferry crossing and recrossing the harbour, and the piers and concrete convention centre complex of North Wanchai, half-enveloped in mist.

In a bedside drawer, Suzy located a Hong Kong telephone directory and *Yellow Pages* and started to draw up a list of useful numbers, beginning with Erskine Greer's headquarters and a string of English- and Chinese-language newspapers.

'I still feel uneasy staying at a Greer hotel,' I said. 'The worst thing is, if they ever want to find out who we've spoken to, they can check out our telephone bill. All the numbers will be logged in the computer. On the other hand, staying here will make our research seem more official. A journalist would only choose it if their article had the official blessing. When I ring people up, they'll assume our room bill is being picked up by Greer's public relations department.'

'I'd still feel safer if we *weren't* here, though. This whole room is seeded with reminders of Erskine Greer. It's creepy, the writing paper, shampoo in the bathroom, even these dressing gowns.' She pointed to the big lilac 'G' embroidered on the pockets.

'What I think we should do is this,' I said. 'I'm going to set up as many interviews as possible for the next couple of days. With luck I'll be able to see a couple of people today, then some more tomorrow. I'm still debating whether or not to ring Bruce McFall. It would be a useful short-cut to the key Chinese journalists, but then again he might tell Greer I'm in town.'

'I think you're mad if you do. Surely you can get to them without him, even if it takes a bit longer.'

'But that's just it. We don't *have* much time. The Federated Aviation deal looks like going through in the next few days. If we hope to expose Greer before then – not to mention everything else, like clearing my name and protecting Cazzie – we've got to get moving.'

The doorbell rang and a Chinese waiter in lilac and grey

uniform wheeled in a steel breakfast trolley, laid up with a tablecloth, china and an orchid in a champagne flute. The coffee cups were thin and delicate with one embossed lilac 'G'.

After he'd gone, I said, 'Suzy, I've had another idea too, which involves *you*. Actually, I thought of this last night on the plane, but you might not want to do it, so I was sort of waiting for the right moment to ask you.'

'What exactly do you mean by "the right moment"?' asked Suzy. 'You mean you were waiting till after we'd been to bed? How typically calculating of you.' Then she smiled. 'All right, let's hear it, your great plan.'

'I want you to ring Erskine Greer.'

'What, just like that? Ring and say what?'

'Tell him his favourite goddaughter is in Hong Kong. Say you're here for a few days, passing through on your way somewhere else, and you'd like to say hello. Chances are, he'll invite you over.'

'Supposing he does, then what?'

'Case the joint. See if you can spot anything incriminating. Ask leading questions. Just get an invitation first.'

'Sounds pretty desperate to me. But OK, I'll try. If he does agree to see me, I can't believe it'll be more cringe-making than the last time. And you never know, he might offer to buy me another leather suitcase.'

At Inns of Happiness there are two telephone lines per hotel room, so I sat at the desk ringing Chinese journalists while Suzy dialled the Greer Corporation headquarters from the bedside phone. I could hear her asking to be put through to Erskine's office, and then explaining who she was to his personal assistant.

'He's in a meeting,' she reported afterwards, 'but apparently won't be very long. His secretary sounded old, but friendly. She said she'd get him to ring me when he comes out.'

I had less luck with the Chinese newspapers. Without a specific name to ask for, I engendered only bewilderment in their switchboards. At the first two papers I rang – the

*Oriental Daily News* and *Wen Wei Po* — the telephonists were so confused by my questions they cut me off.

After that, I simply asked to be put through to the newsroom.

By lunchtime, I had two meetings scheduled for the afternoon, though it was hard to tell exactly who they were with, or what seniority the journalists held. At two o'clock I would visit someone called Chiu Man-hon at the *Sing Tao Jih Pao*, and was due a couple of hours later at the offices of *Ming Pao*, a middle-market Chinese daily which competed with *Sing Tao*.

'Before you go anywhere,' said Suzy, 'I'm taking you to buy some shirts. I noticed a place down near the lobby. And if they sell trousers, you need them too. You can't traipse round Hong Kong in a towelling robe.'

We took the elevator downstairs, past the dragon temple and Scandinavian coffee shop, and inspected a mall of boutiques. There were antique shops selling jade and calligraphic scrolls and reproduction Tang Dynasty camels, and others specialising in sapphires and citrines, and watches and cameras and embroidered silk blouses. Sally's friend Paul would have approved of the gem emporium, I thought; I half-expected to see her blood-orange ruby engagement ring in the showcase.

We bought some clothes and were recrossing the lobby when a familiar voice rang out.

'Kit! Is that really you?'

It was Minnie Vass. She was looking her most formidable in sugar-pink Chanel, with her dyed black fringe held back from her face by an orchid hair-clip.

'I had no idea you were in Hong Kong,' she said accusingly, as though I had purposely concealed it from her.

'Nor I you. What brings you here, anyway?'

'Darling, I'm *always* in Hong Kong. It's literally my second home. So many friends. And so many opportunities — *still*, even with the Communists beating down the door. Seriously, darling,' she said, suddenly confidential.

'Don't tell a soul, but I'm hoping to decorate an apartment for Dickson Poon.'

'Great,' I said flatly. I was furious at running into Minnie Vass. It could blow the whole thing. What was the point of sneaking into Hong Kong, and avoiding ringing Bruce McFall, if you then collide in the lobby with one of the biggest blabbermouths of all time? She was bosom friends with Erskine Greer, for God's sake. If she mentioned to him that I was in town, what hope would we have on his home turf? He'd managed to dispose of Peter Grant five hundred miles into the Brazilian jungle, so I didn't suppose he'd have much of a problem here, if he knew what we were up to.

'If you're still around tomorrow evening,' said Minnie, 'I hope you can both come to my party.'

'What party's that?'

'The party the whole island's talking about, *that* party. It's right here at the hotel, in the ballroom. Ballet Russe cocktails and *dim sum*. It's really to celebrate the redecoration of the public rooms, but the poor Swiss General Manager doesn't know a living soul, so he's handed the whole thing over to me.'

'Sounds great,' I said uncertainly. 'But Suzy and I aren't sure about our plans at the moment.'

'Nonsense,' said Minnie. 'Complete nonsense. Whatever else you're doing, cancel it. Or bring them along too. Wait 'til you hear who's coming: Li Ka-shing, Henry and Tessa Keswick, Erskine of course, David Tang, Stanley Ho and his daughter Angela, Peter and Bessie Woo, the Kadoories ... Listen, which suite are you in? I'll have an invitation delivered to you right away and will be mortified if you don't make it.'

. 'That's blown it,' I said to Suzy after Minnie had gone. 'Now we're truly fucked. We may as well place full-page advertisements in the *South China Morning Post*, announcing our arrival in town.'

'Obviously we won't go to the party.'

'Too right we won't. But Minnie bloody Vass is the

town crier. Now I've lost my job I'm devalued currency, but she could still easily mention me to Erskine.

'Anyway,' I said wearily, 'I'd better head over to *Sing Tao*. My first interview's in twenty minutes.'

'Good luck,' said Suzy. 'I'm going back up to the room to await the call from my wicked godfather.'

I took a cab through Hung Hom, past the perimeter of Kai-Tak airport and drew up outside the *Sing Tao* building on Wang Kwong Road. From outside it resembled a giant high-tech bottling plant, one of the most modern newspaper offices I'd ever seen. Three dozen vans were standing by the delivery bay, engines running, waiting to distribute afternoon editions, while sinisterly silent printing presses completed their run. Up on the roof, the newspaper's logo was lit up in orange neon, overlooking the landing lights of the airport.

A security guard directed me to the fourth floor where Chiu Man-hon would meet me by the elevator. On each floor, the steel doors of the lift slid open on to wide, empty landings with bright plastic signs written in English and Chinese script. The offices reminded me of a hospital, clinical and subdued.

Chiu Man-hon looked twenty-eight, with thick black hair and horn-rimmed glasses. In his dark Istante suit and Breitling Chrono Colt sports watch, both heavily featured in last month's *Man Alive*, he looked more like a futures trader than a journalist. He explained he worked for the *Sing Tao* business section, and motioned me to follow him across the open-plan newsroom where he drew me up a chair alongside his desk.

'So, how can I assist you?' he asked. His accent sounded two parts Chinese to one part Canadian. Man-hon had evidently travelled abroad. His face was round and bland; his only distinguishing feature, just above his lip, was a black mole, out of which sprouted two long black hairs.

Elsewhere in the room about thirty journalists, of both sexes, were tapping away at screens. None showed any interest in my arrival.

'Let me explain. I'm researching an article – a long article, six or seven thousand words – for the British men's magazine *Man Alive*. The subject is Erskine Greer.'

I noticed Chiu Man-hon's eyebrows rise a centimetre before his expression resumed its blanket inscrutability.

'I'm going to be in Hong Kong for about a week, staying at the Inn of Happiness ...'

'That hotel belongs to Mr Greer,' observed Man-hon. 'It is very tall: one of the tallest, I think, in Tsim-Sha-Tsui.'

'Exactly. It's an excellent base from which to interview as many of Greer's friends and business associates as possible. Obviously the peg for this piece is his impending takeover of Federated Aviation.'

'That is one very big deal,' said Man-hon. 'Two point three billion US dollars. Hong Kong people have plenty of respect for Mr Greer.'

'What I'd like to ask you about – and this is for background only, entirely unattributable – is how Erskine Greer is viewed by the business community out here. Is he seen as an Establishment figure – conservative – or more of a buccaneering outsider?'

'Hong Kong people have plenty of admiration for Mr Greer. His companies, you know, began as very small enterprises, maybe thirty years back. Today, everyone in Hong Kong knows the legend of Mr Greer's many ventures.'

'On a more personal level, though. What motivates Erskine Greer? Is he ruthless, does he play dirty in business, that kind of thing?'

Chiu Man-hon furrowed his brow. He seemed to be searching for the right expression.

'I think everyone in Hong Kong,' he said at last, 'respects Mr Greer as a prime mover in Hong Kong business. The decisions he is making are very fast and firm. He has grown his operations overseas into a very strong network, first in Asia and now in China.'

Man-hon and I stared each other out, while I pretended to make notes on my pad. Was it possible he thought these platitudes were remotely helpful, or was this deliberate Chinese stonewalling?

I tried a new tack. 'Who are his enemies? All significant business tycoons have enemies. When your paper has written about Erskine Greer in the past, who do you contact for a more critical take on his deals?'

'Actually, Mr Greer has the respect of everyone in the business community. They look at the way he has extended his operations – from trading to shipping, airlines, hotels, shopping malls – and all must think about him with the same admiration.'

For a moment I considered throttling him, or thumping his head against the flickering green screen of his computer. What was it Bruce McFall had said? 'Ask the Chinese. If you can find any that'll talk to you, that is.' It was infuriating to have to listen to this disingenuous pap.

'One last question, then. What about Erskine Greer's other businesses? The businesses nobody ever mentions out here? I'm sure you know the ones I mean.'

Chiu Man-hon gave me a hard stare. 'Mr Greer has many charitable enterprises, but I don't know details of these myself. For better information, you must consult his office directly.'

At the end of the street I found a callbox and rang Suzy at the hotel.

'Hi, Kit. How's it going?'

'Hopeless. I've just endured twenty minutes of pure frustration. Total waste of time.'

'Then here's some good news. Erskine rang me back.'

'And?'

'He's invited me to lunch tomorrow. At his house. He couldn't have been friendlier. Said he was delighted to hear from me.'

'Well, watch out. It's fantastic you're going, but it could be dangerous.'

'We'll talk about it tonight,' said Suzy. 'I'm off in search of something to wear. Last time Erskine saw me I was in backpacker mode. This time I'd better make more effort.'

The offices of *Ming Pao*, across the harbour from Kowloon on Quarry Bay, are from a different era to *Sing Tao*; situated on the corner of Java Street and Healthy Road, in a low-slung neighbourhood of hardware shops and mah-jong parlours. They occupy a classic old-style Chinese office block: the front entrance and bottom three storeys faced with grey and white marble, the upper floors like a Mongkok tenement with air-conditioning units grafted on to the outside walls, and precarious, droopy wiring.

I waited in reception on a suede sofa while Security rang up to Vincent Leong. Twenty minutes later, when I had almost begun to give up on him, Vincent appeared in the lobby.

'Kit Preston? Excuse me for keeping you waiting but I had a story to put to bed. Unfortunately, just a story, not a beautiful lady.' And he beamed, exposing several prominent gold teeth.

Vincent Leong looked fifty-five: a small, amused man in a white shirt with his hair combed and greased straight back across his scalp. He took me up to the sixth floor in a teak-lined lift, to his office off a teak-panelled corridor. From the many proof pages pinned on to cork boards, I deduced he was the paper's business and social gossip columnist. The paragraph-length items were written in Chinese characters, but I recognised photographs of Joyce Ma, the fashion queen, Sir Run Run Shaw, the tycoon, and Flora Cheong-Leen, the Hong Kong socialite.

'So,' said Vincent Leong, when he'd offered tea, 'you are writing about Erskine Greer for a magazine. May I ask, is this a general article or have you a particular angle in mind?'

'Well, the takeover of Federated Aviation means he's in the news at the moment. So it's going to be a business profile, with hopefully some colour as well.'

Vincent Leong laughed. 'Then I hope they're allowing you plenty of space. Have you seen any of his mistresses yet?'

'Not yet. In fact, I was rather hoping you might give me some background on that kind of thing. I've read the cuttings, but they mostly just concentrate on his business deals.'

'That's the English-language papers. How would they know? You don't read Cantonese, do you? I imagine not. Well, you'll miss my column, then. I must have written about all Greer's mistresses over the years.'

'Actually, I *have* met one of them, I think, an English decorator called Minnie Vass.'

Vincent Leong threw up his hands and shrieked. There was a camp side to him: a Chinese drama queen.

'Minnie Vass! She's a scream. Are you going to her party tomorrow evening? Minnie gives wonderful parties, I clear the whole column for Minnie. But she was never a mistress of Erskine's. Lover, probably. But never a mistress, no. The mistresses are always Chinese.'

'Why's that?'

Vincent tossed his head. 'Because Chinese girls make good mistresses, I suppose. It's one of the things we do well. Ming porcelain, abalone, mistresses. No, there's a reason. Chinese girls don't make trouble. They understand the arrangement. They keep their legs open and their mouths shut.'

'You mean they don't gossip?'

'In the case of Greer, that's essential.'

'Why's that?'

Vincent Leong looked at me, suddenly serious. 'Kit, I can help you with your article. I can tell you things of interest. Things that haven't been told before in English publications. But there are subjects too that I cannot speak to you about. Things from before my time. Erskine Greer has always been helpful to me. People like Erskine are important for my job. When he throws a big party, I need access for my photographer. When I write about his mistresses he doesn't give a damn. It is read only by a Chinese audience anyway. And the mistresses like it.

Sometimes, when there is a new one, they ring me themselves: they appreciate the publicity.'

'What sort of girls are they?'

'Nice girls. Not whore types. Erskine always goes for the same sort, tall, long legs, elegant. And he's generous too: the best clothes, jewellery, nice apartment. When it's over, they get to keep the apartment. That's why the girls like to be with him, they know that. I could name eight apartment buildings with ex-mistresses of Erskine Greer in residence.'

'If I called on them, would they see me?'

'Sure. Why not? But I'll tell you two things: they'll check first with Erskine, to make sure it's OK, and they'll tell you nothing indiscreet. If your interest is his famous bedroom preferences, you'll get nothing from them.'

'I don't know the first thing about Erskine's sexual tastes.'

'You don't?' Vincent looked genuinely astonished. 'In the Chinese community, everyone knows about Erskine Greer. Two girls, three girls, he has a big appetite, that's what they say, anyhow.' He snorted. 'There used to be one special lady. Her name was Wendy: Wendy Lai. Very, very beautiful. When she and Erskine first met, she can't have been much older than fifteen. She came from the New Territories, from a small place near the border with China. She came into Hong Kong to work as a waitress at a restaurant in Wanchai, on Lockhart Road. One evening Erskine came in for a business dinner. Within a week he'd set Wendy Lai up in a nice apartment on Mid-Levels. He bought her everything: French clothes, fur coats, jewellery. Erskine loves to buy jewellery for his girls.'

Vincent's eyes sparkled, and his gold teeth glinted, as he told the story. I could see why he was a professional gossip. And he was right, too, about Erskine loving to buy jewellery for girls. His recorded voice from Anna's answerphone echoed in my head: 'Another thing I should have told you is bring jewellery ... If you forget, I can buy you some out there.'

'For more than a year Erskine took Wendy Lai everywhere,' said Vincent. 'This was highly unusual; normally he pays home calls only on his girls. He doesn't take them out so much. But Wendy he took racing, on overseas trips, even to Greer Corporation functions. There was plenty of speculation that they might get married. Then, one day, another girl came to stay with Wendy at the apartment. Her name was Jacky, and she was a year younger than Wendy, from the same village. Pretty soon she was accompanying them everywhere: Erskine and his two girls. He took them on holiday to Bali, and they stayed with him on the Greer Company junk. You can imagine the scandal: everyone was saying he had sex with both girls at the same time. He bought Jacky clothes and fur coats, and jewellery exactly like Wendy's. This continued for maybe two years. The girls were like twins with their sugar daddy. Then, very abruptly, Erskine dropped them. Overnight, it was over.'

'Why was that, do you think?'

'No one knows for sure. But I have a good idea, and I wrote this in the column. The leadership in Beijing is very conservative. Those old men were doing a lot of business with the Greer Corporation at the time. I think Erskine was warned off. Either drop your teenage mistresses, or you don't get the permission for your shopping malls in Beijing and Guangzhou. Which goes to show,' said Vincent, laughing, 'that Erskine Greer prefers money over sex. He knows the opportunities to make big money don't come along every day. But, with sex, in Hong Kong new potential mistresses arrive every week.'

'Where are they now, Wendy and Jacky?'

'Neither is in Hong Kong. When Erskine finished with them, he wanted them off the island. It had all been too public. But he looked after them, he found husbands for them both. Jacky's in China, married to the Greer agent in Guangzhou. Wendy lives in Manila. Her husband's a very rich Filipino, an old associate of Erskine's, with casinos in Quezon City.'

385

'Do you mind if I change the subject slightly and ask you a question about Erskine Greer's past?'

Vincent frowned.

'Have you ever heard anything about his activities as an arms dealer?'

He stared at me noncommittally, saying nothing.

'This would be right at the start of his career,' I continued. 'During the Vietnam war.'

Vincent Leong looked at his watch, stood up and, without meeting my eye, began gathering armfuls of proofs from his desk.

'So sorry,' he mumbled, 'so sorry. The time. You must excuse me, I have to clear my pages now.'

He hustled me to the lift door and pressed the call button. 'Maybe see you at Minnie's party. It'll be a hot crowd.' And then he hurried away, as quickly as possible, back along the teak corridor in the direction of his office.

After the interview I waited forty minutes by the Quarry Bay expressway without finding a taxi. The sky had turned porridge grey and it looked like we were in for a storm. Several empty taxis drove by, but when I tried to wave them down, they went on without stopping. I felt extraordinarily annoyed and frustrated.

The stuff about Erskine's underage mistresses was all very interesting, had I really been researching a profile, but for my purposes it got me precisely nowhere. What did I even think we were doing in Hong Kong, other than blowing the last of my resources on a forlorn ploy to expose Erskine Greer? Had I really imagined that by cross-questioning a few Chinese journalists I'd discover the key to Anna's murder? All I'd managed to learn in my first day of research was that Greer was impetuous and vaguely amoral in both business and bed. Neither of which are illegal or even, in Hong Kong, particularly noteworthy.

I eventually found a taxi and asked for the pier for the

Star Ferry. From there I'd recross the harbour to Tsim-Sha-Tsui.

I sat in the back of the cab, torpid with jetlag. My escapade with Suzy this morning had exhilarated but also rather alarmed me. I wasn't in a position to embark on a serious relationship, especially with Suzy. My money looked as if it would last for another week at most. We had our return air tickets, but chances were they'd rearrest me at Heathrow airport. I hated the idea of dragging Suzy into all this. She was too nice a girl to deserve it. She needed a reliable, settled man in her life: not a nearly broke, jobless murder suspect on the run.

I bought a ticket for the ferry and sat on a bench next to the window, staring out at the grey, choppy water. All around me were Chinese with canvas bags full of shopping, jabbering in Cantonese. The curse of this thing was that I didn't speak Cantonese myself. How could I hope to breach the Great Wall of mistrust if I couldn't schmooze my interviewees in their own language? Both Chiu Man-hon and Vincent Leong knew much more than they'd been prepared to say, but how I was going to unearth it, I hadn't a clue.

As we crossed the harbour, I once again went over everything I knew about Anna's last night alive, and her relationship with Greer. Barney Weiss had dropped her home at Harrington Gardens; ten minutes later, Anna rang me sounding relaxed and normal. If Greer killed her, he'd have to have done so later that evening or early the next morning: he needed to shut her up quickly before she told anyone else about the arms dealing. So let's suppose he turned up at, say, eight on Sunday morning and rang the intercom. Would Anna have let him in? Of course she would, they'd spent half the previous afternoon in bed together. 'Hi, Erskine. I'll buzz you in, come on up.' It could have been planned, the rendezvous. Erskine would be round for breakfast. No wonder she didn't want to come over to my flat on Saturday night. 'I think I'll pass,' she'd said. 'It's been a long day.'

Would he have killed her himself? I couldn't imagine it, somehow, but why not? Wait until he got close, then a sharp crack on the back of the head to throw her balance, and hands round the windpipe. She'd have struggled, but Erskine was fit. After five or so minutes she'd have stopped struggling. And he'd have had the advantage of surprise. She wouldn't have suspected a thing. Then he could have humped Anna's AppleMac downstairs, in case it contained any incriminating notes, and headed off back to Hyde Park Gate. The whole expedition needn't have taken longer than half an hour. The Filipino maid would swear he never even left home.

I got back to the hotel but Suzy hadn't returned yet, so I lay down on the bed and tried to focus on my next move. What I really wanted was a drink, but I needed a clear head even more. There were still a couple of Chinese journalists to see, but on current form I wasn't optimistic this would achieve much. Maybe Suzy would discover something tomorrow at lunch: but that was ridiculous. What was I hoping for? Invoices for a Vietcong arms deal? A diary confession to murdering Anna, left open on Erskine's desk?

The more I thought about it, the more frustrated I became. Someone in Hong Kong knew something about Erskine Greer. If he'd built his business through trading in weapons, there must be several people who knew about it: clerks, agents, middlemen. But who? And how could I get hold of them?

There was one way, of course. I yanked the telephone on to the bed and, before I could think better of it, dialled Bruce McFall's office switchboard and asked to be put through.

'Bruce McFall.' He sounded less slurred than last time, but only slightly.

'This is Kit Preston. You may remember I rang you last week from England, about an article I'm writing on Erskine Greer.'

'Sure,' said Bruce. 'For a pooftah's magazine, you said.'

'Exactly. Well, I took your advice about doing some legwork in Hong Kong. I'm here now. I've been interviewing Chinese journalists.'

I knew it was a risk mentioning the Chinese press, but I reckoned it was worth taking. If Bruce was going to relay our conversation to Erskine, he'd do so anyway. And I needed to establish my journalistic seriousness if there was any hope of him helping me.

'Did you find them co-operative, the Chinks?' asked Bruce.

'So so. A bit guarded. Some were great, though: gave me some hot leads.'

'Yeah?' Bruce sounded curious. As a resident hack, his professional status would be undermined if I produced a scoop on his home turf. 'What's the angle?'

'Just paydirt. Greer's other businesses et cetera. Probably the same stuff you couldn't publish in the *Economic Review*. And then I'll incorporate a lot of new stuff about the mistresses.'

'Have you interviewed any of them, the girls?'

'Between ourselves, I've made progress. I'll just say one word: Manila.'

Bruce whistled. 'Wendy Lai? You saw Wendy Lai in Manila?' He sounded impressed.

'Look, I can't talk about it over the phone. I'm staying at the Inn of Happiness.'

Bruce was suddenly serious. 'Sure, mate, I understand. How about meeting up for a drink tomorrow morning? We could compare notes, off the record, of course.'

'That's a deal. Bring your stuff on Greer, and we'll trade. Is there somewhere to meet where we won't be overheard?'

'There's a place in Central on Queen's Road. In a basement, opposite New World Tower. Shanghai Bill's. Cocktail place. Nobody goes except in the evening. How about we meet there at eleven a.m. tomorrow?'

After the call, I awarded myself a small pat on the back. The conversation had gone off well. Without actually telling an outright lie, I'd sufficiently intrigued Bruce into meeting me, and bringing along his Greer file. If I strung him along tomorrow, drawing on Anna's taped interview with Erskine and her description of his London house, plus some suitably vague observations about Wendy Lai, I might just get the break I needed.

It was half past six and Suzy still wasn't back. I left a note by the telephone, saying I wouldn't be long, and headed downstairs to the hotel bar. Now that the Bruce McFall encounter was set up, I felt like a proper drink, built by a proper barman, rather than a go-it-alone squirt from the mini bar.

The Tiger's Eye Bar was tucked behind the front lobby: a softly lit, wood-panelled nook got up like the library in an English country house hotel. There were green leather wing chairs with needlepoint cushions, a large squashy sofa covered in red Bennison fabric, and several alcove cupboards displaying Sèvres porcelain. One entire wall was taken up by a panelled bar, the surface of which was dotted with bowls of cashews, olives and deep-fried shrimp balls. The place was already three quarters full, so I found a vacant stool at the bar and ordered a Bloody Mary. A Chinese barman in a white mess jacket made an elaborate show with a cocktail shaker, before sieving the spicy red tomato juice into a salt-encrusted glass goblet.

Although there were a fair number of Chinese businessmen using the bar, it was clear that its main catchment was expat. Groups of British and European stockbrokers and lawyers sat around small, low tables, drinking beer. In a quiet corner, two French brokers, divided by open attaché cases, were sifting through documents, while every so often a whoop of laughter rang out from a table of young Swire's recruits.

'Excuse me? Is anyone sitting here?'

An Englishman in a flannel suit indicated the stool next to my own.

'Sure, it's free. No one's there.'

He nodded his thanks. He was about my age. His

brogues, I noticed, were well polished. I guessed he worked in raw money, in one form or another.

'Mind passing the olives?' he asked after a bit. 'Barman's rather dragging his feet tonight with the service.'

I passed them, and was warmly thanked.

'Live out here?' he asked.

'No, London. What about you?'

'Also London. But chances are I'll be posted to Hong Kong some time next year.'

'Would that be good news?'

'Workwise, yes. It'd be promotion. But there's a bit of unfinished personal business in England I need to sort out first. To be honest, I'm engaged to a wonderful girl, but there are complications.'

There was something disarmingly charming about him. He had an easy manner. Normally, I avoid getting embroiled with strangers in bars, but tonight, on my own, it seemed harmless enough.

'What do you do?' I asked.

'Banking. Mergers and acquisitions, mainly.'

'You're not involved with Erskine Greer's bid for Federated Aviation, are you?'

'No, Morgan Stanley are doing that one. But we've acted for Greer in the past. Interesting chap.'

'I once nearly did a deal with him myself.'

'Then you know the pitfalls. Smooth as butter, but teeth like a barracuda.'

I laughed. Over the years I've met plenty of bankers, most of them uptight, but this guy was OK.

'How do you find him as a businessman?' I asked.

'Odd mix. Brilliant time manager. Gives the impression of doing nothing at all. Always has time for you, never in a hurry. And there's nothing on his desk: no papers, completely clear. Remarkable when you think how many different businesses he's managing. Have you been to his office? Incredible paintings. I'm no modern art buff, but these are phenomenal. Tate Gallery quality, all the way.

'But I'll tell you something else about him. Behind the

civilised exterior, he's bent as a five-bob note. The structure of those businesses: everything's a subsidiary of something else. Holding company's registered in the Netherland Antilles, but he swaps it about. Closing a deal was an eye-opener. Funds appeared from everywhere: fifty million from here, thirty from there. Quite a relief afterwards to move back on to something less hairy.'

'So what deal are you working on now?'

'Can't tell you that – sorry – client confidentiality, but it's not a headline-grabber. Quoted Taipei property company trying to reverse into a Hong Kong family business. Credit Suisse and First Boston are acting for the other side. Pretty routine, nothing sexy.'

'I'm never quite sure what sexy means in a banking context.'

'Simple. If it makes an impact on the outside world, it's sexy. Measure the sex appeal in column inches in the *Financial Times*. Certain deals are automatically sexy: blue-chip companies, high-profile stocks. It's not always the biggest. There's a deal going through at the moment with a French cosmetics company, Mouchette. That's pretty sexy. They employ that supermodel, whatshername, Tigra. And the Greer deal, of course: anything involving Erskine Greer is orgasmically sexy. It was a Bloody Mary, wasn't it? Let me get you a refill.'

While the barman mixed the drinks, my neighbour looked critically round the bar.

'I never really know what to think about Hong Kong, deep down. I mean as a place to live and bring up kids. What's your take?'

I said it seemed OK to me, maybe a bit claustrophobic, but pretty safe and child-friendly.

'You really think so?' He sounded relieved. 'Girl I'm marrying, she's got one child already from the first time round, beautiful little girl, so she's obviously concerned about schools and things. I said I'd ask about a bit while I'm here.'

'So you'll inherit a stepdaughter. Is that a problem?'

'Bonus. Sweetest little thing. We were joking that half the reason I'm taking the plunge with her mother is to get the daughter. It's a package deal. Exaggeration, obviously. But she's great fun. I can't imagine how her father could bear to do a runner.'

'What possessed him to do that?'

'Couldn't tell you. I thought it tactful not to ask too many questions. Can't imagine why they got married at all – from what I've heard they're chalk and cheese. Sal's completely down to earth and straight forward, as well as being very pretty. Her ex has got himself mixed up in all sorts of trouble: dodgy acquaintances, you name it. He's on the run from the police at the moment. But Caz, the daughter, seems pretty unscathed. They're amazingly resilient, children of that age. Look,' he said, oblivious to my mounting incredulity, 'take a look at these ...' He was untying a velvet jewellery roll. 'Pearl earrings. There's a jeweller in the hotel shopping arcade who made them from my own design.' A large cultured pearl was surrounded by smaller pink pearls in the shape of a heart. They were hideous, but I guessed that Sally would love them. 'They're sort of a pre-wedding present for Sal. Her divorce could take ages to come through, so there's no point waiting.'

'None at all.'

'Which only leaves Cazzie, I've got to get something for Caz. Any suggestions? First thing she'll ask me is, "Paul, where's my present?"'

I stood up, my head reeling, and shook him firmly by the hand.

'Thanks for the drink. And very good luck in your marriage. Oh, and for your stepdaughter's present, how about a little salt and pepper set from the aeroplane? I find they always hit the spot with Clapham five-year-olds.'

On the thirty-second floor, Suzy was already in the bath, the bedroom strewn with shiny carrier bags from her shopping trip. I threw off my clothes and joined her in the hot water, hugging and kissing her, so happy to be with her again, and free from my soul-searching of this afternoon.

That night, after we made love, Suzy and I slept together in the same bed for the first time. As we lay entwined, touching feet in the darkness, her warmth, and the gentleness of her breathing, consoled me somewhat.

# 23

I was awakened by a tapping sound somewhere close by, followed by a succession of muffled thumps. The clock radio showed six-fifty and a finger of gruel-coloured light was infiltrating the edges of the curtains. At first I thought someone was forcing the door. But it was closer than that: they must already be inside the room.

Suzy was asleep next to me as I slipped out of bed. Leaving the lights off, I stole across the carpet. If I could reach the upright chair by the desk, I could use it as a weapon.

There was a loud crack from over behind the curtains, and a rasp of metal against metal. *Someone was breaking in through the window.*

I picked up the chair, ran to the window and tore at the curtains. Suzy had woken now and, seeing me sprint past her, screamed. The curtains were heavy and interlined, and could only be drawn by cords along a track. I tugged at them with my full strength, yanking them from the rail. The folds of fabric collapsed on to the floor in a heap, while the plastic track buckled away from the wall.

Four men were outside the window, dressed in black leather. They were suspended on a wooden platform, like a window cleaner's boat on a pulley. The iron bracket of the platform was ramming against the windowpane.

Thirty-two storeys beneath us lay a concrete promenade and the pier from the hover ferry. When they smashed through the window, I'd lunge with the chair legs. With luck, I'd dislodge at least one of them from the platform before they made it inside. I shouted to Suzy to fetch help and she fumbled for the telephone.

The biggest of the men was wearing thigh-length black motorcycle boots with steel toecaps. I was brandishing the chair when he spun round and stared blankly at me through the window.

It was Yando.

Yando and three assistants were perched on the platform surrounded by metal camera cases. An abnormally long lens was trained on a concrete spur at the far end of the hotel, where the supermodels, Tigra and Marja, were precariously posed above Hong Kong harbour.

Tigra was dressed from head to toe in silver Lycra with tottering silver Aladdin Sane boots; Marja, her albino hair billowing out behind her, was naked.

'Jesus, Yando,' I mouthed through the double-glazed sealed pane. But the platform had already been winched lower, and he was gone.

Still panting, we ordered coffee and laid plans. I had my appointment with Bruce at eleven, Suzy was going to be collected from the hotel by Erskine's driver at midday. Suzy's objective over lunch was partly dependent on what I managed to garner from Bruce. If he gave me any good leads, there might be angles Suzy could pursue. What we needed most were informants: disgruntled former employees, defectors. That's assuming they existed. Maybe Erskine arranged to have them all bumped off. In any case, we agreed I'd ring Suzy at the hotel from Shanghai Bill's at ten to twelve, to brief her on how the Bruce meeting was developing. If she didn't hear from me, it meant I couldn't risk interrupting the flow of conversation.

'There's one other thing I'm going to try and find out,' said Suzy, 'though I'm not sure how, yet. The weekend Erskine was in London, the one Anna was murdered. What was he doing on Saturday evening and Sunday morning? We've never known that.'

'For God's sake go gently. We don't want him to know we're on to him.'

'Only if it comes up in conversation, then. I promise I'll be careful, truly. But you've got to admit, it would be helpful to know if there's an alibi. I mean, if he'd been staying up in Yorkshire or something, it would rather rule him out.'

'True. But remember, if he's killed twice, he'll kill again. And there's Cazzie. We've been warned not to ask questions. If anything happened to Cazzie ...'

Suzy took me by the arm and kissed me. 'You're very brave, Kit. Has anyone told you that lately? Well, you are. And everything's going to work out, it just will. You've almost cracked it now, you're so close. You'll see.'

'I wish I had your confidence.' And then I smiled. 'If you're right, and I pray you *are* right, then as soon as this is over, I'm taking you and Cazzie somewhere wonderful. Just the three of us. Somewhere remote and sunny, with palm trees and blue sea.'

'This sounds suspiciously like Arambol beach. It isn't that hermit hut in Goa you're dreaming of?'

I laughed. 'Fuck Goa. No, not a hippie beach. The Caribbean. Tobago. That's where we'll go. An air-conditioned hut on the beach.'

'*Two* huts, I do hope. Where's Cazzie sleeping?'

'One hut. Two bedrooms. Girls in one, me in the other. That's a joke, by the way.' I hugged Suzy. 'Thanks for being here, Suzy. God knows how this thing will pan out, but if we succeed, it'll be largely thanks to you. And now I'd better get dressed.'


The entrance to Shanghai Bill's lay between a camera shop and a branch of the China State Bank. A silver canopy, with an art deco graphic of a cocktail shaker, gave way to a chrome staircase which led down to a dark, cavernous bar reeking of last night's cigarettes. I appeared to be alone there. There were rows of brown corduroy banquettes, and a chrome palm tree growing out of a bed of smooth Japanese pebbles. Around a small dance floor, tables and chairs were stacked on top of each other and I spotted a mop and a pail. In the background, a Pretenders record was playing, 'Back on the Chain-gang'.

'Hello? Hello? Is there anybody here?' I was standing against the deserted bar. 'Hello?'

Behind the bar were crates of beer and mixers, waiting to be unpacked.

'Hello? Excuse me?'

I looked at my watch: ten past eleven. Bruce would arrive before long.

I tried to guess what he'd look like. From his voice, he sounded mid-forties. I envisaged him paunchy and balding, in a flak jacket or safari suit. He'd have a passion for South-east Asia and despise Rupert Murdoch: yer classic Aussie journo.

By half past eleven there was still no sign of him. There was a pay phone next to the chrome palm tree and I rang the *Economic Review*. Bruce wasn't expected back until after lunch. Give him another fifteen minutes.

At twenty to twelve a barman rolled in, looking surprised to find me there. I bought a beer and sat at a table, watching the entrance in case Bruce made it.

At five to twelve I rang Suzy. 'The bastard hasn't shown up. Can you believe it? I've wasted the morning. Now it's all up to you, Suzy.'

Still furious, I paid for my drink and went up to the street. After the gloom of the bar, it took a moment or two for my eyes to adjust.

Suddenly, from behind me, I felt my arms being gripped. There were two men, one on each side.

'Get in the car. *Move.*'

A white station wagon was drawn up at the kerb, with a third man behind the wheel. He began pulling out as they threw me face first across the back seat. I hit the bench with a crack, numbing my jaw.

'Down on the floor. *Move.*'

The accents were Chinese. They were shouting instructions to each other in Cantonese.

I lay face down, feeling the vibrations of the engine as

we shot off into the traffic. One man jammed his heels on my lower back, the other on the nape of my neck. I couldn't see their faces. I tried to shift my position, and was booted hard.

'Don't look up. Don't move a muscle. Or we kill you, understand?'

After that we travelled in silence. At first we drove straight down Queen's Road, and I could hear cars all around us, honking their horns and revving at traffic lights. But then we turned south, deeper into Hong Kong island, and I felt the gradient become steeper. We were climbing through Mid-Levels, and then on, up towards the Peak. I got the impression we'd been going for about fifteen minutes. The higher we went, the thinner the traffic and the windier the road. Where were they taking me? If they were going to kill me, wouldn't they wait until after dark?

It's strange the things that pass through your mind when you're about to die. I wondered how Suzy would settle the bill at the Inn of Happiness, and whether my body would be found. I'd prefer it to be washed up on a beach than disappear altogether. Otherwise there would always be the lingering suspicion I'd done a runner. And I wondered how Sally would explain it all to Cazzie, and what she'd say about me later on. 'Daddy loved you very, very much, Cazzie, but sometimes – through no fault of their own – people become ill, and do silly things.' Silly things like murdering Anna Grant, and getting themselves fired, and committing suicide by drowning in Hong Kong. Silly things like that, Cazzie.

We were turning off the road now and then stopped abruptly. The engine remained running and I heard the driver lower his window. He was saying something in Cantonese to a fourth man. There was a whirr of electric gates opening, and the crunch of gravel as we proceeded up a drive.

'Get up now, and follow this way.'

I got out and looked around. My back was still

throbbing from the kick. Ahead of me stood a two-storey white colonial mansion, with a pillared portico and unobstructed views of the island of Lamma. There was an immense sweep of lawn, impeccably mown, bordered by a yew hedge. Two Chinese gardeners in coolie hats were standing on ladders, trimming a topiary arch. The hillside had been terraced as a backdrop for a collection of enormous Buddhas. A gold Buddha, carved in stone and framed with white azaleas, reclined between two giant granite lingams.

'This way. *Move.*'

One of my captors went ahead, the other behind. We walked along an avenue of pollarded limes, at the end of which lay a thatched pavilion and a table set for lunch. There was metal garden furniture covered by white slip covers, and a white octagonal parasol.

Two people were strolling towards us, holding drinks and talking. A tall, silver-haired man was pointing out some aspect of the view to a blonde girl in a pink sundress. The blonde looked spellbound.

Erskine Greer and Suzy.

Greer saw me and, without breaking stride, called out, 'Kit Preston. My dear chap. Welcome to Hong Kong. Know everybody here, do you? Suzy Forbes, my god-daughter? 'Course you do. Work together, don't you? Or did. How about Cheong Li? Met Cheong Li yet? Must have, in the car. Good man, Cheong Li, *seriously*, but no small talk. Anyway, drink? What'll it be? Glass of champagne, wine, cocktail if that's what you like, all here. Nothing a problem.'

'Er, a glass of white wine, please,' I said mechanically.

Erskine clapped his hands and a butler in a striped waistcoat appeared from inside the pavilion.

'Man Tai – white wine for Mr Preston. The dry French variety, not that sweet pudding wine you keep pushing on us.' He winked, bringing me in on the joke. 'And ice. Masses of fucking ice. And those snacks I asked for. Where are they? They must be ready by now.

'What do you make of the view?' he asked me. 'Like views? Some people don't care for them, too open ended. Suzy likes them, she's already told me so. Pretty good view from your hotel too, actually, when the mist lifts. Man Tai? Music. Put on music.'

The strains of *Madame Butterfly* welled up from the flowerbeds where dozens of miniature speakers must have been buried in the borders.

'Exquisite this bit, isn't it? Goose pimples every time. Give anything for a voice like that.'

Suzy was half a pace behind Erskine, looking astonished. She mouthed, 'What are you doing here?'

I shrugged. I was still feeling shaken up from the car ride. The two heavies had melted into the undergrowth. Man Tai handed me a goblet of wine, and a Chinese maid in a lilac and grey pinafore circulated a plate of *dim sum*.

'Now, *lunch*,' said Erskine. 'Mind eating outside? Seemed the right decision at the time. See that cloud over there, Suzy, the bloody-minded black jobbie, think it's about to piss on us? If it does, we'll move inside. Weather less dependable here than it was in Nassau, right, Kit? Took you scuba diving, I seem to remember, off the boat. Loved that boat. Some Ayrab has it now. Gave it to him in exchange for something or other. Can't remember what, just for the moment.'

Erskine was dressed in cream chinos, docksiders and a long-sleeved light blue shirt with a monogram on the pocket. ESG. Erskine Simon Greer. On the table lay a pair of tortoiseshell half-moon spectacles and a leather folder of letters for signature.

A third place setting had miraculously appeared at the table and we sat down: the men facing each other with Suzy in the middle.

'*God*, it's good to see you again, Suzy,' he said, exuding warmth and charm. 'Last time was Florence, wasn't it? What's the name of that teashop place we went to? Biscottis? Gelattis? Come on, Kit, you should know. Frescos all over the ceiling and rum baba ice cream.

*Delicious*. Anyway, Suzy, what the hell are you doing racketing around the globe with this reprobate?' He nodded in my direction. 'I'm supposed to be your moral backstop, aren't I, all part of being a godfather? Shouldn't I be warning you off him or something? Shacked up in an hotel with a man twelve years older than yourself.'

Suzy looked horrified. How did he know all this, anyway?

'Toast,' said Erskine. 'To Suzy, loveliest of goddaughters. More beautiful than her mother, smarter than her father. Not that that's much of a compliment. Sorry, Suzy, joke, don't run out on me this time.' Erskine draped his arm around her shoulders and squeezed, and her face turned crimson with embarrassment.

Some fish appeared in a black bean and chilli sauce, and the maid in the pinafore served it round the table.

'You both like Chinese food, I hope,' said Erskine. 'Otherwise, I'm sure Man Tai can lay his hands on something else. Love it myself. Always eat Chinese fish for lunch: brain food. Fact. How about you, Kit, have any of these journalists you've been visiting taken you out for a good Chinese meal yet?'

'Er, no. Not yet.'

'Pity. You want to suggest it. Doesn't he, Suzy? Instead of calling on them cold in their offices, trawling for scandal about me, he wants to warm them up a bit first in a restaurant. Surprised you don't know that, Kit. Fundamental.'

The next time I risked meeting Erskine's eye, he was appraising me, like an art dealer with a strange painting. He seemed to be searching for something, my conscience, my soul.

'Mind telling me what you're up to?' he asked. 'Don't mean to be nosy, but one does get a tiny bit curious. Chap flies into one's own back yard, so to speak, rings half the journalists in the place inquiring about one's screwing arrangements, but doesn't have the courtesy to request an interview. Can't help making one a little jumpy, you know.'

Jesus, how the hell did he know about that? Either he'd had me tailed or every journalist on the island was in his pocket.

'I can see it must look a bit odd,' I said, noncommitally. 'The truth is, I'm writing a profile of you for *Man Alive*, the British men's magazine. The peg is your takeover of Federated, of course.'

Erskine's eyes never left my own. Over his shoulder I could see the South China Sea, still as glass, its surface broken only by a lone junk rounding the headland.

'Balls, frankly,' he said at last. 'Utter balls. You know that and so do I. Had my people check with the magazine yesterday, and they flatly denied it.'

'Maybe they spoke to the wrong people.'

'They spoke to everyone. Editor, Managing Director, whole lot. Wanker named Trench. Said you were *persona non grata*, stole a car.'

'That isn't true, about the car.'

'Couldn't give a toss, did or you didn't. Fuck's it matter? But you're evading my question: what are you up to?'

Suzy, rigid with tension, had slipped her hand on to my knee and was gripping it tightly. I could feel her fingers biting into the muscle. Erskine poured wine into Suzy's glass, then mine, then his own. He looked at me expectantly, one eyebrow raised.

And suddenly I was furious. If anyone owed an explanation it wasn't me, it was Greer, having me bundled into cars without apology. How dare he look at me like that, as though he'd caught me out, as though it was me who was the guilty party? Smooth as butter with teeth like a barracuda, Paul had said. Well, I'd show him whose bite cut the deepest. The anger was welling up inside me. At that moment I hated all of them, Bruno, Barney, Erskine: all of them who thought their money absolved them of morality and responsibility. What had Erskine ever done to command my respect or earn him the right to an explanation? Apart from firing Suzy's father and thereby hastening his death, and seducing Anna and then strangling her. Having me hauled off the street and booted in the spine by some Triad hood was only the latest and smallest of his crimes. And fixing me up for murder.

'OK,' I said, 'you've asked me what I'm up to, and I'll damn well tell you.' Suzy's fingers tightened on my leg, warning me to stop, but I was on a roll now, out of control.

'It may interest you to learn that we know everything, or virtually everything. You've done your best to drop me in it, but it hasn't worked. We know it all. The arms dealing with the Vietcong. Murdering Anna Grant to shut her up. Murdering her brother Peter in Brazil. I can't pin that on you directly yet, but we know there's a link. I'm sure the police will find it. And that note you had sent to Cazzie, to a five-year-old child, for Christ's sake. That was despicable. You're sick, you know that? All these young girls you chase after, it's pathetic, an old man like you.' I was really motoring now. 'Well, it's finished. It's all coming out. That's unless you intend to kill us both here, this afternoon. But it won't do any good. I've left a letter with my solicitors in London, in their safe, to be opened if they don't hear from me by a certain time this week. All the evidence is written down.' This last bit wasn't bad for an on-the-hoof insurance policy, I thought. 'So there you are. It's over. Does that answer your question?'

When I'd finished, Erskine looked at me for a long time. We sat in silence. I could hear the breeze rustling the leaves of the shrubs and, far away in the bay, the dull chug of an outboard. Adrenalin was pumping up and down my veins, making me feel nauseous.

And then Erskine laughed. He laughed and laughed until tears started running down his face. He rocked with laughter.

'Kit, that was priceless, *priceless*. If I asked Man Tai to fetch a tape recorder, do you think you could possibly do it again? Word for word? It was just splendid. Vintage stuff.'

Suzy and I exchanged glances. It wasn't the reaction I'd expected. Anger, expostulations of innocence, violence. I'd anticipated the possibility of all three. But not mirth.

'My God, you've drained me, I feel quite weak. Man Tai, more wine. And brandy. Like brandy, Kit? Usen't to touch it myself, filthy Chinese habit. You know, one part of your outburst that especially interested me was your reference to Anna Grant. What on earth made you think I'd killed her?'

'Every good reason. Motive, opportunity. I've heard the tape of the interview – and kept a copy too, in a safe place. You admitted selling weapons to Hanoi. It's all on tape. Think how Congress will react to that. And I know you killed her, so don't bother to deny it.'

'Cloud cuckoo land, whole thing, but don't stop, for goodness' sake. Much too entertaining. But if you know everything, as you claim, you must also know I screwed Anna on the Saturday afternoon before she died. And was planning to again the next weekend in Palm Beach. Looking forward to it, matter of fact. She was a minx, but a lot of fun. And you should know I never, repeat never, kill my ex-girlfriends. In fact, I seem to go on paying through the nose for them for years afterwards.'

Suzy had caught my eye. She looked thoughtful. She hadn't known about Erskine and Anna. My last secret.

'Another reason your theory breaks down, of course, is opportunity. Anna told me she was having supper with you that night with your American boss, or ex-boss, I should say, that vulgarian Barney Weiss. He keeps faxing me incidentally, trying to arrange a meeting. Wants me to be his partner in some valet-parking enterprise in China. Reason I knew about your dinner was I tried to persuade Anna to spend the weekend with me instead, in Scotland with the Keswicks. But she wouldn't jack you for me. Not even when I offered a helicopter ride. So I went on my own. Easily verified. Plenty of people staying that week-end.'

405

'What about the arms dealing, then? You've got to admit it's a compelling motive.'

'Suppose so, if you're interested in ancient history. Can't say it gives me sleepless nights. Easy enough to deny anyway, nothing down on paper, no weak links. People involved either very old or dead, or else still on the payroll. Thing you've got to understand, Kit, is this is Hong Kong. Or *was* Hong Kong, not so sure what it is these days. Changed place. Rules, regulations, written constitution. But *then*: frontier town, literally. Arrive with a few thousand pounds, not even, and thirty, forty years later something to show for it. Reasonably attractive house, garden, bit of a *view* – something for one's goddaughter to gawp at while her old godfather's banging on.' He smiled his easy smile at Suzy. 'Granted, one cut corners in those days, didn't always submit one's every last transaction to the scrutiny of political correctness. But who did? Who'd even heard of PC in those days? PC meant something else anyway: Poking Chinese. Sorry, Suzy, shouldn't say that in front of you. But it's true. Doubtless sold the Vietcong a few catherine wheels and bangers along the way. Probably sold them to the Russians, Iranians too. Chinese. Didn't know the final destination half the time, didn't ask. Reason people came back for more. So you're right in one respect: they'd have squealed like stuck pigs in Washington if Anna had been foolish enough to print unsubstantiated hearsay. But you know something else: *I don't give a tuppenny fuck.* Genuinely.

'Listen,' he said. 'Sorry to bugger you about on your theory. Must be incredibly frustrating when you've put a lot of work into it. Only thing is, you've got the wrong person. Seriously. Don't pretend to be a saint, never have, but murdering pretty girls isn't my thing. Aren't enough of them to go round, as it is, without further depleting stocks. But if there's anything else I can do to help while you're out here, just ask. Car, driver, borrow an office? Betty, my secretary, knows everything. Restaurant reservations, anything, ask Betty. Incidentally, your hotel bill.

When you come to check out, you'll find it's already taken care of. Any problems, speak to Betty. No, no need to thank me, *easy*, already done. Pleasure to see you, both of you. Imagine you'll be at Minnie Vass's event later on anyway, so doubtless see you there. Meanwhile, hope you'll forgive me, need to put in a token appearance at the office. Papers to sign. But don't feel you have to hurry off yourselves. Man Tai's here, anything you need, ask him. Swim. Tennis. When you want to get back down to Kowloon, the driver's round the front. Now that he knows we're all best of buddies, I expect he'll let you sit down properly in the back this time.'

Then Erskine kissed Suzy warmly on both cheeks, shook my hand, and before we could move strode back across the lawn in the direction of the house.


Minnie Vass greeted her guests at the entrance to the Grand Ballroom, dressed as Nijinsky's Faun. A bodystocking had been elaborately painted with brown and black patches, like a pony skin, and on the top of her head was perched a pair of elfin horns.

Suzy and I groaned. We were virtually the only guests not in costume. Two hundred had arrived already, dressed as golden slaves from Scheherazade or creatures from a sylvan glade. Minnie's instruction to 'dress Ballet Russe' had been seriously adhered to.

'Thank God you've arrived,' she hissed as we went inside. 'Get in there both of you and *circulate*. There isn't enough *circulating* going on, I can see that from here.'

Normally used for conferences and corporate hospitality, the ballroom had been brilliantly transformed by Minnie into a Bakstian fantasia. One corner had become a forest, suffused with pale yellow light, while another was got up as an Arab harem with golden drapes and tasselled cushions. Chinese waiters on cloven hooves perambulated with blinis and caviar and large steel samovars filled with chilled vodka, which they dispensed neat from the tap.

'Have you even the remotest idea what we're doing here?' I asked Suzy, irritably.

'Yes. Bucking you up. You were becoming insufferably grumpy upstairs. I'm hoping a party will improve your mood.'

She was right, of course. Since reluctantly suspending Erskine from the suspect list, I'd plunged into a black sulk. It was understandable. Over the last few days, ever since lunch in the pub in Alton, in fact, I'd convinced myself we were on to something. But now where were we? Several thousand pounds poorer and as far from a result as ever.

Elaborately costumed guests were still streaming through the lobby into the ballroom. If there was anything incongruous about a Ballet Russe party hosted by an English socialite and underwritten by the Swiss General Manager of a Hong Kong hotel, then I was the only one to notice. A troupe of jugglers from the Moscow State Circus were threading their way through the crowd, closely followed by a dancing bear, Vincent Leong the gossip columnist and a photographer.

Minnie's social net had been cast far and wide. David Tang, behind a cloud of cigar smoke, was talking to the Chinese department-store millionaire, Dickson Poon. The fashion designer Annalina Lau was there with her backer, C. C. Wang. Half the British grandees of the island had descended from the Peak to support Minnie, and I recognised a large contingent of European and American guests too. Yando and his three assistants, all in dark glasses, were hanging out with the supermodels in backless Versace dresses. I noticed Erskine arrive on his own, dressed as the last Tsar in a sable hat.

'Kit Preston.' Someone was buttonholing me in a French accent.

It was Pierre Roux. What on earth was he doing in Hong Kong?

'Pierre.'

'Quite a coincidence seeing you here,' he said superciliously. 'A lot of people in London are looking for you.'

'And what brings *you* here?'

'Business. There are plenty of interesting commercial opportunities for the magazines. Your regime neglected the Pacific Rim, which was too bad.'

'Probably did, Pierre. How's it all going anyway, enjoying the new job?'

Frankly, I couldn't have cared less, but it seemed civil to ask.

'Plenty to do, year zero management. I don't mean to be critical, but in marketing terms you let things slide. Howard and I have identified big problems there.'

'I'm sure you'll solve them, between the two of you.'

'No question, given time. But in the short term, you know, change is painful. I think you were too indulgent with the editors, no? Micky Rice. You heard Howard let him go?'

'When did that happen?'

'Friday. It was necessary. Micky wasn't a team player.'

He was right about that. And, I had to concede, the news interested me. With Fulger and Gombricht as his new mentors, I'd imagined Micky was safe. Clearly, his damage limitation manoeuvres were less successful than he'd hoped.

'Anyway,' I said, eager to back off, 'you're not missing Mouchette, with all the changes there?'

'Barney Weiss takes over from Fabrice at the end of the month. Then we shall see.' He pressed up uncomfortably close to me and asked, conspiratorially, 'Do you think Jean-Marc LeNoy will be kept on? Tell me candidly, Kit.'

'What do *you* think?'

'Me?' Pierre shook his head. 'Regrettably, I fear he's destined for the chopping board. Everyone is charmed by Jean-Marc, the perfect old-fashioned gentleman. But I tell you frankly, that is no way to move a company forward.'

'How interesting,' I replied. 'I was going to predict exactly the opposite. Don't forget Barney's allergic to marketing, he doesn't believe in it. And he loves French class. I think he and Jean-Marc will get on rather well.'

I left Pierre an unhappier man, staring thoughtfully into his vodka shot.

I dragged Suzy to a table and sat down.

'Sorry, but this is all getting too much. I can't handle it, these people. I'm beat. We might as well just admit it's over. Give up gracefully.'

'Not another outburst. Suppress it, can't you, before it starts.'

A waiter offered us a Molotov Cocktail: Georgian champagne with pepper served from a bucket of dry ice.

'And, anyway,' said Suzy, 'it isn't over. All you've done is eliminate Erskine. That's progress, not defeat.'

'Wrong. Don't you see, we've eliminated everybody? Either that or hit a total brick wall. Bruno Fulger we can't get near. We know he's a shit, but if he's a murderer too, we haven't any evidence. There's a perfectly good motive, but where's the proof? With Erskine, it doesn't work either. Maybe he's bamboozled us. We ought to check out his weekend alibi. But the annoying thing is, I've lost faith in him, I think he's probably innocent. And now there's Micky. If he's been fired, it rather undermines the Micky–Bruno–Gombricht conspiracy theory. Unless, of course, he was acting on his own. That's still a possibility. Micky could simply have strangled Anna. In which case, he's pulled it off.'

'There's one thing you've overlooked, though,' said Suzy. 'That letter to Cazzie. You keep inferring that whoever the murderer is is completely secure, and certain they've got away with it. But that can't be true. Otherwise why threaten Cazzie? Someone would only go to the trouble of sending an anonymous letter if they thought you were getting close. Your questions *must* have rattled them. Somebody you've spoken to, something you've asked, has freaked them.'

'OK, when did that letter arrive? Wednesday afternoon. We've been over this ground before. Who'd I spoken to in the previous forty-eight hours? Nick Gruen, who could conceivably have alerted Bruno. Maruccia Mazzelli, ditto.

Bruce McFall, which is why we're in Hong Kong. The Action First people, about Peter. And of course I broke into Jackson Chalk's flat. He'd have found his front door off its hinges. That could have rattled Micky. But I can't think why, considering I didn't find anything and he didn't know it was me.'

Just then, a very tall man, made taller by his sable hat, loomed across our table.

'Aha, the conspirators hugger-mugger again, I see. What are you planning to accuse me of next? Running a chain of brothels? Smuggling rhino horns into China?' Erskine laughed. 'Looking for you, actually. Mind if I join you for a minute? Something I want to ask your opinion on, Kit.'

'Sure. Sit down.'

'I'll be totally frank, I don't know whether this is a good idea or not. Could be terrible. If it is, tell me straight. Rather know now than six months down the line.'

'OK, fair enough. Fire away.'

'Business magazine. Got this idea for starting a new one. Complete innocent in publishing, but caught the bug a bit. Global. Three editions at least: Asia, Europe, the States. Weekly, fortnightly, could be either. Plenty of spice and mischief. Lot more fun than *Fortune* and *Forbes*, both crashers. Gutsier too. What you reckon? Think it's got a hope?'

'I'd like to think about it, but why not? It'd cost a fortune to launch, though. Fifty million dollars at least:'

'Pencilled in a hundred. But what do I know? Bugger all.'

'You'd want to make it quite gossipy. I don't mean sloppy, but full of conjecture. Who's on the up, who's on the down? Who's going to be the next CEO of Goldman Sachs: runners and riders? Who's the highest paid thirty-year-old stockbroker in Singapore? Erskine Greer and Warren Buffett: which has the biggest dick?'

'Mr Kit Preston?' A hotel flunkie in morning dress was asking for me anxiously. 'Sorry to disturb you, but there's a telephone call. Very urgent. You can take it at the front desk.'

I pushed through the crowd to the lobby, wondering who even knew I was there. That patsy, Bruce McFall?

Reception put the call through to a bank of telephones across the lobby.

'Hello? Kit Preston here.'

'Kit! It's Sally. Thank God I've found you. I've rung about twenty hotels, I didn't know where you were staying.'

'What's happened?' But I knew already: something had happened to Cazzie.

'Cazzie's been knocked down by a car. Outside our house. We were crossing the road, and it came straight for us. It was *deliberate*, Kit. *They tried to kill Cazzie.*'

I felt sick. 'She's not ... dead?'

'No. But both her legs are broken. She was screaming and screaming, Kit, lying on the pavement. It was horrible.'

'Where is she now?'

'Chelsea & Westminster Hospital. They've set the legs and given her a sedative. I'm there now, waiting for her to come round.'

'Sally, I'll be right back. The next available flight.'

'I felt I should tell you, even though you don't bloody well deserve it. But I want you to know what's happened, thanks to you. This is your fault, Kit.'

'Have you reported it to the police?'

'Of course I have. There isn't going to be any more of this messing about. I'm telling them everything.'

'Did you mention I'm in Hong Kong?'

There was a silence at the other end.

'Don't you ever think about *anyone* other than yourself? I don't care if they lock you up for ever.' Now she was crying. 'Actually, they did ask where you are and I said I didn't know. I want you to come home *now* and sort out this whole bloody mess.'

'Thanks, Sally. Now look, I'll be right there. With luck,

there'll be a flight tonight, so I'd arrive some time tomorrow morning. Kiss Cazzie for me, won't you? And Sally, I'm so sorry.'

I rushed back into the party to find Suzy, pushing my way between the guests. Minnie was introducing the Swiss General Manager to various Chinese millionaires, who consented to be photographed shaking his hand for the hotel magazine. Erskine was chatting up a Malay girl who looked seventeen. Pierre Roux was talking earnestly to the hotel PR. I shoved past them all, back to our table.

'Suzy, we've got to leave *now*. Pack and leave. Cazzie's been hurt by a hit-and-run driver. It was intentional. They've broken both her legs.'

We raced up to our room, flinging our stuff into suitcases. I was panicking, I couldn't think straight.

'Shall I ring the airlines?' asked Suzy.

'No, let's just head out to the airport. If need be we'll beg our way on board.'

We checked out in ten minutes flat – Erskine had already waived the bill – and piled into a cab.

'All the flights leave around eleven o'clock,' said Suzy.

'It's nine now. We should make it, if there's space.'

We crawled through Hung Hom, bumper to bumper. The airport road was gridlocked.

I sat in the back fuming and looking at my watch.

'Keep calm, Kit. This isn't helping us go any faster. It's making me anxious.'

'I just wish the driver was a bit more anxious, that's all. Surely we can get off this fucking flyover. Don't they have backstreets in Hong Kong?

'Listen, driver,' I said. 'Here's a hundred dollars. Get us to Kai-Tak by ten and it's yours.'

Money, the great motivator. We exited down a sliproad and weaved through neon-lit alleys. I won't swear there was washing strung across the streets, but it felt that way.

We made it by five to. Trans-Asia was already over-booked, with a long wait list. British Airways only had space in First; too painful to contemplate. Cathay Pacific was also technically full, but it depended on the number of no-shows. I remonstrated with the check-in girl to let us on.

'Listen, Kit, just sit down somewhere, won't you,' said Suzy sharply, 'and leave it to me. You're putting them off.'

Twenty minutes later she reappeared clutching boarding cards. I could have cried. I kissed her. 'How on earth did you manage it?'

'Told the truth, strangely enough. I said our daughter had been run over and rushed into hospital. It was an emergency.'

'*Our* daughter?'

'That's what I said. It sort of added to it, the tearful mother.'

We collapsed into our seats, emotionally drained. 'Fourteen long hours to London,' I said. 'I feel so completely bad about this. Sally's right, it never would have happened except for me. I can't bear it. I'm so guilty.'

'It's not you. It's whoever set you up. It's their fault.'

'But what was Cazzie even doing there, back in Clapham, that's what I want to know? They were meant to be staying with my ex-mother-in-law.'

'They must have come home early. There's no point blaming yourself or Sally. And I'm sure Cazzie will be fine. It's a good hospital.'

'I know. But who the hell did this? Who bloody well did it? I'll kill them, really. I promise you, when I find them, I'll kill them. And I *will* find them too, whatever it takes.' I was starting to raise my voice, and a passenger in the seat in front turned round. 'Those *bastards*. I'll get them. Don't doubt it.'

'I don't doubt it. But for goodness' sake keep your voice down, or they'll chuck you off the plane.'

After we took off, Suzy said, 'Kit?'

'Yup?'

'Why didn't you tell me about Anna and Erskine?'

'Tell you what?'

'That they had an affair. You evidently knew all about it, but whenever we've talked about Erskine, you've never mentioned it.'

It was a fair question. The trouble was, I didn't know the answer.

'I suppose it just didn't seem relevant.'

'For God's sake, you know that's not true.' I'd never seen Suzy really angry before. 'Admit it: you're still in love with her, aren't you?'

'Of course not.'

'I think you are. And it's very hurtful. I'm not naïve.'

'Truly, I'm over Anna now. It was a long time ago.'

'Three weeks,' said Suzy. 'That may be a long time to you, but to me it isn't. Goodnight, Kit.'

Then we slept. Don't ask me how. My dreams that night were violent and hallucinatory. Anna, Bruno, Barney, Howard, Erskine, Micky, Anastasia, Suzy, they loomed and receded, horribly transformed, like creatures from a house of horrors.

'One small advantage of this flight,' I said awkwardly as we prepared to land, 'is that the police are expecting us on Trans-Asia. If they're still looking for me, they'll be watching the Trans-Asia passenger lists. And this flight arrives at Gatwick, not Heathrow. I just hope to God they haven't put out a general alert on the computer terminals.'

We filed down the gantry and followed the signs for Arrivals. As usual, there were plainclothes immigration people at the first desk, watching faces. If they recognised me, would they pull me over there and then, or ring ahead to Passport Control? I wasn't sure.

As before, Suzy took first run at Immigration, and got through without incident.

This time I selected a booth manned by an ashen-faced older officer. He looked tired. Are immigration officials prone to burn-out? I hoped so.

There were still two people ahead of me, then one.

Please God, let me through, please let me through. All I want is to see Cazzie.

The officer took hold of my passport and flicked to the photograph. Then looked at my face, then back to the picture. Then he tapped several digits – my passport number, I imagine – into his keyboard. Do they usually do this? Not to me, they don't.

'How long have you been out of the country?'

Trick question. I could tell he already knew.

'Three days, or is it four? Two nights on the aeroplane, one night in Hong Kong. Three days.'

My voice had a quaver, I was shaking. And my fists were clenched inside my pockets.

I could see Suzy watching us from the head of the staircase, waiting for me. I wasn't sure how angry she still was, after last night.

'What was the purpose of your visit to Hong Kong?'

'Pleasure, mostly. I went to a party.'

'When was that, then?'

'Er, last night.'

'Can't have been much of a party, to go all that way, seeing your flight left Hong Kong at 23.05.'

'It was a cocktail party.' Why the hell was I volunteering all this? For Christ's sake, shut up.

He was flicking through the pages now, looking at old visas. Narita airport, Tokyo. Seoul. Pisa. The stapled stub of an American immigration card.

'Travel a lot, do you?'

'Quite a lot. Mostly business.'

'What business is that?' My God, I was actually leading him now.

'Er, magazines.'

Any second I expected him to make the connection, and haul me in.

'Thank you, sir. Welcome back to Britain.' He handed me my passport and nodded me through.

# 24

We headed straight for the Chelsea & Westminster Hospital by taxi, racing through East Sussex and Croydon towards Central London. After Hong Kong, everywhere looked empty and low slung and tweely half-timbered. And safe. Not the kind of place at all in which small children are run over to intimidate their fathers.

I was desperate to see Cazzie, to hold her in my arms and know she was all right. Her little legs were so brittle, they must have snapped like wishbones. I remembered, when I was teaching her to swim, how she'd cling to the tiled edge of the pool, thrashing her legs behind her. I prayed they'd knit together properly, and that she wouldn't end up with a limp.

And all the time, I was raging at myself for endangering Cazzie. You could get overly philosophical about this: the father as progenitor, provider and protector. If I'd been less punctilious as a provider, pushing the magazines to their journalistic edge, then I wouldn't have failed so completely as protector. And if I didn't nail the killer now, Cazzie would always be in danger. I was furious at my lack of progress.

There must be a solution, there *must*. It could only be a question of concentration and focus. But, right now, I didn't have either. I felt seedy and displaced from the flight.

Sally had got Cazzie into a private room in a public hospital. We found it near the end of a corridor full of toytown plastic signs. Her name was posted on the door: Cassandra Preston.

'I still don't feel I should be here,' Suzy said. 'It should just be her parents. I'm sure I should wait downstairs.'

'Nonsense. And, anyway, I want you with me. To restrain me if I start bickering with Sally.'

Cazzie was sitting up in an adult-sized bed, her legs, both plastered, resting on the bedcover, with her little toes peeping out of the end of the casts. She looked incredibly small, barely filling one third of the bed. Sally was on a chair next to her, reading her a story.

Cazzie saw me through the glass porthole. 'Daddy's here, Daddy's here. *Hooray*. Have you brought me back a present, Daddy?'

'Hi, darling.' I kissed her on the forehead, and perched myself on the edge of the bed. 'How are the legs?'

'Well, yesterday they were very hurty, but this lady, one of the nurses, gives me special sweets if I swallow my medicine. I can choose one from a basket, whichever I like.'

I looked at Sally. 'We came as fast as we could. You know Suzy, don't you? I'm sorry you had such a problem reaching us in Hong Kong. I've been so worried: what does the doctor say?'

'About her legs? He thinks they'll be OK. They're clean breaks, thank God. But we won't really know 'til the plaster comes off. In about six weeks.'

'And it happened in Clapham, outside the house?' I asked as nonjudgementally as possible. Suzy will back me up on that.

Sally's eyes narrowed. 'Yes, *actually*. We *were* outside our own house in Clapham. I know you ordered us out, and there's no need to rub it in. We spent three very nice days with Granny in the country, but then we came home. We couldn't stay down there for ever, for goodness' sake. My poor mother, she's not running a boarding house.'

'I'm not being critical, genuinely. I understand. I'm just interested to know exactly what happened, that's all.'

Sally cast a sidelong glance at Cazzie, who was scribbling on her plastercast with felt-tip pens.

'There's not much extra to tell you,' said Sally. 'We'd just arrived back from the New Forest. Cazzie was tired and didn't want to get out of the car. I was trying to undo her seatbelt and unload the suitcases, all at the same time. We were crossing the road and Cazzie was dragging her feet, you know how she can be. Suddenly this car pulled out from the kerb and drove up on to us. It hit Cazzie for six, there was this terrible thud, and she was thrown on to the ground. For a ghastly moment I thought she was dead. She didn't move. Then she started screaming.'

'And the car?'

'Drove off. At top speed. I didn't even get a proper look. It was grey, a Citroën, I think.'

'And you didn't notice the registration?'

'*Of course* I didn't. For Christ's sake, Kit, my daughter – our daughter – was lying in the road. She could have been dead, for all I knew. Do you honestly imagine I was thinking about numberplates?'

'Sorry. I just thought you might have noticed the first letter or something. Out of the corner of your eye.'

'Well, I didn't. I was more interested in calling an ambulance, as a matter of fact.'

'So would I have been,' said Suzy, tactfully. 'Any mother would.'

Sally rounded on her. 'And how would *you* know a mother's reaction?' She stared at her accusingly.

Just then a pretty nurse in a blue uniform appeared through the door carrying a tray of tea.

'I've just made this,' she said. 'I thought you might like it. Tea for three and a glass of milk for Cazzie. But would you like me to fetch more cups, for the policemen?'

'Policemen?'

'They're on their way up now. Didn't anyone tell you?'

They were on to me. I'd be back in the bowels of Chelsea police station and this time they'd make the murder accusations stick.

I bolted into the corridor, shouting goodbye over my shoulder. 'See you soon, Cazzie. And, Suzy, I'll ring you later at home. Go straight there.'

Instead of heading back to the lifts, I went the other way, following signs to a fire exit. The one good thing about this modern fixation for over-signposted emergency exits is that you can't miss them.

At the end of the corridor was a pair of double doors. They were locked with a chain, but there was a glass box on the wall, with a key inside. 'In case of emergency, break glass.'

I removed a shoe and shattered the glass with the heel. Somewhere along the corridor, an alarm started ringing.

The key fitted and I pushed the steel bar. It opened. Miraculous: whenever there's a blaze in a cinema or nightclub, the emergency exits are padlocked on the outside too.

There was a flight of stone stairs with a plastic banister rail. I was already three storeys down when I heard voices above me.

'He's on the back stairs. Somebody ring Security.' It sounded like Superintendent Barratt. Then there was a clatter of feet on the staircase. They were coming after me.

I reached ground level but the stairs continued down to a basement. I decided to chance it by heading on down. If it was a dead end, I was cornered.

There was a wide, tiled corridor with steel food trolleys parked against the wall. Beyond lay swing doors with portholes, leading into the hospital kitchen. Porters in green overalls were humping boxes of vegetables.

I ran into the kitchen, doing my best to look as if I belonged there. About twenty chefs, mostly Bengalis, were working at a steel counter. There was a strong smell of minestrone soup and overcooked lentils. At the far end of the kitchen was a second set of doors. With luck, these might lead to the outside world.

I had almost reached them when the doors from the corridor swung open.

'There he is.' Sergeant Crow was accelerating down the gap between the counters. 'Stop. Police.'

'The police.' A murmur went up from the cooks and kitchen porters. I got the impression most of them were working illegally. Several men bolted across Crow's path, trying to make it to the exit before him.

'Get out of the effing way,' Crow blustered. 'You're letting him get away.'

There was a cloakroom behind the kitchen, full of lockers and clocking-in machines. And an open door leading down a narrow rampway to a covered delivery yard.

Lying under a bench was a pair of rollerblades. They looked about my size, and there was no sign of their owner.

I kicked off my shoes and pulled on the skates, fumbling with the clips. My hands were shaking so much I could hardly do them up. Any second now, Crow and Barratt would be on top of me.

'There he is.' The door swung back hard against its hinges.

The blades were on now and I skeetered down into the yard, gathering speed on the ramp. Normally, I feel unsteady for the first few seconds, before I find my equilibrium. But today there was no time.

I could hear the pounding of the policemen's feet behind me. They were only fifteen seconds away, maybe less.

Ahead lay a wider ramp up to the street. A porter was delivering a crate of tomatoes on a trolley. The gradient looked steep, almost forty degrees. Unless I got some decent speed up, I'd never make it to the top.

I accelerated across the yard, pushing out with all my strength. The wheels were shooting sparks on the concrete floor. If I toppled now, I was finished.

There were only twenty yards to the ramp and I didn't think I'd gained enough momentum. Crow was still shouting at me to stop and give myself up.

Five yards. I'd reached the ramp and was clattering uphill. Push out, push out towards the top. There was a bend coming up, so I leant into it.

I could feel myself slowing down.

Ahead lay the street. There were still another ten yards of ramp, then some flat, then freedom. I had to make it over the hump.

I was beginning to tire. Keep pushing, damn you, keep pushing. I had almost come to a complete stop. Any moment now I'd roll back down the ramp.

I propelled myself forwards, scrabbling at the concrete floor. I was doubled over on all fours, the wheels slipping and sliding beneath me. Inch by inch, I levered myself forwards by my fingertips. Four yards to go. Three. The police were ten yards behind and closing.

I reached the hump and hauled myself upright. Then skated for dear life.

A delivery truck was backing towards the ramp, almost blocking the exit. I placed my feet in front of each other, like a monoski, and glided through the gap.

I'd emerged into Netherton Grove and swerved up towards the Fulham Road. In the distance I could hear police sirens. I cut up the traffic into the Hollywood Road, jumped the kerb and accelerated along the pavement in the direction of Earls Court. It must have been the adrenalin, but I've never done it so well or so fast in my life before. Or since, come to that. If Anna could have seen me now, I thought, she'd be amazed. They could put me into that rollerblading fanzine of hers.

I didn't know where I was heading, I just wanted to get the hell out of there. But I knew I'd have to dump the skates. Before the police radioed out my description.

On the corner, near the Underground, was a public callbox, pasted with Day-glo advertisements for tarts. I dialled Suzy and heard the phone ringing into an empty flat. Maybe she was so fed up, she'd given up on me. I'd try again later.

I sat on the steps of a student hostel, wondering exactly

how I was going to approach the rest of my life. Was evading arrest a separate offence, or simply a subsidiary of a murder conviction? It probably didn't make much difference.

It was only a matter of time now before they picked me up. For one thing, where was I going to sleep tonight? Not at my flat or Suzy's, even if she let me. We could check into a hotel on plastic, but wouldn't the police alert the credit card companies? One swipe and they'd pounce.

Back at the telephone box, I tried Suzy, who was still not home, and left a message at Joanne Pratchett's office. If I was going to turn myself in, I may as well do it properly, with Joanne or Bob Ostler as referee. Joanne's assistant said they were both in Leicester until this evening.

I skated into a patisserie and bought coffee and some pistachioed Arab cake. Just then, I needed the caffeine like a diabetic needs insulin. The place was full of Kuwaitis and Yemenis kicking their heels, and dehydrated Australians with backpacks. I found a table at the back and raked over now familiar territory.

From the start, Anna's killer had needed two things: motive and opportunity. Establish both, I'd reasoned, and I'd find the killer. But it hadn't worked out like that. They all had a motive, and they all had the opportunity if you allowed the probability of subcontracting. The problem with these fat cats is they don't do their own dirty work. Even Micky had the witless Jackson Chalk.

It could still be Erskine. He had the most to lose financially with Anna alive. However much he tried to downgrade the impact of her revelations, I wasn't sure the great Washington liberal establishment would see it that way. Or the Republicans, either. But the Federated takeover would go through today, might already be a done deal. A victory for the crafty old freebooter.

And he could have killed her, quite irrespective of arms dealing. He'd admitted going to bed with Anna on Saturday afternoon. What if he'd returned on Sunday morning for a second helping and accidentally strangled her? It's been known. I could visualise Erskine easily enough with nipple clamps and a bag of tricks. Until I'd checked his alibi, I couldn't rule him out. Suzy was right, I still hadn't fully come to terms with the fact that Anna and Erskine were lovers. There was scar tissue.

But if it was simple sexual misadventure, why the break-in two days later, or the warning letter and attack on Cazzie?

Bruno remained maddeningly out of reach. I don't know what he pays Gombricht, but he's worth every Deutschmark. Bruno had the lot: unambiguous motive and opportunity. He didn't leave London until Sunday evening. And he had a track record.

Not that any of this helped. If Bruno killed Anna, I couldn't prove it.

Which left Micky. I still felt it could have been him and Jackson in Harrington Gardens in the masks. They were the right build. But without the imprimatur of Bruno and Gombricht, what was their motive for being there?

For the fiftieth time, I rehearsed Anna's last known movements. She'd arrived at my flat on the river at five to five: the flat already under surveillance by Fulger's thugs from the schloss. We'd driven directly from there to the Dorchester. I didn't think we'd been tailed at the time, but we might have been. Fulger's men could have waited outside the hotel, and later followed Anna home. But why? Her address was no secret, it was in the phone book. I suppose, if they were going to bump her off that night, they needed to establish where she was staying. After all, she could have been laying over with me. Or with Erskine.

I bought another coffee and a Middle Eastern pudding made of shredded wheat and honey. A man in the queue had the *International Herald Tribune*. Over his shoulder, I read: 'Greer Corp wins Federated' and, further down-page, 'LoCo exits publishing, diversifies into custom parking, cosmetics'. There was a photograph of Barney looked suitably stentorian.

After dinner, Barney had dropped Anna home in his limo, and we'd spoken again on the phone a few minutes later. The last established conversation. The last person to *see* her alive, of course, was Barney. Barney and the chauffeur.

Barney got his cars through Belgravia Limousines. More accurately, Suzy ordered them for him on the Weiss Magazines account. The editors and certain contributors were entitled to use executive cars to appointments. For Barney, though, it was always a top-of-the-range Mercedes or six-door presidential hearse.

I wondered whether the driver had spotted anything when he dropped Anna home. A figure in the shadows, or a suspicious vehicle tailing them down the Cromwell Road. It was worth a try.

'Belgravia Limousines.' A woman answered at the first ring. Their office was above a garage in Hay's Mews; there was always a line of Daimlers double-parked outside, being chammied up by elderly chauffeurs.

'This is Kit Preston speaking, Managing Director of Weiss Magazines.'

I reckoned they wouldn't have clocked the change in management yet, and I was right.

'The reason I'm calling you,' I said, 'is I need to clarify an invoice. Saturday June 23rd. One of your drivers was with our owner, Mr Weiss. He was staying at the Dorchester.'

'Hold the line please, I'll look it up in the book. Yes, here we are. The booking specified wait-as-required. The chauffeur that night was Albert.'

She went on to give me chapter and verse on the invoice. Poor Albert must have spent most of the weekend dozing over the wheel, hanging around for Barney.

'That all sounds perfectly in order,' I said. 'I'll authorise an immediate cheque. Oh, one other thing. I might need Albert myself later on today. Do you know where he is and whether that's feasible?'

'We're very booked up at the moment, Mr Preston. But

I'll check.' I hung on while she consulted her ledgers. 'No, I'm afraid Albert's already out on a job today. Wait and return outside Claridge's. With Mr Weiss, as a matter of fact. Can I arrange one of our other drivers for you?'

'Don't worry, I'll ring back a bit later when my schedule's clearer.'

Then I tried Suzy again. This time she was in.

'Kit, where on earth are you? The police are ballistic. They're all looking for you now, I heard the Sergeant radio a general alert.'

'Suzy, listen, I want you to meet me outside Claridge's in half an hour. In Brook Street, directly opposite the ballroom entrance. But whatever happens, don't get tailed. If you think there's anyone following you, head somewhere else.'

'I'll be there. But what's up?'

'Explain later, but I really need you and your charm.'

I bladed along the Old Brompton Road to South Ken, then up the length of Knightsbridge and cut through the park to Park Lane. Down the underpass and up the other side into Mayfair. There was a traffic cop on a motorbike on the corner of Mount Street, but he sped past oblivious.

Outside Claridge's were a dozen cars with chauffeurs, but I spotted Albert at once. He was sitting behind the wheel of the longest stretch in the street. Albert had once driven me in it to a film premier, with a bunch of journalists and clients; it had fitted twelve comfortably. Typical of Barney, with the shortest legs, to insist on maximum leg-room.

Suzy turned up five minutes later in a taxi. I noticed, rather enviously, that she'd managed to change into fresh clothes. My own kit was ripe from the flight and the escape.

I briefed Suzy and we approached the limo from different sides. Albert was listening to the cricket. He was a delightful, white-haired old boy who'd been driving for Belgravia Limousines for thirty years. He was garrulous too, given the chance. One of his hobby-horses was how his present clientele – mostly Arabs and South Americans – lacked the elegance of his British theatre parties in the 'fifties. The money, he always concluded, was in the wrong hands. These sociological homilies were, I suspected, shameless warm-ups for a nice tip.

Suzy opened the front passenger door and stepped in while I slipped into the back.

'Albert, we need to talk to you. It's important. But no one must see us. I want you to pull out and circle Grosvenor Square. Got that?'

Albert, confused, said, 'Who is this? What are you doing in my car?' Then he recognised me. 'Oh, it's you, Mr Preston. I'm driving Mr Weiss today, but I expect you know that, seeing as you work for the same company.'

'Don't worry, Albert. Mr Weiss won't be out for another hour at least. He said it was fine to ask you some questions.'

'You're never putting me in an article, an old fellow like me?' He looked excited. 'I always said someone should write me up. The people I've driven over the years: Terry Thomas, Cassius Clay, lords and ladies, so many I can't remember the names half the time. The Duchess of Argyll, she was one I do remember, only lived round the corner from here. And Moira Lister, the actress. She was another. That nice girl who writes for your magazines, I'll forget my own name next, Anna Grant, she was always on at me to write down my recollections. "Oh Albert," she'd say. "Go on. It's a piece of social history." Which I suppose it is, in its way.'

'Actually, it's Anna Grant I need to talk to you about.'

We were circling the American embassy in the direction of Duke Street.

'Do you remember the last time you drove Anna? It was nearly a month ago, a Saturday night. You dropped her back home with Mr Weiss.'

Albert thought for a moment. ''Course I do,' he said. 'Wait-as-required outside the Dorchester. Daft job, really. People order cars, round-the-clock cover, then don't use them. You just sit outside, listening to the wireless. Costs them a king's ransom, and they don't get the benefit. Not that I'm complaining: it was Wimbledon week and I enjoyed myself.'

'Albert, I want you to think hard about that Saturday evening. After dinner, you and Mr Weiss dropped Anna off at her flat near the Gloucester Road. Do you remember?'

'That's right. Down near that modern hotel. Behind the Cromwell Road.'

'Now, when you got there, do you remember noticing anyone hanging about? Any suspicious-looking people lurking in the shadows? Think carefully, it could be important.'

Albert thought. 'To be truthful, I didn't notice a thing. I always like to see my passengers safely in through their front door. There are so many odd types about these days, it's part of the job. With women especially.'

'And you noticed nothing unusual?'

'Not in the street, no.'

Something about Albert's manner made me suspect he was holding something back.

'What about *during* the journey, then?'

He looked troubled.

'Don't worry, Albert, we already know Mr Weiss got rather fresh with Anna. She told me that herself.'

'Well, I wasn't going to say anything. But Mr Weiss did get rather friendly with her, or tried to. Made a bit of a pest of himself, to be honest. I wasn't sure, at the time, whether or not to say anything. Miss Grant was such a lovely girl, always remembered to thank me when I drove her anywhere. But she managed very well: told him to keep his dirty hands to himself.'

'And how did Mr Weiss take that?'

'Seemed to accept it. Asked her some questions about some article she was writing, far as I remember.'

'Article about what?'

'I couldn't tell you, I'm afraid. I never eavesdrop on my passengers, you see.'

'But roughly,' said Suzy, sweetly. 'Was it an article about a person? Erskine Greer? Anastasia Fulger? Do either of those names ring a bell? It really could help.'

'I think it was all about pygmies in the jungle or something. I remember thinking how surprising it was, Mr Weiss being so knowledgeable. He was asking Anna about them, but seemed quite an expert himself.'

'Pygmies?' said Suzy. 'Are you *sure*?'

'Quite sure. They were talking about these out-of-the-way areas of the jungle, where they've lived for millions of years, and how foreigners are coming along and stealing the herbs and berries.'

'Listen, Albert,' I said, suddenly excited. 'I want you to think back very, very carefully. When Anna and Mr Weiss were in the car, and you'd just left the Dorchester, who was it who began the conversation about the pygmies? Was it Anna who began it or was it Mr Weiss?'

'It was Mr Weiss. But I got the impression it was something they'd talked about earlier, at their dinner. Mr Weiss was encouraging her to put an article in one of the newspapers, telling people what was going on, so they could put a stop to it.'

'Barney Weiss said *that*: that Anna should write an article?'

'Yes, he was encouraging her, giving her ideas.'

What was it Anna had said to me later that evening on the telephone? 'He put on his pseudo-sensitive face and talked about journalism. He was actually quite high minded.'

I remembered Anna making some reference to the rainforest over dinner that evening, and how the big cosmetics companies were moving in. But Barney had shown no interest at all. In fact, he'd made a dismissive comment about iguana tails being ground into face cream.

It was all coming at me in a rush. Anna had even

mentioned a specific company: Mouchette. 'They're real sleazoids at Mouchette. I've got this bearded brother who's a conservationist out in Brazil and he says they're doing terrible things in the rainforest.'

At the time of the dinner, Barney must already have had agreement in principle with Fabrice to buy the company. He certainly held eleven per cent of the stock. So the last thing he needed was a full-blown exposé of environmental terrorism. The way the market's reacting these days, sales could have halved overnight.

'So, after Anna told Mr Weiss to keep his hands to himself, he asked her further questions about these pygmies?'

'Oh yes, he was very interested. Asked lots of questions, went on and on.'

'And what about Anna's brother, Peter? Did she say anything about him at all?'

'I believe she did, now you mention it. Lives out there or something, doesn't he? I remember thinking to myself, "Rather him than me, miles from anywhere with those cannibals and their poison blowpipes." But from what Miss Grant was saying, her brother was quite fond of them.'

I had a sudden memory of Fabrice Mouchette's dinner party in New York, and talking to the French wife of the General Manager for South America. The Indians, she'd said, were causing problems at the research station: 'Whenever Henri's scientists choose to use this new plant or flower, they say it's sacred.'

We were making our sixth lap of Grosvenor Square, and beginning to attract the notice of the traffic cops outside the embassy.

'One final question, Albert, before you go back to Claridge's. After you'd dropped Anna home that evening, you did take Mr Weiss straight back to the Dorchester?'

'Oh no. He wanted to go to that casino, next to the gates of Kensington Palace. The Connoisseur Club, that's what they call it.'

430

It was a place in Kensington High Street, about half a mile from Harrington Gardens.

'And how long did Mr Weiss stay there, at the club?'

'That I couldn't tell you. He found his own way back, you see. Told me not to wait, said he'd find a taxi outside.'

'Did that surprise you?'

'It did surprise me, yes. Seeing as I'd spent all day parked up outside the hotel, doing nothing.'

# 25

Barney didn't emerge from the hotel for another hour.

Suzy and I waited nervously in a doorway in Brook Street, watching the entrance. I'd bought a pair of black loafers in a shop in South Molton Street and dumped the rollerblades in a public bin. Barney thought of himself as a street fighter, but he'd never admired street fashion, and I needed to make exactly the right impression.

'I hope this works,' said Suzy. 'It's just *got* to work.'

Each time the revolving door began to spin, we stiffened. If we missed him, I was finished. Albert had said he was driving Barney straight from Claridge's to the airport, where the Gulfstream was on standby to fly to Chicago, and I knew that once he'd left the country, I'd have lost him for good.

At ten past two he stepped out on to the pavement. Two porters, supervised by the head doorman, began loading suitcases into the trunk of Albert's limousine. I hadn't seen Barney since he'd exited Smith & Wollensky's with the lobster claw, and he looked paunchier and more dissolute than I remembered.

'Barney! It's *great* to see you.' I was pumping him by the hand. 'I'd no idea you were in London. You should have rung me, I'd have bought you lunch.'

Barney regarded me suspiciously. But then, evidently deciding to take me at face value, he said, 'Hello, Kit. I've been spending a couple of days here at one of my favourite inns. My schedule called for some business meetings in London, so I reckoned I'd make the most of it at the Claridge.'

'You're certainly all over the newspapers, Barney. Front page of the *Trib* today, I notice.'

'Oh, you saw that,' said Barney, preening. 'Well, the journalist called me, so what can you do? I guess he was pretty impressed by everything we're doing.'

'This is a real coincidence, running into you,' I said. 'Because I was thinking about you earlier today. I was going to call your office in Chicago to set up a meeting.'

'You were?' Barney eyed me narrowly.

'By the way, you remember Suzy Forbes, don't you?'

Suzy, looking her sexiest in her fringed cowboy jacket and short suede skirt, joined us on the pavement.

'Hello, Mr Weiss. My godfather, Erskine Greer, was singing your praises yesterday.'

'He was?' Barney looked suddenly interested.

'He said he's hoping to start some big company with you in China. He thinks it'll make millions.'

'Erskine said that?' You could see Barney clocking up the competitive advantage. 'I didn't know Erskine was your godfather.'

'My dad used to run one of his businesses. He's an old family friend.'

'I see,' said Barney, visibly reclassifying Suzy in the social food chain.

'Where are you off to now, Barney?' I asked. 'Paris to review Mouchette?'

'Nah, back to Chicago. Lola's committed me to some fancy fundraiser tonight. Ten thousand bucks a plate. We're saving the Bosnians, or the Red Indians. One or the other. It's on the ticket.'

'Barney,' I said, 'listen, we do need to talk. It's important.'

'Now, Kit, if this is about your severance ...'

'It's not. It's to do with Mouchette. I've heard some disturbing things about the company. Serious things. From before your time.'

'Mouchette,' he said airily. 'This is a new business for me. Steep learning curve, but sweet margins. If you've got any observations to make, you can fax them through to my secretary.'

The porters had slammed shut the boot of the limo, and were hovering for tips.

'I mean it, Barney. This could affect the stock price.'

Barney shot me a hard look. He was trying to assess how much, if anything, I knew.

I held his gaze, while doing my best to appear guileless. I said, 'Can we go inside the hotel? This will only take half an hour.'

'Impossible. We've got clearance for take-off in sixty minutes.'

'Why don't we travel with you to the airport and talk on the way? If we clarify everything now, we won't have to arrange another meeting.'

I could tell Barney was reluctant, but he was also intrigued. I was banking on his curiosity overcoming his caution. There was also his considerable arrogance to factor in. If I really did know something, Barney would reckon he could talk his way clear.

'OK,' he said. 'Come for the ride.'

We climbed into the back of the limo, Barney sitting on the bench with Suzy, having directed me firmly on to the jump-seat.

'You know,' he said, slipping a fat paw on to Suzy's knee, 'where Mouchette's concerned, I still feel like the virgin in the cat house. But I'm sure having fun learning.' He winked at her. 'One thing I've figured already, in this industry there are more opportunities for screwing the customer than in any other business I've been involved with previously.'

'Barney,' I said. 'While I've got you here, I wonder if you'd object if I did a bit of fundraising? I appreciate you're out of magazines now, but I hope you'll still contribute to the Anna Grant Memorial Prize.'

Barney looked at me sharply, and moved his hand off Suzy's leg. 'Anna Grant, that girl you brought round to the Dorchester Hotel?'

'That's right. The one who was killed. You dropped her back to her flat after dinner. Her mother and I are setting up a journalism award in her memory. Actually her brother Peter was going to be a trustee of the prize too, but he died a week ago in South America.'

'That's too bad,' said Barney. 'Anna had a brother who died? I didn't know that.'

'Maybe you met Peter,' I said. 'He lived out near the Mouchette research station in Brazil. Near Manaus.'

'No way you'd catch me in Brazil. Leastways, not in the jungle. As Lola says, we find the Hôtel de Crillon in Paris uncivilised enough. Their power showers dribble like an old man at a urinal.'

'But you'll subscribe to Anna's award, Barney?'

'I'll need to talk first with my accountant about that. Now that we've withdrawn from publishing, I'm not cognisant of the tax position on donations made outside of our sector.'

'Even five hundred dollars would help. It's nothing. You blow that in two minutes at a casino.'

'Not me, boy,' said Barney. 'Gambling's for boneheads, I never touch it. At least not with my own money. And never at a casino.'

'Really? I'm so sorry. Somehow I'd got the impression you're a high-roller. Someone even saw you at the Connoisseur Club the night we had dinner. The night Anna died.'

Barney was momentarily wrong-footed. 'Aw, *that* place,' he said. 'I guess it is a casino, though it hardly merits the description. The maximum stakes there are a joke: the ceiling's lower than a chicken coop. But at least they'll sell you a drink.'

'You really *should* do something for the Anna Grant fund. Especially since you were the last person to see her alive.'

'Aside from her murderer, of course. I guess he – or she – was the last.'

'Of course. The murderer would have been the last.'

An awkward silence lay between us, until Suzy said brightly, 'Mr Weiss, do you mind if I ask you a question about make-up? I know you've only just become the owner of Mouchette, and obviously probably don't know the details about what actually goes into it, but I'm interested in the new skin rejuvenator you're bringing out. Is it true it's made from these amazing new plants from the Amazon?'

'You'd have to ask our scientists about that. But they tell me this stuff's pretty effective. It'd better be: it's cost enough to develop.'

'And what about the sacred roots and things? Everyone's saying it's made from these rare ingredients the Indians worship.'

A look of apprehension crossed Barney's face.

'Do you mind telling me where you heard that information?'

'About the roots? I'm not sure exactly. It could have been from Anna Grant originally. Or her brother, the one who died. I really can't remember. Anyway, it's what a lot of people are saying now.'

'Well, that's horse feathers. In fact I'm giving my attorneys instructions to litigate. If people want to start that rumour, we'll initiate proceedings.'

'I think you're right,' I said to Barney. 'If the media manipulate all this in the wrong way, it could turn nasty.'

'How do you mean?'

'I was thinking of the Peter Grant rumour. It's what I wanted to talk to you about. There's a story going round that he was murdered, hacked to death in the jungle. People are speculating it was the cosmetics companies who were behind it, because he was championing the Indians against them.'

'That's crap,' said Barney. 'Peter wasn't hacked to death. He died of snake bite.'

It took Barney three long seconds to recognise the implications of that last remark, then he swung back into action.

'I've only now made the connection,' he said. 'Nobody mentioned that the hippie in the jungle and that prick-tease at the Dorchester were brother and sister.'

'Didn't they, Barney? I thought that you and Anna discussed Peter all the way back in the limo that night.'

'Well, you thought wrong.'

'Barney, you'll be telling me next you don't remember sending the driver home from the Connoisseur Club.'

'What is this? He'd been hanging about all day. I was doing the guy a favour, goddamn it.'

'And doing yourself a disfavour at the same time.'

'I don't follow you.'

'So who's to say, now, at what time you left the casino for the Dorchester? Or even whether you went into the club at all?'

'For Chrissake, you can check up with the croupier.'

'I don't doubt you made some gesture they wouldn't forget: a thousand dollars on your birthdate or some such. But you didn't stay long, did you? You returned to Anna's flat. Isn't that what happened?'

Barney raised his eyebrows. If he was rattled, he was showing no sign of it. But I was panicking badly. We were drawing up at the gates of the private airfield at Bushey, fifteen minutes from Heathrow. Barney had made a couple of slips, but I was well short of a confession. The fact was, I'd blown it. In a short time he was going to leave the country, and that would be that.

Albert had clearly made the journey to the airport countless times before: he slowed at the security post, waved some documentation and we drew up at a customs and departures shed. Parked along the edge of the runway were several dozen small planes: Falcons, Gulfstreams, Westwings with corporate liveries.

The crew were waiting for us in the shed: a pilot and a heavily made-up stewardess. The stewardess was dressed in a short, blue fitted suit with big red plastic buttons with the LoCo Inc. logo.

'You guys ready to make a move?' asked Barney through the limo window.

'Just as soon as they'll give us a slot, chief,' said the pilot. 'Seems pretty busy here today. I've been on to air traffic control, and they're saying it'll be another forty, fifty minutes.'

'Goddamn it. Just keep on their arses. I've no intention of hanging around in England.'

I guess Barney had reached that stage, that a lot of very rich people eventually arrive at, when the laws of any one country stop counting for much. It's like hotels. You mess the linen in one place and check on out to the next. There was something dangerous but also elated in his demeanour, as though my accusations had served only to sharpen his wits.

Barney swung open the door and heaved himself out of the car. I cursed. I'd lost him now, he was out of my reach, leaving me with no suspect and a theory that I doubted was going to impress the police. As if he'd read my thoughts, Barney smiled mockingly and turned to go.

Just then, Suzy said brightly, 'Mr Weiss. Isn't that your Gulfstream parked over there?'

'My new Gulfstream. The new V model.'

'But they're *amazing*. Godfather Erskine was telling me all about them. He's thinking about getting one too, but says they're *incredibly expensive*, even for him.'

Well done, Suzy. Barney swallowed the bait.

'You tell your godfather that you get what you pay for. Irrespective of market segment: jet plane, plastic beaker, investment art, the price–quality ratio's a constant. Took me twenty years to figure that. That's why I went for the Gulfstream. There are less expensive aircraft, certainly, but when you're talking value ...'

Suzy said, 'Could you possibly show us inside? Erskine's over next week, and I'd love to be able to tell him I've seen one. Not even he has. It would really annoy him!'

Barney looked doubtful, then gestured at me. 'Providing

you can stop this guy exercising his fertile imagination. Not another word, OK?'

Barney stared hard at me, and then he lumbered towards the shed with us in tow, while Albert and the pilot took care of the luggage.

'We'll be a couple of minutes, Bob,' he called to the man in shirtsleeves behind the counter. 'My pilot's taken care of the paperwork already.'

'Off to see the Gulfstream, are you?' The man nodded and returned to a large sheaf of blue and green forms. We followed Barney on to the tarmac.

'These aircraft,' said Barney, 'open doors. They're the best. You meet people who question the capital cost. But you know something? They're not big-picture people. They don't factor the time–money ratio. There've been studies done. Business jet owners regularly outperform their non-owning competition.'

'I'm sure you're right,' said Suzy. 'With all those different companies of yours, it wouldn't be practical to fly scheduled.'

Barney wrapped his arm around her waist and squeezed. 'I like that. You're a smart cookie. Maybe you can work for me as my European assistant. I need a confidential young lady this side of the pond.'

'*Really*, Mr Weiss?' said Suzy, wide eyed. 'What an opportunity. Let's talk about it on board.'

The interior of Barney's jet reminded me of an Atlantic City casino: the walls and ceiling were upholstered in black leather, with black leather blinds above the porthole windows. There were wide-bodied black leather seats with matching footrests, acres of black carpet, and walnut and brass tables and cabin dividers.

Barney plonked himself in a plump seat and ordered three highballs. The stewardess reappeared with tall cut-crystal tumblers, pretzels, blue steaks and miniature hot dogs.

'Well, you know what they say about girls who enjoy hot dogs,' exclaimed Barney.

'No, what do they say, Mr Weiss?' asked Suzy, ingenuously.

'Aw,' said Barney. 'I thought all the girls knew that one.

'Here's another argument for company jets,' he went on. 'Drinks before take-off. The airlines make you wait until after you're airborne. Isn't that right, Carleen?'

'Perfectly right, Mr Weiss.'

'But you don't make me wait, do you, Carleen?'

'No way, never, Mr Weiss.' And she wiggled her hips in his face.

She poured him another large whisky while Barney bragged to Suzy about specifications. I heard him describe the Honeywell flight management system, and the GPS – Global Positioning System – which he said enabled the pilot to know precisely where they were at all times.

'I wouldn't like Lola to get hold of one of those gadgets,' he rumbled. 'I reckon she'd attach it to the seat of my pants. But then she couldn't catch me, this bird can fly Seattle to London nonstop. A one-hop trip, no goddamn wait while they refuel. Los Angeles–Beijing, Helsinki–Sao Paolo, Perth–Jo'burg. All direct.' He reeled off half a dozen improbable routes, while Suzy looked suitably impressed.

'Carleen,' shouted Barney. 'Will you ask the pilot where the hell our take-off slot's disappeared to? I'm fed up waiting. And tell him to go rev the engine or something, show them we're getting impatient.'

Shortly afterwards, the jets growled into life making the glasses rattle on the table.

'Feel that,' said Barney. 'Rolls-Royce Tay engines. Goes straight to the testicles.'

Just then, as though our conversation in the back of the car had never been interrupted, Barney turned on me.

'Before I let you off my plane, Kit, you'd better promise to keep your mouth shut. You maybe don't realise this, but you're crazy. Bitter and crazy. You screwed up those magazines, got yourself fired, and now you're on some

440

crazy vendetta. That's what any courthouse would conclude. Wouldn't even *reach* the courthouse. Your motive's clear as daylight.'

How *dare* he say I'd screwed up the magazines? Barney's sole contribution for his seventy million dollars profit was contaminating the editorial with his friends' houses, and murdering the star contributor.

'If we're talking motive,' I said, 'if you really have the gall to mention motive, then let's talk motive. How about silencing the girl who was about to blow the lid off Mouchette? It was lucky for you, wasn't it, that I brought Anna to dinner that night: lucky for *you*, tragic for her. She made an allusion to Mouchette that went over my head, all that stuff about her brother in the jungle. But it didn't go over yours. You knew exactly what she was referring to, and knew it was trouble. And what neither of us realised was that you'd already taken a big position in Mouchette, with more to follow. So you gave Anna a lift home, found out how much she knew, realised it was a lot, got dropped off near the flat, and then came back and killed her, before she had a chance to blow the whistle in the newspapers.'

Only Barney's eyes, which darted nervously about the cabin, betrayed any sense of unease.

'Let's get one thing straight, shall we?' he said evenly. 'I'm not in the business of justifying myself to just anyone who comes along with a grudge and a dumb-ass theory. Principal reason I took Suck-U-Like private was to dispense with the analysts asking smart-ass questions on matters that don't concern them. And, let me tell you, I'm not about to embark on a game of catch-me-out with you either.

'But I'm prepared to cut a deal with you.' He leaned forward confidentially. 'Maybe with hindsight, there could have been a provision for your severance, Kit. I'm not saying there *should* have been – there's no admittance of liability here – but maybe we could revisit that situation.

441

Contractually, Bruno Fulger assumed all employee liabilities, and it's a matter for him. But how does a million dollars sound to you? Payable anywhere you choose – Cayman, Bermuda – to avoid the tax implication.'

'And if I don't accept?'

'If you don't accept, your life will get complicated, particularly if you keep asking stupid questions about Anna Grant. In fact, let me give you a piece of free advice. If you don't stop asking questions, something bad will happen.'

That was Barney's big mistake, that's what the bastard wrote to Cazzie: *If you don't stop asking questions, something bad will happen.*

Until then I'd managed to keep my fury in check. But now I flipped.

'No way are you buying me off, Barney. Absolutely no way. And I'll tell you what I'm going to do. I'm getting right off this plane and I'm turning you in. For the murder of Anna Grant. And Peter Grant. I'm sure you had a hand in that too.'

'Sorry to disappoint you,' said Barney, 'but you're not going anywhere. In case you didn't notice, this aircraft belongs to me. Nobody leaves unless I say so.'

Suddenly he lunged at Suzy, grabbing her round the neck in the crook of his short, fat elbow. Then he picked up a steak knife from the plate and held it to her throat.

'This young lady,' he said, 'this very attractive young lady, it would be a tragedy if she got hurt.' He moved the point of the blade to Suzy's cheek, ran it lightly from her earlobe to her lips, then back to her throat.

Barney pressed the call-stewardess button in the panel above his seat, summoning Carleen from the forward galley. She must have seen the knife at Suzy's throat, but evidently didn't think it worthy of comment.

'Carleen. Could you please inform the pilot that as soon as we've got clearance, I'd like to switch destinations. Instead of Chicago, we're going to Brasilia.'

'Surely, Mr Weiss. I'll inform the captain.'

Barney smiled smugly at me and, for the briefest of moments, allowed the point of the knife to leave Suzy's throat.

Suzy took her chance. Deflecting the blade with her left arm, she rammed her right elbow into his crotch.

He doubled up, while she tried to scramble out of his reach. She was edging into the aisle when Barney grasped the fringe of her cowboy jacket.

'Come back here, bitch,' he shouted, yanking her towards him.

Suzy struggled and Barney's highball glass crashed to the floor, sending splinters across the cabin.

Suzy, breaking free, stumbled into the arms of Carleen.

'Grab her,' Barney ordered. 'Grab the bitch.'

Carleen forced Suzy on to the floor, locking her arms behind her in a full-nelson, and pressing her knee into the small of her back. 'Get off me,' Suzy was screaming. 'Just let me go.'

The stump of the broken glass was rolling between us in the aisle, and Barney stooped and snatched it up. The base was still intact, but the rim was dangerously jagged. I leapt up from my seat. Barney advanced on me, waving the glass in front of him, forcing me to retreat towards the back of the plane.

'Let me tell you something,' Barney said, still advancing. 'If I take risks I make them work, whatever the costs.'

'Even when it means murdering two people?'

'Two, four. Do you even know the scale of investment I've made in Mouchette? Or the number of employees, all round the world, whose livelihoods and families depend on the success of this new skin paste? No, I guessed not. Well, sometimes in business the only choice is to move forward and make things happen. But I don't expect you to understand that one.'

'So what are you proposing to do? Slit our throats and dump us in the jungle?' I was yelling at him, making sure Carleen could hear every word.

I've never been so scared as I was at that moment.

Barney continued coming at me up the aisle, and I knew now that he would kill us. He hadn't planned to, but it was the only option.

In Brazil, the Gulfstream would land at some out-of-the-way airstrip, where he'd have every trace of the fight expunged from the cabin. Our bodies would be bagged up and taken off the plane as garbage. I didn't doubt Barney's competence as a murderer. If he'd convincingly set up Peter's death as snake bite, he could devise a disappearing act for us too.

Barney looked completely deranged. He was waving the broken glass in front of him, his fat face glistening. I had backed off as far as I could, and was pressed up against the walnut cabin divider.

Suzy was still struggling to break free, and I decided to appeal directly to Carleen.

'Carleen,' I shouted. 'Have you any idea what you're getting into? This man's a murderer. For God's sake, let Suzy go. He killed two people, he's just admitted it. He's mad. He tried to kill my five-year-old daughter.'

'Let me go, *please*,' Suzy implored. 'Don't you see, if he kills us, you'll be next. You'll be a witness.'

Carleen looked appealingly at Barney's back, but he didn't see her. He was concentrating on me, edging still closer with the stump of glass. When he lunged, I would try and grab his wrist, but in the confined space of the cabin I knew I didn't stand much chance.

'I warned you,' Barney was saying, 'I warned you to keep out of this. That Grant girl and her brother didn't get a warning, they were in too deep.'

He loomed over me, raising the glass level with my throat. At any moment, he'd make his move. I was up on my toes, pressed back against the wall. He slashed out at my face and I put up my arm to protect myself. I felt the glass carve into the fleshy pad of my left hand, and a spurt of blood ran down my sleeve.

'Fuck you,' said Barney. 'Fuckheads like you. You don't understand anything.'

'For God's sake, let me *go*.' Suzy was begging Carleen. 'He's going to kill all of us.'

I saw Carleen relax her hold on Suzy, who clambered up and sprinted up the aisle towards Barney. Suzy was right behind him now. She was holding a silver-plated drinks tray she'd grabbed from the table, and lifted it above her head.

It came down with a thud on Barney's head.

He stumbled towards me, losing his grip on the tumbler which smashed on to the floor. Then he regained his balance, hurling himself on top of me. The impact pitched me sideways, and down on to the floor. Tiny splinters of glass covered the carpet and dug into my head and neck. Barney raised his fist to punch my face. I braced myself for the blow. It was all over.

Then I saw Suzy over Barney's shoulder.

She raised the silver tray, for a second time, and brought it down with an almighty crack.

Barney swayed, and then collapsed on to me like the carcass of a great ape.

He was out cold.

Just then there was another crack as the cabin door was flung open and four uniformed police officers burst on to the plane. Moving at speed up the aisle, two of them grabbed Barney from behind. A third took hold of Suzy and frogmarched her into the galley at the front of the plane.

Superintendent Barratt gripped my arm above the elbow.

'You,' he said grimly, 'have a lot of explaining to do.'

# 26

The last twenty months have been so crazy, I've scarcely had time to stop and take stock. Suzy and I moved to Hong Kong four months before the launch, but still haven't got the apartment sorted out. The view from our balcony across to the Shek O peninsula is magnificent, but we're living out of packing cases.

I worked out that last year we spent more than a hundred nights in hotel rooms. Taipei, Seoul, Washington, Seattle, Singapore, Hamburg: Suzy and I must have done it in a dozen different cities. In theory, now that the magazine is up and running, and the network of overseas bureaux established, things ought to settle down a bit, but somehow I doubt it.

The launch of *Hot Money* has certainly been a *succès d'estime*. Ellen Durlacher, who's joined us as global PR, tied up front-page stories in three continents and the business cable channels plagiarise us remorselessly every fortnight. Objectively, the Asia-Pacific edition is performing best, and is the only one making decent money. The European edition should move into the black some time next year. The United States is going to take much longer, as I warned Erskine it would from the start.

My days have assumed a kind of structure now: talking to the American office before breakfast and London and Hamburg in the evening. Operating in three time zones means never being off call. Erskine talked me into overseeing both sides of the magazine, as editor-in-chief and publisher, and it certainly fills the day.

I had reservations about working for Erskine Greer, but on the whole they've proved groundless. He's a civilised owner. I'm under no illusions: if I screw up, I'm out. But he doesn't throw his weight about, and he listens and he believes in editorial integrity. I was concerned that his other businesses might constrain us journalistically, but it hasn't happened so far. When C. C. Wang threatened to pull Annalina Lau's boutiques from Erskine's Sha Tin and Guangzhou shopping malls, following something we wrote, he didn't even bother to mention it. And he didn't miss a beat when we ran a critical take on his stewardship of Federated Aviation.

Suzy and I are summoned up to the Peak for lunch or dinner about once a month. I'm well aware of Erskine's fondness for Suzy. I'm sure he'd find it rather rejuvenating to bonk his own goddaughter. Suzy plays up to him, but claims not to fancy him one bit.

Mr and Mrs Paul Leys live across the island in a modern residential enclave on Shouson Hill, so we get to see Cazzie most weekends. Her legs healed up perfectly, you'd never guess there'd been a problem. When I watched her win first prize in the fifty metres freestyle at the Kellett School swimming gala, I knew everything was OK again.

We socialise more with Paul and Sally than I'd ever have expected. My girlfriend and ex-wife have gone out of their way to get along for Cazzie's sake, and we've fallen into this routine of having Sunday-night supper together as a foursome at a Korean barbecue place in Wanchai. Sometimes, at weekends, we all join up and take Cazzie for a trip over to Lamma on the Flemings or Greer Corporation junk.

Paul's good company and certainly good for Sally; she's a lot less uptight these days. The money is probably a factor too. When someone told me the size of Paul's 1995 bonus, I nearly fell overboard. Not that you'd ever hear about it from Paul, he's the original low-key Englishman in that respect.

As for Sally, I've almost – almost – forgiven her for shopping me to the police that morning at the hospital. It's a subject that we never, ever mention. In point of fact, the police are a bit of a touchy subject all round. Far from applauding my forced confession from the murderer, Superintendent Barratt claimed to have been wrong-footed by my intervention, caricaturing me as a loose cannon who might easily have scared Barney off. He said the police had been pursuing several separate lines of inquiry, and been on to Barney for a couple of weeks. It had always been their intention to arrest him leaving the country, so they'd been dismayed when Suzy and I rolled through the gates of the airfield in the back of his limousine. They'd been stalling his take-off slot until a warrant for Barney's arrest was issued.

Suzy, loyal girl that she is, point blank refuses to believe it, and says it's just an arse-covering manoeuvre by Superintendent Barratt. But I have to confess that Barratt's version has a ring of authenticity, galling as it is.

Despite my best intentions to cut loose, one way or another I still hear quite a lot about my old firm. Howard Trench lasted eight months before falling out with Fulger, who instructed Gombricht to fire him with three months' salary, though they dressed it up as early retirement. Howard's become a freelance consultant, and a sad old man of industry committees. He sits on the boards of the Advertising Association and Old Ben, a charity for destitute news vendors.

Kay Lipschwitz Anderson is Managing Director of Fulger Publications now, the first woman and the first American in the company's history. By all accounts, she's doing a fine job. The magazines certainly look healthy, whenever I come across them. Kay's first act as MD was to oust Pierre Roux, though the press release specified resignation. Pierre found a new job almost immediately at British Airways, where he's part of the marketing unit responsible for repositioning Club World and refining the frequent-flyer programme.

Barney Weiss, following his conviction for the murder of Anna Grant, was sentenced to life imprisonment. Last I heard, he was still in Wormwood Scrubs, though he's scheduled for a transfer to Whitemoor prison in Cambridgeshire. Suzy and I were both called to give evidence at the trial, which attracted enormous media interest. The *Daily Mail* got it into its head that I was unofficially engaged to Suzy, causing a lot of gratuitous embarrassment at the time.

Barney's two hit-men on the roof at Harrington Gardens got eighteen and thirty months respectively; the longer stretch going to the driver of the car who broke Cazzie's legs. When the sentences were handed down, there was a brief outcry in the press at their leniency. Even the Home Secretary, responding to a Parliamentary question, said he regretted that they weren't stiffer.

The second charge against Barney – the murder of Peter Grant – was unsustained through lack of evidence. Right to the end, he insisted he had nothing to do with it, despite confessing to me on the plane. Throughout the trial, this stubborn denial on Barney's part annoyed me very much. But Bridget Grant, who watched the proceedings every day from the visitors' gallery, was stoic. 'We know what happened,' she'd say. 'And he knows himself. And so does God above, who knows everything. It really doesn't make any difference now, does it?'

Peter's body had eventually been repatriated, and is buried alongside Anna's in the Golders Green cemetery in North London.

I've lost count of the breakfasts, lunches and dinners at which Suzy and I chewed over everything that happened to us. Not that, in the end, it was particularly complicated. Most of it we'd established already.

The men in the park and watching my flat had definitely been working for Bruno Fulger. When they'd broken in and stolen Anna's notes that Sunday afternoon, they'd been searching for her tape of the Anastasia interview. And had evidently found it too. No wonder Gombricht had been so heavy with his legal action; he knew the critical evidence for my defence was securely locked away inside his safe.

Barney had returned to Anna's flat in Harrington Gardens forty-five minutes after I'd spoken to her on the telephone for the last time. I presume he'd walked the half-mile from the Connoisseur Club, in case he was later identified by a taxi driver. No doubt, on arrival, he'd simply rung the bell and Anna had let him in. I don't like to dwell too deeply on her motive here. Of course, everything that was said in court about the murder itself was pure conjecture, but it sounded convincing enough. He'd gone upstairs to the flat, grabbed her by the neck, then strangled her. The whole exercise probably didn't take much longer than ten minutes.

Then Barney had made off with Anna's AppleMac, which he guessed would contain her notes on Mouchette. It never was established exactly where he'd dumped the computer. The streets off the Gloucester Road are seldom short of builders' skips.

It must have been after he'd returned to Chicago that Barney started to panic. Were there any floppy disks or letters that he'd overlooked? Peter could easily have sent his sister something in writing. And if the police decided to make a thorough search, he couldn't know what they might turn up.

One thing that did emerge at the trial was the hit-men's brief: a thousand pounds each to break in and strip the place of every last document and disk. And we learned about Barney's reaction when they reported back on my presence in the flat. That had given him one hell of a shock. My assailants had described me well enough, so Barney knew exactly who it was who'd been there that night. By the time he summoned me to lunch in New York, he had an additional motive in offloading the magazines quickly: removing himself from my orbit.

Mouchette itself went back on the market even before the onset of the trial. In preparation for the worst, Barney decided to liquidate his assets. Several multinationals, including Unilever and Procter & Gamble, expressed interest in acquiring it, but in the end it was bought by

Vendôme, the luxury brands holding company which also controls Cartier and Dunhill. The Mouchette jungle station at Manaus, made infamous by the trial, was disbanded and the research and development team relocated to the South of France, close to Jean-Marc LeNoy's villa at Juan-les-Pins.

Anastasia and Bruno, after a year-long separation, got back together, having racked up an estimated four million dollars in lawyers' fees.

Their back-together-again thirteenth wedding anniversary dinner at Schloss Fulgerstein merited eighteen pages in *Hello!* and a six-spread salute by Bob Colacello in *Vanity Fair*, photographs by Yando.

Erskine was invited to the dinner and seated between Bianca Jagger and Mrs Rudolph Gombricht, who had complained about me from the minute they sat down. 'A really *unusually* tiresome woman,' Erskine said. 'Wouldn't shut up about some motorcycle you borrowed from the stables. As if I give a damn.'

Bruno's libel suit against me was dropped, to my immense relief, at the time of the great reconciliation. Even Gombricht accepted that, under the circumstances, they couldn't really drag me through the courts.

I follow the progress of Fulger AG with an attention bordering on obsession; I've only to think about Bruno and Gombricht to become angry. I have never been one of those people who automatically despises everyone richer and more powerful than themselves, but Fulger is an offence to the species. Part of my frustration lies in the knowledge that I couldn't even get near him, and I'm quite aware that, had Fulger murdered Anna, I'd never have been able to prove it. I've already told our bureau chief in Hamburg, Karl Heine, that as soon as we've got the ammunition, we're going to run an annihilating cover story on the whole rotten Fulger empire. Believe me, it's going to be World War Four when that's published. Even Rudolph Gombricht can't hold back the tide for ever.

Micky Rice, as I predicted, wasn't overwhelmed by job

offers after his fall from grace at *In Society*. He certainly wasn't invited to the Fulger party. Instead, he's writing a history of club culture in London (1978–96), with picture research by Jackson Chalk. The Embassy Club, the Titanic, Heaven, Blitz, the Wag, the Fridge, the Ministry of Sound: street-cred anthropology. Colin Burns has optioned serialisation for the style section of the newspaper.

I am one hour into a flight between Taipei and Hong Kong. In a minute I'll begin work on a stack of page proofs that were faxed through to the hotel during the night. In Europe, fashion week must have come round again, because there's a photograph on page nine of today's *Herald Tribune* of front-row customers at the Givenchy show. I can just make out Mrs Taubman and Mrs Gutfreund, sitting on either side of Mrs Bruno Fulger and Tina Turner. At moments like this, it's always Anna who rushes first into my thoughts: I can't wait to show this to Anna, won't Anna find this hilarious. And then I remember, and am always surprised by the strength of my feeling of loss.

Erskine has taken on the sponsorship of the Anna Grant memorial prize, now officially named the Anna Grant–Greer Corporation Journalism Award. 'You see,' Erskine said when I'd talked him into it, 'didn't I tell you I go on paying for old girlfriends for years afterwards?'

One evening, after I'd been working for Erskine for about a year, and Suzy and I were part of a large dinner party on the Peak, he drew me aside into his study and closed the door. The walls were glazed blood red as a backdrop for his collection of Mayan and Jain sculpture, each piece individually lit by a pinhead halogen beam.

'Been clearing out some old papers and came across this. Thought it might amuse you,' he said, handing me a single sheet of rice paper. It was covered with typewriting in a language I didn't recognise, and a variety of impressive rubber stamps. At the bottom of the sheet were two signatures, one of them Erskine's. It was dated September 1966.

452

'One of my first arms deals. You'll recognise the signature of the then chief of military procurement in Hanoi.'

Then, with a chuckle, he whisked it out of my grasp, set it alight and lobbed it into the grate.

Only much later, when I was relating the incident to Suzy, did I realise the document could have been anything: an old visa for all I knew. It looked flimsy for a contract.

Another hour and we'll have landed at Kai-Tak; home in under two. Suzy is playing tennis today at some country club and is going to pick up our supper on the way back.

We're planning on getting married some time next summer, at least I think we are. With the move out East, we've been too busy to have a proper conversation about it. But I overheard Suzy discussing children's car seats with Sally the other day, and I know for a fact that her mother wants us to get a move on. If we do get married, I expect we'll be very happy.

I believe I only have one real secret from Suzy now, which is tucked inside a book on a high shelf: a photograph of Anna rollerblading in Kensington Gardens. Technically, it isn't a great picture. But it captures something – a particular look, a smile – that no other picture has. I can remember the precise moment when I pressed the shutter on a warm May afternoon. Sometimes, when I can't sleep at night, I slip out on to the balcony and lose myself in that photograph, until the sky begins to lighten over the South China Sea.

I don't want to give the wrong impression here. I mean, I don't have some big problem about Anna. I'm perfectly capable of getting on with my life, and there are plenty of good things to look forward to.

It's just that I still miss her so much sometimes, that's all.